You're invited to a

CREEPOVER

This book is a work of fiction. Any references to historical events, real people, or real locales are used fictitiously. Other names, characters, places, and incidents are the product of the author's imagination, and any resemblance to actual events or locales or persons, living or dead, is entirely coincidental.

SIMON SPOTLIGHT
An imprint of Simon & Schuster Children's Publishing Division
1230 Avenue of the Americas, New York, New York 10020
This Simon Spotlight bind-up edition July 2022
Truth or Dare . . . , *You Can't Come in Here!*, *Ready for a Scare?*, *The Show Must Go On!*
Copyright © 2011 by Simon & Schuster, Inc.
All rights reserved, including the right of reproduction in whole or in part in any form.
SIMON SPOTLIGHT and colophon are registered trademarks of Simon & Schuster, Inc.
YOU'RE INVITED TO A CREEPOVER is a registered trademark of Simon & Schuster, Inc.
For information about special discounts for bulk purchases, please contact
Simon & Schuster Special Sales at 1-866-506-1949 or business@simonandschuster.com.
The Simon & Schuster Speakers Bureau can bring authors to your live event.
For more information or to book an event contact the Simon & Schuster Speakers Bureau
at 1-866-248-3049 or visit our website at www.simonspeakers.com.
Truth or Dare . . . text by Ellie O'Ryan
You Can't Come in Here! text by Michael Teitelbaum
Ready for a Scare? text by Heather Alexander
The Show Must Go On! text by Michael Teitelbaum
Series designed by Nicholas Sciacca
The text of this book was set in Manticore.
Manufactured in the United States of America 0522 FFG
10 9 8 7 6 5 4 3 2 1
Library of Congress Control Number 2022935296
ISBN 978-1-6659-1841-1
ISBN 978-1-4424-2158-5 (*Truth or Dare . . .* ebook)
ISBN 978-1-4424-2157-8 (*You Can't Come in Here!* ebook)
ISBN 978-1-4424-2904-8 (*Ready for a Scare?* ebook)
ISBN 978-1-4424-2906-2 (*The Show Must Go On!* ebook)
These titles were previously published individually in hardcover and paperback by Simon Spotlight.

You're invited to a

CREEPOVER

Truth or Dare . . .

You Can't Come in Here!

Ready for a Scare?

The Show Must Go On!

written by P. J. Night

SIMON SPOTLIGHT

New York   London   Toronto   Sydney   New Delhi

Truth or Dare . . .

PROLOGUE

Up and down the aisles she wandered, and though so much was familiar, there were small and unexpected differences: The lights seemed brighter, the colors looked bolder, even the sounds were louder. She smiled a little, to think how fascinated she was by a grocery store. How many times had she been in one before and hardly noticed a thing about it? Felt bored, even?

Now that seemed like a long time ago.

And here she was, drinking it all in, appreciating it, even appreciating the people around her, who weren't paying her any attention as they hurried past one another, obviously preoccupied.

Then she saw them, two girls around her age, one tall with long, straight chestnut hair; the other a little shorter, her blond hair pulled back from her face. She watched how they giggled together, how the taller one leaned down to whisper something, a secret that they shared, their heads nearly touching. She wished she knew what they were talking about. It wasn't hard to tell that they were best friends; and a pang of longing made her want to look away. But she didn't. Instead she stared harder.

Did they have any idea how lucky they were?

CHAPTER 1

Abby Miller stared at the contents of the grocery cart. "Okay, we've got soda, we've got veggies and dip, we've got popcorn," she said. "Do we need anything else?"

"What about chips?" Leah Rosen, Abby's best friend, asked.

Abby nodded. "You go get some chips and I'll find something good for breakfast."

Leah disappeared around the corner, leaving the cart behind for Abby. Abby wandered through the store to the frozen food section and stood in front of the breakfast case, weighing the waffle options: plain or buttermilk or blueberry or apple cinnamon or—

Suddenly Abby had the creepiest feeling that she was being watched. In the chrome edges of the case, she thought she saw something move.

But when she glanced behind her, no one was there.

She was the only person in the frozen food aisle.

Abby turned back to the freezer case and opened the glass door. She was reaching for a box of buttermilk waffles when—

"BOO!"

Abby shrieked as she felt a swift tug on her hair. She spun around to see Leah grinning at her.

"Gotcha!" Leah exclaimed. "Wow, I really spooked you, huh? You have goose bumps!"

"Yeah, from the freezer." Abby laughed, gesturing to the frosty air pouring out of the open case.

"Sure, Ab. Whatever you say," Leah replied, her eyes twinkling. "Check out what I got!"

Abby wrinkled her nose. "Barbecue chips? You know I don't like barbecue!"

"More for me," Leah said with a grin. "Don't worry, you're covered." She tossed a bag of tortilla chips into the cart and placed a jar of salsa next to it.

Abby added two boxes of frozen waffles. "We'll order the pizzas after everybody else gets to my house, so I think that's about everything we need."

Leah frowned. "You're forgetting one essential—dessert!"

"What's wrong with me?" Abby said, laughing. "What should we get? Cookies?"

"Brownies?" suggested Leah. The girls exchanged a glance.

"Both!" they said at the same time.

"Come on, desserts are in the next aisle," Leah said as she pushed the cart around the corner. Suddenly she backed up—right into Abby!

"Leah! What are you—," Abby began.

But Leah frantically waved her hands at her friend and whispered, "Shh! Shh!"

"What? What is it?" Abby asked as she followed Leah to the opposite end of the aisle.

Leah leaned close to Abby's ear and whispered, "Max! Max Menendez! He's right over there getting candy! Do I look okay?"

Abby reached out and smoothed out the bumps in her friend's blond ponytail. It was no secret that Leah had a major crush on Max. Every time she was around him, she got so nervous that she could barely speak. "You look great," Abby assured Leah. "Want to go say hi?"

"Are you crazy?" Leah gasped as she tried to get a

glimpse of her reflection in the freezer case's shiny silver handle.

"Come on!" Abby urged her friend as she gave Leah a little push. "This is a perfect opportunity to talk to him! I'll come with you."

But Leah shook her head. "I'll probably say something stupid," she replied. "Let's just wait here until he leaves."

"Come on, Leah!" Abby whispered. "How will you two ever go out if you won't talk to him? And this'll be a great story to tell Chloe and Nora at the party tonight."

"Party? What party?" a voice asked.

Leah and Abby spun around.

It was Max!

He smiled at the girls. "You're having a party and you didn't invite me?"

Abby looked at Leah, thinking it would be the perfect time for her friend to say *something* to Max. But Leah just stood there—as frozen as the peas across the aisle. Her eyes were so wide that she even looked a little scared.

"Um . . . of course we didn't invite you," Abby said, grinning playfully as she tried to save the situation. "It's a sleepover party. No boys allowed."

"Well, *fine*," Max said, pretending to be hurt. "I'm busy, anyway."

"Oh yeah?" asked Abby. "Doing what?"

"Wouldn't you like to know?" Max said with a laugh. "Nah, I'm just messing with you guys. I'm going to a movie with Jake and Toby. I thought I'd snag some candy before the show."

"That's cool," Abby said as her eyes lit up. She didn't notice the way Leah began to watch her. "What are you guys gonna see?"

"Don't know yet," Max replied. He laughed. "I mean, obviously some snacks were the priority, you know?"

"Well, have fun," Abby said. "We've gotta go. See you later, Max."

"See you guys," Max said. "Hey, Leah—heads up!"

Leah jumped as Max tossed a candy bar to her. "I got too much," he said with a smile. "You want one?"

"Uh, yeah, sure," Leah stammered. "Th-thanks, Max."

Max flashed another grin at the girls as he sauntered down the aisle. As soon as he was gone, Leah grabbed Abby's arm. "*Wow! He gave me a candy bar!*"

Abby smiled at Leah's excitement. "Kind of," she pointed out. "You still have to pay for it."

But Leah was too distracted to pay attention to Abby. "Max is so cute!" she gushed. "I wish I didn't get so tongue-tied around him."

"Just relax," Abby said to her friend. "He's only a boy."

"Only a boy!" exclaimed Leah. "How are you not as in love with him as I am?"

Abby thought for a moment about Max's spiky black hair and his big smile. He was definitely a hottie—but there was a guy at school who Abby thought was even hotter. "Yeah, he's pretty awesome," she said carefully.

But Leah gave Abby a piercing look. "You think there's somebody cuter than Max?" she asked. "Who?"

Abby pressed her lips together and shook her head. Her crush was top secret—and she wanted to keep it that way.

"Oh, come on, Abby," Leah begged. "I told you a million years ago that I liked Max. You owe me!"

Abby laughed. "I'm not telling. It's not my fault you can't keep your own secrets."

"I'll figure out who it is," Leah said. "It's not Toby, is it?"

"Not even close," Abby replied. "Now would you please stop? I'm not telling!"

Leah clapped her hands. "I know! I know! It's Jake, isn't it?"

Abby's mouth dropped open. "No! Why would you even think that?"

"*Jake?*" squealed Leah. "Seriously? You like *Jake?*"

"No way," Abby said firmly. "Please, can you drop it? I mean it, Leah."

Leah sighed. "Fine, be that way. But I *will* find out for sure who you like."

Abby was silent as she pushed the cart toward the produce aisle to get some strawberries for breakfast. She knew that when Leah was determined to find something out, there was no stopping her.

And Abby also knew that even though Leah was her very best friend, she couldn't keep a secret. Leah might be shy around boys, but she wasn't shy when it came to gossip. Abby knew she meant well, but telling Leah something in confidence was as good as posting it online.

Before long, the whole world would know it too.

After Abby and Leah finished buying everything they needed for the sleepover, Abby's mom drove them to Abby's house. They had just started unloading the groceries when there was a loud knock at the door. Chester, the

Millers' oatmeal-colored cocker spaniel, jumped up and ran toward the door, yipping in excitement.

"Woo-hoo!" Abby exclaimed as she hurried out of the kitchen. She flung open the front door to find her friend Nora Lewis waiting there, holding a purple duffel bag, a pink sleeping bag, and a stack of DVDs.

"Am I too early?" Nora asked as she walked inside. "My brother had to drop me off before he went to work."

"No, you're fine," said Abby. "Leah and I were just getting some snacks ready."

"Hey, Nora," Leah said, pouring the tortilla chips into a bowl. "Which movies did you bring?"

Nora's brown eyes lit up. "I raided my brother's DVD stash!" she said excitedly as she spread three DVD cases across the counter. "What do you think?"

Abby grabbed one of the cases and read the title. "*Attack of the Bee People?*" she asked.

"Oh, it's *sooo* funny," Nora said. "It's this movie from forever ago, and it was supposed to be really scary, but the special effects are horrible! It's hilarious!"

"What's this one?" asked Leah curiously. "*A Love Beyond?* Seriously?"

Nora sighed. "*Very* romantic. This guy dies, but he

never stops loving this girl, even though she tries to go on with her life. My brother would kill me if it got out that he owned this."

Abby picked up the last DVD case, which had a black cover with a pair of spooky green eyes on it. "*The Hole*," she said as she read the title aloud. "This one looks scary."

"It is," Nora said, nodding. "It's about a cursed grave that can never be closed, and whenever anybody visits the person who was buried there, they get sucked into it too."

"Cool!" Leah exclaimed. "I love scary movies! Let's save that one for right before we go to sleep."

Abby shook her head as she dropped the DVD back on the counter. "No way," she said firmly. "If we watch that one last, I'll be way too scared to sleep."

Leah laughed. "Exactly! Then we'll stay up all night for sure!"

There was another knock at the door.

"Got it," Abby said as she darted into the hallway. When she opened the front door, she found her friend Chloe Chang waiting on the front porch. Chester barked in greeting.

"Hi, Abby!" said Chloe as she stepped inside. "Hi, Chester."

"I'm so glad you're here!" Abby exclaimed. "Leah and Nora are in the kitchen."

"Excellent," Chloe said as she gave Chester a pat on the head and followed Abby into the house. "I've been looking forward to this sleepover all day!"

"Hey!" Leah said as she waved to Chloe. "Abby, did you unpack the cookies and brownies? I can't find them."

Abby shook her head. "Maybe we left a bag in the car," she replied. "I'll go check." She grabbed her mom's car keys and hurried outside.

Abby's brown hair fluttered in the cool, damp breeze; in the distance, dark clouds threatened to bring a rainstorm before morning. She unlocked the car and found one last grocery bag that had fallen under the backseat.

Then Abby felt it again: that spooky sense that someone was watching her, just as she'd felt in the grocery store.

In the silence, she heard a crackling sound, like the crunch of fallen leaves. Almost like footsteps.

But that's not possible, she thought. Abby's house was located at the end of a suburban street, next to a woodland nature preserve where people were forbidden to trespass. In all the years she'd lived there, Abby had never seen anyone in the woods.

She'd never stepped foot in them either, not with all the large NO TRESPASSING signs, bright orange warnings that were impossible to miss.

But as she stood in the driveway, Abby couldn't shake the feeling that someone was standing just beyond the trees, watching her.

Then she heard another sound coming from the woods. This one was familiar, but she couldn't place it. It was sort of like the rusty squeak of an old swing set on a stormy day, when the wind pushes the swings like invisible hands.

But there weren't any swing sets here.

Abby took a deep breath and spun around. "Hello?" she called loudly. "Who's there?"

The noise suddenly stopped. The silence was overwhelming.

Someone heard me, she thought.

"Hello?" she called again. A few moments passed. As she glanced at the nature preserve, Abby started to feel silly. *Are you some kind of baby?* she scolded herself. *Why are you getting all freaked out for absolutely no reason?*

Suddenly a creature burst out of the trees. The black blur took to the sky, cawing noisily, beating its wings with tremendous power as it flew away from the forest as fast as it could.

A crow, Abby thought with relief; she almost laughed out loud. *It was just a crow.* She grabbed the grocery bag and slammed the car door shut. She turned toward the house. She was eager to get inside and forget about the fear that had spread through her whole body as she stood, all alone, by the car.

The first thing Abby saw when she opened her door was Chester standing by the front window, growling quietly. She wanted to believe he was growling at the squirrels in the yard, but she couldn't help but think that the same thing that had spooked her had also spooked her dog. No matter how hard she tried, Abby couldn't stop thinking about the strange squeaking sound coming from somewhere in the woods, just beyond the trees.

And she couldn't shake the feeling that someone— or something—had been watching her.

CHAPTER 2

The kitchen was bright and cheery when Abby returned with the missing grocery bag. She grinned at her friends as she joined them at the table, where they'd already started digging into the snacks. Abby had decided not to tell anybody about what had happened out by the car. But she kept glancing out the window at the woods.

"How many pizzas should I get?" Leah called as she held the cell phone up to her ear. "Two? Three? The phone is ringing and—Hello? I'd like to place an order for delivery."

"Two pizzas," Abby said. "One plain and one pep-peroni?"

"Sounds good to me," Chloe said as Nora nodded.

"Hey, check this out," Chloe continued as she dug

around in her backpack. "Guess what I brought?"

"Your teddy bear?" teased Abby.

"Ha, ha," Chloe said sarcastically. "A makeover kit! It has every color lipstick you can imagine and a hundred shades of eye shadow."

Nora smiled. "Score!"

"Okay, the pizzas will be here in thirty minutes or less," Leah said as she ended her call. "What should we do until then?"

"Let's go down to the basement," Abby suggested. "We can move the furniture and set up the sleeping bags and stuff, and by the time we're done the pizzas should be here."

She grabbed the DVDs off the counter and followed her friends down the stairs. The awesome sleepover she'd been planning all week was about to begin.

And Abby couldn't wait!

After they were completely stuffed with pizza, the girls returned to the basement. It was one of Abby's favorite rooms in the house. It was set into a gentle hillside so that only part of it was underground; the other half of the basement had large windows that opened onto the backyard and the nature preserve on the side of the house. There was an overstuffed L-shaped couch covered with lots of squishy throw pillows. It was the favorite spot of her mom's black cat, Eddie, who spent most of his time in the basement avoiding Chester. Across from the couch, a large flat-screen TV was mounted on the wall. The rest of the walls were covered in cool vintage movie posters that Abby's parents had collected over the years. When all the colorful sleeping bags were spread out on the floor and the side table was covered with platters of yummy snacks, the basement turned into the perfect place for a sleepover party.

"Makeover time!" Chloe announced as she placed a pink case on the table in the middle of the room. The other girls crowded around as Chloe flipped open the lid to reveal three levels of trays, each one cluttered with a rainbow of cosmetics. The bottom of the case had a large drawer jammed with dozens of hair accessories.

"Is that *blue* mascara?" Leah asked, grabbing a tube. "I have to try that."

"Anyone want to give me a manicure?" asked Chloe. "My nails are a mess."

"Sure," Nora replied as she reached for a nail file. "What color do you want?"

Chloe frowned. "Purple?" she asked as she considered her choices. "Or pink? Or maybe silver?"

"Nora, can I do your hair?" Abby asked. "It's so gorgeous."

Nora shrugged. "Sure. But good luck. These curls do their own thing."

Leah stared into the mirror. "What do you guys think? Too much?"

Abby tried not to laugh as she glanced at Leah's crazy-heavy eye makeup; in addition to the blue mascara, she'd added purple eyeliner and two shades of glitter eye shadow. "Well, it depends what look you're going for," she began. "Cute girl on a Saturday night? Yeah, a little much. Going back in time to a disco in the seventies? Then you look perfect!"

Leah reached for the bottle of makeup remover. "I always go overboard with the eye shadow." She sighed.

"Just remember, less is more," Nora advised.

"Except when it comes to your hair, Nora," Abby said as she struggled with a round brush.

Nora laughed. "Hey, don't say I didn't warn you!"

An hour later the girls were just about done with their makeovers. Abby had never seen so many wild eyeshadow pairings and outrageous hairstyles. At least, not since her last sleepover.

"You know what? I think it's time for a little Truth or Dare," Leah suggested slyly, twirling one of her high pigtails around her finger.

"Ooh, yes!" squealed Chloe. "I *love* Truth or Dare!"

"I'm game," said Abby. "How about the person with the craziest hairdo has to go first?"

Chloe started laughing uncontrollably. "Then no doubt you're up, Nora."

"This mess on my head is all Abby's fault," replied Nora, "but sure, I'll go."

"All right, then, Nora," Chloe began, her eyes twinkling. "Truth or dare?"

Nora bit her lip as she thought about her options. "Dare," she said. "What have I got to lose now?"

"Great. I have a good one." Chloe grinned at her. "I dare you to go into the front yard and pretend you're a chicken. And I mean squawking and bawking and everything. For one whole minute."

Abby frowned slightly, remembering the spooky

feeling she'd had when she grabbed the grocery bag from the car earlier in the evening. "We don't have to go outside," she said quickly. "Nora can just do the dare down here."

"But it's way more embarrassing if she does it outside," Chloe pointed out. "I mean, somebody could *see* her!"

"No kidding," Abby said. "Did you forget that Jake Chilson lives right across the street?"

"But Jake's at the movies with Max and Toby," Leah reminded her. "And it's Chloe's dare. She gets to set the rules—no matter how heartless they are."

As everyone laughed, Nora rolled her eyes. "Whatever. It's dark. No one will see me." She held her head confidently as she climbed up the basement stairs, with everyone following behind her. When the girls walked outside, Abby saw that Nora was right about how dark it was. The moon was hidden behind some storm clouds; it was so pitch-black that she could barely see her own yard.

Or the trees looming at the edge of the nature preserve.

"Don't start yet," Chloe said. She turned to Abby.

"Do you guys have any lights in the front yard?"

"Yeah, I'll go turn them on." Abby ran over to the side of the house and flipped the big utility switch. Suddenly the front yard was flooded with light that spilled into the street, all the way over to Jake's yard. Abby snuck a glance at the sprawling red house; even though the curtains were drawn, she could tell that the lights were on in the living room. She had lived across the street from Jake for her entire life; in fact, one of her earliest memories was of the two of them digging around in the sandbox in his backyard. They had played together a lot when they were younger, but Abby hadn't been over to his house since the fifth grade. She wondered briefly if Jake still had the same spaceship wallpaper in his room, and smiled to herself as she rejoined her friends in the front yard.

"Oh, man," groaned Nora. "Abby! I didn't know your house had, like, floodlights!"

"That's not all!" Chloe announced as she whipped out her cell phone. "Smile for the camera, Nora!"

"What!" Nora cried. "You're going to *film* me?"

"Absolutely," Chloe said wickedly, holding the cell phone up so the camera would catch all of Nora's chicken impression. "Don't worry, you look fabulous!"

Nora frowned. "No fair!"

"I never said that I *wasn't* going to film you," Chloe protested. "But I guess I can skip it, Nora. If you're feeling *chicken*, I mean."

Nora gave her friend a look. "Ha, ha. Very funny, Chloe. Let me just start so I can get this over with." She walked onto the grass and began to strut around like a chicken, flapping her arms like wings and clucking, "Bawk, bawk, bawk, bawk!"

Abby and the rest of the girls didn't stop laughing until Chloe stopped filming and said, "Okay, that's one minute. Way to go, Nora. You do an awesome chicken impression."

Even Nora started to laugh as she took a bow. "That was seriously the longest minute of my life!" she complained as the girls traipsed back through the kitchen.

"Here you go, Nora," Abby said as she handed her friend a brownie. "You earned it!"

"Thanks," Nora said with a grin. "Better bring the whole tray downstairs. Truth or Dare isn't over yet!"

As soon as the girls were settled back in the basement, Leah announced, "Okay, since Nora was so brave to make a total fool out of herself—"

"*Bawk, bawk!*" clucked Chloe.

"It's her turn to ask someone," Leah finished. "Go on, Nora."

"All right, I choose our hostess. Truth or dare, Ab?"

Uh-oh, Abby thought as everyone turned to her. *I am definitely not in the mood to act like a chicken!* "Truth," she said firmly.

After all, Abby figured, Truth could never be nearly as embarrassing as the dares her friends could dream up.

Or so she thought.

"All right, Abby," Nora began. "Who do you like?"

Abby's face fell. She noticed Leah sitting across from her, beginning to smile and clearly looking forward to the answer.

"Do I *have* to answer that?" Abby pleaded, already knowing what Nora would say.

"Yes," Nora said matter-of-factly. "You picked Truth, and now you have to answer any question I ask. Those are the rules."

As much as she hated to admit it, Abby knew that Nora was right. "If I tell you . . .," she said slowly. "If I tell you who I like, you have to *promise* not to tell anyone. *Ever.*"

"Oh, we promise," Nora said as she made an X over her heart. "Cross my heart and everything!"

Leah nodded, and Chloe added, "Of *course* we won't tell anybody, Abby. You can trust us!"

"Okay." Abby sighed as her face turned redder. "I . . . like . . ."

No one made a sound as they waited for Abby to confess her crush.

"Jake!" she said at last, covering her face with a pillow.

"I *knew* it!" Leah crowed. "I *knew* you were acting weird in the supermarket earlier!"

"Jake Chilson?" asked Chloe. "Oh, he's supercute!"

"Please don't tell anybody, you guys," Abby begged. "I would die if he found out. Seriously."

"We won't say a word," promised Nora.

"Definitely not," Leah agreed.

There was an awkward pause, and Abby wondered if everyone else was thinking about what had happened last year too.

Suddenly Leah pulled her cell phone out of her pocket.

"What are you doing?" Abby asked suspiciously.

Leah looked up innocently. "I thought I could text Jake and say hi," she said, her eyes wide.

"No!" cried Abby. She lunged for Leah's phone, but Leah was too quick; she jumped out of the way and ran to the other side of the room.

"Please don't text him, Leah," Abby begged.

"Why not?" asked Leah. "I only want to help you like you helped me at the market. Like you said, how will you ever have the chance to go out with Jake if you don't talk to him? I can get the conversation started."

"No!" Abby pleaded. "I *really* don't want you to text Jake!"

"Well, *you* could always text him instead," Nora suggested.

"Oh, no. Absolutely not," replied Abby immediately. "What would I say?"

"Well, you'll never know if you don't try," said Chloe. "Maybe Jake would love it if you texted him."

Abby sighed. She knew her friends were right in a way. It would be great to text Jake if he wanted to text her, too. But what if he didn't want to? Abby decided it was a risk she was willing to take. "Fine! Fine, I'll do it!" she said as she pulled her own phone out of her back pocket. *Jake and I are friends*, Abby thought. *We've known each other forever. It won't be totally weird for me to text him. Probably.*

Abby plunked down on the couch as her friends crowded around her.

"What are you going to write?" Chloe asked excitedly.

Abby shrugged. "I'm not sure," she admitted. "What do you guys think?"

"How about this?" suggested Nora. "Dear Jake, I l-o-o-o-o-ove you. . . ."

Abby frowned playfully and grabbed a pillow and tossed it at Nora.

"Just write, 'Hey,'" Chloe suggested. "Maybe he won't even get the text right now. Maybe his phone will be off."

"Maybe," Abby said. But she didn't sound very hopeful. She sighed again as she typed HEY into her phone. Then she took a deep breath and hit send.

For a few moments, everyone was quiet with anticipation. Then, suddenly, Abby's phone pinged. All the girls shrieked.

"He wrote back! He wrote back!" Abby cried, forgetting her embarrassment as she read Jake's message aloud. "'Hey, Abby! What's up?' Aaaah! What should I write back?" she asked her friends.

"Just say, 'Nothing. What's up with you?'" Chloe advised her.

"That works," Abby replied as she started typing.

Everyone waited anxiously for Jake to reply.

Ping!

When Abby's phone beeped, all the girls screamed in excitement again. This time the cat dashed up the stairs, frightened by the commotion. "Sorry, Eddie," Abby apologized to the cat.

Suddenly the door at the top of the stairs creaked open—and everyone screamed for a third time!

"Girls?" Abby's mother asked. "Is everything okay?"

"Yeah, Mom," Abby said quickly as her friends dissolved into giggles. "Sorry if we're being too loud."

"It's okay, honey," Mrs. Miller replied. "Just try to keep it down after eleven o'clock, okay?"

"Sure," Abby said. "Good night, Mom."

As soon as Mrs. Miller closed the door, Leah reached for Abby's cell. "What did he say?" she asked excitedly.

"Hang on," Abby said, holding the phone away from Leah. She peered at the screen. "He's hanging out with Max and Toby at his house!"

"*What?*" squealed Nora. "Leah said they were all at the movies!"

"I guess they—"

Ping!

Abby read the text to herself, then started laughing so hard she couldn't speak.

"What did he say?" Leah asked, bouncing up and down a little.

Abby glanced up from her phone. "He says they were wondering if Nora is feeling okay!" she cried. "I guess they saw your little chicken dance."

"*Nooooooo!*" groaned Nora. "Chloe, you are so dead! I can't believe you made me do that stupid dare where everybody could see it. And with all those lights on!"

"Sorry," Chloe said with a shrug, but she had such a big smile on her face that the other girls knew she didn't mean it.

Abby didn't say anything as her fingers flew over the keypad.

"What did you write back?" asked Nora.

"I just told him that you felt like dancing." Abby giggled. "You know you've got all the coolest moves!"

"You guys, this is so awful!" Nora moaned. "If they tell everybody at school on Monday, I will die."

Ping!

This time, Abby started laughing before she even finished reading the text. "Jake says they thought Nora was trying to defeat the evil Octopus Girl!" she shrieked. "I think he means you, Leah!"

Leah's hands flew up to her crazy hairdo as everyone turned to look at her. "Eight pigtails!" she groaned. "Oh man, they really *do* look like octopus tentacles!"

Ping!

Ping!

Ping!

Ping!

"What did he say?" Leah asked. "Anything more about any of us?"

Abby held out her phone so everyone could see Jake's latest texts for themselves.

BATTLE OF THE CENTURY

SUPER CHICKEN VS OCTO-GIRL

FOWL MEETS FISH

WHO WILL WIN?

Abby was howling with laughter along with the other girls when a terrible thought struck her. Had Jake and his pals noticed her own wild hairstyle? The double French braids Nora had attempted to give her were so lumpy that they practically looked like stegosaurus spines.

Abby didn't want to know whatever awful nickname

the boys had dreamed up for her. She turned back to her cell phone and sent one more quick text to Jake.

G2G, C U MONDAY! B4N!

Then Abby turned off her phone.

"Abby!" cried Leah. "Why'd you do that? Things were just getting interesting."

"I figured we should quit while we were ahead. You know, before the guys had a chance to nickname the rest of us. Let's watch a movie now," Abby said, trying to change the subject. "*Attack of the Bee People*, anyone?"

"Awesome," Nora said. "I promise you won't be disappointed!"

While Leah set up the DVD, Abby turned off the lights. Then she joined the rest of the girls on the couch. As the movie started, she checked her cell phone to make sure she had turned it off.

Several hours later the basement was dark and quiet. There wasn't a single sound except for the deep, calm breathing of the sleeping girls.

Suddenly the basement was filled with an eerie green glow.

BZZZZZZZZZZZZZZZZZ!

BZZZZZZZZZZZZZZZZZ!

BZZZZZZZZZZZZZZZZZ!

Abby rubbed her eyes as she started to wake up. What *was* that noise? It sounded familiar.

"What's that?" mumbled Leah.

"The bee people!" Chloe gasped, sitting straight up in her sleeping bag.

"No, no, that was just a movie," Abby said sleepily. "I think it's my phone."

BZZZZZZZZZZZZZZZZZ!

BZZZZZZZZZZZZZZZZZ!

Abby fumbled around on the floor near her sleeping bag, but she couldn't find her phone anywhere. "Guys, where is my phone?" she asked. "I left it right here when we went to bed."

BZZZZZZZZZZZZZZZZZ!

BZZZZZZZZZZZZZZZZZ!

"Abby, is that it?" Nora asked, pointing across the room. Sure enough, Abby's phone was sitting on the table by the stairs, glowing in the darkness. It rattled across the table every time it vibrated.

"Sorry, everybody," Abby apologized as she crawled

out of her sleeping bag. "I swear, I thought I turned it off."

"Who would text you in the middle of the night?" Chloe asked.

"I don't know," Abby said as she picked up her phone. She squinted her eyes as she peered at the message, trying to read what it said.

Her eyes swept across the screen, and before she could stop herself, she gasped in horror.

"Abby! What's wrong?" Leah asked as she stood up. "What does it say?" She grabbed the phone out of Abby's hand as the other girls gathered around, and held it up so that everyone could read the mysterious text message that Abby had received. It said:

LEAVE HIM ALONE. HE'S MINE!!! DON'T MAKE ME TELL YOU TWICE!

CHAPTER 3

"What?" Chloe cried as she grabbed the phone from Leah.

"Somebody get the lights," Nora said nervously.

In the darkness, Leah stumbled over to the stairs and flipped the light switch—but the soft glow from the lamps didn't make the text any less scary. One look at her friends' faces told Abby that they were as terrified as she was.

"Who sent that text?" Abby asked as she reached for her phone, her hands shaking so much that she almost dropped it on the floor. "I don't know this number. Do you guys recognize it?"

One by one, her friends stared at the screen, then shook their heads.

"Did you—did you do anything to upset anybody?" Nora asked, her voice unsure. "Whoever sent this text sounds mad—*really* mad."

"No—I mean, not that I know of," Abby replied, her eyes glued to her phone, reading the creepy text again. "And if I did, I would want somebody to, you know, tell me—not send some freaky message in the middle of the night."

"Why would someone text you at four o'clock in the morning, anyway?" asked Leah.

"And why would they say *that*?" Chloe chimed in. "I mean, who is 'him'?"

No one answered her—but Abby could tell that they were all thinking of Jake. Could it be a coincidence that she'd received this strange message just hours after she had confessed her crush? *I wish I'd kept my mouth shut*, she thought with regret.

Abby wrapped her arms around herself and shivered. "This doesn't make any sense," she said. "What was my phone doing over there on the table? I *always* sleep next to it. And how did it get turned on? I *know* I turned it off before we watched the movie. I don't understand—did one of you—"

"I'm sure nobody messed with your phone," Nora tried to reassure her. "Maybe you just forgot about checking it before bed, and you accidentally left it on the table or something."

Abby shook her head. "No, I don't—"

"You know what?" Leah said suddenly. "Maybe it was a wrong number."

"Maybe," Abby said slowly. "But that still doesn't explain why . . ."

She trailed off, and Leah spoke up. "Listen, here's how I *know* it's a wrong number. Because you're, like, the nicest girl in the world, and nobody who knows you would *ever* send you a message like that." Leah smiled at her friend.

Abby tried to smile back.

"I mean, it's actually really funny, when you think about it," Leah continued. "Since this is obviously a wrong number, whoever sent it thinks she told somebody off—when she really didn't!"

Leah was on a roll. "Oh, I told *her*," she said in a silly high-pitched voice as she imitated the anonymous girl who'd sent the text. "That girl will *definitely* leave my guy alone now!"

There was a brief pause, and then everybody started to giggle.

"You really think it's no big deal?" Abby asked.

"Of course," Leah said confidently. Then she yawned loudly. "Come on, let's go back to sleep. The sun's not even up yet."

Abby turned her phone off and held it for just a moment. Then she put it back on the table by the stairs before returning to her sleeping bag.

For some reason she couldn't quite explain, Abby didn't want to sleep anywhere near it.

The sun was shining brightly when Abby and her friends finally awoke for the day. As the girls ate waffles and strawberries for a late breakfast, Chloe suddenly said, "Maybe it wasn't a wrong number. Maybe it was a prank!"

"Huh?" asked Leah sleepily as she rubbed her eyes.

"That weird text Abby got last night," Nora reminded her. Then she turned to Chloe. "What do you mean?"

Chloe shrugged. "Well, Abby was texting Jake last night, and Jake was hanging out with Max and Toby," she explained. "Maybe one of them thought it would be funny to send her a scary message in the middle of the night. You know those guys. They can act like total idiots sometimes."

"Maybe it was Jake!" Leah exclaimed.

"No," Abby said, shaking her head. "Jake's too nice. He wouldn't do that."

"He might be nice, but he has a wicked sense of humor," Leah said knowingly. "Remember when he and Max convinced Joey Abrams that everybody was going to do the wave in math class, and Joey had to start it since he sat in the first desk? And then Joey jumped up with his arms in the air, but nobody else did?"

"And Ms. Garcia was all, 'Joey? Are you okay?'" remembered Chloe as she cracked up.

"Oh, and remember that time when they broke into Brandon Murphy's locker and covered all his books in sparkly pink wrapping paper? And he had to carry them around like that all day, until he could go home and re-cover them!" added Nora.

The girls laughed at the memory of Brandon shuffling from class to class with his shiny pink book covers grabbing everyone's attention.

"Those pranks were pretty intense. And Joey and

Brandon are some of Jake's best friends!" Leah continued. "Yeah, I totally wouldn't put it past Jake to prank you. After all, you *did* text him first last night! And maybe this is his way of telling you that he likes you."

Abby blushed at the thought that Jake liked her, too, but she wasn't convinced that it'd been him who texted her last night.

Chloe recognized the look on her friend's face. "Don't worry, Abby, I don't think Jake did it. He doesn't seem like the type of guy who would do something like that to a girl, you know? I still think it was just a wrong number."

"Well, there's one way to find out," Leah said. "Why don't we call the number back and see who picks up?"

"No way," Abby said at once. "Whoever sent that text was obviously really upset. I don't want to make them any madder."

"We could ask Jake if he sent the text," suggested Nora. "Come on, Abby, aren't you curious?"

"Nope," Abby replied, shaking her head. "Not that curious, anyway. I don't want anyone to know about it. I'm serious."

Her friends exchanged a glance.

"What would be so bad about that?" asked Nora.

"Because it was weird," Abby said. "Even if it was just a wrong number, even if it was just a prank, it was creepy, and I don't want anyone else to know about it, okay? From now on, consider it a secret. It doesn't leave this house. Just like you swore you wouldn't tell *anyone* that I like Jake. Swear it, okay?"

"Sure," Nora replied, as Chloe nodded in agreement. Then all eyes turned to Leah.

"Leah?" Abby asked.

"Whatever you want, Abby," Leah said loudly. "I swear I won't tell a single, solitary soul!"

"Won't tell what?" asked Mrs. Miller as she walked into the room. "Good morning, girls."

"Oh, I can't tell you, Mrs. Miller," Leah said, widening her eyes innocently. "What happens at Abby's sleepover, *stays* at Abby's sleepover!"

Everyone laughed as Mrs. Miller poured herself a cup of coffee. "Sounds serious," she joked. "I hope you all had fun last night."

"We did," Chloe replied. "Thanks for letting us sleep over."

"Oh, anytime!" Mrs. Miller said.

Just then a car horn honked outside. Chester barked in reply, and Abby peeked out the window. "Hey, Chloe, your mom is here," she said.

"Ack! I still have to pack up my makeover kit!" Chloe cried as she scurried downstairs.

"I'll help you," Nora said, following her.

"So what are you doing today?" Leah asked Abby. "Any awesome plans? Any awesome plans that would be even more awesome with me?"

"Nope," Abby said. "Homework. I have a ton, and I haven't even started yet."

"Boo! You're no fun," Leah said, pouting.

"What about you?" Abby asked. "Did you finish all your homework already?"

"No," admitted Leah. "But that's what Sunday *night* is for—not Sunday *day*."

"Yeah, well, I'll probably still be working tonight," Abby said. "I've barely started my English paper."

"Oh, good, neither have I," Leah said brightly. "I'll text you when I get writer's block!"

There was another honk outside. "That's my mom," said Leah, picking up her plate and putting it in the sink. "Thanks for an awesome sleepover, Abby!

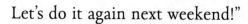

Let's do it again next weekend!"

"Maybe," Abby said with a smile. "I'll talk to you later, okay?"

"You know it," Leah said, grinning over her shoulder at Abby.

After all her friends went home, Abby trudged down the hall to her first-floor bedroom to start her homework. But her bed looked so comfortable that she decided to lie down for just a moment. The next thing she knew, she heard her mother calling her for dinner. *Oh, man,* Abby realized as she blinked her eyes sleepily. *I slept all afternoon! Now I'm going to be up late doing my stupid homework.*

Abby ate dinner as quickly as she could, then hurried back to her desk and logged onto her computer. Just as she opened a new document to start writing her report, an instant message flashed onto her screen. It was from Leah.

Leah601: HEY!!! HOW IS YOUR HOMEWORK GOING? ALMOST DONE?

AbbyGirl: UGH, NO. I FELL ASLEEP AND HAVEN'T EVEN STARTED YET.

Leah601: WELCOME TO MY WORLD.

AbbyGirl: DID U SLEEP ALL AFTERNOON TOO?

Leah601: NO . . . I JUST COULDN'T GET STARTED. I WASN'T IN THE MOOD.

AbbyGirl: WHEN ARE YOU EVER IN THE MOOD FOR HOMEWORK?

Leah601: ☺

Leah601: I JUST COULDN'T STOP THINKING AFTER LAST NIGHT . . .

AbbyGirl: ?

Leah601: I WAS THINKING ABOUT HOW YOU LIKE JAKE.

AbbyGirl: WHAT ABOUT IT?

Leah601: IT MADE ME THINK ABOUT . . .

Abby frowned at the screen. *What's up with Leah?* Then she heard a *ping*; Leah had sent her a link. Abby clicked on it and waited for the website to load. When she saw what was on the website, her heart sank. She knew exactly why her friend had sent her that link. The *ping* of a new message rang through Abby's room.

Leah601: WELL? DID U CHECK IT OUT?

AbbyGirl: YEAH.

Leah601: AND?

AbbyGirl: I KNOW WHAT U MEAN.

Leah601: IT'S STILL SO SAD.

AbbyGirl: DEFINITELY.

Leah601: ANYWAY, I BETTER GO. HOMEWORK CALLS. SEE YA TOMORROW.

Abby closed the IM window, but she didn't start her report. Instead she found herself clicking back on the website Leah had sent her: the homepage for the Sara James Memorial Scholarship Foundation. As Abby looked at the large picture of Sara on the website, she felt a strong pang of sorrow. She remembered when that picture was taken—almost one year ago, on last year's school picture day. When Sara sat on the metal stool and smiled for the camera, she didn't know that it was the last picture anyone would ever take of her. She didn't know that she had just weeks to live.

Sara and her family had moved to Riverdale two years ago. At a large school like Riverdale Middle, a new student wasn't usually a big deal, but Sara was special. With her long red hair, sparkling green eyes, and mysterious smile, everyone was fascinated by her—especially the boys. It seemed like everybody wanted to get to know her, but Sara was totally into Jake. They had become a couple almost immediately, and Abby hardly ever saw them apart. Abby could still remember them sitting together at a corner lunch table, Jake's head bent low as Sara whispered a secret into his ear, her sleek red hair brushing against his cheek. While most of the other guys in their class were goofing off and acting totally immature, Jake seemed to really be falling in love.

Then everything went terribly wrong one foggy autumn evening as Sara walked home alone after studying at Jake's house. A car rounded the corner just a little too fast, lost control, and swerved onto the sidewalk, slamming into Sara and killing her instantly. Abby remembered all too well the awful days that followed: the small groups of students crying quietly at school; the funeral that was unbearably sad; the scholarship foundation that Sara's grieving parents had started to make sure their beloved daughter would never be forgotten.

And Abby remembered something else, too: the heavy cloud of sadness that seemed to follow Jake everywhere last year. In fact, it was only recently that Jake had started to seem like his old self. It seemed like his summer away at baseball camp had really lifted his spirits. Abby was so happy to see her old friend smiling again. And she started to realize that she liked him as more than just a friend, and maybe he liked her that way too.

But as she looked at the photo of Sara, Abby felt her hope fade. *Even if Jake is ready to go out with someone else, I'm totally not his type. I'm* nothing *like Sara James.*

Suddenly the light on Abby's desk burned out with a loud *pop* that made her jump. In the darkness of the bedroom, the computer monitor gave a spooky glow to Sara's photo on the website. Abby shook her head as she closed the site and went to the basement to find a new lightbulb.

But it was impossible for her to forget those luminous green eyes, gleaming in the darkness.

CHAPTER 4

Arriving at school the next morning, Abby and Leah found a cluster of kids just inside the entrance, blocking the front doors. Abby raised her eyebrows as she looked at Leah. "What's going on?" she asked.

"Must be something important," Leah said as she craned her neck, trying to get a glimpse over the crowd. "Or something exciting!"

"Exciting? Here? Yeah, right." Abby laughed as they slowly made their way into the lobby. Just beyond the doors, they saw what all the fuss was about: a large poster announcing the first dance of the school year.

Leah grabbed Abby's arm. "A dance!" she squealed. "I can't wait! And it's the perfect excuse to get a new outfit. What are you going to wear?"

"Let's see," Abby mused. "My gray hoodie and my favorite jeans."

Leah frowned. "You're kidding," she said bluntly. "That is the worst outfit for a dance."

"But it's perfect for lounging around and watching TV," Abby said. "Which is what I will be doing instead of going to some stupid dance."

"Don't be like that," Leah complained. "I know the dances were boring last year, but this is the first dance of this year. That's kind of a big deal."

"Whatever," replied Abby. "Every dance is the same, Leah. They play the same lame music and serve the same nasty cafeteria hot dogs every single time. And all the girls stand around just waiting for *anybody* to ask them to dance while all the guys end up shooting hoops. No thank you. Come on, I need to go to my locker before homeroom."

But Leah hovered near the poster. "Well, here's something different," she said slowly. "It says here that proceeds from the dance will go to the Sara James Memorial Scholarship Fund. You know what that means, right? You-know-who will definitely be there, so—"

"Shhh!" Abby hissed, glancing around to make sure

no one had overhead Leah. "You promised you wouldn't mention that ever again."

"All right, all right," Leah said. "I just want you to come to the dance! It won't be any fun without you. Please?"

"I'll think about it," Abby finally said, just to stop Leah from badgering her.

"That sounds like a yes!" Leah said, clapping her hands. "Now, seriously, what are we going to wear?"

"I'll think about that, too," Abby promised with a laugh. She couldn't stay annoyed with Leah, not after being her best friend since kindergarten—even if it meant suffering through another awful dance in the gym.

But as the days passed, it started to look like Leah was right to be excited. The whole school was buzzing with rumors about the dance, like that the student council's events planning committee had actually hired a DJ and promised to order better food. After school on Wednesday, Abby and Leah joined a group of kids who had gathered around Morgan Matthews, the class president. Morgan was in the process of describing all the improvements she had planned for the dance. "It's the *least* we can do in memory of Sara," she gushed.

Abby resisted the urge to roll her eyes. "Um, I don't think a pizza upgrade is a really special way to remember Sara," she whispered to Leah.

Just then she felt someone tug on her backpack. She turned around to see who was behind her.

It was Jake!

Oh, no, Abby thought in a panic. *Did he overhear me?*

"You know what?" Jake asked in a low voice. "I couldn't agree more."

"Hi, uh, hey, Jake," Abby stammered. "Yeah . . . it's kind of weird, huh?"

"A little bit," Jake said, nodding. "What are you doing now?"

"I was just about to head out for the bus," Abby said.

"It's such a nice day," Jake began. "I was wondering if you'd like to walk home with me."

"Um, yeah," Abby said as her heart started to pound. She shot a quick glance at Leah. "I'll see you later, Leah?"

"I'll call you!" Leah exclaimed as she gave Abby a little wave. "Bye, Abby! Bye, Jake!"

As Abby and Jake crossed the wide school lawn toward the sidewalk, Abby couldn't think of a single thing to say. Finally she blurted out, "So how's your school year going?"

"It's good, so far," Jake replied. "A lot more work this year, huh?"

"Tell me about it," Abby said. "I have *hours* of homework every night."

"Me too!" exclaimed Jake. "I already can't wait for summer vacation."

"Well, that's only eight months away," Abby pointed out.

"Don't remind me," Jake groaned.

Abby smiled at Jake and looked down at her feet. She couldn't remember the last time she'd been so happy to walk home.

"So that dance," Jake began, "it's turning into kind of a big deal, I guess."

"I guess," Abby said carefully. "Everybody seems really excited about it."

"Are you?" Jake asked, shifting his backpack to his other shoulder. "I mean, are you going?"

"Um, yeah," Abby replied. "I think so."

"That's cool," Jake said. "Me too. Do you want a ride?"

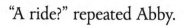

"A ride?" repeated Abby.

"Yeah," Jake said. "My mom's going to drive me, so we could give you a ride. If you want one."

"Yeah, sure," Abby said quickly. "That sounds great."

Jake smiled at her, and Abby felt like she had a hundred butterflies fluttering in her stomach. "Great," he repeated. "We'll come over at seven on Saturday."

"Okay," Abby replied. "I'm, um, looking forward to it."

"Me too," Jake said. Then, lowering his voice, he added, "I heard a rumor that there's even going to be *pizza*."

As they rounded the corner of Elmhurst Lane, Abby started to laugh. "Do you mean *really* amazing, *really* delicious pizza?" she asked, imitating Morgan. Jake's laughter told Abby that her impression was spot-on.

"Well, here's my house," Abby said.

"Right," Jake said. "I'll see you around. Later, Abby."

"Bye, Jake," Abby replied as Jake turned to cross the street. She couldn't stop grinning as she walked along the path to her house. When she had almost reached the front door, she dared to glance behind her.

Jake was standing across the street, looking at her—and smiling! When he saw Abby peeking over her

shoulder, he held up his hand in a wave. Then he turned away and walked over to his own front door.

Abby opened the door as slowly and calmly as she could, just in case Jake could still see her. But when she got inside, she raced down the hall to her room, smiling so broadly that her cheeks started to ache a little. As she expected, she already had two voice mails, an e-mail, and IMs from Leah.

Leah601: HELLOOOOOO!!

Leah601: WHERE ARE YOU? I AM DYING HERE!!!!!

Abby grinned as she sat down at her computer. She quickly typed a message back to Leah.

AbbyGirl: I'M HERE!!

Leah601: WELL?!?! WHAT HAPPENED?!?!

AbbyGirl: JAKE IS GONNA GIVE ME A RIDE TO THE DANCE!

AbbyGirl: HELLO?

AbbyGirl: DID I LOSE U?

Leah601: SORRY, I FAINTED AND FELL OFF MY CHAIR. R U SERIOUS?! ABBY! U HAVE A DATE W/ JAKE!!!

AbbyGirl: NO, IT'S NOT A DATE, JUST A RIDE :)

Leah601: WHATEVER!! IT'S TOTALLY A DATE. I HATE U SO MUCH. U R SO LUCKY.

AbbyGirl: OH PLZ. IT'S JUST A RIDE.

Leah601: COME ON, HE'S SOOO INTO U! AND U DIDN'T EVEN WANT TO GO TO THE DANCE!

AbbyGirl: LOL, I WANT TO NOW!

Just then Abby heard her mom's voice. "Honey, can you take Chester out?" Mrs. Miller called from the living room. "He won't stop barking, and I'm expecting a phone call any minute now."

"Sure, Mom," Abby called back. Then she typed one more message to Leah.

AbbyGirl: GOTTA TAKE CHESTER FOR A WALK. CALL U LATER?

Leah601: U BETTER! WE HAVE SO MUCH TO DISCUSS! BYE!

Abby bounded down the hall. "Chester!" she said. "Let's go for a walk, cutie!" Chester trotted up to Abby, wagging his tail. She fastened a red leash to the dog's collar and walked toward the front door.

But as they approached the door, Chester's fur

suddenly bristled. His mouth twisted into a snarl as he started growling, a long, low, menacing sound that sent chills up Abby's spine.

"What's the matter, boy?" Abby asked as she moved closer to the door and glanced outside. Across the yard, golden sunlight streamed through the trees in the nature preserve. It looked like a beautiful autumn afternoon—and completely ordinary. Abby couldn't imagine why Chester seemed so tense, but there was definitely something outside that was making him growl so fiercely.

"Shhh, it's okay, Chester," Abby said soothingly as she stroked his head for a few seconds. Eventually he stopped growling, though he wouldn't take his eyes off the door.

But the minute Abby reached for the doorknob, Chester started barking so furiously that Mrs. Miller called out, "Abby! I'm on the phone!"

"Okay, okay!" Abby replied as she scooped up Chester and hurried through the front door. Once they were on the sidewalk in front of the neighbor's lawn, the dog calmed down immediately, but Abby couldn't stop wondering what had bothered him. "Was it a squirrel, buddy?" she asked. "Or another dog, maybe?"

Chester just trotted alongside her, wagging his tail happily. Abby shook her head and gave up trying to figure out what had spooked her pup; she decided to think about more important things as she turned off Elmhurst Lane, like imagining what she and Jake could talk about at the dance. But that made her nervous. She could feel her palms start to sweat. *Why are you being so silly?* she thought. *You've known him forever.* She smiled at her foolishness and started mentally rummaging through her closet instead, analyzing each potential outfit she could wear. *Definitely not a dress,* she mused. *I don't want to look like I'm trying too hard. Maybe my new skirt?*

As dusk began to fall, Chester started to seem a little tired from their long walk. Abby started heading back home. As soon as they got inside, Chester curled up in his dog bed in the living room and fell right asleep.

Abby walked into the kitchen, where her mom was making a big green salad. Eddie was lounging on the kitchen floor, clearly happy that the dog wasn't around. "Mmm, something smells good! What's for dinner?"

"Your favorite—lasagna," her mom said.

Abby's stomach growled. "Score! Can I help?"

Mrs. Miller shook her head. "It's already in the

oven," she explained. "Dinner will be in about half an hour, okay?"

"Yum. I can't wait," Abby said, grabbing a handful of baby carrots from the colander on the counter. Then she paused. "Um, Mom? I have to ask you something."

"Go ahead, honey," Mrs. Miller said as she chopped a tomato.

"Um . . . ," began Abby awkwardly. "There's a dance at school this Saturday night, and, uh . . . Jake Chilson said he could give me a ride—er, his mom would drive, of course—so . . . is that okay?"

Mrs. Miller looked up, smiling at her daughter. "Of course, Abby!" she said. "That's exciting! Is Jake your date?"

"Um, maybe," Abby said, looking down and squirming a little. "It's just a ride to the dance, you know? It's not like a big deal or anything."

"Do you want me to pick you two up when the dance ends?" Mrs. Miller asked.

"Uh, I think Mrs. Chilson will pick us up, but I'll ask Jake," Abby said. "Anyway, I'm going to get started on my homework."

"Okay, sweetie," Mrs. Miller said. "Don't forget to set the table before dinner."

When Abby got back to her computer, she had another instant message waiting from Leah. It said:

Leah601: I FIGURED OUT WHAT U SHOULD WEAR TO THE DANCE, CUZ I'M BRILLIANT! YOUR NEW BLUE TOP (THE ONE WITH THE BELT). IT'S GORGEOUS AND J WILL LOVE IT!

A smile spread across Abby's face. She knew just the top Leah was thinking of; it was pale blue with a skinny black belt that looped around the waist. She pulled the top out of her dresser and tried it on, then examined her reflection in the mirror. The color was a perfect contrast against Abby's dark brown hair. *Leah is brilliant!* she thought happily as she twirled in front of the mirror.

Then, out of the corner of her eye, Abby thought she saw a flash of color in the mirror's reflection. She spun around just in time to catch a glimpse of red outside. She raced over to the window for a better look.

In the twilight, she saw the shadowy figure of a girl running away from the window, right through her yard.

The girl had long red hair.

CHAPTER 5

Abby yanked off the top, threw on a T-shirt, and ran outside as quickly as she could, her heart pounding wildly. She was determined to catch up with that girl and find out who she was—and why she was looking in Abby's window.

"Hey!" Abby yelled, careening out the back door. "Who are you? What are you doing here?"

But there was no answer.

She can't be far, Abby thought as she strode through the yard. "I said, *who are you?*" she shouted again.

Still no response.

Abby paused as she reached the edge of the nature preserve. She looked back at her neighbors' yards but didn't see anyone running through them. There was only one possibility: The girl must have disappeared into the woods.

Abby hesitated for just a moment as she glanced at the neon orange sign that read WARNING: TRESPASSERS WILL BE PROSECUTED. She had never set foot in the nature preserve before.

Then again, she'd never caught some stranger staring into her window, either.

Abby took a deep breath and stepped through the wild and overgrown brush. The trees cast long, looming shadows that made Abby shiver—from fear as well as from the sudden chill in the air. The sun was setting. It would soon be dark.

The thought pushed her forward.

"I just want to talk to you," Abby called. "I just want to find out why you were looking in my window."

But the only sound was the crackle of dry, dead leaves being crushed beneath Abby's feet as she walked deeper into the woods. As night seemed to fall faster and faster, she paused. She started to reach for her cell phone.

Suddenly she heard footsteps behind her!

Abby sucked in her breath sharply as she spun around, ready to face whoever had been peeking in her window.

"Hey, kiddo!" Mr. Miller said from the edge of the nature preserve, his suit coat slung over his shoulder. "What are you doing in there? Don't make me call the police to report a trespasser!"

"Ha, ha!" Abby said, so relieved to see her dad that she actually laughed at one of his dumb jokes.

"I thought I saw you run back here when I got home," Mr. Miller continued. "What's going on?"

"Nothing, Dad," Abby said, hoping that her voice sounded normal. With one last glance into the nature preserve, she walked back to her yard. She knew that with her father standing right next to her, there was no hope of finding the mysterious red-haired girl or figuring out why she'd been staring in Abby's window.

"Come on, let's go inside. It's starting to get chilly out," Mr. Miller said. "How was school today?"

"Good," Abby replied. "Mom made lasagna for dinner."

"Fantastic!" exclaimed Mr. Miller as they walked inside. "That sounds delicious."

"Abby, honey, did you set the table?" Mrs. Miller called.

"In a minute, Mom," Abby replied as she reached for

her cell phone, dying to tell Leah all about the strange red-haired girl.

"Abby, it's almost time to eat," Mrs. Miller said as she poked her head out of the kitchen. "Can you please set the table now?"

With a sigh, Abby shoved her phone back into her pocket and walked into the kitchen, where she grabbed a stack of plates and a handful of silverware.

"Did you tell Dad your big news?" asked Mrs. Miller as she carried a platter of sliced bread into the dining room.

"I don't have big news," Abby replied, confused.

"Well, of course you do!" Mrs. Miller exclaimed. "Bob, Jake Chilson asked Abby to go to the dance with him!"

"Mom!" Abby cried. "Why are you making a huge deal out of this?"

"Wait a minute—do I need to have a talk with Jake before you guys head out to the dance?" asked Mr. Miller. He frowned, but Abby could tell by the twinkle in his eyes that he was teasing her.

"Dad, it's just Jake," Abby said. "And he's *just* giving me a ride."

"Still, perhaps I should have a chat with him before—," began Mr. Miller.

"Ugh!" Abby groaned. "Absolutely not! Why are you—"

"Kiddo, I'm just fooling around." Mr. Miller grinned at Abby. "I'm sure you'll have a lot of fun."

Abby sighed once more as she placed the last fork on the table. Then she slipped down the hall to send Leah an instant message in peace.

"Don't get sucked into the Internet, honey," Mrs. Miller called after her. "Dinner is in five minutes!"

"I just have to go hang up my new top, Mom!" Abby replied, rolling her eyes since she knew her mom couldn't see her. "I'll be right back!"

She ducked into her room, closing the door behind her as she breathed a sigh of relief. Then she stopped and sniffed the air, catching a whiff of—what was it? A flowery scent, like jasmine or gardenia, but more exotic. It reminded her of something. Something that she couldn't quite place, a memory that she couldn't quite recall. With a slight frown, Abby sat down at her computer and sent an instant message to Leah.

AbbyGirl: JUST CAUGHT A RED-HAIRED GIRL STARING IN MY WINDOW!!!

Leah601: WHAT???!!!

AbbyGirl: I FOLLOWED HER INTO THE WOODS BUT SHE DISAPPEARED.

AbbyGirl: HER HAIR LOOKED JUST LIKE . . .

Leah601: ???

AbbyGirl: I KNOW IT SOUNDS CRAZY, BUT HER HAIR LOOKED LIKE SARA'S. I'M REALLY WEIRDED OUT.

Leah601: K, SETTLE DOWN. TAKE A DEEP BREATH.

Leah601: EVERYBODY HAS BEEN TALKING ABOUT SARA A LOT, W/ THE DANCE AND ALL . . .

Leah601: AND U PROBABLY FEEL A LITTLE STRANGE FOR GOING ON A DATE W/ JAKE . . .

Leah601: I AM SURE U JUST IMAGINED IT.

Abby's fingers flew over the keyboard as she wrote back.

AbbyGirl: BUT HER HAIR . . . IT LOOKED JUST LIKE SARA'S!!!

Leah responded again in seconds.

Leah601: THAT'S HOW I KNOW U R IMAGINING IT. SARA'S GONE. SO THERE IS NO POSSIBLE WAY THAT THIS REALLY HAPPENED. I PROMISE.

Abby paused for a moment as she considered what Leah had written. Was it possible that she had imagined the girl? She had seemed so real, running away from Abby's window. But by the time Abby had reached the backyard, the girl had vanished without a trace.

It would make sense, she realized, if the girl didn't exist at all, if Abby had raced outside to chase a figment of her imagination. After all, it was possible that the red hair Abby thought she saw was just a trick of the light from the setting sun. She felt her cheeks grow warm at the thought.

AbbyGirl: IT SEEMED WAY TOO REAL TO BE MY IMAGINATION.

AbbyGirl: BUT IT'S OVER NOW, I GUESS.

AbbyGirl: DON'T TELL ANYONE, OKAY? I FEEL SOOOOOO STUPID.

Leah601: YOUR SECRET IS SAFE W/ME, SILLY! JUST RELAX AND BE HAPPY.

Leah601: YOUR DREAM GUY ASKED U OUT TODAY! THAT'S SO AWESOME! U SHOULD BE CELEBRATING, NOT FREAKING OUT OVER NOTHING.

AbbyGirl: GOTCHA. LISTEN, I GOTTA GO EAT DINNER. TALK LATER?

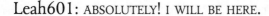

Abby stood up and pushed in her desk chair. Then she turned around to pick up her top from the floor.

But it wasn't there.

Abby frowned. *I know I tossed it on the floor when I changed to run outside,* she thought, *so where is it?*

She looked in the hamper in the corner of her room, peeked under her bed, and even rummaged through her dresser drawers.

Her beautiful new top was nowhere to be found.

Okay, this is bizarre, Abby thought as she bit her lip. *Where could it be?*

"Abby!" her mom called.

"Be right there!" she yelled back.

Then she glanced at her closet. The door was closed.

A sudden feeling of fear washed over Abby. *I know I didn't close the closet door,* she thought slowly. Step by step, she walked across the room, her heart thudding loudly in her chest. Her hand started to shake as she reached for the smooth brass doorknob; she dreaded opening the door. Who—or what—would she find behind it?

Just do it, she told herself. *One—two—three—*

Abby took a deep breath and yanked open the door. She peered into the dark closet and saw . . .

Her clothes, hanging neatly. Her shoes, arranged in careful pairs on the floor. Her suitcase, tucked in the corner.

Abby was so relieved that she started to laugh out loud. *I can't believe that I was scared to open my own closet door,* she thought. *I have got to chill out.*

Then she saw something blue jammed in the corner of the closet. She reached down to pick it up and realized that she was holding the sleeve of her new top.

Only the sleeve.

The rest of the top, ripped down the middle, was stuffed under her suitcase.

CHAPTER 6

AbbyGirl: U STILL THERE?!?!?!?!

Leah601: YEAH, WHAT'S UP?

AbbyGirl: SOMETHING CRAZY IS DEFINITELY GOING ON! I JUST FOUND MY BRAND-NEW TOP RIPPED UP!

Leah601: HUH?

AbbyGirl: BEFORE I RAN OUTSIDE TO FIND THAT GIRL, I CHANGED OUT OF MY NEW TOP, BUT WHEN I GOT BACK TO MY ROOM, I COULDN'T FIND IT.

AbbyGirl: FINALLY I LOOKED IN MY CLOSET AND MY TOP IS RUINED! IT'S BEEN TORN INTO PIECES! SOMETHING REALLY SCARY IS GOING ON!!!

Leah601: OKAY, OKAY, CALM DOWN. THERE HAS TO BE A REASONABLE EXPLANATION FOR THIS. MAYBE CHESTER GOT IT AND CHEWED IT UP.

AbbyGirl: RIGHT, SO AFTER CHESTER RIPPED UP MY TOP, HE SHOVED IT IN THE BACK OF THE CLOSET AND SHUT THE DOOR?!?!

AbbyGirl: COME ON, HE'S A DOG, THAT DOESN'T MAKE ANY SENSE!!!

Leah601: DON'T YELL @ ME! I'M JUST TRYING TO HELP!

AbbyGirl: SORRY, I'M JUST REALLY FREAKED OUT.

Leah601: MAYBE YOUR MOM CLOSED THE CLOSET DOOR?

AbbyGirl: BUT SHE WOULD HAVE TOLD ME IF SHE CAME IN MY ROOM.

AbbyGirl: AND SHE WOULD HAVE NOTICED IF CHESTER ATE MY SWEATER.

AbbyGirl: AND SHE'S BEEN IN THE KITCHEN THIS WHOLE TIME, COOKING DINNER. IT'S NOT POSSIBLE.

Leah601: THEN I DON'T KNOW WHAT TO TELL U. I MEAN, NO OFFENSE, BUT IT SEEMS LIKE U R TRYING TO FREAK YOURSELF OUT.

AbbyGirl: WHAT DO U MEAN?

Leah601: NEVER MIND.

AbbyGirl: NO, SERIOUSLY, TELL ME WHAT U MEAN.

Leah601: JUST FORGET IT.

AbbyGirl: I CAN'T FORGET IT! SOME CRAZY STUFF IS HAPPENING TO ME, AND MY BEST FRIEND IS ACTING LIKE I'M

MAKING IT ALL UP! THX A LOT.

Leah601: WHAT DO U WANT ME TO SAY? THAT SOME STRANGE GIRL WITH RED HAIR MUST BE STALKING U? THAT SARA'S GHOST IS AFTER U?

Leah601: IT'S NOT ENOUGH FOR U THAT THE GUY U LIKE ASKED U TO THE DANCE, NOW U HAVE TO MAKE UP THIS BIG DRAMA SO U CAN BE THE CENTER OF ATTN?

Abby sat back as suddenly as if she'd been slapped in the face. Her eyes darted back and forth as she read Leah's words again. Then, with quivering fingers, she sent another message back to Leah.

AbbyGirl: I DIDN'T KNOW U FELT THAT WAY. I WON'T BOTHER U ANYMORE.

Leah601: ABBY, WAIT. I DIDN'T MEAN IT LIKE THAT. LET'S TALK ABOUT IT, OKAY?

But Abby didn't want to talk to Leah anymore. With a fast click of her mouse, Abby shut the chat window and stepped away from her computer. Just then her cell phone buzzed.

Leah, give it a rest! Abby thought angrily as she picked

up her phone. The screen was blinking with a green light to announce that there was a text message waiting for her.

It wasn't from Leah, though. A wrinkle of confusion crossed Abby's forehead as she stared at the phone number. She didn't know whose number it was, but that long combination of digits seemed familiar.

Abby pushed a button so she could read the text. In angry-looking capital letters, the message flashed onto the glowing screen.

I'M WARNING YOU. STAY AWAY FROM HIM!!!! NEXT TIME I WILL DO SOMETHING MUCH WORSE!

As Abby gasped in shock, the phone fell from her fingers; it skidded across the floor until it disappeared under her bed. Another text! After everything that had happened this afternoon, enough was enough. Abby's first instinct was to get to her computer and type the phone number into a search engine to see if she could learn anything about its owner.

She fell into the chair at her desk and tried to type the number into the text box, but her fingers were shaking so much that she kept hitting the wrong keys. She took a deep breath and tried again.

She hit enter.

But the search didn't go through.

With a frown, she hit enter again, but nothing happened. She tried to move the cursor—but her computer was frozen.

"Oh come *on!*" Abby exclaimed as she slammed the keyboard in frustration. She needed to know what was going on *now*. She didn't have time to waste by restarting her computer.

Maybe I can look the number up on my phone, Abby thought as her heart sank. She dreaded seeing that scary message again, but she knew that she had no choice. She dropped to her knees and stuck her head under the bed.

The phone, still glowing, was under the exact middle of Abby's bed. She stretched her arm out to grab it, but the phone was just beyond her reach. With a sigh, she lay down on her stomach and crawled under the bed as far as she could, extending her arm as she reached for the phone.

The minute Abby's fingers curled around her phone, the screen went dark. A freezing blast of air surrounded her; she tried to get out from under the bed but couldn't wiggle free. It was like an unseen hand was holding her down, in the dark, in the cold, and Abby couldn't escape, couldn't move, couldn't breathe.

All she could do was scream!

CHAPTER 7

"ABBY! Abby! What's wrong?" cried Mrs. Miller as she burst into the room, with Mr. Miller and Chester following right behind her.

"Mom!" Abby screamed. "Mom! Help! I can't get out!"

"Honey, honey, calm down," Mrs. Miller said, and Abby felt the warm, comforting touch of her mother's hand on her back. "Let me see. Your T-shirt is caught on the bed frame, honey. Hold on . . . there. You can get out now."

Abby shot out from under the bed, blinking back tears of terror and relief. She wiped her eyes with her hands as she exhaled in a long, jagged sigh. Chester gave her a big lick on the face.

"Kiddo! What's going on? You really scared us," said

Mr. Miller, an expression of concern on his face.

Abby looked at her parents and knew that she needed to tell them everything. "I—I don't know what's happening," she began. "I was trying to look something up online, but then my computer froze, and my whole room got freezing cold and I couldn't get out from under the bed!"

Mr. Miller walked across the room to Abby's computer. "So this old thing's giving you trouble?" he asked. "I can take a look at it after dinner—but you remember how to restart it, right?"

"Dad! That's not the point," Abby exclaimed. "All this weird stuff happened at the same time! I went under the bed and it got *so* cold in here—the air was like ice—"

Mrs. Miller reached out and rested her hand against Abby's forehead. "Are you feeling all right?" she asked. "You don't feel feverish to me."

"You're not listening—," Abby began shrilly as she ducked out from under her mom's hand.

"You know, Abby, this is an old house," Mr. Miller interrupted her as he poked his head under the bed. "There are all sorts of drafts in just about every room. I can see about adding some insulation under the floorboards before winter comes. That would probably help."

"Sweetie, what were you doing under the bed in the first place?" asked Mrs. Miller. She and Mr. Miller exchanged a glance, and in their eyes, Abby saw it: that awful look of parental humoring. They thought she was overreacting, like a small child who was afraid of things that go bump in the night.

That was when Abby realized that there was nothing she could say or do that would convince her parents to take her seriously.

So why even bother?

The text messages, Abby suddenly realized. *I could show them those awful texts.* But then a new thought occurred to her. What if her parents freaked out and took away her phone?

It didn't seem worth the risk.

Abby sighed. "I just . . . I was trying to get my phone. It fell under the bed. It's not important. Forget it."

"Come on, Abby, let's go eat dinner," Mrs. Miller suggested. "I've been calling your name for the last five minutes! Didn't you hear me?"

Abby shook her head as she followed her parents

out of the bedroom. She didn't have much appetite, but she was eager—desperate, even—to get out of her room and away from everything that had just happened there.

Bolstered by a good meal and feeling courageous, Abby hurried back to her bedroom after dinner, but she made sure to leave her door open. If Leah and her parents weren't going to take all these strange things seriously, then Abby would have to figure them out by herself.

Abby's computer hummed to life as she restarted it and logged onto the Internet. For once, she didn't bother checking her e-mail or signing into IM. Instead she opened up Google and searched for the phrase "proof of ghosts."

Dozens of websites flooded the page, promising everything from certified ghost hunters to scary horror movies. But one site in particular caught Abby's eye. She clicked on the link and tapped her fingers impatiently as she waited for the page to load.

When the Paranormal Gets Personal

The only people who can afford not to believe in

ghosts are those who have never been troubled by them. It takes but one encounter with the other world to know that though death waits for us all, the spirit is eternal. Electrical interference, sudden drops in air temperature, unexpected— and unexplained—visions are all calling cards from beyond the grave. Even the most pragmatic disbeliever will find it difficult to explain away all manner of paranormal phenomena, especially when they occur simultaneously.

As she read, Abby started nodding her head. Everything in the article sounded very familiar.

For most spirits, the journey to the other side is an easy one; the gentle letting go of the earthly life is simply part of the natural cycle of being. But some spirits are unprepared for death and find it impossible to tear themselves away from their earthly concerns. This is especially true for those who have suffered untimely death; instead of accepting that their lives were cut short, these spirits long for more—more time with their friends, more time with their families, more time with their loved ones. They are overcome by the sense that they have been cheated of their due; the drive to live becomes like a drug, addictive and intoxicating. With all their strength, these spirits resist the pull of the beyond, desperate to cling to the lives they once lived.

Abby felt a chill run down her spine. She hugged herself tight and glanced at her bedroom door to make sure it was still open . . . just in case.

Sadly for these spirits, there is no going back; once the life force has been extinguished, they find themselves nearly powerless in the earthly realm, unable to be seen or heard (in most cases). This virtual invisibility grows increasingly painful for them, especially as they see their loved ones move through the stages of grief and eventually begin to resume their lives. With a sad and silent farewell, many reluctant spirits will, at this point, resolve to pass over; it is simply too painful for them to watch life from the sidelines.

But some spirits find themselves enraged by these developments, especially if they think that they are being forgotten or replaced. This small number of vengeful spirits should not be confused with those that are simply trying to relay one last, perhaps vital, message to a loved one. Rather, the spiteful spirit will do anything to reclaim his or her former territory, channeling large amounts of electromagnetic energy in an attempt to regain the power of the physical world. Highly charged ions are known to interfere with electronic devices, and clouds of electrons can alter the temperature of the air; scientists have proven this. What modern science has been unable to explain is why sudden, strong pockets of electromagnetism seem to develop out of thin air. Perhaps the air is not as thin as it seems.

With enough practice and motivation, a spirit can summon a quantity of electromagnetism sufficient to scatter paper, knock down books, and create all manner of mischief that generally confuses, befuddles, or frightens the living. There have even been documented reports of "sightings," in which the image of the deceased appears as real as if he or she were still alive. If you have found yourself on the receiving end of such unwanted interference from a restless spirit, be assured that you are not crazy. Read on for suggestions on how to help this misguided spirit find its way to the other realm.

Abby eagerly clicked on the link to read more. What she learned convinced her that she was not imagining things or overreacting. She sat back in her chair, deep in thought. Then she opened up her e-mail and started typing.

To: Leah601
From: AbbyGirl
Subject: Sorry
Hey Leah,
First, I'm sorry I just disappeared like that. I'm really stressing out. So many weird things have been happening and some of them you don't even know about. So I'm going to tell you everything. Please hear me out before assuming it's just my imagination. I wish it was. Because then I could control it and make it STOP.
So right before my party started, I was outside and I had the creepiest feeling that someone was watching me from the woods. And then I got that scary text message in

the middle of the night. And my phone was on—not the way I left it when we went to sleep. This afternoon, I had that creepy feeling that someone was watching me again—and I saw a red-haired girl running away from my window! When I got back to my room, my top was NOT where I left it and I found it shredded in my closet. All that stuff is VERY weird. Don't you agree?

Then things got even scarier. Leah, I got another freaky text message from that same strange number! And this time, I wanted to know who sent it, so that maybe I could stop them from sending another. But when I tried to look the number up online, my computer froze for no reason. Then my room went icy cold. I was terrified. If just one or two of these things happened, I would think it was a coincidence. Or maybe even my imagination. But all of them, together . . . I mean, how could I imagine those texts? Or my top getting ripped up? Those things are completely real, and you can come see them for yourself if you don't believe me.

I need to make this stop NOW, and I have an idea, but I'd like your help. Can you meet me at school tomorrow morning before class starts? Like, eight a.m.? You are my best friend, Leah. Please help.

<3

Abby

Abby read her e-mail to Leah twice before she took a deep breath and sent it. She didn't know how Leah would respond, but she also knew that if Leah wouldn't take her seriously, she'd have to move forward on her own.

No matter how terrifying or dangerous it would be.

CHAPTER 8

Thursday morning dawned cool and cloudy; Abby woke up earlier than usual after a long and restless night. Even with her bedroom door wide open and Chester sleeping peacefully at the foot of her bed, she had tossed and turned, alert to every little noise in the night. When she finally got out of bed just before her alarm went off, Abby stepped over to the window and saw damp mist seeping out of the woods into her backyard. She shivered as she pulled the gauzy curtains back across the window. She knew that she couldn't be too careful; there was no telling who—or what—might be out there.

Then she walked over to her computer to see if Leah had e-mailed her. By the time Abby went to bed, Leah hadn't responded, which was so unusual it made Abby even more anxious. Abby didn't know anyone who was more addicted to the Internet than Leah, so there was no possible way she hadn't received the e-mail. The only explanation for her lack of response was that Leah was ignoring her.

To Abby's relief, though, she saw that she had an e-mail waiting from Leah. It was short, but Abby didn't care.

To: AbbyGirl
From: Leah601
Subject: Re: Sorry
Hey Abby,
Everything is going to be fine. I'll meet u @ the flagpole. L.

Abby got dressed and grabbed a stack of pages that she'd printed off the Internet the night before. When she went to the kitchen, she found her mom drinking coffee and reading the newspaper at the table.

"Morning, Abby," Mrs. Miller said. "How did you sleep last night? Was your room warm enough?"

"Uh, yeah," Abby said as she grabbed a box of cereal out of the cupboard. "It was fine."

"You're up early today," Mr. Miller remarked, walking into the room.

"I'm meeting Leah before school," replied Abby. "We, um, have a project to work on. That reminds me, can she come over after school today?"

"I don't see why not—as long as it's okay with her parents," Mrs. Miller said. "Dad and I are going out to dinner with the Takahashis, remember? So we won't be here. Do you mind heating up some leftovers for dinner?"

"Sure," Abby said, grateful that her parents would be out. "Leah and I will mostly be working on that project."

"Well, we'll probably be home around eight. Then we can drive Leah home," Mr. Miller said. "Speaking of rides, do you want me to drive you to school? I'm headed out for work in a few minutes."

Abby smiled at her dad as she quickly ate her cereal. "That would be great. Thanks, Dad." When she was finished, she put her bowl in the sink and said, "Okay, I'm off. See you tonight, Mom."

"Bye, Abby," Mrs. Miller replied. "Have a good day!"

Abby pulled on her coat and picked up her backpack as her mom went back to the newspaper. Standing in the cozy, cheerful kitchen, it was hard to believe that such scary things had been happening. Abby wished, briefly, that they would just stop on their own. That life would go back to normal.

But she knew that that wasn't going to happen—unless she did something about it.

During the car ride with her dad, Abby noticed how much emptier the streets and sidewalks were at this early hour. As the car neared the school, she started to feel more and more nervous about meeting up with Leah. What if Leah didn't want to help her? What if Leah laughed at her plan?

That's just a risk I have to take, Abby told herself.

The schoolyard was empty when she walked through the heavy black gate, though the lights were already on and she could see teachers arriving in the faculty parking lot. She sat on the round concrete base of the flagpole and glanced up at the cloud-covered sky; overhead, the flag flapped loudly as gusts of wind blew in from the west. Abby glanced at her watch.

Leah was late.

Abby had a sinking feeling that Leah wasn't going to show up. *Maybe she forgot*, she thought. *Or maybe she was never going to come in the first place.* She didn't know what had happened to make Leah so mad at her, but she really needed her best friend now.

As she waited, Abby's feet started tapping, then her knees started jumping, until she was suddenly too anxious to sit still for another minute. She stood up and started pacing near the flagpole, watching silently as more students arrived for the school day. *Where is Leah?* Abby wondered frantically. *Has something happened to her? What if Sara's ghost—*

Abby couldn't finish that thought.

With just five minutes left before homeroom, she had to face the truth: Leah wasn't coming. For the first time in her life, Abby actually hoped that Leah had blown her off; that would be better than the other possibilities that wouldn't stop running through her mind. She stood up and was slipping the strap of her backpack over her shoulder when she heard someone call her name.

"Abby!"

It was Leah.

"You're here!" Abby exclaimed, rushing up to Leah. "I was so afraid! I thought you—"

"I'm fine. I just overslept," Leah said, her voice full of concern. "You have to relax."

But Abby noticed that Leah wouldn't meet her eye. The girls stood there awkwardly for a moment. Then they both spoke at the same time.

"So what do you—," Leah began.

"Did I do something—," Abby said.

They exchanged a smile. "You first," Leah said.

Abby took a deep breath. "Did I do something to upset you?" she asked bluntly. "I don't know why you were mad at me last night."

Leah looked away. "Just—it's not important," she said. "I read your e-mail."

"I know," Abby said quietly. She waited for Leah to continue.

"It's not that I don't believe you," Leah said. "But here's what I *don't* believe in: ghosts. I mean, they're really creepy and spooky to think about, but they're not real, Abby. Dead is dead. And Sara is dead. That's it."

Abby was silent for a moment. Then she reached into her pocket and pulled out her cell phone. She scrolled through her most recent text messages and shoved the phone at Leah. "I *know* Sara's dead!" Abby cried. "But read this latest message. Just read it!"

Leah's blue eyes flicked back and forth as she glanced

at the screen of Abby's phone. "So you think this message is about Jake?" she asked.

"Who else would it be about?" Abby asked. "Whoever is sending those messages wants me to stay away from 'him' and Jake is the only 'him' I'm into. And the only people who know that are you, Chloe, and Nora—and you guys would never do this to me."

"You're right about that," Leah replied.

"So who could it be?" Abby continued. "And what about when my computer froze or the cold air I felt in my room? I'm telling you, after what I read last night, this has to be a ghost."

Leah sighed. "So what's your big plan? Assuming that it's Sara's ghost, which I just can't believe. I mean, have you even thought that through? I don't think ghosts have wireless plans, you know?"

"Look, don't worry about it," Abby said. If Leah really couldn't believe in the possibility of this all being Sara's ghost, there was no point in her helping. "I'll figure something out."

"No, really," Leah persisted. "I can tell you're upset, and I want to help, Abby, I really do. And I'm sorry for what I said in the IM last night. I didn't mean it at all.

I don't even know why I said it."

The bell rang. Abby looked at Leah. "Come on—we're going to be late for homeroom."

"Okay, fine," Leah gave in. "But if you change your mind, let me know."

"I will," Abby replied. "Whoa—was that a raindrop?"

"Let's go!" Leah exclaimed. As the rain started to fall, the two girls raced toward the school. By the time Abby sat down in her seat for homeroom, she was out of breath and soaked. But not even the drenching rain and the rush to homeroom were enough to make her forget for a second about the strange experiences that had been haunting her.

That evening, as it started to get dark out, Abby put her plan into motion. The website had said that the séance would work better if two or three people were involved, but Abby would just have to make do on her own. Leah just didn't understand.

In the quiet of her room, she cleared off the top of her dresser and placed a photo of Sara in the very center of it. She surrounded the photo with a circle of softly glowing lights and white rose petals. *Sara should still be alive, like me and Jake and Leah*, she thought suddenly. *She shouldn't exist only in photos and memories.*

But Abby knew that there was no way to undo the tragedy that had cut Sara's life short. So if Sara's spirit was having trouble crossing over to the other side, Abby was determined to help her.

Next, Abby draped a dark cloth over the mirror. Whatever it might reflect in the next hour, she didn't want to see it—not when she was all alone. With the lights off and the door closed, her room suddenly felt as dark and cramped as a crypt. She closed her eyes and reminded herself that this was the only option she had. There was no point in letting fear get the better of her— not when she'd been so frightened already.

Abby sat on her bed and forced herself to stare at the photo of Sara. Her green eyes gleamed in the soft light, as if they held a secret that no one else knew. After counting backward from one hundred, Abby took a deep breath and started to speak.

"Sara?" she asked softly. "Are you there? Please give me a sign if you can hear me."

Abby waited in the quiet darkness, but no sign came.

"Sara," she repeated. "I want to help you. Please, give me a sign."

This time, in the quiet, Abby started to feel a little foolish. But she pressed on.

"Give me a sign, Sara," she said, her voice growing louder. "Give me a sign."

Tap-tap-tap-tap.

Abby's whole body stiffened. "Sara?" she asked, her voice shaking. "Is that you?"

Tap-tap-tap-tap.

The sound was coming from the window.

Tap-tap-tap-tap.

Abby slowly got off her bed and walked over to the window, which was covered by the curtain. Was that a shadow on the other side of the window—or was it just her imagination? Her heart pounded wildly as she reached for the curtain with a trembling hand. She mustered all her courage, and with one swift, sudden yank, she pulled back the curtain.

On the other side of the window, a pale face stared back at her!

CHAPTER 9

"Leah!" Abby screamed as she recognized her friend. "What are you doing here?"

"Open up!" Leah yelled back, her voice muffled by the glass. "It's wet out!"

Abby unlocked the window and pushed it open. "You scared me to death!" she exclaimed. "Why were you hanging outside my window?"

"Because you wouldn't come to the door," Leah replied as she climbed into the window. "I was ringing the doorbell for, like, five minutes."

"The doorbell's broken," Abby said. "Have you ever heard of knocking?"

Leah shrugged. "What's the big deal?" she said. "I figured you'd be in your room, and here you are." Then she glanced around Abby's bedroom. "Whoa. What are you doing?"

"Nothing," Abby said quickly as she felt her face grow hot. "Just—let's go down to the basement and watch TV or something."

"Is that a *shrine*?" Leah asked incredulously as she walked over to Abby's dresser. She stared at Sara's picture, the rose petals, the gleaming lights. "Abby, did you make a *shrine* to Sara?"

"I don't want to—," Abby began.

Leah looked concerned. "This has definitely gone too far. I think you're starting to get obsessed. What are you up to here?"

"Why should I tell you?" Abby shot back. "You'll just laugh."

"No, I won't," Leah said. "I promise."

"I was trying to have a séance," Abby admitted. "I wanted to make contact with Sara to help her get to the other side."

Neither girl spoke for a moment.

"So you're really convinced that Sara's ghost has been bothering you?" Leah asked.

"It's the only explanation I can think of," Abby

replied. "I did this research on the Internet, and everything that has happened can be explained as 'paranormal phenomena.' That's the technical term, I mean. And I saw this one site that said spirits can have trouble moving on, especially if they weren't ready to die. So I . . ."

"Go on," Leah said encouragingly.

Abby sighed. "If Sara's spirit hasn't been able to move on, then I want to help her," she finished. "Go ahead. Laugh."

But Leah looked at Abby without giggling or even smiling. "That's intense," she finally said. "And you were going to hold a séance all by yourself? Weren't you scared?"

"Yeah," Abby said. "But I figured it couldn't be any worse than everything else that's been going on. I felt like I had to do something, you know?"

"So what happened?" asked Leah.

"I had just gotten started when you came along and knocked on my window!" Abby exclaimed as she started to laugh. "I was asking for a sign, and then I heard this *tap, tap, tap.*"

Leah started laughing too. "No wonder you were so freaked out!" She got serious again. "You know what?" she asked. "Maybe *I'm* the sign. Maybe I'm the sign that you need two people for a séance."

Abby shook her head. "No, that's okay," she said. "Besides, séances don't work unless everybody believes."

"Come on, Abby!" Leah said. "You already got everything ready. And if Sara's spirit really is hanging around, it's a nice thing to do, helping her move on. Let's give it another try."

"Okay," Abby said slowly. "But no messing around. I don't want to do it unless we both take it seriously."

"Absolutely," Leah promised. "So, what do we do?"

Abby glanced at the printouts next to her bed. "We sit across from each other and hold hands," she told Leah. "That's to make some sort of energy connection. And then we just think and talk about Sara, and all our memories of her, to channel her spirit."

For several minutes the only sound in the room was Abby and Leah's quiet breathing. Then, with her eyes closed, Abby started speaking. "I remember Sara's first day at school," she said in a quiet voice. "Everyone wanted to meet her. Everyone wanted to be her friend."

"I remember when Sara read a poem that she wrote in English class," Leah spoke up. "It was about the ocean, and it was amazing."

A rumble of thunder sounded in the distance as

another storm approached. Rain started to fall again, harder and harder, the sound of the raindrops hitting the window like a message in a secret code. The wind moaned, low and lonely, as the shadows of quivering tree branches danced around Abby's room.

Abby knew that it was time to make contact.

"Sara, if you're there, I hope you can hear me," she began. "I know you've been trying to reach me, and I want you to know something: You will never be forgotten, Sara. Not by your family, not by your friends, not by Jake. And not by me, even though I didn't get to know you very well. I know why you're angry. It's not fair that I'm here and you're not. It's not fair that Jake is taking me to the dance and not you. We both know that if you were still alive, he would have asked you."

A jagged bolt of lightning illuminated the dark room, followed by an immediate clap of thunder that was so loud it made both girls jump. But Abby, her eyes still closed, pressed on.

"But you're not here, Sara. If you cared about Jake, and I know that you did, you would want him to go on with his life. That doesn't mean he'll forget you. But don't torture yourself by clinging to a life that's over, Sara. Move on. Move on into the spirit world. Move on."

Abby was quiet for a few moments, listening to the storm rage outside. Then, finally, she opened her eyes. To her surprise, Leah's eyes were tearing up. "Hey," she said gently. "You okay?"

"Yeah," Leah said with a loud sniff. "I just—I felt so sad for her, all of a sudden. You're right, Abby. It's *not* fair."

"No," Abby said sadly. "It isn't."

"Did you feel like Sara's spirit was here?" Leah asked. "I tried to believe, but I didn't feel anything that was, like, a ghost or anything."

Abby shrugged. "I don't know," she said. "But we did what we could."

Ping!

"That was my computer!" Abby exclaimed as she laughed nervously. "Uh, I guess the séance is over." She turned on the monitor and clicked on her e-mail. For a moment she didn't say a word.

"Anything interesting?" Leah asked as she pulled the cloth off Abby's mirror and started fixing her eye makeup.

"Leah?" Abby asked. Her voice was high and tight. "Can—can you come look at this?"

"Sure. What's up?" Leah asked. She peered over

Abby's shoulder at the computer screen. At the top of the e-mail window, the girls read:

TO	FROM	SUBJECT
AbbyGirl	sarajAmEs	READ IF YOU DARE

"Whoa. What is that?" Leah asked slowly.

"It's—it's Sara's old e-mail address," Abby stammered. "But this e-mail was just sent!"

"You'd better open it, Abby," Leah said. When Abby hesitated, Leah reached forward and clicked on the e-mail. In an instant, it filled the whole computer screen.

PRESENT FOR JAKE IN YOUR TOP DRESSER DRAWER.

"Oh, no," Abby whispered. "This séance was a terrible idea."

"Maybe not," Leah said hopefully. "I mean, maybe Sara had a message that she needed to give to Jake, and by contacting her you made that possible! Maybe now her spirit will be free to go to the other side!"

But Abby was filled with horrible dread. "I don't

think so, Leah," she said. "I have a really bad feeling about this."

"Just go see what it is," Leah encouraged her. "Just go see if there's even anything there."

Abby walked over to her dresser, where Sara's picture stared back at her, still illuminated by the glowing lights. She pulled open the top drawer and looked inside.

Socks. Her bathing suit. Old T-shirts for sleeping in.

Nothing unexpected.

Nothing unusual.

Abby was so relieved she started to laugh. "Leah, there's nothing here—," she began. But her voice trailed off when she saw it: the corner of a pale purple piece of paper. She didn't remember ever putting something like that in the drawer. She moved a pair of socks out of the way and found a carefully folded piece of paper with Jake's name on it, written in tiny, perfect letters.

"What do I do with this?" Abby asked anxiously. "Give it to Jake? What would I say? 'Hey, Jake, I found this in my sock drawer and I think it's for you?'" She picked up the paper and suddenly caught a whiff of that strange, exotic flower again. "Do you smell that?" she asked Leah abruptly.

"Smell what?" Leah asked impatiently as she grabbed the paper out of Abby's hand. "I want to read it."

"Maybe we shouldn't," Abby wondered aloud. "It could just make things worse."

But it was too late. Leah had already unfolded the paper. Abby watched her eyes move back and forth as she read whatever was written there.

"Well? What does it say?" Abby asked.

Leah crumpled the paper into a ball and threw it in the trash. "Never mind," she said firmly. "It was stupid. It was nothing."

"Forget that," Abby said as she reached into the trash. "I want to know what it said!"

"Abby, don't—," Leah began.

Abby smoothed out the wrinkled paper. She stood completely still as she stared at the note. The message on it wasn't long.

Truth time, Jake. What do you see in Abby? You can do better!

Abby inhaled sharply. She wanted to forget every word of the note, but she knew that the message was burned into her memory forever. She stared into the dresser drawer so that Leah couldn't see the tears that filled her eyes.

"I'm so sorry. I wish I hadn't read it. I wish *you* hadn't read it," Leah said miserably. "It was so mean. And so harsh. And totally not true! I never knew Sara was so mean. Abby? Abby? What's wrong? You look like you're going to pass out!"

Abby reached into the drawer, picked something up, and turned toward Leah. "There's something else in here," she said, her voice hoarse.

Abby held out her hand to Leah and uncurled her fingers.

A lock of long red hair tied together with a purple bow gleamed in her palm.

CHAPTER 10

"Gross!" Leah exclaimed, jumping back. "What is that?"

"It's hair," Abby said with a shudder. "Red hair. Leah, if you can come up with a reasonable explanation for this, I'm dying to hear it."

Leah just looked at her with wide eyes. "Abby, I don't know what to say," she replied. "You . . . haven't started collecting other people's hair, have you?"

Abby turned away. "This isn't funny," she said coldly. "Sorry if my sense of humor is failing me right now."

"No, *I'm* sorry," Leah replied as she stared at the floor. "I didn't mean for that to sound sarcastic. You need a totally supportive friend now more than ever, and I've been an epic fail in that department. This is all just very hard to believe."

"Tell me about it." Abby sighed. "It seems obvious, though, that Sara's . . . spirit has been here. She was probably here the night of my sleepover, too, when she moved my cell phone and turned it on and all that."

Leah sighed too. "Abby?"

"Yeah?"

"I . . . never mind," Leah said awkwardly. But there was something about the expression on her face that made Abby narrow her eyes and take a closer look at her friend.

"What is it?" Abby asked.

"Forget it," Leah replied.

"Leah, if you don't tell me right now—," Abby said, her temper starting to rise.

"Okay, okay, I have to confess something," Leah said as she held up her hands. "At your sleepover, after everyone went to bed, I couldn't sleep, and I was wondering if Jake had texted you back. Maybe he had told you that Max mentioned me. So I got up and I, well, borrowed your cell. Just to see if Jake texted you again."

"You went snooping around in my phone?" Abby cried.

"No! Not exactly. Well . . . kind of," Leah admitted.

"I know, I know. I didn't have any right to do that. But I was really curious, and honestly, I didn't even know if you would tell me if he *did* text you again. You're so secretive sometimes."

"I can't believe you did that," Abby said. "It was *none* of your business. No wonder I'm secretive when you're always invading my privacy."

"Ouch," Leah said. "That was mean."

"But true," Abby said. "So did you send me that scary text message, too?"

"No!" exclaimed Leah, looking genuinely hurt. "Abby, I would never do something like that."

"So all this time when I was wondering how my phone got moved, how it seemed to turn on by itself— that was you?" Abby asked, shaking her head. "And you just let me keep wondering about it instead of confessing?"

"I was embarrassed," Leah said. "But do you understand now why I kept telling you that there had to be a reasonable explanation? Because those things *seemed* really creepy, but there was a perfectly rational explanation for them."

"Except for the scary message—I mean *messages*,"

Abby pointed out. "And the ripped-up top, and this hair in my drawer, and—"

"I get it," Leah cut her off. "And I can't explain that stuff, Abby. I wish I could, but I can't."

There was a pause as Abby tried to think of something to say. Suddenly Leah continued. "You don't understand, Abby. It's so *easy* for you."

"Excuse me?" Abby asked. "Easy for me that I have some crazy *ghost* stalking me?"

"Not that," Leah said, shaking her head. "You can text Jake. You can talk to him like it's no big deal. And then, surprise, he asks you to the dance. But I've had a crush on Max *forever* and he barely knows that I even exist."

"Because you never talk to him!" Abby exclaimed.

"Because I'm scared I'll say something stupid!" Leah retorted.

Abby sighed. "Do you want me to talk to Jake? Find out who Max likes?"

"No. Maybe. I'm not sure," Leah replied. "I'll think about it. But speaking of Jake, what are you going to do?"

"Do?"

"Well . . . you know . . .," Leah said, gesturing to the photo of Sara on Abby's dresser. "Are you still going to go to the dance with him?"

For a moment Abby didn't answer as she turned away from Leah and stared at Sara's picture. Then she picked up the photo and slowly tore it in half with a loud, satisfying *riiiippppp*.

"You bet I am," she replied as she dropped the torn photo in the trash. "I'm not going to let some *ghost* keep me from living my life."

Leah raised her eyebrows. "Wow," she said. "Go, Abby. You're so brave."

Abby glanced at the lock of red hair and the crumpled-up note that had accompanied it. "What choice do I have?" she asked.

CHAPTER 11

By the time Saturday evening came around, though, Abby's courage began to waver. Friday and Saturday were thankfully uneventful, but Abby hadn't gotten a good night's sleep since her sleepover. She was exhausted as she got ready for the dance. She peered at herself in the mirror and frowned. "There's not enough makeup in the world to get rid of these circles," Abby said as she dabbed concealer over the dark shadows beneath her eyes.

"Don't be silly. You look beautiful!" Mrs. Miller replied as she reached for Abby's hairbrush. "Let's put your hair up a little. Just to see how it looks."

"Mom. My hair is fine," Abby said. "Leave it alone."

"Okay." Mrs. Miller sighed. "It just looks so pretty

when you clip it up. See what I mean?"

"But I want to wear it down," Abby argued, pushing away her mom's hands.

"Okay, okay! Honey, you seem so nervous," Mrs. Miller said, her voice filled with concern. "Jake is such a nice boy. Just try to relax and have fun tonight!"

If she only knew, Abby thought. "I will, Mom," she replied, hoping that her voice sounded normal. "Sorry I snapped at you. I'm a little stressed."

"You look wonderful, and you're going to have a great time," Mrs. Miller said. "I just know it!"

I hope so, Abby thought as she tried to smile at her mom. But she wasn't so sure.

Just then there was a loud knock at the front door. "That must be Jake," Abby said as she jumped up. "I've gotta go."

From the hallway, she could hear her father's voice. "Hello, Jake. Why don't you come inside and sit down for a minute? I thought we could have a nice chat before you whisk my daughter away into the night."

A look of horror crossed Abby's face. "Mom, *no!*" she whispered. The absolute last thing Abby wanted Jake to deal with was her dad and his sense of humor—or lack thereof.

"Hurry," her mom said, patting Abby's arm. "I'll get your coat."

Abby darted into the living room. "Hi, Jake," she said with a little wave. "Well, we better get going. See you later, Dad!"

But Mr. Miller wasn't quite done. "You'll have her home by nine thirty, of course," he said to Jake, raising an eyebrow at him.

"Um, yes, absolutely," replied Jake. "My mom's picking us up at nine fifteen, so that won't be a problem."

"No, I didn't think it would be," Mr. Miller said, with a twinkle in his eye.

"Come on! Let's go!" Abby exclaimed as she grabbed the sleeve of Jake's coat and pulled him toward the front door.

"Here you go, Abby," Mrs. Miller said as she handed Abby her coat. "Have fun!"

Abby breathed a sigh of relief as she and Jake stepped outside into the twilight.

"Hey," Jake said as he flashed Abby a smile. "You look nice."

"Thanks," she said, blushing as she followed Jake out to his mom's car. "Sorry about my dad." But one thing Abby wasn't sorry about was the lock of hair and the note that were crammed in the trash can in her room—presents for Jake that he would never receive.

As she buckled her seat belt, Abby felt her cell phone buzz with a text message. She reached for it, but suddenly stopped herself. *It's not Mom or Dad,* she thought. *And if it's Leah, I'll see her in five minutes. So I'm not even going to look at this text.*

The short drive to the school passed quickly, thanks to Mrs. Chilson's friendly chatter. "Bye, kids," she called out as Abby and Jake climbed out of the car. "I'll pick you up in front, okay?"

Abby and Jake thanked her for the ride and walked around the school to the gym, where the dance was being held. As Jake held open the door for her, Abby gasped in delight. The gym had been transformed! The walls were covered with shimmering dark purple fabric; thousands of twinkling lights looped across the ceiling like constellations from another galaxy. At one end of the gym, a row of refreshment tables was decorated with garlands of white roses that perfumed the entire room.

"It's beautiful!" Abby exclaimed, her eyes shining happily. She had never imagined that the gym could be transformed into such a romantic and magical place.

The dance was already about a hundred times better than any dance she'd been to before.

But when Jake didn't respond, Abby turned to glance at him. The look of dread on his face told her that the dance was the last place in the world that he wanted to be.

"Jake?" Abby asked quietly. "Is—um—is something wrong?"

Jake shrugged and tried to smile at her. "No, no," he said. "Ready to go in?"

"Sure," Abby said, trying to sound friendly. Trying to sound normal.

Jake hesitated for just a moment, then reached for her hand. His fingers were smooth and warm as he entwined them with hers.

Abby's heart started pounding so loudly that she was sure everyone in the gym could hear it. She felt the blood rush into her cheeks and was grateful that it was too dark for anyone to notice. Because in that sweet moment, and despite everything that had happened in the past week, Abby was overcome with such happiness that it almost made her dizzy.

Inside the gym, she could see Morgan Matthews fluttering around anxiously, making sure that everything was set up perfectly. And across the room, she spotted Chloe and Nora. Her friends smiled and waved to her. Then Abby saw something that made the biggest, brightest smile stretch across her face: Max Menendez, carrying two cups of fruit punch, walking over to Leah. Abby giggled when she saw the look on her friend's face—somehow her expression was a combination of astonishment, excitement, and utter delight. Abby realized that she'd never seen Leah look so happy . . . or so pretty. *We're gonna be on the phone all night for sure,* Abby thought, thrilled that Max and Leah were finally spending time together.

But as Jake and Abby moved farther into the gym, the smile faded from Abby's face. She saw, then, what Jake had noticed the moment they had arrived: an enormous portrait of Sara hanging from the ceiling, watching all of them with her haunting green eyes. The portrait had been painted in such a lifelike style that Sara's eyes almost seemed to glow. Abby glanced at Jake's face and saw that he couldn't take his eyes off the portrait, try as he might.

Does he see what's really there? she wondered suddenly. To Abby, those green eyes seemed evil. The thin red lips were pursed in anger. She could find no trace of beauty in Sara's portrait anymore.

Maybe it was the lack of sleep.

Maybe it was the culmination of her week of fear.

But Abby knew that she couldn't do this—not here, not now, not with him.

"I'm sorry," she whispered to Jake as her hand fell out of his. "I can't."

Then Abby turned away and ran from the room.

CHAPTER 12

"Abby, wait!"

She heard Jake calling after her but she kept running, away from the gym, away from the portrait, away from the boy who was so clearly still crazy about a dead girl. With a ghost.

"Please, Abby!" Jake begged as he caught up to her in the hallway and grabbed her arm. "Give me—"

"No," Abby said, shaking her head. "You can't—"

"Try to understand," Jake interrupted her. "I knew that the money from the dance was going to her scholarship, but I didn't expect the gym to be turned into such a huge memorial to Sara, okay? The purple decorations? Her favorite color. The white roses? Her favorite flower. And that portrait . . . Living in this town, going to this school, there are reminders of her *everywhere*. I can't even take a girl I *like* to a dance without feeling like Sara's watching me."

"Because she is!" Abby exploded. Then she clapped her hands over her mouth in horror.

"What did you say?" Jake asked.

"Never mind," Abby said quickly. "I'm just going to call my mom and get out of here, okay?"

"No," Jake insisted. "I want to know what you meant by that."

Abby's resolve wavered as she looked into Jake's eyes. *He deserves to know the truth*, she thought. *But can he handle it?*

Then Abby realized that that wasn't her decision to make.

"I don't even know where to begin," she said slowly. She took a deep breath. And she told Jake everything.

Everything.

Jake listened quietly, never interrupting her, but Abby couldn't help noticing the way his eyes narrowed and his lips grew thin and sullen. Near the end of her story she realized that she had made a huge mistake.

But there was no turning back now.

"I know it sounds crazy," Abby finished. "I know it does. But there is no other explanation that I can figure out. Sara's spirit hasn't moved on. She's still in love with you, Jake, and she doesn't want anyone to take her place in your heart."

Abby held her breath as she waited for Jake's response. For a moment he looked angry. But then his anger melted away.

"Abby," he said gently, "it doesn't just sound crazy. It *is* crazy."

Abby sighed. "Okay," she said. "I'm going home now."

"Wait," Jake insisted. "I know you didn't know her well, but Sara was a really nice person. Like, genuinely nice. She would never try to scare someone or upset them in any way. I mean, you've known *me* forever. Do you think I'd go out with someone like that?"

Abby grabbed her cell phone and shoved it at Jake. "I haven't even read this text yet," she said. "But I can guess who it's from."

Abby held her breath as Jake's eyes flicked over the screen of her phone. One look at his face told her she was right. But then he shrugged as he handed the phone back to her.

"There's no proof that this message is from Sara," Jake said. "I don't even recognize the number it came from."

"But who—," Abby began.

"Don't get me wrong," Jake continued. "It's terrible that you're getting messages like this. I just don't believe that they're from Sara."

Abby looked down at the screen so Jake wouldn't see the tears in her eyes. At last, she read the message for herself.

DO YOU DARE GO TO THE DANCE WITH JAKE? HERE'S THE TRUTH: IF YOU GO TO THE DANCE WITH HIM, YOU WILL BE SO SORRY.

"I mean, whoever is sending these messages is just a bully," Jake said. "Don't give in. Come back to the dance with me, Abby. Or we could get out of here altogether— go get some pizza or something—just you and me, and forget all about what we saw in there."

As if he could sense Abby's hesitation, Jake pressed on. "Listen. I can tell you're convinced that Sara's ghost is behind those messages," he said in a rush. "So make her prove it. Write back and ask for *proof*—something that only Sara could tell you."

"Fine." Abby sighed. Her fingers fluttered across the

keypad as she typed, IS THIS REALLY SARA? PROVE IT! Then, before she could lose her nerve, she hit send.

Abby and Jake were quiet for a moment as they waited for a response. Seconds stretched into minutes until Jake suddenly laughed so loudly that Abby jumped.

"See?" he said joyfully. "It was just a prank. Whoever was sending those messages has nothing to say now! So how about it, Abby? Want to go—"

BZZZZZ!

The buzzing of Abby's phone silenced Jake and wiped the grin from his face. "Well?" he asked, with just the hint of a tremor in his voice. "What does it say?"

Abby glanced at the screen as her face filled with confusion. "I don't understand what this means," she said, shaking her head. She handed the phone to Jake so he could see for himself. "It's just numbers—a seven, a four, and a two."

The phone slipped from Jake's hands, clattering loudly on the linoleum floor. His face was like a mask, empty of all emotion except for terror.

"What is it?" Abby asked in a panic. "What's wrong?"

"It's *Sara!*" he gasped.

CHAPTER 13

"Jake?" Abby asked urgently. "Jake! What does that mean?"

But Jake just stared at her with wide, scared eyes.

"Jake!" she cried again, grabbing his arm. "Tell me what it means!"

Abby's touch seemed to snap Jake out of his daze. He opened his mouth, closed it, shook his head. "I can't—," he began. "It's not possible—"

"What's going on?" Abby begged.

Jake closed his eyes as he sighed heavily. "It was our secret," he said. His voice was halting, unsure. "Sara and I had this secret code. Every night before I went to bed, I'd send her an e-mail that said, 'XOXO 24/7.' And when I woke up in the morning, I always had an e-mail waiting from her that said, '7-4-2, OXOX, a mirror of my message.' After a while, she started texting me the number 7-4-2 during the day, after classes, on the weekends—you know, whenever. It was her way of telling me that she— that she was thinking about me. And no one in the world knew what it meant, except for the two of us. I never told anyone except for you, right now."

Abby sucked in her breath sharply. This, more than anything else that had happened, confirmed her deepest fears.

"Listen," Abby said slowly. "Don't freak out. But I have an idea."

"What is it?" asked Jake.

"You asked for proof—and you got it," Abby continued. "So let's take this to the next level."

Abby bent down to the floor and picked up her phone. She started typing a text message as Jake stared over her shoulder.

SARA, JAKE IS HERE. HE MISSES YOU. CAN HE SEE YOU?

"Abby, wait—," Jake began.

But it was too late. Abby had already pressed send.

"Why did you do that?" Jake exclaimed. "What were you thinking?"

"Jake, this has to end," Abby said. "I can't have Sara's spirit *haunting* me like this. And it doesn't matter if you stop liking me—she'll just do it to the next girl you like. And the next, and the next, and the next."

Jake shook his head. "I don't want to see her, Abby."

"She needs to move on," Abby replied. "And I think she needs your help to do it."

"But I already said good-bye to Sara—at her funeral, and every day for the last year," Jake said. "I don't want to say good-bye again."

Abby opened her mouth to reply when—

BZZZZ.

Abby read the incoming text without saying a word. Then she held the screen up to Jake so he could read it too.

I'M @ ST. RAYMOND'S CEMETERY. COME SEE ME IF YOU DARE!

Jake and Abby exchanged a glance. They were both familiar with St. Raymond's Cemetery. It was where Sara had been buried nearly a year ago.

"Come on, Jake," Abby said gently. "Let's go."

"Okay," Jake said at last. "I'll come with you. But only because it's time to put an end to this—for your sake and mine."

Abby stared at Jake's face for a moment, and the way the light had gone out of his eyes. He looked tired and angry. "What?" she asked. "You don't believe it's Sara anymore?"

"No," Jake said firmly. "And I can't believe you do either. There's no such thing as *ghosts*."

"But—," Abby began.

"Here's the other reason," Jake interrupted her. He tapped the screen of Abby's phone. "This doesn't even *sound* like Sara. She really was a sweet and wonderful person. She'd never say anything like that. . . . 'Come see me if you dare.'" Jake sighed. "If it was really Sara, she wouldn't have to dare me. She'd know that I would be there in a heartbeat."

"Right," Abby said awkwardly, feeling a flush of embarrassment for liking Jake when it was so painfully clear now that his heart belonged to someone else: a dead girl. "Let's get this over with."

Abby and Jake didn't speak as they walked down the

long hallway toward the door and stepped into the crisp, clear autumn night.

Finally Jake's voice interrupted the silence. "Abby?" he said. "I want to—I want to tell you that I'm sorry."

"For what?" Abby asked.

Jake waved his hand vaguely. "For all this," he replied. "For everything. This is not exactly what I had in mind when I asked you to the dance."

"Me neither," Abby said. And then, to her surprise, they both laughed.

"I really like you, Abby," Jake said shyly.

In the moonlight, Jake smiled at her, and Abby's heart skipped a beat, the way it always did when he looked at her. But then, slowly, his lips fell into the same sad expression that had grown so familiar to her over the last year.

This time there was something else, too: tension in his muscles and a hint of fear in his eyes as they looked past Abby.

And in that moment, she realized where they were: just steps away from the marble archway of St. Raymond's Cemetery. She shivered as the hair on the back of her neck rose, but she forced herself to look beyond the entrance, where the tombstones stood in long, silent rows, illuminated by the pale moonlight. The close-cut grass; the stone-paved paths; the carefully-carved grave markers; all of it seemed so dark and lonely on this cold, starless night. But what Abby really hated about grave-yards was the flowers. They seemed so out of place with their gaudy colors and sweet scents—especially when it was just a matter of time before they, too, died, their petals falling like tears.

Of course, worst of all were the forgotten graves, where no one bothered to leave anything.

Abby inhaled sharply. *All right. Time to go in*, she thought. She turned to Jake. "Are you ready?" she asked.

Jake nodded in reply.

Abby took a deep breath, and together they stepped into the cemetery. For a few moments, they walked in silence. Then Abby said, "Jake? I don't—I don't remember where Sara's grave is."

"It's near the back," he said. "By the border of the nature preserve."

"Oh," was all Abby said. But she thought, *Of course it is. And my house is right on the other side. How easy for Sara to—No. I won't go there. I can't.*

A cool breeze kicked up, ruffling Abby's hair and sending chills down her spine. She pulled her jacket tighter around her, but the cold creeping through her body wasn't just from the night air. As they approached the area near Sara's grave, every muscle in her body resisted, and her steps grew heavy, leaden. She wanted to run, out of the cemetery, back to the school, anywhere away from this place of deathly stillness.

But Abby knew that she had come too far to turn back now. And, of course, there was Jake. He needed her. She wouldn't let him down.

No matter how afraid she was.

She forced herself to keep walking, one step after another, remembering the feel of Jake's hand in hers back at the gym, the way her own hand had felt warmer from his touch. In this dark, quiet graveyard, that memory told her something essential: that she and Jake were alive. It seemed a silly thing to focus on, but it was exactly what Abby needed to take those terrifying steps.

Suddenly Jake stopped. He stiffened. "You—do you see that?" he asked. "Abby, please tell me you see that."

Abby's heart started pounding as she followed Jake's gaze to a gravestone that was as white as a pearl, with a single rose carved into its front. But it wasn't the stone that had captured Jake's attention; it was the pale hand resting atop it. A hand that was connected to a slender arm, one that belonged to a girl.

A girl with gleaming red hair—a bright spot of color in the dark and dreary cemetery.

CHAPTER 14

Is it Sara? Is it Sara? Abby was only vaguely aware of Jake's hand gripping hers tightly.

Abby tried to remember how to talk, how to breathe, but those ordinary abilities seemed lost to her as the girl turned to face them, standing in a beam of moonlight. And Abby knew, all of a sudden, with brilliant clarity:

It wasn't Sara.

The realization hit Jake at the same moment; Abby could tell from the way he sighed and from the way his shoulders fell, the tension in them replaced by a great relief.

The resemblance was uncanny, though. The girl had Sara's long red hair, and her creamy skin, and even her glowing green eyes. But her nose was narrower and her chin pointier; all around, the girl seemed somehow sharper and more angular.

And far more alive. That was certain.

Jake spoke first. "Who are you?" he asked, and his voice was harsh. Angry.

"My name is Samantha," she said in a clipped English accent. "Hello."

"Hello?" Jake asked. "Hello? You're going to have to do better than 'hello.' Because you have a *lot* of explaining to do."

Abby placed her hand gently on Jake's arm. Then she turned to face the stranger. "Who are you?" she asked. "I mean, really—who *are* you?"

Samantha sighed. "I'm Sara's cousin," she replied. "I live in London with my mum. But she's on special assignment for her work, traveling through Africa, so I've come to live with my aunt Stacy and uncle Steven for six weeks."

"Sara's parents?" asked Abby. Next to her, Jake nodded.

"I was so excited," Samantha said. "I'd never been to America before. I was going to go to a new school and make new friends and everything. And Mum told me that Aunt Stacy and Uncle Steven couldn't wait for me to arrive. They hadn't seen me in years and their house had been too quiet since . . ."

Samantha looked down at Sara's grave. Then she cleared her throat and continued speaking. "But at the airport I could tell everything had gone wrong already. Aunt Stacy burst into tears the moment she saw me."

"Because you look so much like Sara?" Abby guessed.

Samantha nodded in response. "I was supposed to go to school here. Your school. But by suppertime Uncle Steven told me that wouldn't be possible. He said it would upset the students too much to see me, so I'd have to be homeschooled. They didn't even think I should leave the house. Suddenly I was to be like a prisoner in their home for six weeks, with nowhere to go and nothing to do except schoolwork all by myself, and I couldn't even reach my mum to tell her how awful it was. All my dreams for my visit were ruined. And every time she saw me, Aunt Stacy started to cry. It's been horrible.

"I started spending all my time in Sara's room, with the door closed," Samantha continued. "Just to spare my poor aunt Stacy the sight of me. And I did something bad. I started reading Sara's diary. And her e-mails. I learned all about her school and her friends and her boyfriend. She did all the things I might have done here if only I didn't look so much like her," she added bitterly.

"So you went through all of Sara's stuff," Jake finally spoke up. "And then what? You wanted to, like, take over her life?"

"You have to understand. I haven't seen Sara since we were, like, three years old," Samantha replied, visibly upset with herself. "So of course I was sad to hear that she died, but I didn't *know* her. I didn't even know anything about her until I started living in her room. Aunt Stacy and Uncle Steven hadn't changed a thing about it. Even Sara's e-mail account was still active. And it wasn't hard to guess her e-mail password—JAKE."

Samantha turned to Jake. "I know I never should have done it," she said. "But I read all the e-mails you sent her. You were always so sweet and funny and really lovely to her. Nothing like the boys at home. I wanted to meet you more than anything. Because I thought if you'd liked Sara, maybe you might like me as well."

Abby spoke quickly, before Jake could respond. "I don't understand. If you were stuck in Sara's room, how did you even know about me or that Jake and I were . . ."

"One day I couldn't take it any longer," Samantha explained. "I simply *had* to get out of that house. Uncle Steven was out, and Aunt Stacy was asleep, so I pinned my hair under a cap and put on my sunglasses and snuck out! I took Sara's bike out of the garage and just rode down the street, feeling the sun, breathing the fresh air, and then I came to a bunch of shops, and I went into one—a grocery store, it was. And—you were there, Abby. You and your friend . . . the blond one . . ."

"Leah," Abby said.

"And you both seemed so happy, and I wished so much that I was going to your sleepover party that night." Samantha covered her face with her hands. "What I did next . . . I'm so embarrassed. I followed your mum's car home, Abby. I thought that maybe even if I couldn't really attend your party, I could still listen to all the fun you and your friends would have."

Abby suddenly remembered something. "Were you in the woods early in the evening?" she asked.

Samantha nodded miserably. "I heard you call out, but I couldn't answer, of course. And then once the sleepover started, I sat by the basement window. And then I overheard you talking about Jake and I ran back home. By the time I got back to Uncle Steven's house, I was so angry and so jealous. Because if Jake started to go out with you, what chance was there for me?"

"So you texted me," Abby continued for her. "In the middle of the night, from your own phone. That's why I didn't recognize the number."

"I just wanted to frighten you enough that you'd stay away from Jake," Samantha admitted. "But then I was hanging around outside the school a few days later and I saw you walking home with him and I followed you. I heard every word you said. You'd be surprised how easily you can follow someone and never be noticed. Neither of you ever even knew I was there!"

Samantha paused. "Well, that's not quite right, actually. Because I followed you all the way to your house, Abby, and later I even peeked in your window. You looked so happy, modeling that beautiful top in the mirror, and I was so angry! And then you nearly saw me. When you ran out of your room I climbed in the window, ripped your top, and put that note in your drawer. I don't know what happened to me. I've *never* done anything like that, *never*. It all got so out of hand. I'm so sorry, Abby. I'll buy you a new top. I promise."

Abby was so shocked by all of Samantha's confessions that she couldn't think of a thing to say. Jake, though, didn't have that problem at all. He glared at Samantha.

"You're terrible," he said, and the quiet anger in his words made them sound even harsher. "You go through Sara's personal, private things, you follow people around, and you do all that terrible stuff to Abby? You break into her house and you destroy her shirt? You send those nasty, awful messages to scare her? What's *wrong* with you?"

"Jake," Abby spoke up, but he was too angry to stop now.

"If you didn't look just like Sara, I never would have believed you were related to her," he continued loudly. "You thought you could take over her life, but you were so wrong. You could never be as sweet and nice as Sara, and that was what really made her beautiful. That was the real reason why everybody liked her so much."

"Jake, stop," Abby said firmly.

But Jake's words hovered in the air even after he finished speaking, almost echoing off the gravestones around them. A single tear slipped down Samantha's face as she nodded.

"You're right," Samantha said. "It's all true, and I

deserve it. I was so lonely—I can't begin to tell you how lonely I was—it's not an excuse, but it is an explanation, and I am so, so sorry. I wish I could go back in time and undo it all."

Abby thought suddenly of what it must have been like for Samantha—thousands of miles away from her home and family and friends, stuck in a dead girl's room, surrounded by what remained of the dead girl's life. It sounded like a nightmare. Abby wondered how she would have handled it. If it would have made her do things that were otherwise unthinkable.

"Hey," Abby said as Samantha self-consciously wiped away another tear. "Listen, I forgive you. Try not to—don't be upset. It's over."

"Abby—," Jake began.

But Abby turned to him and cut him off before he could say anything else. "What do you think Sara would do right now? Wouldn't she forgive Samantha, Jake?" she asked in a quiet voice, and in Jake's eyes, Abby saw that he agreed.

Abby gave Samantha a small, sincere smile. "Would you—would you like to hang out sometime?" she asked, with just a touch of hesitation. "I, um, might have a sleepover at my house next weekend. Do you want to come? You could meet some of my friends, and my mom can talk to your aunt and uncle and make sure it's okay for you to stay over. If you want."

Samantha's eyes were bright with surprise. "R-really?" she asked.

"Well, sure, why not?" Abby asked. "After all, you already know where I live."

There was a moment of silence, and suddenly Abby and Samantha laughed, just a little. Even Jake cracked a smile.

"Come on," Abby said with a last glance at Sara's grave, so silent and cold in the moonlight. "Let's get out of here."

EPILOGUE

Nearly a week later, Abby found herself back in her basement, surrounded by sleeping bags, a plate of double-chocolate brownies, and her best friends. But this time, there was a new face in the group: someone who looked a little familiar, sounded a little different, and was slowly, shyly, getting to know everyone.

Samantha.

"What do you guys think?" asked Chloe as she lugged her enormous makeup kit over to the table. "Makeover time?"

"*Only* if we're absolutely, positively *not* going outside again tonight," Leah said firmly. She was sitting on the couch scratching Eddie's belly. The cat was purring so loudly that she was having trouble hearing her friends' chatter. "I swear I heard Toby call me Octo-Girl in gym this morning."

"No, what he *said* was, 'Watch out, girl!'" Nora laughed. "Because you were totally in the way!"

"Hey, I can't make any promises we won't go out-side," Chloe said, her eyes twinkling. "I mean, maybe we'll play Truth or Dare later. And *anything* can happen during Truth or Dare."

"No, no," Abby spoke up, shaking her head. "I think we've played enough Truth or Dare for a while."

"What's the matter, Abby?" Leah asked with a giggle. "Are you worried somebody's going to ask all about your big date with *Jake* tomorrow?"

Abby grinned as the rest of the girls shrieked with excitement. "Nope," she replied. "That's not a secret. I'll tell you guys whatever you want to know."

"Well, here's what I want to know," Nora said loudly. "Everything!"

"Yeah!" cried Chloe as she plunked down next to Abby. "What are you going to wear?"

Abby caught Samantha's eye and smiled. "Samantha and I went shopping yesterday after school," she began, "and I got this great top. It's pale blue, and it has a skinny black belt. I love it."

"It looks so gorgeous on you," Samantha spoke up, and the two girls exchanged a grin.

"So what are you and Jake going to do, anyway?" asked Chloe.

"We're going to the movies," Abby said. "And then I think we're going to get ice cream after. You know, at the place down the street from the movie theater."

Leah sighed. "That sounds *so* awesome."

"Want to come?" Abby asked, her eyes twinkling.

"You know I can't." Leah giggled. "Because Max and I are going out for pizza!"

"What?!" screamed Chloe and Nora at the same time, and everyone cracked up.

"He just asked me this afternoon!" Leah said excitedly. "I couldn't believe it! I couldn't even think of anything to say, so I finally just nodded!"

"What are you going to do if that happens on your *date* tomorrow?" asked Nora.

Leah suddenly got serious. "Well, I already made a list of things we could talk about," she said. "I'm not, like, going to bring it with me or anything. But hopefully writing them down will help me remember them later!"

"You'll be *fine*," Abby said. "And if you get really stuck, just text me! We could all meet up for ice cream or something, especially since Max and Jake are best friends too."

"Well, obviously makeovers for you two are a top priority," Chloe announced. "We want you guys to look really great tomorrow night." She patted the floor in front of her. "Leah, you're up."

Leah scrambled across the room and sat cross-legged in front of Chloe. She closed her eyes as Nora reached for a container of lavender eye shadow. "I think this color will look amazing next to your pretty blue eyes," Chloe said.

"Want to try those French braids again, Nora?" Abby asked. "But maybe just one this time?"

"Sure," Nora said as she grabbed a hairbrush.

"Hey, Samantha," Abby continued. "Can I do your hair?"

"Oh, of course," Samantha said quickly. She sat down in front of Abby, and as she did, Abby smelled that exotic floral scent again. Suddenly she remembered where it was from, and her eyes lit up with recognition.

"Are you wearing Sara's perfume, Samantha?" Abby asked.

The room got very quiet as everyone looked at Samantha.

She shook her head. "No, this is my perfume," she said. But then she realized something. "Oh! We gave a bottle of this perfume to Sara every year for Christmas! Did she like it?"

Abby nodded, with the hint of a smile on her face. "She loved it. She wore it all the time. Once I asked where she got it, because I wanted to buy some, but she told me that it wasn't available here."

"It's not," Samantha said. "We buy it from a small perfumery in London. They make all the fragrances there." She paused. "I could send you a bottle, if you like. When I go back home."

"That's okay," Abby replied. "I think I'll try to find my own fragrance." She started running her fingers through Samantha's long red hair, the silky tresses slipping through her hands like water. "Your hair is so beautiful. I only wish my hair was this shiny!"

"Thank you," Samantha said, and Abby could tell from her voice that Samantha was smiling.

"Where did you cut it, anyway?" asked Abby. "It's all so straight and even. You can't even tell that you cut some off."

There was a pause.

"Cut some off?" Samantha finally asked in a puzzled voice.

"Yeah, when you left that lock of hair in my dresser drawer," Abby said. "With the note?"

"I put a note in there—for Jake," Samantha said. "But that was all."

"Wait a minute," Abby said as her hands fell away from Samantha's hair. "Are you saying that you *didn't* put a lock of hair under the note? Long red hair, tied with a purple ribbon?"

"Absolutely not!" Samantha announced as she turned around to face Abby. "I'd *never* cut off my hair. I haven't had it cut since I was four years old."

Abby's eyes grew wide as she stared at Samantha. "But if you didn't leave me a lock of red hair," she said slowly, "then who *did*?"

WANT MORE CREEPINESS?

Then you're in luck, because P. J. Night has some more scares for you and your friends!

MIRROR MESSAGE

Sara James has a message from beyond the grave. Do you want to know what it is? Hold this page up to a mirror. Then have a friend read it in the mirror to find out what Sara has to say!

I AM STILL IN LOVE WITH JAKE. HE NEEDS TO KNOW. WILL YOU HELP ME?

Answer: I AM STILL IN LOVE WITH JAKE. HE NEEDS TO KNOW. WILL YOU HELP ME?

YOU'RE INVITED TO . . .
CREATE YOUR OWN SCARY STORY!

Do you want to turn your sleepover into a creepover? Telling a spooky story is a great way to set the mood. P. J. Night has written a few sentences to get you started. Fill in the rest of the story on the lines provided and have fun scaring your friends.

You can also collaborate with your friends on this story by taking turns. Have everyone at your sleepover sit in a circle. Pick one person to start. She will add a sentence or two to the story, cover what she wrote with a piece of paper, leaving only the last word or phrase visible, and then pass the story to the next girl. Once everyone has taken a turn, read the scary story you created together aloud!

It was a dark and stormy night. The rain was tap, tap, tapping against my window and the trees were groaning in the wind. Everyone in the house was sleeping peacefully . . . except for me. There was a loud clap of thunder and then I heard something in the kitchen. It sounded

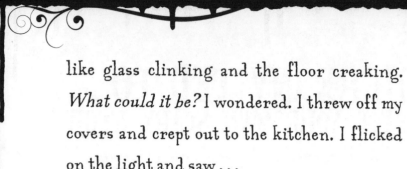

like glass clinking and the floor creaking.
What could it be? I wondered. I threw off my
covers and crept out to the kitchen. I flicked
on the light and saw...

_____

_____

_____

_____

_____

_____

_____

_____

_____

_____

_____

_____

_____

_____

THE END

You Can't
Come in Here!

CHAPTER 1

The tall, black-clad man stepped slowly toward the sleeping woman who was stretched out on the couch. Behind him, pale light from a mist-shrouded moon trickled in through a broken window. In the distance, the mournful wail of a wolf split the deathly still night. The man strode one step closer, brushing past a spiderweb, sending the eight-legged creature scurrying up its silvery strands. Reaching the couch, the man parted his brilliant red lips, revealing two long, sharp, gleaming white fangs.

"And now, my dear," the man said softly, leaning down toward the woman's exposed throat, "you will be mine—forever!"

As the man's fangs closed in on her neck, the woman suddenly awoke. Her eyes shot open in horror as she stared up at the beastlike jaws moving quickly toward her.

"AAAIIIEEEEEE!" she screamed, but her cry went unanswered.

Almost.

"Emily? Is that you? Is everything all right? I heard a scream," said a voice drifting down the basement stairs. Downstairs, in her family's home theater, Emily Hunter hit the pause button on the DVD's remote.

"Yeah, Mom, I'm fine," Emily replied, shaking her head. *Why does she always interrupt me just at the good part?* she wondered, staring at the horrific image frozen on the big screen in front of her.

"Well, I'm home, honey," Emily's mom called down. "You watching a scary movie again?"

"Yeah, Mom. I like scary movies, remember?" Emily shouted up the stairs.

"Okay, dinner will be ready in about half an hour," her mom replied. "Dad will be home any minute."

Emily glanced at the clock. It read 8:10. She shook her head.

"I bet I'm the only kid in the entire country who eats dinner at eight thirty," Emily mumbled to herself. Then she shrugged and hit play.

Up on the screen, the man had the woman locked in his supernatural gaze. She was spellbound by his stare, unable to move, trapped by his dark, penetrating eyes. He bit down hard, sinking his teeth deeply into her neck. She went limp in his arms, not dead, but no longer truly alive. The vampire's victim had been ushered into the world of the undead.

"Cool!" Emily said. Then she hit rewind and watched the scene again.

"Hey, Em, I'm home!" came her dad's voice from the top of the stairs.

"Hi, Dad," Emily shouted up to him, pausing the movie again.

"How was your day?" her dad asked.

"Good, thanks."

"Great," her dad said. "I'll see you in a few for dinner."

As she went back to the movie, Emily thought about the long hours that both her parents worked. Her mom was a lawyer. Her dad, a vice president of a pharmaceutical company. Emily knew that without all their hard work she would not be sitting in a state-of-the-art home theater watching one of her favorite horror movies. And if letting herself in after school, spending a few hours alone, and eating dinner at eight thirty instead of six like the rest of the world was the price, well, she figured she didn't have it all that bad.

As the undead man and woman on the screen stepped from the old gothic mansion in search of fresh victims, the credits rolled, and Emily's mom called her for dinner.

"On my way, Mom!" she shouted, flipping off the TV and bounding up the stairs.

"So what did you do at school today?" her dad asked as he passed Emily a bowl of mashed potatoes.

"Nothing too exciting," Emily replied, scooping potatoes onto her plate next to a mound of string beans. "I had to climb the rope in gym. You know how much I love that. But chem lab was fun. Ethan and Hannah were lab partners. And Ethan put too much red powder in with the blue powder, and white smoke and bubbles started pouring out of the beaker, all over the lab table and the floor. It was so funny!"

"I always said Ethan was a born scientist," her father teased. "Hey! How about we play some Wii after dinner?"

"Can't," Emily replied through a mouthful of string beans. "Going across the street to hang out at Drew and Vicky's."

"So late?" her mom asked. "We're getting up early tomorrow to drive to the beach."

"It's Friday night, Mom. And besides, I'll be home by my nine thirty curfew and I'll go straight to bed," Emily said. "I promise."

"It seems like you're always going over there," her mom said, shaking her head. "Are you embarrassed by your own house?"

"Of course not. Drew and Vicky just feel more comfortable at their own house, I guess."

"I don't know how anyone could feel comfortable in that house," her mom said. "It's a wreck."

"That house has been a wreck for all the years we've lived here," Emily pointed out. "That's not their fault."

"Yes, but it was empty for a long time," her mom said. "When I heard that someone had bought it and was moving in, I was thrilled. I figured they'd fix it up. But the Strigs have been there for a few months now, and they haven't done a thing. The siding is still ripped up. The old shutters hang from the windows. The porch is about to collapse, and the next big storm we get will probably take that roof down. The lawn is brown and dead. They haven't planted a single flower. It's just a disgrace to this neighborhood. Your father and I and the rest of the people on this street work hard to have a nice place to live, and a nice community."

Emily looked away for a second, then she turned back to her mother. "I just think you don't like Drew and Vicky," she said. "But you only met them once for, like, two minutes. You don't even know them."

"Oh, honey, it's not true that I don't like Drew and Vicky," Mrs. Hunter explained. "But it is true that I've never even *seen*, much less *met*, their parents. Normally I'd insist on meeting them before you hung out at their house, but I guess it's okay since you're only right across the street."

"You know that there aren't any other kids in the neighborhood, Mom," Emily said. "Everyone's old, even older than you and Dad, and now I finally have some kids my own age around here. They're a lot of fun to hang out with and I just want to be friends with them. So what if I go over to their house all the time?"

Emily's mom sighed. "All right, go have fun," she said, knowing how much Emily missed having other kids around. Then she scowled slightly. "But I still wish their parents would fix up that house."

"I'll tell them that, Mom," Emily joked, getting up

from the table and bringing her plate into the kitchen. Then she kissed her mom and hurried across the dining room. "Bye. See ya later."

Emily bolted out the front door before her mom could say anything more. She glanced up and down the block. House after house looked pretty much the same. The soft glow of streetlights and porch lights revealed muted-color siding, sliding glass doors leading onto decks, nicely mowed lawns, landscaped gardens, and blacktop driveways.

And then there was the Strig house.

Looking across the street, Emily saw the ramshackle old place. The last few flakes of paint on the original wooden clapboard danced in the wind. The sun-bleached shutters dangled on rusty nails. Most of the windows were broken, and those that weren't were boarded up. Green moss spread across the roof. The front lawn had died long ago, and even the weeds seemed to be struggling to survive.

Emily realized that her mom was right. The place looked as if no one had lived there for years. But she knew better. She knew that a family with two kids was living there. And they liked her. They wanted to hang

out with her, and she liked hanging out with them. They had a lot of cool stuff in their house. And that was good enough for Emily.

She walked across the crunchy brown lawn and stepped up onto the porch. Ancient floorboards creaked as she approached the front door. Emily was about to knock when she felt a tap on her shoulder. She jumped at the touch, spun around, and found herself face-to-face with Drew Strig.

Drew was taller than Emily, and very thin. His face was pale. His jet-black hair sprang out in every direction and looked as if it hadn't had even a chance meeting with a hairbrush in years. His black T-shirt and jeans looked slightly too small for his body.

"You scared me!" Emily exclaimed, and started to laugh. "I didn't hear you step onto the porch."

"Sorry about that," Drew said. "I wasn't sure you were going to make it over tonight."

"Yeah, my mom gave me a hard time," Emily explained. "You know, the usual. 'It's so late. Why are you always going over there?'"

"Maybe she doesn't like us," said a voice from above.

Looking up, Emily spotted Drew's sister, Vicky, sitting on a branch in an old gnarled tree that spread out across the front yard and overhung the tattered porch. Vicky looked very different from her brother. Her hair was pure white, but not old-lady white, more like glowing platinum. It hung down to her shoulders in perfectly straight strands extending from the part in the middle of her head. There was never a strand out of place. Her skin was the same color as her hair, and her thin lips had an odd purplish tint to them.

She was as skinny as her brother and almost as tall. Her black oversize shirt extended below her waist. The sleeves were so long, they hid her hands. Her clothes were dirty, but she didn't smell bad. She smelled kind of sweet and earthy, like the way the dirt smelled when Emily's mom churned up the garden each spring. To Emily, Vicky looked like some kind of goth-hippie hybrid. In fact, Emily thought that both Drew and Vicky dressed like rock stars. Emily, with her long, curly, reddish brown hair, sneakers instead of boots, and often sunburned face (from always forgetting to put on sunscreen before she went outside), never thought she looked as cool as these two.

"Nah," Emily responded. "It's not that she doesn't like you guys. I think she just doesn't like your house."

Vicky nodded and pushed herself off the branch. She dropped down onto the porch without making a sound and without the slightest stumble.

"Nice move," Emily said. "You should try out for the school gymnastics team."

"But I don't go to your school," Vicky said, lifting herself onto the porch railing, which shifted slightly even under her light weight.

"You could probably still join the team though," said Emily. "It's a bummer you guys are homeschooled. Any chance that'll change next year?"

"Not likely," Drew answered. "Our parents would just rather have us stay home and teach us themselves."

Emily shrugged.

"Your parents around tonight?" she asked, glancing up at the house and noticing that every window was dark.

"Yeah," Drew said. "Somewhere in the house."

Emily nodded as Vicky slipped off the railing and walked past her without making a sound. She followed, noticing that the floorboards creaked loudly beneath her own clumsy feet.

Drew pushed open the front door. It swung inward

with a woeful squeak. Emily followed Drew and Vicky inside.

"Drew, Vicky? Is that you?" called out a woman's voice.

"We're upstairs," added a man's voice.

"Ah, Mom and Dad," Drew said to Emily. "Told you they were around here somewhere." Then he cupped his hands around his mouth and shouted, "Yeah, it's us, Mom! Emily's here. She's gonna hang out for a while."

"Hi, Mr. and Mrs. Strig," Emily called up as she closed the front door.

Emily followed Drew and Vicky deeper into the house. This was not the first time she had been inside, but the weird layout of the place always surprised her a bit. It was so different from her own house right across the street. Just inside the front door, there were two narrow hallways, formed by unpainted Sheetrock walls. One turned to the left. The other led to a large room that was made entirely of wood paneling. And not just the walls, but the floor and ceiling too, as if someone had found a bunch of the stuff on sale and decided to build a whole room out of it.

"Ah, the famous Strig rec room," Emily said as they stepped in.

"We like it," Vicky said, somewhat defensively.

"Hey, I like it too," Emily replied quickly. "Who wouldn't?"

The room looked as if it had been magically transported here from a college dormitory. Its main furnishings were a Ping-Pong table and a foosball table, plus a couple of ripped-up chairs and a table with an old-fashioned rotary dial phone. A line of electric guitars and amplifiers stood in a row along one wall. A stereo, complete with a record turntable, sat in one corner. Next to it stood stacks and stacks of vinyl LPs. Drew turned on the stereo and put an album on the turntable. Punk music filled the room.

"Don't your parents mind you playing music so loud?" Emily shouted as she flipped through the stack of albums.

"Nah," Drew replied. "Whose records do you think these are?"

"Ready to lose?" Vicky asked, stepping up to the foosball table and grabbing the handles on one side. Emily took the other side and spun her players a few times.

"Game on," she said, dropping the ball onto the table.

Emily and Vicky slammed and twisted the game's

handles, making the little plastic players they controlled kick the ball. Vicky reacted instinctively when Emily fired a shot at her goal. Her goalie blocked the shot, then she deftly passed the ball through Emily's defense and fired it into the goal.

"Ugh," Emily moaned, spinning a handle in frustration. "How are you so good at this game?"

Vicky smiled at her friend. "I've had a lot of practice. Don't worry, once you've played as much foosball as I have, you'll beat me. Another game?"

Emily sighed. It was nice that Vicky tried to make her feel better, but she knew that she could practice all day and all night for weeks and she'd never be as good as Vicky. "Sure, why not."

As Emily and Vicky played another game, Drew chose the music, playing a song or two from one album, then another. When Vicky had beaten Emily two more times, Drew turned off the stereo and picked up a guitar.

"Wanna play some tunes?" he asked Emily, gesturing to another guitar.

"Or I could just beat you at Ping-Pong now," Vicky added.

Tough choice. Emily's dad had taught her to play a

little guitar, but she didn't practice as often as she would have liked, since it was kind of boring playing alone. She loved playing guitar with Drew and Vicky, who had been playing for far longer than she had. She always had a great time with them, and she could feel her playing improve. On the other hand, she'd love nothing more than to pay Vicky back by thrashing her at Ping-Pong.

But before Emily could decide, her cell phone sounded with a text message alert. Pulling out her phone, she saw that the message was from her mother. It simply said, IT'S NINE THIRTY.

"Ah, my mother, the human alarm clock," Emily said. "Sorry, guys, I promised her I'd be home by nine thirty."

"See you tomorrow night?" Drew asked.

"Can't," Emily said. "My parents have the whole week-end planned. We're spending all of Saturday and Sunday at the beach. Kind of a 'summer's almost here' thing."

"Bummer," Vicky said. "But we'll see you Monday?"

"Definitely! See you later."

Emily hurried across the street and slipped into her house. Her mother and father were in the living room watching TV. Franklin, their black cat, was curled up on her father's lap.

"I'm here!" Emily announced. "Nine thirty-two on the dot. Just like we agreed."

"Cute," her mom said. "Thanks for coming home right away. Did you have fun? What did you do?"

"Played games and stuff, you know," Emily replied.

"Video games?" her mom asked.

"No, they don't have a TV, actually," Emily said. "We played foosball."

"Foosball?" her dad said. "I played that all the time in college. Great game. I am definitely a master. Maybe I could join you some time?"

"Dad!" Emily groaned.

"Just kidding," her dad said.

"All right, hon," her mother said. "Time for you to get some sleep. I'm going to wake you at seven tomorrow morning."

Emily grimaced. Waking up early was not her thing. "Really? That early?"

"The early bird doesn't get stuck in traffic," her father reminded her.

Emily smiled as she trotted up the stairs to her room. That was one of her dad's signature corny phrases.

After brushing her teeth and changing into her

pajamas, Emily flopped onto her bed, popped in her earbuds, and turned on her iPod. She imagined playing the guitar chords herself. It wasn't long before she got sleepy and took out her earbuds. Emily snuggled under the covers.

A-hooooo! Ow-ow-w! came a loud, gut-piercing howl. Emily felt the blood freeze in her veins, then remembered the DVD she had been watching. *Dad must have turned on that movie. Jeez, he scared me half to—*

A-HOOOOO! OW-OW-W!

This time the howl was louder, and Emily knew instantly that it wasn't coming from the basement and it was too loud to be coming from the TV. The bone-chilling shriek was coming from outside.

She dashed across her room, stumbling over a stack of books she had left on the floor. Catching herself on her windowsill, she peered out the window. There, on the Strigs' brown front lawn, a huge wolf loped toward the house. It had to be bigger than a car. The wolf's back legs were long and slender, its chest round and muscular. Matted gray fur extended down its powerful front legs in mud-stained clumps.

But it was when Emily caught sight of the wolf's jaws

that her heart rose into her throat. Was that blood on the animal's long snout? The wolf opened its mouth wide and howled again, revealing long white fangs flecked with specks of red.

A little yelp escaped from Emily's throat as porch lights up and down the block flicked on. Seeming to sense her watching it, the wolf glanced over its shoulder, then quickly turned back toward the Strigs' front door. Crouching low, as if it were stalking prey, the wolf slowly climbed the stairs onto the front porch.

"Drew and Vicky," Emily muttered in horror. "It's gonna hurt Drew and Vicky!"

She turned and dashed from her room. Practically flying down the stairs, she exploded out the front door. Running across the street, she felt her heart pound as she watched the wolf lunge toward the door.

"Get away from there!" Emily shouted.

At the sound of her voice, the wolf turned and stared right at her, baring its razorlike teeth and growling. Then the snarling beast turned back, pushed the door open with its snout, and walked right into the house.

"No!" Emily cried, running faster now. Reaching the porch, she took the stairs two at a time, then stopped

175

short at the front door. She pushed the door open slowly, straining to see inside without actually sticking her head through the doorway. Pushing back against the terror shooting through her body, and shoving aside all thoughts of her own safety, Emily burst into the Strigs' house.

CHAPTER 2

"Drew, Vicky? Is that you?" Mrs. Strig called out from upstairs as Emily stepped through the doorway.

"We're upstairs!" Mr. Strig shouted.

"Mr. Strig! Mrs. Strig! You've got to get out of here!" Emily cried. "There's a wolf in your house!"

She got no reply.

Oh no! Emily thought in horror. *I hope the wolf hasn't gone upstairs and cornered them! Where are Drew and Vicky?*

Emily crept slowly toward the rec room. As she walked, she strained to hear any sound coming from the end of the hall.

She heard nothing.

She also felt the rush of courage she had experienced wearing off—quickly.

What am I doing? she wondered, inching closer to the rec room. *What can I possibly do against a wolf anyway? I must be crazy.*

She reached the room, her heart pounding wildly in her chest. Gripping the doorknob, Emily wondered why she heard no sounds in the house. No growling, no howling, no screaming in terror—nothing.

She took a deep breath, then another. She steadied herself, then she twisted the doorknob, thrust the door open, and burst into the room.

The door swung open faster than she thought it would. She lost her balance and tumbled to the floor, landing facedown. She rolled over, looked up, and found herself face-to-face with—Drew and Vicky.

The Strig kids both had puzzled looks on their faces as they glanced down at their friend completely sprawled out on the thick rec room rug.

Drew extended a hand and helped Emily up to her feet.

"Nice of you to come over," Vicky said. "I find that knocking on a door usually works better than somersaulting into a room. But that's just me."

Emily looked around the room in a panic. There was

no sign of the wolf and no evidence of a struggle or fight of any kind.

"Where did it go?" Emily asked, her heart still pounding.

"Where did what go?" Drew asked, looking at Emily as if she had three heads.

"The wolf!" Emily cried. "I saw it from my bedroom window. It came right through the front door!"

"You were spying on us from your bedroom window?" Vicky asked.

"No!" Emily protested, growing frustrated and more than a little confused. "I heard a howl coming from outside. When I looked out the window, I saw a big wolf. And it had blood on its fangs. It looked right at me and growled. Then it just walked into the house. I thought you guys were in trouble, so I ran over."

Drew and Vicky stared at Emily. Vicky raised her pencil-thin eyebrows and opened her eyes wide.

"Guys!" Emily moaned, hearing for the first time just how crazy her own words sounded.

Then she remembered Mr. and Mrs. Strig.

"Your parents!" she cried frantically. "They said hello when I came in, but then didn't answer when I warned them about the wolf. Maybe it went upstairs. Maybe it got them."

"Whoa, calm down," Drew said, extending his hands, palms out. "I'll go up and check to see if Mom and Dad have become wolf chow. Wait here."

Drew slipped out the door Emily had come through.

"So what were you doing when you heard this big bad wolf?" Vicky asked.

Great. She's making fun of me, Emily thought. "I was lying on my bed, listening to music. I got sleepy and decided to call it a night when I suddenly heard the wolf howl."

"You were lying on your bed and you got sleepy?" Vicky repeated.

"Yeah."

"And what did you tell me you had been doing earlier in the evening?" Vicky asked, as if she was a lawyer cross-examining a witness.

"Watching a scary movie," Emily replied, realizing where Vicky was going with this line of questioning. Emily started to blush.

"And is it possible that there was a wolf howling in said movie?" Vicky asked, crossing her arms in front of her, really getting into the whole lawyer-interrogating-a-witness thing.

"Yes," Emily admitted, sighing.

Vicky spun quickly and began speaking emphatically to an imaginary judge. "And so, Your Honor, I suggest that the witness did not see a wolf, but had, in fact, simply dozed off and had a dream about the wolf she had seen in that movie! No further questions. I rest my case."

"All right, all right," Emily conceded. "When you put it that way, I suppose I could have dreamed it all."

Drew rushed into the room, red faced and panting.

"It's terrible! It's horrible!" he cried.

"What happened?" Emily shrieked, rushing to his side.

"The wolf ate Mom, but—but—it didn't like the way Dad tasted, so it spit him out," Drew said, dropping his chin to his chest. "Dad feels so rejected."

Then he lifted his head and smiled at Emily.

"I get it, guys," Emily said, shaking her head. "I fell asleep. I had a dream. There was no wolf."

"Oh, Mom and Dad say hi, by the way," Drew added.

Emily nodded.

"Tell them I say hi back. And now that I've totally embarrassed myself, I'm gonna head home and see if I can get to work on a better dream."

"Don't worry about it," Vicky said sweetly, her usual edge softening a bit. "It happens to the best of us."

"Thanks," Emily said, thinking how great it was that Drew and Vicky accepted her even when she made a fool out of herself.

"Watch out for the wolf," Drew said as Emily headed for the door.

"Cute, real cute," Emily said.

She stepped from the house, closing the front door behind her. As she walked away she heard the muffled sounds of Mr. and Mrs. Strig talking to Drew and Vicky. A few seconds later, she was quietly opening the door to her own house, breathing a sigh of relief that her parents hadn't noticed her being gone.

Back in bed, Emily tossed and turned a bit before finally drifting off. Her dreams, while not scary, were fitful, filled with a sense of unease. She kept finding herself in unfamiliar rooms, trying to figure the way out, but running into one locked door after another. A feeling of dread pulsed through the dreams like a faint heartbeat. The last thing she remembered before the dreams finally stopped was the distant, lonely cry of an animal.

CHAPTER 3

BLEEP! BLEEP! BLEEP! BLEEP!

A terrible noise filled Emily's ears. Her eyes shot open wide and she bolted upright in bed. Then she glanced at the alarm clock on the night table next to her bed, saw that it was seven a.m., and realized that this was the source of the hideous noise. She slapped the snooze button so hard that the clock tumbled onto the floor. Dragging herself from the bed, the horrible reality of the situation dawned on her. It was Monday morning and she had to get up for school.

Emily had tried all different ways of getting herself to wake up for school. At first she set her iPod to wake her up with music. But when the wake-up music started blaring, she would just drift back to sleep, falling into a new dream based on the tune she had selected to awaken her. Then she had her mother call up to her room, but that just resulted in a grumble, a moan, and another plunge into slumber. So, in time, Emily realized that it had to be this loud, incredibly annoying clock that forced her up and out to start her day.

The weekend had flown by so fast. After she'd played beach volleyball with her dad all day Saturday and eaten way too much saltwater taffy yesterday, Friday night's wolf incident had pretty much faded from her mind. When it did circle back into her thoughts, she alternated between recalling just how real it had seemed and just how dumb she'd felt when she realized that it had only been a dream.

Emily got dressed, gulped down a bowl of cereal, and hurried off to catch the school bus. As the bus pulled into the school parking lot, she spotted Ethan Healy and Hannah Young, her two best friends. The three of them had been in school together since kindergarten. Here in middle school, they were not in all the same classes, but they always ate lunch together.

"Hannah! Ethan!" Emily called out as she bounded from the bus. "Wait up!"

"Hey, Em!" Hannah shouted back as the three friends fell into step together, heading for the school's main entrance. Hannah had short brown hair and a round face. When she smiled, her eyes twinkled mischievously, as if she was cooking up some kind of scheme. Hannah would do anything for Emily, and Emily felt the same way. Whoever came up with the abbreviation "BFFs" most definitely had Hannah and Emily in mind. "How was the beach?"

"Did your weird neighbors come with you?" Ethan jumped in, stepping in front of the two girls and walking backward.

Ethan was taller than Emily and Hannah. He had a mop of bright red hair that hung down into his face and shook when he walked. His hair was definitely the first thing anyone noticed about him, but it was his sense of humor that Emily and Hannah knew best.

"They didn't, but I did hang out with them on Friday night, Mr. Smarty Pants," Emily said. "They happen to be really awesome. But you wouldn't know that since you've never met them."

"Well, I met them, Em," Hannah piped up, "when I went with you to their house a couple of weekends ago. I usually like anyone you like, but they were kind of cold to me. And that house—I was really creeped out by that place."

"I know," Emily said. "But Hannah, you get spooked by butterflies, remember?"

"How could anyone forget?" Ethan chimed in. "You were the best part of our class trip to Butterfly World. From your reactions, you would have thought that you were being attacked by flying zombies or something, not little butterflies with pretty wings."

"All right, all right, are you guys done?" Hannah asked, shaking her head. "Am I ever going to live that down?"

"Nope," Ethan said matter-of-factly.

"Butterflies disturb me," Hannah continued. "All that fluttering around my face—ugh! Anyway, that doesn't have anything to do with what we were talking about."

"What *were* we talking about?" Ethan asked.

"Drew and Vicky," Emily reminded him.

"Right," Hannah said. "I was creeped out by their house. And I don't see what's so great about them anyway."

"They're nice and fun to hang out with, that's all," Emily explained. "You just have to give them a chance."

Before Hannah could reply, the bell rang, signaling the time when all students had to be inside.

"See you guys at lunch," Emily said, scooting into the building with her friends, who each went in a different direction.

Emily hurried down the hall. The last thing she needed was another tardy caused by standing outside the building, yakking away with Hannah and Ethan.

The rest of the morning dragged on, as Monday mornings always did. Emily made it through math, English, and gym. Lunchtime finally arrived.

As she headed to the cafeteria, she thought about what Hannah had said before school. So Hannah was a little creeped out by Drew and Vicky's house. So what? She shouldn't hold that against them. Emily wondered how she could get her friends to like one another. Invite everyone over all at once? Emily smiled to herself. A party wasn't a bad idea.

By the time she reached the cafeteria, the usual lunchtime pandemonium was well underway. She filled her tray, then deftly navigated her way between tables of screaming and laughing kids, ducking under a few flying trays and stepping around the odd container of spilled milk or splattered glob of Jell-O.

Spotting Hannah and Ethan at their usual table in the

corner near the window, Emily slid into a seat beside them.

"What'd you get?" Ethan asked, leaning forward, sticking his face right over her tray and scanning it, like a hungry hawk searching for prey on the ground below.

"Get your nose outta my food!" Emily said, gently shoving Ethan's forehead away. "I got the lasagna. It's the usual gloppy cheese, dried-out sauce, and some green things that perhaps were once vegetables."

"I got the meat loaf," Ethan said proudly. "I like not knowing what's in my lunch."

"You are so strange," Hannah chimed in, looking right at Ethan and picking up a forkful of salad.

"You've been saying that since we were six!" Ethan complained.

"Well, it doesn't make it any less true," Hannah shot back. Then she turned to Emily, as Ethan picked apart his meat loaf. "How was gym?"

"Rope again. Need I say more?"

"I know! If people were meant to climb ropes—"

"We'd have wings, right?" Ethan interrupted.

"What's that supposed to mean?" Hannah asked.

"Well, you know, so we could fly up the rope instead of having to climb it?" Ethan explained. The girls started giggling at the thought of Ethan with a pair of wings.

"Well, at least you won't have to climb the rope for too much longer," Hannah began. "The school year's over in just three more days, not counting today or our random day off on Thursday."

"What are we going to do to celebrate the end of the school year this weekend?" Ethan asked. "We could go to Ride World again. That was great—especially seeing your face on the roller coaster, Em!"

"As I recall, Ethan, I was not the one who lost his lunch when the Ferris wheel got stuck with us at the top," Emily replied.

"So I learned that I don't like heights," Ethan said defensively. "And that fried chicken sandwiches with peanut butter on top don't like me. That's a mistake I won't make again."

"I have a different idea for this year," Emily said, trying to steer the conversation back to reality and away from the strange planet known as Ethan's brain. "I was thinking we could have a big party. I'm sure I could talk my mom into letting us have it at my house."

"Ooh, fun!" Hannah squealed. "We haven't had a big

party in forever. Wait a minute. How about making it a sleepover?"

"An end-of-the-school-year sleepover party!" Emily cried. "I love it! Hannah, you are a genius!"

"I've been telling you that for years," Hannah said, hiding her face behind her hand, adding, "Please, no autographs."

"And that will be a perfect chance for you both to get to know Drew and Vicky better," Emily added. "You'll see that they're really cool."

"Wait," Hannah said, dropping her genius routine and staring at Emily. "You're going to invite them to our sleepover?"

"Yes," Emily replied quickly. "They *are* my friends."

"But they don't even go to our school," Ethan pointed out.

"They don't even go to *any* school," Hannah added.

"All the more reason to invite them, then, isn't it?" Emily asked. "This will be a chance for them to meet all my other friends, to help them feel like part of the gang. It's got to be hard when your parents homeschool you. It'll be a great time for everyone to get to know each other."

"Well, I don't—," Hannah started.

"Great, then it's settled," Emily continued, not allowing Hannah an opportunity to protest. "I'm glad we all agree."

"You're forgetting one thing," Ethan said, inhaling the last crumbs of his meat loaf. "I'm a boy."

"Really?" Emily replied in mock surprise. "I just thought you were a really weird-looking girl."

"Seriously, Em," said Ethan, rolling his eyes. "Hello! There's no way your mom will allow a coed sleepover!"

"Good point," Emily said, a bit surprised that she had completely overlooked this fact.

"How about the boys have to leave around ten or eleven?" Hannah suggested. "It can be a regular party, and then the boys can go home and the girls get to stay for the sleepover."

"That'll work!" Emily said, greatly relieved. "Hannah, you're—"

"—a genius, yes, we've already established that."

"Good idea, Hannah," Ethan said. "I'll bring the fried chicken with peanut butter sandwiches!"

BRIIING!

The bell rang ending lunch period, and the three friends got up, cleared their trays, and headed from the cafeteria with the stampede of the rest of the students.

"Call me tonight and we'll start planning the party!" Emily said to Hannah as the three friends headed off to three different classes. "See ya, guys."

Emily was bursting with excitement as she hurried off to history class. *Hannah and Ethan are going to love Drew and Vicky*, she thought. *The five of us are going to have the best summer together—and it all starts at this party. I can't wait!*

CHAPTER 4

"How was school today, honey?" Emily's mom asked as the family sat down for dinner that evening.

Emily glanced at the clock and saw that it was 7:55. *We're eating early tonight*, she thought as she dug into her dinner. *For us, anyway.*

"It was okay," she replied to her mom. "You know, the usual. Lunch with Hannah and Ethan, surrounded by a few classes."

"Funny," her dad said. "I guess I don't have to ask what your favorite subject is."

Since they were on the topic of lunch and Ethan and Hannah, Emily thought this might be a good time to mention the plan they had cooked up. She didn't think it would be a problem, but after all, there could be no party without her parents' permission.

"So, Hannah, Ethan and I were talking at lunch," Emily began. "You know, about what to do for the end of the school year?"

"How about finish your schoolwork and get good grades?" her dad suggested.

"I mean, *after* we do all that, Dad," she replied, smiling. There had been a time when her dad's dumb little jokes would have really bothered her. She took it as a sign of her ever-growing maturity that she could ignore them—like Mom always did.

"Another trip to Ride World?" her mom asked.

"Nah, we talked about that, but we wanted to do something different this year," Emily explained.

"How about a thrilling outing to Miniature Golf Palace?" her dad chimed in. "They have eight different courses, and you haven't lived till you've played them all twice."

Emily's mom gave her a look and smiled. "Here we go again."

"I aced the clown-face course," her dad continued. "Every hole is a different clown face. Put the ball in the last clown's mouth and his nose lights up!"

"Actually, we were thinking of having a party," Emily said, cutting right to the chase before the entire evening slipped away. "A sleepover party."

"Oh," said her mom, thinking this over. "Where? Here?"

"Of course," Emily said quickly. "You guys are the best. You know Hannah's parents are super uptight about everything, and Ethan's grandmother has an apartment in his basement so there's nowhere for us to hang out. Plus, everybody's so comfortable here."

"Everybody except Drew and Vicky, it seems," her mom said. "Will you be inviting them to the party?"

"Sure," Emily said. "I really want all my other friends to meet them."

"Well, that's fine, but I would really like to officially meet them and their parents, especially if they're going to be sleeping over in my house," her mom said.

"Well, Vicky will," Emily corrected her. "Drew and Ethan and any other boys who come will have to leave at some point, of course."

"Well, yes," her mom said.

"And you'll meet Drew and Vicky and their parents, I promise," Emily said, hoping she could keep her word. "Speaking of which, I told them I would go hang out tonight. See ya at nine thirty."

"Have fun, honey," her mom said as Emily got up from the table.

"I still think Miniature Golf Palace is a great idea!" her dad shouted as Emily slipped out the door.

A few minutes later Emily was in the Strigs' rec room, strumming on an electric guitar.

"Ready to rock out?" Drew asked, cranking up the volume on his amp.

"I'm just ready to try to keep up with you guys," Emily said, tuning the final string on her guitar.

"All right, enough talk," Vicky said. "Here we go. One-two-three-four!"

Counting off the tune, Vicky began bashing out power chords on her guitar. Emily, who was still a relative newcomer to the instrument, did her best to follow the chord changes as Vicky sped through the song.

Meanwhile, Drew played lead guitar, his fingers flashing up and down the fret board. He played a run of superfast notes, then bent some very high notes until it sounded as if the strings would pop right off.

As she struggled to keep up, Emily continued to be impressed by how well it seemed these two did everything. The first song ended, and Emily felt good that she had at least known how to play all the chords that Vicky was strumming.

"Wow! You guys are really good," Emily said, catching her breath. "I know it seems like I say that every time I come here, but it's true."

"We do get to practice a lot," Drew said.

"It comes with hanging out at home most of the time," Vicky added.

Emily took this as an opening. "So, about that. What would you say about coming to a sleepover party at my house this Saturday?" she asked.

"We'd have to check with our mom," Vicky replied. "She's a little weird about stuff like that."

"Stuff like what?" Emily asked.

"Sleeping over other people's houses," Vicky replied. "They like us being home."

"Well, here's the thing," Emily continued. "It's an end-of-the-school-year party and I really, really want you guys to come. My friends Hannah and Ethan will be there, and I'd love for you to get to know them so we can all hang out together this summer. Drew, all the boys have to go home around eleven, but Vicky, you can stay over."

Drew and Vicky looked at each other. They seemed to be genuinely surprised by Emily's announcement. They also looked slightly confused.

"It's nice of you to ask us," Drew finally said after an awkward few moments of silence.

"Of course," Emily said. "But the thing is, my mom wants to meet you and your parents first, you know, like now, before you come for the party, so the sooner you can convince your parents to say yes, the better it will be."

"I'll talk to them later," Vicky said. "They're busy now."

"How are they putting up with our loud guitar playing?" Emily asked, smiling.

"They love it," said Drew. "Seriously. And speaking of which, let's play another tune."

The trio broke into another song, and Emily was blown away by how Drew seemed to get better with each note he played. *He's better than half the musicians I hear on the radio,* she thought. *And he's only a kid. He has a chance to be a pro when he grows up.*

Again, Emily pushed herself. She could almost feel her playing improve as she concentrated intently. The song ended, and Drew gave her a high five.

"Nice!" he said. "You are getting so much better, Emily. We should go on the road!"

The road? Emily thought. *This guy isn't even allowed to leave his house!*

"Just kidding!" Drew said quickly. "Want to do another?"

"Sure, but first I need to use your bathroom," Emily announced. She pulled the guitar over her head and placed it on its stand. Then she headed for a door on the far side of the rec room.

Emily reached out to open the door.

"Don't open that!" Vicky cried out in panic.

Emily jumped in fright, pulling back her hand as if she had just received an electric jolt. "I'm sorry!" she said automatically, her heart still pounding in her chest, though she couldn't figure out what she had done wrong.

"No, *I'm* the one who should apologize, Emily," Vicky said, looking more pale than usual. "I didn't mean to have such an extreme reaction, and I didn't mean to scare you. It's just that that bathroom is broken and it has to be fixed. The last time someone went in there and used it, water went everywhere and the whole house was flooded for a week."

"You could go outside and pee in the woods behind our house," Drew suggested, flashing a big smile. "That's what I do."

Emily grimaced. "Gross! You sound like my friend Ethan. I'll just wait until I get home."

"So, Ping-Pong?" Vicky asked brightly. "I owe you a chance to get revenge for the foosball games on Friday night."

"Sure, why not?" Emily said.

The two picked up paddles from the Ping-Pong table set up in the corner of the room and began to volley back and forth. Drew continued to pluck out riffs on his guitar while the two girls smacked the ball over the net.

Emily held her own for a while. But then Vicky seemed to shift her game into a higher gear and put her away, winning easily.

"It's a good thing I really like you guys," Emily said, tossing her paddle onto the table. "Otherwise I would hate you for being so good at everything."

"You'll get there," Vicky said.

"Nice of you to say," Emily sighed. Glancing at her phone, she noticed that it was 9:20. "I think I'll head home a couple of minutes early and shock my mom when she sees me without having to text me to tell me what time it is. And I also gotta . . . well, you know." She gestured toward the door to the broken bathroom.

"Okay, so your homework, young lady, young man, is to work on your parents," Emily said, doing her best impression of a grown-up voice. "Then you all have to come over and meet mine. And then you can come for the sleepover and meet my friends. It'll be a great start to an awesome summer! See ya."

Emily headed over to her house. She hoped that maybe her little jokey encouragement would get Drew and Vicky to convince their parents to let them come over. Just before she reached her own front door, she heard a faint sound coming from across the street.

A-hooooo! Ow-ow-w!

She stopped short, the blood seeming to freeze in her veins.

"The wolf!" she whispered to herself. "That's the same howl I heard the other night. And now I know I'm awake."

A-hooooo! Ow-ow-w!

The sound came again, and this time Emily could pinpoint where it was coming from: the woods behind the Strigs' house.

"I've got to find out if I'm imagining things or figure out what in the world is going on here." She hurried back across the street, slipping past the Strigs' front porch, then circled around behind their house. Pausing for a moment at the edge of the thick grove of trees, she plunged into the dark woods.

"What am I doing here?" Emily wondered aloud as she picked her way past craggy branches, her feet crunching on fallen leaves and dried-out twigs.

Deeper she went, feeling the darkness close in all around her.

Something ran right past her. She actually heard the sound of something tearing through the woods a split second before she saw the streak.

"Yah!" she screamed, backing up and crashing into a tree.

Whatever it was flashed past her again, then disappeared, swallowed up by the darkness and silence.

Was it the wolf? Where did it go?

Deciding not to wait around to find out, Emily turned and ran. The woods were not very big, but panic made her doubt her usually reliable sense of direction. No. She was not about to get lost in the tiny woods she had been playing in since she was a little kid.

"Ah, there's the exit," she said to herself, breathing a sigh of relief. "And I can see streetlights between the leaves."

Just before she stepped out of the woods, Emily caught sight of something fluttering in the breeze up ahead.

"What is that?" she wondered aloud. When she got close enough to see, Emily gasped in horror. She was staring at a tuft of fur dangling from a tree branch—wolf fur—covered with blood.

CHAPTER 5

Emily put her head down and ran, her legs pumping, her arms shoving branches out of the way. She crashed through the last bit of woods that stood between that tuft of fur and safety, bursting out onto the sidewalk.

Glancing back over her shoulder toward the Strigs' house, she wondered if Drew and Vicky had heard the howling this time. Maybe they even had seen her running in fear from the woods she knew so well. Or maybe they saw whatever she had spotted running through the woods. But their house was dark. There was no sign of her two friends.

Emily dashed across the street to her front door and then paused.

Gotta catch my breath, she thought. *Can't let Mom*

and Dad see me all freaked out like this.

She wiped the sweat from her forehead with her sleeve and pushed her hair back into some sort of order. Then she took a deep breath and reached for the front door.

"Everything's fine. Everything's fine," she whispered, hoping this mantra would calm her down. "Everything's—YAH!"

She was startled by the text message alert coming from her cell phone—her mother's curfew reminder. She opened the door and stepped into her house.

"I almost beat your text tonight," she said, forcing a big smile—maybe a bit too big. "I was right outside the door when I got it."

"Everything okay, honey?" her mom asked. "You look . . . Did something happen tonight at Drew and Vicky's?"

"Nothing out of the ordinary," Emily replied, trying hard to pull herself together. "You know, we, uh, played guitar, then Vicky whipped me at Ping-Pong. The usual."

"Did they ask their parents about the party?"

"They're working on it, Mom," Emily said, heading for the stairs. "I'm pretty beat. I'm gonna head up to bed. G'night."

"Okay. Good night, honey. You sure everything's okay?"

"Peachy!"

Peachy? Emily thought as she bounded up the stairs to her bedroom. *I never say "peachy." Where'd that come from?*

Stretched out on her bed, she wondered if she was losing her mind or if there might actually be a deadly creature roaming around her neighborhood. And what exactly was it? A wolf? Not that it ever would have happened, but what if she had followed Drew's advice and went out to pee in the woods?

Then she remembered that the first time she'd heard and saw the wolf at the Strigs' door, porch lights all along the block came on as if others had heard it too. She could check with some neighbors. Maybe they remembered that night. But that was just a dream . . . or was it?

These questions kept her tossing and turning until she finally drifted off to sleep. Once again her dreams were filled with anxiety, though when she woke up Tuesday morning she could not remember any of them.

That morning in school Emily felt distracted. She

had not told Ethan or Hannah about the wolf incident from Friday night, figuring it was just a dream, despite how real it seemed. Now, after last night, she really wanted to tell them, but she also knew just how strange it was going to sound.

She debated with herself all morning, barely hearing what her teachers were saying and thankful that none of them called on her during any of her classes. As she walked to the cafeteria, Emily knew what she had to do. These three best friends had never kept secrets from one another—which was one of the reasons they had remained best friends for so many years—and now was not the time to start.

"I have some great ideas for the sleepover," Hannah said as Emily sat down at their usual lunch table.

"Me too!" Ethan added, flashing his partly jolly and partly demented grin.

"Seeing how far we can throw rolls of toilet paper from the upstairs windows hardly qualifies as a sleepover activity," Hannah pointed out.

"My brother's friends did it," Ethan grumbled, shrugging.

"That was for Halloween, Ethan," Hannah pointed

out. "And as I remember, more than a few angry neighbors stopped by the next day."

"No angry neighbors, please," Emily said, glad for the momentary distraction, but still bursting to tell her friends what had happened.

"So, here's what I came up with," Hannah continued.

"Hannah, before you tell me your ideas, I have something to tell you guys," Emily said.

"No! The party's canceled. Your mom said no, your dad—"

"No, no, no, the party's on. This has nothing to do with the party." Emily took a deep breath, then went on. "Last Friday I had this dream, or at least I think it was a dream. It's all so confusing now."

"Dreams usually happen when you're asleep," Ethan volunteered.

"Thanks for that valuable piece of information," Hannah said. "Now let Emily talk."

"So anyway," Emily continued, "I had been hanging out with Drew and Vicky. I went home and was on my bed when I heard howling. It sounded like it was coming from outside. I went to my window and saw . . . well, I saw a wolf!"

"A wolf?" Hannah asked in disbelief.

"Like a real wolf? Not like a big dog or something?" Ethan added.

"Yes, a real wolf," Emily said. "It was huge and horrible and had bloodstains on its mouth and teeth."

"They sell a special toothpaste for that now, you know," Ethan joked.

"Ethan!" Hannah shouted.

"I saw the wolf go into Drew and Vicky's house," Emily continued. "I panicked and ran across the street to save them."

"Wait, you went into the house?" Hannah asked, grabbing her head with her hands. "You thought you saw a bloodstained monster go in and you thought it was a good idea to just follow it and what? Fight it with your bare hands?"

"I know, I know. It's nuts," Emily said, sighing. "I don't know what I was thinking. But just let me finish, because it gets weirder."

Ethan leaned forward, placing his elbows on the table and resting his chin in his hands. "Weirder is good," he said. "Go on."

"Okay, so I followed the wolf into the house, but it

wasn't there. Drew and Vicky were there, just hanging out. They didn't hear or see any wolf. And I found no evidence that the wolf was ever there. When I told Vicky all about this, she convinced me that I had fallen asleep on my bed, dreamt all about the wolf, then woke up and ran over to her house. And that made sense."

"Sounds about right," Hannah said, shrugging. "So can I tell you about my party idea now?"

"Not yet," Emily replied, holding up her hands. "It did make sense, and I had pretty much forgotten about it, until last night."

Ethan leaned in even closer.

"I was playing some music with Drew and Vicky. When I left their house to go home, I heard the howling again. This time it was coming from the woods behind their house. So I went into the woods."

"Wait! Time out!" Ethan said. "You heard this wolf a second time and followed it again?"

"That's right."

"Okay, I have just one question, and it's a simple one. ARE YOU COMPLETELY INSANE?"

"Ethan, I had to find out. I had to know."

"And what did you find, Em?" Hannah asked, starting

to take this whole thing seriously for the first time.

"Well, I didn't exactly see the wolf. But I did see something moving very fast through the woods."

"Like a bunny?" Ethan asked.

"This was no bunny," Emily continued. "It was big, but it flashed past me so quickly, I couldn't see what it was. I was starting to run home when I saw a bloody tuft of fur hanging from a tree. It looked like wolf fur."

"Really?" Hannah asked skeptically. "Are you sure it had blood on it?"

"Pretty sure," Emily replied.

"I think maybe you're starting to get spooked from hanging around with Drew and Vicky all the time," Hannah said.

"I think Hannah's right," Ethan added. "Maybe hanging around with those two has got you seeing stuff. I mean, a fox, yeah, but there aren't any wolves for, like, a hundred miles."

"I guess you're right," Emily sighed. "But what's been making that howling sound?"

"It was probably just a neighbor's dog or something," suggested Hannah.

"And the bloody fur—that could have come from

anywhere," Ethan assured her. "Maybe two squirrels got in a fight."

Emily let out a deep breath. "Thanks, guys. I'm probably just making too big a deal out of nothing."

"Forget about it for now," Hannah said. "Let's talk about something fun, like my idea for the party—make-your-own ice cream sundaes!"

"I love it," Emily said.

"Excellent," Hannah said. "Now, for games I—"

The bell sounded, ending lunch period.

"Games will have to wait," Emily said. "Can't be late for history. We'll talk later."

"See ya," Hannah said, grabbing her tray and hustling from the table.

"Don't talk to any wolves on the way home, Em, okay?" Ethan added.

"Good-bye, Ethan," Emily replied.

As she walked to class, Emily found her thoughts turning back once again to the wolf. Despite her friends' reassurances, something didn't seem right to her. She just couldn't let it go. And even though Hannah didn't like them, she wasn't ready to give up her friendship with Drew and Vicky. She wanted them all to come to

the sleepover. She was sure that once they all had some fun together, away from that creepy house, Drew, Vicky, Hannah, and Ethan would become friends.

But first she had to find out, once and for all, whether there really was a wolf or if she was simply losing her mind.

I'm going back into the woods tonight, Emily decided. *And this time I'm taking Drew and Vicky with me!*

CHAPTER 6

"So the sleepover party is definitely happening?" Vicky asked that evening when Emily went over to hang out. Vicky had just finished beating Emily in a game of Ping-Pong. They were each stretched out across a different tattered, overstuffed chair with their legs dangling over one of the chair's thick arms and their heads resting against the other. Drew looked on from the corner of the room, where he was restringing his guitar.

"Yep, everything's on," Emily replied. "My friends and I always do something special at the end of the school year. Last year we went to an amusement park. This year we thought a party would be fun and a sleepover party would be extra fun. What'd your parents say? You guys allowed to come?"

"I'm not sure," Drew said, never taking his eyes off the neck of his guitar. He tightened a string, then pulled another one from the package.

"What do you mean?" Emily said. "I thought you guys wanted to come. You know, since you don't go to school, this is a way you can be part of a group of friends."

Vicky looked at her brother, then at Emily. "We do want to come," she said. "It's just that we haven't been able to nail our parents down about going over to your house."

"Why not?" Emily asked. "You know my mom won't let me officially invite you to the sleepover until she's spent more than two minutes with you. And she'd really like to meet your parents, too. What's the problem?"

"You know, they're weird," Vicky replied, slightly defensively. "Lots of people have weird parents. I mean, are *your* parents totally normal?"

Emily shook her head. She couldn't figure out what the big deal could be with Mr. and Mrs. Strig, but it wasn't worth pushing too hard and risking her friendship with Drew and Vicky. "No, of course not," she said. "My parents are weird just like everyone else's. I mean, the other day my dad asked if he could come over with me and play foosball with you guys. And when I told him about the idea for the sleepover, he suggested we go play miniature golf instead. He is *such* a weirdo!"

Vicky and Drew both laughed.

"Anyway," Emily continued, "there's something else I wanted to talk to you both about."

Vicky sat up. Drew continued working on the guitar's sixth and final string.

Emily went on, "Last night, when I left your house, almost as soon as I stepped out, I heard—I heard—oh, boy, I just realized how weird this is going to sound. Well, I heard the wolf again."

Vicky's eyes opened wide. "The wolf from your dream?" she asked.

"It sure sounded like the same one," Emily explained. "But I didn't actually see it."

Drew put down his guitar and walked over to the girls. "Well, at least we know you weren't dreaming."

"Unless, of course, you were sleepwalking when you were over here."

"Vicky!" Emily cried.

"Just a joke. So what did you do when you heard the wolf?"

"Well, the sound was coming from the woods behind your house," Emily began.

"Really?" Drew interrupted.

"Without a doubt," Emily said.

"That's strange," Drew said. "I didn't hear a thing."

"Me neither," Vicky added. "So what did you do?"

"I went into the woods to see what was going on," Emily replied, as if it were the most natural thing in the world. "I know, you're going to say, 'Are you crazy, going into the woods by yourself to find a wolf—a huge, man-eating monster?'"

"No," Vicky said. "Actually, what I was going to say was that you're pretty brave for doing that and I wish I had been there with you. Sounds like a cool adventure."

"Oh," Emily said, pleasantly surprised.

"Did you see anything in the woods?" Drew asked.

"Nothing I could identify. I saw something big move very quickly past me. Then I heard the howling again. I got scared and ran from the woods. That's when I saw something hanging from a tree."

"What?" Vicky asked.

"Fur from an animal. A wolf maybe. And it was covered in blood."

"You're not making this up to get back at us for making fun of your dream, are you?" Drew asked.

"If it really was a dream," Emily said with renewed conviction that maybe she *had* seen a wolf that first night. "And no, I'm not making it up. In fact, I think we should go back out into those woods right now and find out once and for all if there is anything creepy and dangerous lurking in there."

Drew and Vicky looked at each other. They both shrugged.

"Let's do it," Drew said, setting his guitar onto a stand and heading for the back door.

Outside, the night was quiet. The three friends hurried across the unkempt lawn and paused at the edge of the woods. Emily nodded to the others, then continued ahead into the darkness.

Leading the way, with Drew and Vicky close behind, Emily moved quickly but carefully through the thicket of trees and bushes. She shoved aside branches and squeezed her way around thick tree trunks.

Emily stopped short in front of an old tree with sharp bare branches sticking out on all sides. "This is it," she said. "I'm sure of it. This is where the bloody tuft of fur was."

A bright light suddenly blazed to life, sending Emily stumbling backward, crashing into a tree.

"Who's there?" she cried.

"Um, sorry, it's just me," Vicky replied, waving a flashlight around. "I guess I should have warned you that I was turning on the flashlight, huh?"

"Yes! No surprises, please! We're in the woods, in the dark, hunting a monster, remember?" Emily screamed in an adrenaline-fueled shriek. She had been keeping her composure pretty well considering all this wolf-and-blood-and-creepy-woods craziness—until that moment.

She took a deep breath. "Okay, maybe I overreacted a bit. Anyway, now that you've got that thing on, shine it at the tree."

Vicky trained the flashlight's beam on the bare tree. She lit up the branches, moving her light up and down. Emily examined each branch. She saw no sign of the fur she had seen the night before.

Finding nothing on that particular tree, the trio moved deeper into the woods. The night was still. Even the usually fluttering leaves made no sound in the windless darkness.

"So what are we looking for now?" Drew asked, ducking under a branch.

"I don't know," Emily replied. "Something. Anything. Whatever it was I saw last—"

The sound of footsteps tearing through the woods stopped Emily short.

"Here it comes!" she whispered. "It sounds like what I heard last night. But I don't see anything."

The woods grew silent again for a moment, then the sound returned.

"Whatever it is, it's running through the dead leaves on the ground, kicking up a storm," Drew said, staring into the darkness, trying to find the movement that went along with the rustling and running sounds.

"There!" Vicky said a few seconds later, aiming the flashlight at the ground. The brilliant beam picked up a scurrying movement.

"That's it!" Emily cried, relieved to learn that she was not imagining things. There really was something out there.

The creature froze in the intense circle of light, then turned and flashed its dark eyes right at Vicky.

"Um, Emily, that's a raccoon," Drew said.

The small creature stared up at the friends, looking

at first puzzled, then annoyed. When it flashed a set of sharp-looking teeth, Vicky turned off the light, allowing the critter to go about its nocturnal business in private.

"*That's* what this was all about?" Vicky asked. "A raccoon in the woods at night?"

"No!" Emily snapped defensively. "I don't know. Maybe we should just—"

A-hooooo! Ow-ow-w!

Emily stopped talking and clutched Vicky's arm. "That's the sound—the exact sound, I swear," she said in horror. "It's the wolf! Shine your light! Shine your light!"

Vicky fumbled clumsily with the flashlight, trying to turn it on as quickly as she could.

Emily's frantic insistence didn't help. "Come on! Come on!" she cried.

A-hooooo! Ow-ow-w!

The howling came again, closer this time. Vicky dropped the flashlight onto the ground.

"It's getting closer!" Emily whispered.

Vicky dropped to her knees. She began to feel around desperately among the leaves and twigs. Emily knelt down beside her and helped with the search. If they were going to get torn apart by a wild beast, the least they could do was see the thing.

"Got it!" Vicky cried after a few more seconds of panicked searching.

A-HOOOOO! OW-OW-W!

The howling was right upon them now. Vicky lifted herself to one knee and flipped the switch. Her light blazed to life, and she aimed the beam right at the sound, which now seemed to be directly overhead, ready to pounce down onto them.

A-HOOOOO! OW-OW-W!

In the circle of light casting skyward, perched on a thick branch, stood an owl. The bird cocked its head as it peered down at the kids looking up at it.

"*A-HOOOOO! OW-OW-W!*" the owl screeched again. Then it spread its wings and took off into the night.

"Well?" Vicky said questioningly to Emily. "Seen enough? Do you need any more proof that there is no wolf, no monster, no bloodthirsty beast?"

Emily sighed. She still could not explain all this, but she also couldn't continue to search for something that most likely did not exist. "Yeah, let's go home. Sorry, Vicky. Sorry, Drew."

But Drew didn't respond. "Drew? DREW?! Vicky, where's Drew? He's gone."

"Drew!" Vicky called out.

"Drew!" Emily cried, their voices echoing through the trees.

"What are you two yelling about?" Drew said suddenly from behind them.

"Where were you?" Emily asked sternly, like a frightened mother reprimanding a child.

"I had to pee," Drew explained. "Did I miss anything?"

"You missed Emily being attacked by a killer owl. *A-hooooo! Ow-ow-w!*" Vicky did a pretty good impression of the owl.

"That's it, guys," Emily said, throwing her hands into the air. "I'm done with all this wolf stuff. I promise. I'm sorry I dragged you out here."

"It's no big deal," Vicky said. "It's a nice night for a walk."

Vicky had barely finished her sentence when the first drops of rain began to fall. The trio picked their way back through the woods. By the time they emerged into Drew and Vicky's backyard it was pouring.

"Sorry again, guys!" Emily said through the teeming

raindrops. "I'll see you soon." Then she ran across the street.

Pausing under the awning at her front door, she glanced back at the Strigs' house. She saw Vicky slip through the front door. Then she heard the all-too-familiar howling again. Leaning to one side to get a better angle on the woods, Emily saw something running—something larger than a raccoon or an owl.

She turned quickly away. "No," she muttered to herself just before stepping inside. "I am done with all this wolf stuff!"

CHAPTER 7

Emily tossed and turned, trying to force herself to fall asleep. She knew it was hopeless.

"I'm done with all this wolf stuff. I'm done with all this wolf stuff," she kept repeating over and over, hoping that she could convince herself it was true, or at the very least use it to help her fall asleep; kind of like counting sheep or listening to music.

No luck. The more she tried to push the weirdness out of her mind, the more it clawed at her. Sure, she could put on a brave face to Drew and Vicky and Ethan and Hannah, saying things like "I know it was only a dream," and "Yes, I love scary movies, and yes, I know I have an active imagination." But in her heart, she didn't buy it. Not for one second. There was something strange going on in her neighborhood, across the street, in the woods beyond the Strigs' house.

And at that moment Emily knew for certain that she had to find out what it was. She had to do this by herself, and she had never been surer about anything in her life. Jumping from her bed, she quickly got dressed. She glanced at the clock and saw that it was three forty-five a.m.—no time for anyone in their right mind to be getting dressed and going outside for any reason, much less to search for a monster.

Then again, Emily was far from sure that she was still in her right mind.

A-hooooo! Ow-ow-w!

The howling drifted through her window, as if somehow the creature knew that she was coming after it, and calling her to join it. Emily found it strange that this sound didn't scare her. In fact, it didn't even surprise her. She felt as though she had an appointment with the beast to settle their score. To end this.

Moving swiftly but as quietly as she could, Emily hurried down the stairs and slipped out the front door. She had never been outside this late before. There was that time when she was nine, her family had to make a trip to visit a sick aunt, and her dad decided it would be better to drive all night than to fly out the next day. But other than that and a few restless nights before big tests, Emily had never really seen what three forty-five a.m. looked like. But now she was out in it.

Her safe, comfortable neighborhood felt odd. The quiet was startling. No cars, no music or TV sets, no one mowing the lawn. Only her footsteps tapping against the blacktop as she crossed the street.

Without pausing, she walked right onto the Strigs' front yard, went around to the back of the house, and reached the edge of the woods.

A-hooooo! Ow-ow-w!

"I'm coming," Emily said boldly. "And I'm not afraid of you."

Emily had been in these woods so many times that she felt she could almost find her way around blindfolded. And she might as well have been, given how dark it was. Fearlessly she pushed through the thick branches, annoyed at their latest attempts to scratch her. She couldn't see or hear the wolf, but she felt she knew exactly where to go to find it.

Deeper and deeper she plunged until she came to a

slight clearing that she somehow knew was right in the center of the woods. Emily looked in every direction, peering into the dense growth just beyond the small opening in which she stood.

"Where are you?" she muttered. "Show yourself. Show me that you are real!"

Snap.

A small twig snapped behind Emily. She spun around and spotted a thick, hairy paw emerging from the undergrowth. The paw was followed by a leg, then the wolf's large head and long jaws slid out from the thicket.

The creature turned its head sideways and narrowed its eyes, as if it were sizing Emily up. She stood her ground. She had not come this far to turn away now. Emily had never felt so brave. She met the wolf's gaze with a penetrating stare.

The wolf drew back the skin around its mouth, revealing the same bloodstained teeth Emily remembered from the first time she had seen the animal—in that so-called dream that clearly was no dream.

Crouching low, the wolf let out a deep, low-pitched growl. Brave as she was trying to be, Emily began to feel afraid . . . very afraid. The creature seemed to sense this change of emotion, from her rock-steady conviction to the overwhelming fear that now threatened to hold her paralyzed where she stood.

That's when the wolf sprang forward, charging at Emily, its eyes wild with rage, its jaws wide open, trailing long strings of blood-flecked saliva.

Emily turned and ran, crashing back through the dense woods. She gave no thought now to being brave, or to proving to everyone else that the wolf was real. Her only thought was to survive.

Branches tore at her face and arms as she ran. No matter how fast she pushed herself, she could hear the wolf close behind. Its powerful legs pounded into the ground, propelling the beast forward, growling and snarling as it ran.

Emily's ankle caught a low branch. A jolt of pain shot through her leg as she tripped and tumbled to the ground, twisting and landing on her back. The wolf increased its speed, seeing that its prey was vulnerable now. It leaped into the air, ready to come down right on top of her.

In the split second that the wolf was airborne, Emily

rolled over, the pain in her back and shoulders matching the ache in her ankle. The wolf slammed to the ground beside her, landing just inches away from her face. It slid along the fallen leaves and twigs and crashed into the base of a tree.

Emily pushed herself up from her stomach and stumbled forward, shoving the pain aside. Behind her, she heard the wolf scramble back to its feet and continue its close pursuit.

Jumping over low branches and ducking under higher ones, Emily maneuvered through the woods like some combination gymnast and high-hurdles track star. Ahead she spotted a thin ribbon of light through the trees. She allowed herself to feel hopeful.

The streetlights! she thought. *I'm almost there, almost home.*

Emily emerged from the woods into the Strigs' backyard. She glanced toward the door, hoping that maybe the noise from the chase would have awakened someone.

The Strigs' house was dark and still.

She glanced back over her shoulder. The wolf was still just a few feet away.

Dashing across the street, Emily made for her front

door, like a runner sprinting for the finish line. Her legs felt like lead, her ankle throbbed, and she began to tremble as she ran.

The wolf drew closer and closer.

Emily hit the front steps and took them two at a time. She grabbed the front door, threw it open, and ran inside. But the beast was right there, leaving her no time to close the door and keep it out.

She bounded up the stairs, but the wolf was right behind her, nipping at her heels. If she could only make it to her room. But what about her mom and dad? Even if she could make it to safety, the wolf would surely get them.

Trying to force herself to move faster, Emily stumbled on the top step and hit the landing, sprawled out on her back. The wolf was next to her in a flash, its paw on her shoulder, pinning her down.

The wolf lowered its jaws toward her face and began to change shape. While becoming no less menacing, it morphed into a human shape.

As the creature came closer, Emily got a good look at its face—its human face.

She was stunned.

The face was shockingly familiar. She knew this face. But who? Whose face was it?

The human monster still had long fangs, which it now lowered toward Emily's neck.

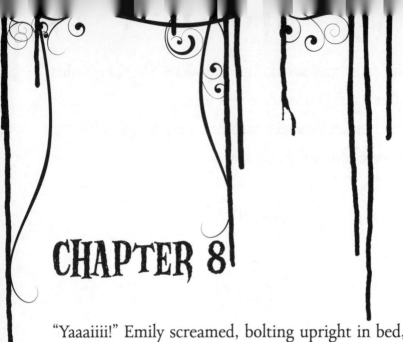

CHAPTER 8

"Yaaaiiii!" Emily screamed, bolting upright in bed, covered in sweat. She flung the covers off and rolled to the floor to get away from the monster attacking her. Then she realized that there was no monster. She was alone. It was not three o'clock in the morning, but rather seven a.m. The sun was shining. Sitting on the floor, panting, out of breath, Emily slowly realized that she had just had the worst dream of her life.

"The whole thing, the howling, the woods, the chase, the changing from a wolf into a person—it was all a dream, a long, terrible dream," Emily muttered to herself. She looked down and saw that she was sitting on the floor beside her bed, completely tangled up in her blankets. "Okay, Emily, first . . . get up off the floor."

She rolled to one side, then pushed herself up, tossing the blankets back onto the bed in a heap. Sitting on the edge of her bed, she tried to make sense of the crazy nightmare. She felt as if someone had been shaking her and shaking her, refusing to stop. The actual events of the previous evening slowly came to her, as if a fog in her head was lifting. She could once again begin to distinguish between reality and the dreamworld in which she had been spending far too much time lately.

Emily remembered searching the woods for real—she believed—with Drew and Vicky, and finding nothing. Nothing except for a few small animals that belonged there. She recalled deciding that she had had enough of all this wolf business and vowing to put it out of her mind. But apparently her mind had other plans.

It's one thing to believe you saw a wolf strolling through the neighborhood, Emily thought as she tried to remember what day it was. *At least that is possible, even though it's not very likely. But a wolf shape-shifting into a person?*

She had read enough science-fiction books and seen enough scary movies to think that the idea was pretty cool. But the "fiction" part of "science fiction" meant that it wasn't real! And whose face was that in her dream

anyway? She couldn't recall any details other than the overwhelming feeling that this person-monster-thing was someone she knew.

"Emily! Are you up? Breakfast is ready!" her mother called from downstairs.

"Be right down, Mom!" she yelled back. Emily knew she had better get moving before she missed the school bus.

Hurrying through her shower, Emily tried to wash away the sickly feeling that still lingered from the dream. After dressing quickly, she bounded down the stairs, looking forward, more than usual, to the normal, boring breakfast chitchat that she sleepwalked through most mornings. She, of course, had decided to tell no one about her dream.

Slipping into her chair at the breakfast table, Emily began shoveling spoonfuls of cereal into her mouth.

"So how's the sleepover planning going, honey?" her mom asked.

"Okay," Emily replied, guzzling down a glass of orange juice. "Hannah and Ethan have come up with some pretty good ideas for the party. Well, Hannah has, anyway."

"Well, you just be sure to let me know if there's anything I can do to help. I used to love sleepovers when I was your age."

"Thanks, Mom."

"What about Drew and Vicky?" Emily's mom asked.

Emily felt herself tense up. Her mind shot back to their expedition in the woods and then to her horrible dream.

"What's the matter, honey?" her mom asked.

Emily quickly realized that her expression must have changed.

"Did you and Vicky have a fight or something?" her dad asked, looking up from his phone.

"Have you invited Drew and Vicky to your party yet? Are they planning on coming?" her mom added.

"No, no, we didn't have a fight," Emily answered her father. "Sorry, my mind wandered for a second. I did invite them, and I really hope they come. But they haven't had a chance to talk to their parents. Mr. and Mrs. Strig are kind of funny about Drew and Vicky going anywhere. I guess that's why they're homeschooled."

At that moment, Emily felt as if a lightbulb had switched on in her brain. "Homeschooled!" she repeated. "Of course. That's it."

"That's what?" her mom asked.

"I've been going about this all wrong," Emily said. "I've been overlooking the obvious. I'm the one who has to talk to Mr. and Mrs. Strig about Vicky and Drew coming over. They work a lot of nights and weekends, but they have to be home during the day because Drew and Vicky are homeschooled."

"O-kay," her mom said slowly, raising her hands and shaking her head.

"Don't you see?" Emily asked, smiling as her dream begin to fade from her mind. "We have no school tomorrow. Some end-of-the-year teacher conference thing, but for Drew and Vicky it'll just be another regular day of homeschooling—with their parents! I'm going to go over there tomorrow and ask them if it's okay for Drew and Vicky to come to the party. And I'll invite the whole family over to meet you and Dad tomorrow night. It's perfect!"

Emily jumped up from the table and grabbed her books. "Bye, Mom. Bye, Dad," she said, kissing each of them. "Thanks!" Then she hurried toward the door.

"You're welcome?" her mom replied questioningly, wondering exactly what Emily was thanking her for.

That day at school was a bear for Emily. Not only

did she have two finals scheduled, but her math teacher sprang one last pop quiz on the class as well. By the time she got to lunch, she was completely stressed.

"Em!" Hannah called out from their usual table. "We've got some serious party planning to do."

"Can't," Emily said, pausing at the table but not sitting down at her usual seat. "Gotta cram for the history final. It's on the Civil War."

"The North won," Ethan volunteered, being his usual helpful self.

"Seriously, guys, I gotta study, but no worries. We're off tomorrow, remember? So let's hang out, okay?"

"I have my first soccer practice for the summer team in the afternoon," Ethan said.

"And I've got to watch my little brother when he comes home from morning preschool," Hannah added.

"So let's hang out in the morning," Emily suggested. She knew that she had to go talk with Mr. and Mrs. Strig tomorrow. But there would be plenty of time to do that in the afternoon. After all, her parents didn't get home from work until late anyway.

"Okay with me," Ethan said. "You wanna meet at the lake?"

"Sure," Hannah said. "Ten?"

"Great. See you guys then."

Emily slid into a seat at an empty table and pulled out her history book. She hardly ate any of her lunch, cramming Gettysburg and Appomattox into her brain rather than mac and cheese into her belly.

When her excruciating day finally came to an end, Emily was exhausted. She had planned to maybe go play guitar with Drew and Vicky that evening, but she felt herself dozing off at the dinner table. She watched about ten minutes of *Attack of the Zombies*, a "true classic" as she described it to her parents, then headed up to her room.

Emily checked her e-mail to see how many of her friends had RSVP'd to her party invitation. Two additional people said they would be coming, bringing the total so far to twelve. This was going to be a great party, but at the moment, all Emily could think about was going to bed. She slept like a rock and had no dreams, scary or otherwise, that she could remember.

The following morning she had the great pleasure of sleeping until she woke up on her own. She had remembered to turn off that annoying pest known as her alarm clock. Her parents were long out of the house by the time she stirred. She fixed herself a bowl of cereal, which she ate while watching the rest of *Attack of the Zombies*. Then she took a shower, threw on some clothes, and hopped on her bike.

During the twenty-minute bike ride from her house to the lake, Emily's mind focused on the sleepover. She had been so consumed with studying for her tests, not to mention all this wolf nonsense, that she had hardly had any time to really think about the party, which was now just two days away. She was really looking forward to kicking around some ideas with Ethan and Hannah. Then later in the day she would finally officially meet Mr. and Mrs. Strig and work it out so that Drew and Vicky could come to the party. It was all good.

Coasting down the final hill approaching the lake, Emily saw that Hannah was already there. She slowed to a stop beside the dock, then lowered her bike to the ground.

"Hey, Em," Hannah said, tossing a small rock into the water and watching the ripples spread out. "How was the history final?"

"I think I did okay," Emily replied. "The North won, right?"

"Cute!"

"Who's cute?" asked a voice from behind them. Ethan crouched down at the edge of the dock and dangled his feet just above the water. He lived the closest to the lake of all three friends and could easily walk there.

"You are, Ethan," Hannah said, blowing silly exaggerated kisses at him. "Don't you think so, Em? Ethan is *sooo* cute."

"Guys!" Emily cried, holding up her hands. "Please, no flirting. I just ate."

"Okay, down to business," Hannah said. "Here's what I have in mind for the sleepover. We all agreed on make-your-own ice cream sundaes."

"Check," Emily said.

"For a theme—"

"A *theme*?" Ethan interrupted. "We need a theme for the party? How about summer's here and everybody hangs out and has fun? Is that a good theme?"

"It's so sad, Ethan, really," Hannah said, the fake sympathy practically dripping from her voice. "You obviously know nothing at all about throwing a successful party."

"Oh yeah?" Ethan said defensively. "Well, one time Roger, Chuck, Sid, and I ate so much kettle corn and drank so many milk shakes that Roger ended up puking all over Chuck's bathroom. And Sid had to go the hospital to get his stomach pumped. Now *that* was a fun party."

"Delightful," Hannah said. "Sorry I missed that."

"Yeah, me too," Emily added. "Be sure to send me an invite the next time you guys decide to test the limits of the human stomach."

"Okay, back to my theme," Hannah said. "You ready? Camping out, indoors! We set up tents in your home theater. We eat dinner sitting around that DVD your parents have of a fireplace burning."

"Ugh, that thing," Emily said, scrunching up her face. "My dad insists on putting it on every Christmas."

"But you guys have a real fireplace," Ethan pointed out.

"Please. Don't I know it," Emily said. "But you know my dad. He thinks the fire looks so real in HD that he insists on playing it every year. It's so silly."

"But for us, it can fill in as our campfire," Hannah jumped in. "Sleeping in tents, eating around the fire."

"Making s'mores in the microwave!" Emily chimed in, starting to get excited about the idea. "And—oh, this is great!—we can tell scary stories! Just like a real campout. Hannah, I'm loving this!"

"Have you been getting replies to your invite?" Hannah asked.

"Yup, we're up to twelve, including you guys," Emily reported. "My mom said she'd like to limit it to about fifteen."

"Oh, I know what I wanted to tell you, Em," Ethan said, picking up a stick and poking it into the water near a school of small fish. The tiny minnows scattered, moving as a group. "My cousin Declan will be visiting me the weekend of the party. Okay if I bring him along? He's pretty cool, like me."

"I don't know if we could handle two kids who are as cool as you, Ethan," Hannah joked, playfully poking Ethan in the ribs.

"Sure, you can bring Declan, no problem," Emily replied. "So that brings us to thirteen."

"Does that include Drew and Vicky?" Hannah asked.

"No, not yet. I'm hoping that they'll fill in the last two spots."

"What's taking them so long to get back to you?" Ethan asked.

"They haven't been able to get their parents to give them permission to come," Emily explained. "But all that is going to change." She told her friends about her plan to talk to Vicky and Drew's parents later that day. "I'm telling you, after today, everything with Drew and Vicky will be different. You'll see. You'll like them."

CHAPTER 9

Satisfied with their party planning, Emily, Hannah, and Ethan left the lake, heading their separate ways. Hannah hurried home to watch her little brother, and Ethan ran off to the school for soccer practice.

As Emily rode her bike home she began to get excited, but also nervous, about her plan to barge in and introduce herself to Drew and Vicky's parents. In the months she'd been hanging out at Drew and Vicky's, she'd called up to them a bunch of times, but she'd never actually met them face-to-face. What was she going to say to them?

"Hi, Mr. and Mrs. Strig. I'm Emily Hunter," she rehearsed aloud as she pedaled toward home. "I'm your neighbor, you know, from across the street. The house with the green shutters and white—"

Emily smiled to herself. *They don't need a detailed description of your house. They'll know who you are. You've been hanging out there, like, every day for the past few months.*

She tried again. "Hi, Mr. and Mrs. Strig. I'm Emily Hunter, you know, Drew and Vicky's friend? You've probably heard me playing guitar with them? I hang out at your house sometimes?" *Jeez, Em, just get to the point!*

"Mr. and Mrs. Strig, I would like to invite you and Drew and Vicky to my house so you can meet my parents. And I would also like Vicky and Drew to come to my sleepover party on Saturday. Well, Vicky will actually be the one sleeping over. All the boys will be leaving at eleven and—"

Emily sighed. *Forget it. You'll figure out what to say when you get there.*

A few minutes later she turned into her driveway and slowed to a stop. Leaning her bike against the garage door, she took a deep breath and walked quickly across the street.

Emily climbed the lopsided steps leading onto the Strigs' porch and walked across the creaky floorboards to the front door. Then she knocked on the door.

No reply.

Again she knocked. Again, no sound from within.

"Maybe they're in the back of the house. Of course, if they had a doorbell . . ."

Emily thought about turning around and going home, but she knew she would regret it. She'd gotten herself psyched to do this and she would not get another chance before the sleepover.

She grabbed the ancient doorknob and turned it. The door squeaked open with a pitiful groan.

"Drew, Vicky? Is that you?" a woman's voice said.

"We're upstairs," added a man's voice.

Why aren't Drew and Vicky home being homeschooled? Emily thought.

"Mr. Strig! Mrs. Strig! It's Emily Hunter from across the street. Drew and Vicky's friend. May I come in and talk with you?"

The Strigs remained silent.

What is with these people?

Emily backed up onto the porch and closed the front door. *Should I just go home?* she wondered. *But I can't chicken out now. I just need to go upstairs and talk to these people. After all, they're just people, right? What can they do, bite my head off?*

Emily opened the door again.

"Drew, Vicky? Is that you?"

"We're upstairs."

Now Emily was really confused. Wasn't that the same thing they'd called out when she came in the first time? And why hadn't they answered her when she called up to them? And that's when it hit her. She'd heard Mr. and Mrs. Strig say the same thing each time Drew or Vicky opened the front door. She closed the door, then opened it again.

"Drew, Vicky? Is that you?"

"We're upstairs."

"Okay," Emily muttered. "What's going on here?"

She opened the door fully and stepped inside.

Instead of walking straight down the hallway, as she always did to go to Drew and Vicky's rec room, Emily turned left. She followed the narrow hallway around a curve and came to a large wooden staircase. It had obviously once been a grand stairway fit for a mansion. She could picture a bride walking down its long sweeping stairs, trailing the train of her wedding gown behind her.

But, like everything in this house, the staircase had fallen into terrible disrepair. Emily carefully adjusted her weight as she took every step, making sure that each stair would support her before she committed fully to moving up onto the next one. Every stair moaned as if it resented being used after so many years.

Reaching the landing, Emily found another hallway, similar to the one on the first floor. This hallway also looked as if it had been thrown together quickly using some unpainted Sheetrock that someone had just found sitting around. At the end of the hallway, a single door stood closed.

"Mrs. Strig?" Emily called out in the direction of the closed door. "Mr. Strig?"

No answer.

Reaching the door, she knocked, her raps echoing into the room beyond.

Emily psyched herself up. "Just do it, Em. Open the door."

She nodded to herself, then opened the door and stepped into the room.

Somehow the fact that the room was practically empty did not surprise Emily. The walls had long ago crumbled. Pieces of plaster lay scattered on the floor, exposing the beams that held what was left of the house together. A single piece of furniture, a small table, sat in the corner. But what was that on the table?

Crossing the room carefully to avoid falling into one of the many holes in the floor, Emily reached the table. Inspecting the small, square device on it, she realized that it was an old-fashioned telephone answering machine, the kind people used before voice mail.

A cassette tape sat inside the answering machine. Emily had seen these types of answering machines in movies from the 1980s. She pressed a button labeled OUTGOING MESSAGE. The cassette tape rolled, and two voices came out of the machine's tiny speaker.

"Drew, Vicky? Is that you?"

"We're upstairs."

When the message finished, Emily saw the tape rewind so it was ready to play again when the next phone call came in—or in this case, the next time someone opened the front door.

Emily walked completely around the table and discovered a wire coming out of the back of the answering machine. She followed the wire down to where the wall met the floor. From there it ran toward the door.

Tracing the wire, she followed it out of the room, along the hall, and down the stairs. At the bottom of the staircase, the wire crossed the floor and ran up to the door hinge, where it disappeared into a small plastic box. Emily pulled the cover off the box and found two batteries inside. The answering machine's wire was wrapped around a metal post. A second wire led from the box to a small speaker mounted on the wall at the top of the stairs. This was obviously where the message came out when the door was opened.

Emily sat down on the bottom step, trying to make sense of what she had just seen. For some reason, Mr. and Mrs. Strig had set up a phone answering machine to play their voices whenever anyone opened the door. But why? And where were they? They were supposed to be here, homeschooling Drew and Vicky.

Drew and Vicky. Where were *they*?

Emily got up and walked down the hall. Reaching the rec room door, she paused, then knocked.

"Drew? Vicky? It's Emily. I'm off from school today."

Silence.

She opened the door and stepped into the rec room. She saw the usual array of guitars and amplifiers, the foosball and Ping-Pong tables, but no Drew or Vicky. Again she called out. "Drew? Vicky?"

Again, no reply.

Emily had always known that there was something different about the Strigs. She knew that Drew and Vicky were not like her other friends. She wondered why Mr. and Mrs. Strig were being so weird about a simple thing like letting their kids hang out at a neighbor's house.

But this—this was more than she could make sense of. What about the whole homeschooling thing? If Drew and Vicky were not here getting lessons, then where were they? And what was the deal with the answering machine? Why were Mr. and Mrs. Strig trying to fool people into thinking they were home when they weren't?

WHERE WAS EVERYBODY?

Emily's mind raced in frustration. Then she spied the bathroom on the far side of the rec room—the door that Vicky had thrown a fit about when Emily had tried to open it. Her confusion and concern quickly gave way to a rush of curiosity. She crossed the room, grabbed the doorknob, and opened the door.

What Emily saw when she stepped through the doorway was almost more than her brain could comprehend. This was no bathroom. It wasn't even a room. It was an open expanse with a dirt floor, raw beams, and crumbling walls. The rest of the house, beyond the rec room, barely existed as anything more than a shell. Giant cobwebs filled every corner. Mice scurried along the dirt floor, pausing and sniffing, then resuming their search for food. A mass of insects crawled slowly, making the floor appear to be alive and moving.

Before Emily's mind could wrap itself around this sight, and just when she thought this whole thing couldn't get any weirder, it did. Sitting on the dirt floor were three long wooden boxes. As she moved closer, Emily's eyes widened in fright.

"C-coffins!" she stammered. "Three coffins!"

CHAPTER 10

Emily backed away from the coffins and stumbled, landing hard on the dirt floor, her face just inches away from a line of crawling bugs.

"Ah!" she screamed, scrambling to her feet. She ran back into the rec room, through the hallway, and out the front door. As she hurried across the street, she wondered for a second if she had remembered to close the front door and the door leading from the rec room to the room with the coffins.

The room with the coffins.

Nothing unusual about that, Emily thought. *Just a typical suburban room with a dirt floor, cobwebs as big as SUVs, and the usual three coffins. It's all the rage this year. "What! You only have two coffins in your dirt room? Please. Everyone is going for* the three-coffin look this season. I saw it on the cover of Better Homes and Coffins *magazine*."

"Calm down, Emily," she said aloud. "If you are going to completely lose your mind, the least you can do is have the courtesy to wait until you are in your own home."

Emily threw open her front door and ran inside.

Good thing her parents were not home. Emily knew that there was no way she could hold it together and keep what had just happened from them. She slammed the front door shut, locked it, scooped up the cat for comfort, and then ran up to her room. She sat on her bed, then immediately got up and started pacing. Franklin watched her as she moved back and forth.

"How could I have been such a fool? Was I just impressed by how good those two were at everything? I thought Drew and Vicky were a little weird, but not *that* weird. There's a big difference between being a little weird and living in a house that's not really a house, having a coffin or three in a secret room that they were freaked out about me possibly discovering, with parents who only exist on a recording, and—"

Emily stopped pacing, lost in her thoughts. *Could it be that there is no Mr. and Mrs. Strig? That they died, and for* some reason Drew and Vicky don't want anyone to know, so they set up this complicated hoax? Do the coffins belong to Mr. and Mrs. Strig?

Emily started to turn green—this wasn't just creepy, it was downright gross. *Why? Why? Why? Why would you hide the fact that your parents are dead? And why three coffins?*

She sat back down on her bed and forced herself to take a deep breath. She really didn't know what was going on. She felt duped, taken, lied to. Whatever the deal was with Drew and Vicky, they were not who they appeared to be. Hannah had seen that there was something creepy about Drew and Vicky, but until now Emily couldn't see it. Or maybe she just hadn't wanted to.

Well, that was about to change. She was through with them. She didn't ever want to go back into that freak show of a house, and she certainly didn't want them in her house. It went without saying that Drew and Vicky would most definitely *not* be coming to her sleepover.

Emily snatched up her cell phone and started tapping out a text message to Hannah. She had no intention of telling anyone about what she had just seen, but she did want her other friends to know that Drew and Vicky would not be coming to the party.

HEY, HANNAH. THINGS DID NOT GO SO GOOD AT DREW AND VICKY'S. THEIR PARENTS REFUSED TO ALLOW THEM TO COME TO THE PARTY. THEY DON'T EVEN WANT ME TO HANG OUT WITH THEM ANYMORE.

Emily sent the message. A few seconds later she got a reply:

SORRY, EM. I KNOW YOU LIKED THEM (EVEN IF I DIDN'T!).

Emily wrote back:

THANKS. THE REALLY WEIRD PART IS THAT DREW AND VICKY DIDN'T EVEN SEEM TO MIND. GUESS I'VE SEEN THE LAST OF THEM. CU LATER. . . . E

Emily felt better that she had at least told Hannah something. She felt bad about lying to her, but she didn't know what to make of all this herself. She was not about to try to explain what she had seen to Hannah or Ethan or especially to her parents. She was too embarrassed about everything. She could say that she had gotten into a fight with Drew and Vicky. She could say that Mr. and Mrs. Strig didn't want their kids hanging out with her anymore. That would get her mom's back up. She would have a hard time believing that anyone wouldn't want their kids hanging out with her daughter.

Emily smiled at the thought of how loyal her mom was.

She began to feel a little better. The burden of trying to get Drew and Vicky to fit in with all her other friends, plus the pressure of getting the Strigs to meet the Hunters before the party, had obviously been weighing on her more than she realized. Having all that lifted off her shoulders felt like a real relief. Emily began to relax. She slid down, stretched out on her bed, and dozed off.

Bing-bong! Bing-bong!

Emily awakened to the sound of the doorbell ringing. She glanced at her clock and saw that it was eight fifteen. The sun had already set. She had slept the afternoon away.

Emily tiptoed down the stairs, dreading the two people she knew would be on the other side of the door. Franklin stood at the top of the stairs, hissing, his back arched.

"Emily, it's Vicky!" Vicky shouted as she began banging on the door.

"And Drew!"

"We finally talked to our parents, and it's okay. They want to meet your parents, and they're going to let us come to the sleepover party. Just open up and let us in."

Emily ignored them.

They pounded on the door. "Emily! Emily!" they called urgently from the other side. "Let us in! Please let us in!"

Emily felt a small pang of guilt. After all this time, Drew and Vicky finally wanted to come over. They wanted to come to the sleepover, and now she was the one resisting.

Then the image of the coffins popped into her mind, and a cold chill ran down her spine.

No. The friendship was over. Whatever was going on in that house, she had no intention of being part of it any longer.

Finally, after a few minutes, the knocking stopped. Emily peeked through the curtains and watched as Drew and Vicky headed back across the street and into their house.

Emily walked back up to her room and grabbed a funny book from her shelf. She just wasn't in the mood to watch a scary movie as she waited for her parents to get home.

When dinner was finally ready at nine o'clock, Emily slunk down the stairs and into her seat. She didn't even complain that dinner was especially late tonight. Her mother and father hadn't gotten home until just a few minutes before.

"You okay, honey?" her mom asked as Emily pushed some take-out pasta around her plate.

"I'm fine, Mom. I just don't think I'll be hanging out with Drew and Vicky anymore."

"Did something happen today?" her father asked.

Emily took a moment to gather her thoughts. She knew she had to tell her parents something, but she wanted to make sure that it was the same story she had told Hannah.

The last thing she wanted was to get caught lying to the people she cared about the most.

"Their parents said that they didn't want them to come to the sleepover," Emily said. "And the thing that upset me the most was that Drew and Vicky didn't seem to mind."

"I'm sorry, honey. That's no fun," her mom said. "But maybe someday Drew and Vicky will come around and you can all be friends again."

"I doubt it," was all Emily said in reply.

After dinner, in her room, Emily was listening to music, trying to put the unreal events of the day

behind her. Her cell phone sounded with a text message alert.

The message was from Vicky:

HEY, EM, WHAT'S GOING ON? HOW COME YOU DIDN'T ANSWER YOUR DOOR? . . . V

A few seconds later a message came in from Drew:

EM, MOM AND DAD SAID OKAY. WE CAN COME TO THE PARTY! . . . D

Emily sat with her thumbs poised above her phone's keys. A hundred things she wanted to say flashed through her mind. Finally she tapped out:

WHAT'S UP WITH THE COFFINS?

She stared at the message and decided not to send it. She really didn't want to have anything to do with Drew and Vicky, starting right now.

But another message came in just a few seconds later:

ARE U MAD AT US? . . . D

"How do I answer that?" Emily wondered aloud. "I'm not mad at them, that's not it. I just don't really want to be friends with people living in half a house filled with coffins and parents who exist only on tape."

Emily knew that she had to send them some kind of

explanation. She typed out a new message:

I SAW THE COFFINS. PLEASE DON'T BOTHER COMING TO MY PARTY. YOU'RE NOT INVITED ANYMORE. LEAVE ME ALONE.

She sent the message.

A minute passed, then five, then ten. Emily dozed off an hour later, having received no reply from either Drew or Vicky. It was over. She'd let them know that she had seen the weirdness that was their life and wanted no part of it.

The following morning, Friday morning, the last day of school, Emily checked her phone. No messages. She could turn her full attention to the party, which was now only a day away.

CHAPTER 11

On Saturday morning Emily woke up and looked at her alarm clock.

"Six thirty!" she groaned. "That can't be right." She was wide awake, her brain buzzing.

On school mornings she could hardly drag herself out of bed at seven, and that was with her alarm set super loud. On weekends she barely budged before ten. But now here she was at six thirty on the first day of summer vacation, awake, alert, and positive that there was no way she was going to fall back asleep.

She threw off her covers and slipped out of bed. "Six thirty," she muttered. "Even the birds don't set their alarm clocks for this early."

Over breakfast, Emily ran through the checklist of

stuff she had to do that day. "Let's see—decorate the home theater, set up trays and bowls for munchies, go with Mom to pick up the pizza and ice cream."

Emily's mom drove her to several stores. By the time they got back, Hannah and Ethan had shown up to help with the preparations.

"I am so excited that this is really happening!" Hannah cried, hugging Emily.

"So we have to turn this house into a jungle?" Ethan asked as he stepped inside and looked around.

"Not a jungle, Ethan," Emily said, giving him a hug. He returned a halfhearted pat on Emily's back. "A forest. And not the whole house, just the home theater downstairs."

"Hello, Hannah, Ethan!" Emily's mom said, stepping into the entryway. "Thank you so much for coming over to help Emily."

"No problem, Mrs. Hunter," Hannah said. "The three of us cooked up this idea together, and we're going to see it through as a team."

"I came up with an idea for eating really gross food," Ethan said proudly. Then his expression soured. "But the girls voted it down."

"That's a shame, Ethan," Emily's dad said, joining the group. "I know that's always my favorite part of camping out."

"When did you ever camp out, Dad?" Emily asked skeptically.

"One time in college, when I locked my keys in my car and had to spend the night in a parking lot," Mr. Hunter said defensively.

"That's what I figured," Emily said, heading for the door leading down to the basement. "We've got work to do! See ya later, Dad."

"Have fun making your jungle," Mr. Hunter said.

"Dad! It's a forest!"

Hannah and Ethan followed Emily downstairs and they got right to work. In keeping with the theme of camping out, they took branches from trees that had recently been trimmed and hung them from the ceiling with clear fishing wire. They placed a few large potted plants around the room to act as the bushes. Emily then placed her collection of stuffed animals in and around the potted plants. The indoor wildlife included assorted bunnies, cats, and a polar bear.

"So, give me the details of what happened with Drew

and Vicky," Hannah said as she carefully placed a stuffed cougar into a tall plant to make it look as if the cougar was hiding as it stalked its prey.

"You know, Hannah, I don't really know," Emily said, feeling bad about continuing her fib. Maybe one day she would tell her friends the whole story. Or maybe not. What she did know was that if she told the whole story to them now, it would be all they could think about, and that would ruin the party for them. "I think it has a lot to do with their parents. Mr. and Mrs. Strig refused to allow Drew and Vicky to come to the party. They had no interest in meeting my mom and dad. But the thing that made me realize that Drew and Vicky were just not worth all the trouble was the fact that they couldn't have cared less that they wouldn't be coming to the party. In fact, it seemed to me that they didn't care about whether or not we were even friends."

"And who needs friends like that?" Ethan added as he placed the stuffed polar bear on the couch. "Especially when you have great friends like us who come over and help you set up a forest—er, complete with a polar bear."

Emily giggled. "Thanks, Ethan," she said. "You guys

are real friends. You'd never do anything to make me feel bad."

A short while later the decorating was all finished.

"This looks amazing!" Emily said, glancing around her former home theater and current private campground. "Thank you, guys, so much for helping."

"And now, I've got to scoot home and change for the party," Hannah said as the trio headed up the stairs.

"Change?" Ethan asked, sounding truly baffled. "I have to change?"

Hannah and Emily both turned around and stared at Ethan. He was dressed in a shirt that might have once had sleeves and a collar, but now looked like it stayed on Ethan's body only because it was too tired and tattered to care enough to fall to the ground. He wore gym shorts—last year's gym shorts, which were so faded the school logo was illegible. On his feet he wore sneakers with no socks. His big toe peeked out of the side of the left sneaker.

"No," Hannah said dryly. "You look fine." Then she and Ethan headed for the front door. "See ya tonight, Em!"

When Hannah and Ethan had gone, Emily went

back downstairs. The room really did look like a small forest. She headed back upstairs to help her parents prepare the food. Soon everything was ready. Now came the hard part—sitting around waiting for the guests.

CHAPTER 12

Six o'clock finally rolled around. The doorbell rang. Emily ran for the door, followed by her parents. It was Hannah, of course. Emily knew she would be the first guest to arrive.

"Welcome to the campout!" Emily cried, opening the door and giving Hannah a big hug, as if she hadn't seen her in months.

"Can you believe it's finally here?" Hannah squealed joyously. "This is going to be so great!"

"Nice to see you again, Hannah. Long time, no see," Emily's mom joked.

"Come on in," her dad added.

"Hi, Mr. and Mrs. Hunter," Hannah replied.

She gave each of them a quick hug. "Thanks again

for letting us use your house for the party."

"You know that Emily's friends are always welcome here," Mrs. Hunter said. "And you kids did a fabulous job decorating the downstairs."

"Yeah, it really looks like a forest," Mr. Hunter added. "I had to take my GPS with me when I went down there so I didn't get lost!"

Emily was in such a good mood that even her dad's corny jokes seemed funny today.

A few minutes later, the doorbell rang again. Emily opened the door and saw Ethan standing there with another boy. This boy was not as tall as Ethan, but his hair was also bright red, though he kept it shorter and neater than Ethan did.

"Em, this is my cousin, Declan," Ethan said. "Declan, Emily."

"Hey, Declan, come on in," Emily said. "Ethan, on the other hand, you can wait outside."

"You're very funny, as always," Ethan said. Then he followed Declan into the house.

"Thank you for inviting me, Emily," Declan said. "I know how much Ethan likes you."

"All right, all right!" Ethan said, pushing Declan

through the door. "That's enough of that Ethan-likes-you stuff."

Emily laughed. "Well, I really can't stand him," she said.

"Hi, Mrs. Hunter," Ethan said, handing a grocery bag to Emily's mom. "Here are the toppings for the ice cream sundaes."

"Thanks for bringing those, Ethan," Mrs. Hunter replied.

Over the next hour the remainder of the guests arrived. By seven fifteen everyone was down in the home theater and the party was in full swing.

As everyone munched on pizza, the talk turned to teachers the kids had this year and who they might have next year. Some kids talked about their plans for the summer.

"I'm off to Camp Cheapskate again in a couple of weeks," Roger Higgins announced.

"Is that really the name of the place?" Emily asked.

"Nah, it's really Camp Chesapeake, but everyone calls it Camp Cheapskate because the guy who runs it is so cheap," Roger explained. "His idea of a camp T-shirt is a white undershirt with 'Camp Chesapeake' written on it in Magic Marker."

"Sounds like my kind of place!" said Ethan.

"Ice cream time!" Emily's mom called out from the top of the stairs. "Make-your-own sundaes."

The kids all charged up the stairs, as if they hadn't eaten in a week. On the kitchen counter, Emily's mom had set up three flavors of ice cream, plus cherries, M&Ms, sprinkles, chocolate syrup, and a spray can of whipped cream.

One by one, the kids scooped ice cream into bowls, then tried to defy the laws of physics by cramming twenty ounces of toppings into a ten-ounce bowl that was already filled with ice cream.

Ethan picked up the can of whipped cream, shook it vigorously, then sprayed a stream right at Declan. Reacting as if he knew the whipped cream attack was coming, Declan ducked. The stream of white foam shot over his head and struck Roger in the face.

Rather than get mad, Roger picked up his spoon, scraped the whipped cream off his cheek, as if he were shaving, and shoved the spoon into his mouth.

One of the girls, Sarah Cooke, winced. "Em, what time did you say the boys were leaving?"

When everyone had finished their ice cream, the

kids all tromped back downstairs.

Emily pulled out a bunch of tents. "Time to go camping!" she announced. The girls each grabbed a tent and began to set them up, with the boys lending a hand occasionally.

The girls set their tents up in a circle near the TV, under the dangling branches. Then Emily popped in her dad's fireplace DVD, complete with a crackling fire in realistic surround sound.

"This is so dorky!" Ethan exclaimed.

"So it's perfect for you," Emily shot back.

Declan laughed. "I think it's cool."

"Thank you, Declan," Emily said. "You are welcome here anytime. Now who's got a scary story?"

"What kind of scary story?" Sarah asked.

"Any kind," Emily said, shrugging.

"How about monsters chasing people through the woods?" Ethan suggested.

"Or maybe a wolf chasing someone through the woods," Hannah chimed in, making a scary face and curving her fingers into the shape of claws. "Or how about a scary story about creepy neighbors?"

Emily shot a look of mild annoyance in Hannah's

direction. The last thing she wanted was to be reminded of her wolf hallucinations, or the Strigs.

"She's talking about Drew and Vicky, right?" Ethan asked.

"Right," Emily replied.

"Who?" Declan asked.

"Did you notice that creepy old house across the street when my mom dropped us off?" Ethan asked.

"Yeah."

"Well, the kids who live there are really weird," Ethan explained. "Or so I've heard. I've never actually met them."

"What's so weird about them?" Declan asked Emily.

"Oh, nothing," Hannah jumped in. "Just the way they're always together and the fact that they never seem to leave that house. The one time I met them, they never made eye contact with me. Not for one second. It was like they were somewhere else, even though we were in the same room."

"And their house is filled with all sorts of old, dusty things," Emily added.

That was all she would say. Just as she had promised herself earlier, she was not about to reveal the truth about just how weird Drew and Vicky really were.

"But enough about them," Emily continued. "Who has a scary story?"

"I do," Declan said. "It's a tale all about vampires."

"Cool, I love vampire stories!" Emily exclaimed.

"Me too," Declan said.

"Did you ever see *Vampire Babysitter?*" Emily asked. "That's one of my favorite movies."

"Only a dozen times," Declan replied. "It's a true classic."

"Agreed. So, what's your vampire story?"

Declan cleared his throat and began. "Five hundred years ago in a remote mountaintop village—"

"In Transylvania, right?" Ethan interrupted his cousin.

"In the Swiss Alps, actually," Declan explained.

"Ethan, no interrupting!" Emily scolded him. "Go ahead, Declan."

"This particular *Swiss* village," Declan continued, looking right at Ethan, "had been plagued by a series of brutal murders. Victims were found dragged from their homes, lying dead in the snow. All of the victims were bitten in the neck. But the odd thing was that some appeared to have been bitten by a person and some by an animal."

"So the murderer had a vicious dog that helped him," Ethan jumped in. Emily said nothing this time. Asking Ethan to stop interrupting was like asking him to stop breathing.

"Not necessarily," Declan went on. "Because as it turned out, these were no ordinary murders. They were the work of a vampire. The villagers knew this because one by one the bodies of the victims started disappearing from the cemetery. People started reporting seeing their dead relatives walking through the village at night."

"But what about the human and animal thing?" Ethan asked.

"Well, that was just further proof that the killer was a vampire. What most people forget is that vampires can shape-shift. They can change their form to look like other people, but they can also change themselves to look like animals. Some vampires actually prefer to hunt and feed in their animal forms."

"Like as a mean, vicious dog?" Ethan asked.

"A dog, maybe, but also a wolf or a jackal, or, of course, the classic bat."

"A hamster?" Ethan asked.

Hannah giggled.

"Not usually, no," replied Declan seriously, totally ignoring Ethan's joke. "Anyway, one day, during a particularly bad snowstorm, a local villager huddled in front of a blazing fire in his hearth. Shortly after the sun set, a sharp knocking came at his door, cutting through the constant howl of the wind outside. Peering out his window, the man spotted a stranger standing in the raging storm. He wore only a thin coat and no hat or gloves. He shivered and shook as snow piled up on his shoulders and head.

"'Please let me in,' the stranger cried. 'It's cold and I've traveled such a long way.'

"Now, the villager knew of the recent attacks, so he hesitated. Again the man outside pleaded with him.

"'Please let me in!'

"The villager had a good heart, and the man outside looked so cold and tired. He looked as if he couldn't hurt anyone. And so the villager opened the door. 'Come in and get warm, my friend, before you freeze to death.'

"As soon as the stranger was inside, he began to change shape. He grew taller and stronger-looking. Well, the villager was never seen again. When his friends came to see what had happened to him, they found one set of footprints leading up to the door, and two sets leading away."

"If the vampire was so strong, why didn't he just bust into the guy's house and bite him?" Ethan asked.

Declan shook his head. "He couldn't. If a vampire catches you wandering around outside, he can do as he pleases. But the only way a vampire can enter a person's home is if that person invites the vampire in. Otherwise the vampire cannot enter."

"That wasn't so scary," Ethan said.

"I liked it," Hannah said. "How about you, Em? You're the big scary movie fan." Hannah looked over at Emily. Her eyes were opened wide, and her face had turned pale.

"What's the matter, Em? I never figured you for one to get so scared by a story."

Emily's mind raced. She felt as if her brain was going to leap right out of her head. The story was set so long ago, but so much of it seemed . . . familiar. It all made sense now. Everything. The coffins, the wolf, never seeing Drew and Vicky during the day, the homeschooling, the fake parents, the way they pleaded to be let in once they decided they wanted—what? What did they want?

Oh no, I know what they wanted, Emily thought. *They wanted someone to fill that third coffin. They wanted me. It's all so clear to me now. Mr. and Mrs. Strig weren't lying in those coffins. They don't even exist. Those coffins belong to Drew and Vicky, because Drew and Vicky are vampires!*

CHAPTER 13

"I'm fine," Emily said, waving Hannah away. She struggled to regain her composure. She was not going to let this ruin her party. Besides, she had never let Drew and Vicky in. She was safe. She pushed all this craziness aside and invited someone else to share a scary story.

A couple of other kids told stories. One was about an alien abduction. Another, about the ghost of a sailor doomed to sail the seas forever.

The storytelling was interrupted by Emily's mom calling down from the top of the cellar stairs. "Okay, guys, it's eleven o'clock. Time for the boys to go home and for the girls to go to sleep. Ethan, your mom is here to pick up you and Declan."

"Okay, Mom," Emily called back up.

The boys said their good nights and thanked Emily.

"Another successful end-of-the-year event," Ethan said as he headed for the basement stairs. "Although not quite as memorable as puking at the top of the Ferris wheel."

"Thank you so much for inviting me, Emily," Declan said as he followed his cousin up the stairs. "I had a great time."

"You're welcome," Emily replied. "Thank you for the vampire story. That was great. I hope I get to see you again soon."

When the boys had all gone, the girls gathered in a tight circle and chatted about summer plans, what they might do at the end of the next year, and about how charming Declan was.

"Okay, girls, lights-out time," Emily's mom called down.

Emily turned off the TV, putting out their campfire, and one by one, the girls slipped into their tents. Just before she went into her tent, Emily glanced toward the basement window. There appeared to be a face peering in at her. She knew the face. It was Vicky!

She blinked and rubbed her eyes. When she opened them again, Vicky was gone. There was no one at the window. *It's been a long day*, Emily thought. *Just go to sleep.*

She crawled into her tent and slipped into her sleeping bag. She was exhausted from the day's events but was still wired from the excitement and the evening's startling revelation.

Vampires living across the street from her. Now that she thought about it, it sounded ridiculous. There had to be some logical explanation, right? There were no such things as vampires. But she must have believed it to some degree, since she felt so relieved that she had never officially invited Drew or Vicky in. And in the last text she sent them, she'd specifically told them they weren't invited to her party. Still, Emily thought about that third coffin and shuddered. She hugged the sleeping bag around herself tighter. Eventually she drifted off to sleep.

Emily's jumbled dreams were shattered by the sudden, jarring ring of her cell phone. She groped around the dark tent until she found her phone. "Who is calling at one eighteen in the morning?" she muttered to herself. Then she saw the caller ID.

She answered the call. "Ethan, are you out of your mind?" Emily whispered.

"Just listen, Em! Listen!"

Emily could clearly hear the panic in Ethan's voice. She had never, ever heard him sound like this. She knew that this was no joke.

"What happened, Ethan? What's wrong?"

"It's Declan," Ethan cried, his voice choking. "We found him."

"Found him?" Emily repeated, moving deeper into her tent, turning away from the flap and trying to keep her voice down so she didn't wake up anyone else. "What do you mean, found him? He left here with you and your mom."

"No, he didn't. He was never at the party. He was not at your house tonight."

"What? What are you talking about?"

"A little while after we got home, Declan said he had to go to the bathroom. He stayed in there forever, so I knocked on the door but got no answer. When I went in, I saw that he was gone and the bathroom window was wide open. I searched around outside, but he wasn't there. When my mom finally opened the hallway closet, she found him. He was unconscious and all tied up. He's okay, but he was really shaken up."

"Did he tell you what happened?"

"He said that shortly before we left for the party, while my mom and I were out at the store picking up ice cream toppings, someone grabbed him. Someone very strong. The next thing he knew, he was waking up in the closet when we found him."

"So then, who was at the party with you tonight?"

"I was," said a voice from behind Emily, startling her, causing her to drop the phone.

She had not heard anyone enter her tent. She spun around and there he was, looking down at her . . . Declan!

CHAPTER 14

"Who are you?" Emily gasped, her hand reaching instinctively to her neck. "Who are you?"

She watched in horror as Declan slowly changed shape. His features blurred, rippling like wax on a melting candle. Then the process unfolded in reverse. The wavy unclear face re-formed, and Emily found herself staring up at Drew.

"Drew!" she exclaimed.

Every instinct told Emily to run, to push past Drew and get out of that tent. Then her eyes met Drew's dark, penetrating stare. His eyes burned deeply into hers. Emily tried to scream, but her voice choked in her throat, as if invisible hands were clutching her neck. She tried to get up, but found she couldn't move. Some unseen force held her in place as panic rose up through her, filling her very being.

"Hello, my dear, dear Emily," Drew said, in a calm, soothing voice. "Thank you for inviting me into your house earlier this evening. Oh, I know you thought I was that boy Declan, but that doesn't matter. You invited me in, and as I explained to you earlier, vampires cannot come into a home unless they are invited in by the person who lives there."

Vicky suddenly appeared next to her brother in the tent. "Or if they are invited in by another vampire," she said, smiling down at Emily, adding her intense supernatural stare to Drew's.

Emily suddenly felt her panic ease. The edges of her vision blurred. Only the deep black circles of Drew's eyes remained in sharp focus. Everything else faded. An odd calm washed over her as she looked up and listened to the two oddly comforting voices.

"I know what you're thinking, Emily," Drew continued. "Why did we wait so long to come into your house? Why didn't we just make you a part of our family during one of the many evenings you were in our house?"

"We had to be sure," Vicky explained. "We had to spend time with you, to see if you were the one—the right one to spend the rest of eternity with us. You see, Emily, we like you very much. You are special, so special that when we met you, we considered expanding our little family for the first time."

All of this made perfect sense to Emily in her state of unnatural calmness. Strangely, she felt honored, even anxious, to join them. Some tiny part of her brain realized that the vampires' power included mind control as well as control over her muscles. But she didn't care.

"By now you have figured out that Vicky and I are not really brother and sister," Drew went on. "I wandered alone for centuries until I found one worthy of joining me."

"And now we have found another," Vicky said. "But it took a long time. That's why we were reluctant to come over to your house. We knew that once we were invited in we would take that opportunity to have you join us. You see, we don't like to leave the comfort of our house and our coffins, and when we do, it has to be for something very important. We didn't want to waste the chance before we were sure."

"Unfortunately, just at the time that we decided you were the one, you chose not to see us any longer," Drew explained. "And we are sorry you had to see your coffin before you were ready to enjoy it. Once you refused to come to our house anymore, we had to get you to invite one of us in."

"You feel at peace now, don't you, Emily?" Vicky asked. "You are ready. The time has come. And speaking of time, now you'll have all the time in the world to learn to beat me at foosball and Ping-Pong and learn to play every riff ever played on the guitar . . . and those that haven't even been created yet."

Vicky opened her mouth, revealing long, sharp fangs. She moved closer.

Emily was suddenly distracted by the sight of Drew slowly morphing again. This time he lost his human shape and changed into the form of a wolf—the very wolf she had seen again and again, complete with blood-specked fangs and a snarling growl. Then slowly the wolf transformed back into Drew, just as he had in Emily's dream.

It was Drew all along, she realized. He was the wolf. He left his house in this form to feed at night. Emily was so distracted by the astonishing transformation that she hardly noticed the sensation of Vicky's fangs sinking into her neck.

She felt a rush of warmth flood her body. The last bits of fear and apprehension washed away in a gentle wave. Then everything went dark.

EPILOGUE

The last rays of sunlight disappeared in smears of red and orange behind the distant mountain. As darkness blanketed the world once again, Drew and Vicky stepped from their house into the cool evening.

Years had passed since the night of the sleepover, and much had changed. Drew and Vicky no longer lived in the same town. As the two had done many times before, they moved to an abandoned house in a new town where no one knew them. Where they would be safe. And where they could make new friends.

"I'm certain about Billy," Vicky said as they kept to the shadows of their dark street.

"It's been a few months and he's come over almost every night," Drew remarked.

"And I agree with you," Vicky continued. "It's her turn. And he seems particularly drawn to her."

"Yes," Drew replied.

They walked up to a house just down the street from where they now lived. Vicky rang the doorbell.

A boy who appeared to be about Vicky and Drew's age opened the door.

"Hey, Drew, Vicky," said the boy. "What's up?"

"We realized that we've been friends all this time and we've never even seen your house," Vicky explained.

Billy looked around, gazing past Drew and Vicky. "Hey, where's your sister?"

"Right here!" called out a voice from behind Drew. "Have my brother and sister been giving you a hard time?"

"Hey, Emily!" the boy said, his face lighting up.

"Hi, Billy," Emily said. She flashed a big smile at him. "Can we come in?"

WANT MORE CREEPINESS?

Then you're in luck, because P. J. Night has
some more scares for you and your friends!

P. J. Night has a secret message for you and your
friends to discover at your creepover. Simply use
the code to fill in the blanks of the secret message.

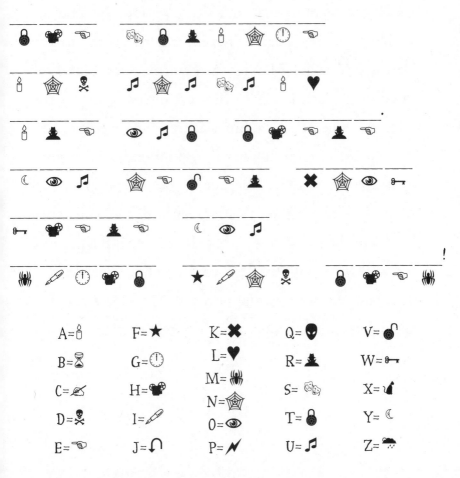

YOU'RE INVITED TO . . .
CREATE YOUR OWN SCARY STORY!

Do you want to turn your sleepover into a creepover? Telling a spooky story is a great way to set the mood. On the next page, P. J. Night has written a few sentences to get you started. Fill in the rest of the story on the lines provided and have fun scaring your friends.

You can also collaborate with your friends on this story by taking turns. Have everyone at your sleepover sit in a circle. Pick one person to start. She will add a sentence or two to the story, cover what she wrote with a piece of paper, leaving only the last word or phrase visible, and then pass the story to the next girl. Once everyone has taken a turn, read the scary story you created together aloud!

When my mom was a little girl, she lived next door to an old, abandoned farmhouse. According to the other kids in the neighborhood, no one had lived there in more than one hundred years. But that didn't mean things didn't happen in there. Every night my mom would see lights turn on and off in different rooms. Her parents didn't believe her, until one night when . . .

_____

_____

_____

_____

_____

_____

_____

_____

_____

_____

_____

_____

_____

_____

_____

_____

_____

_____

_____

_____

_____

_____

_____

_____

_____

_____

_____

_____

_____

_____

_____

THE END

Ready for

a Scare?

PROLOGUE

At first, all she felt was the cold.

Each crystal of snow pierced her bare skin, stinging like an electric volt. A sensation so violent, so torturous. Frigid wetness seeped through the fabric of her pretty red dress. Her body tried to double into itself, to search for what little internal warmth lingered in this coffin of cold.

Then the coldness was gone. In its place a heaviness, a numbness remained.

She tried desperately to move but couldn't. The wet snow pressed on her body. Forcing her down. Pushing her on all sides. Unseen hands dragging her away, away from the light, from the air, from life.

Fight. She had to fight. *This can't be the end,* her brain screamed.

Desperately she tried to force open her ice-crusted eyelids, but the weight of the snow had created a mask, encasing her face, her head, and her body.

She concentrated on her fingers. It took every ounce of energy to connect her brain with her right hand, to will her knuckles to bend ever so slightly. She had to free herself. She forced her hand to move, to scrape at the icy blanket smothering her. But each little movement caused the avalanche of snow to press down harder. To bury her deeper.

She moaned, though she knew no one could hear her. Why had she come? Why had she listened?

It seemed impossible that across the yard, people were still drinking steaming mugs of hot cocoa, singing carols, and eating dainty cookies cut into precious holiday shapes. Only minutes ago she had been in the warmth of the house, part of her aunt's party, accepted, included.

Unfair. It was all so unfair.

She scraped her fingernails violently against the snow that encased her. Eyes sealed shut, she could visualize her red polished nails clawing at the bright white snow. Someone would pay, she decided. Someone would have to.

"Miss Mary? Is that you, Miss Mary?"

She shuddered as the voice on the phone echoed in her head. Why had she answered? She should have known that any call this far from home was trouble. She should have refused the kindly old woman who'd handed the receiver to her. "*Miss Mary.*" Just by the way her name was said, she should have known. She never should have followed the directions. Never should have left the party. Never should have strayed from the house decorated with candy canes.

Darkness pressed on her. Her thoughts became fuzzy. She could sense that her hand was still reaching, still scratching though the snow, but she felt disconnected from her arm. Disconnected from the world. Deep in the darkness.

In the haze of snow and cold, her brain grasped at a sudden sensation, a smell that invaded her muddled thoughts. Peppermint. The spicy aroma surrounded her just as the snow did. The smell came from the necklace of mints she wore around her neck. A string of peppermints meant as a garland for the tree that, earlier in the evening, she had strung around herself instead. A festive gesture of a young, carefree girl. A girl full of life and promise.

She relaxed her frigid muscles. The smell seemed otherworldly. As if telling her that everything would be all right. That there would be justice. That someone would pay for her misery.

I will not be forgotten, she vowed.

CHAPTER 1

"They're not coming back," Ryan Garcia announced.

"What?" Kelly demanded. Gray slush from her boots fell in clumps onto the woven mat by the front door, leaving behind small pools of water. The warmth of the house felt good. The bus was like a freezer on wheels, and she was starving. Friday was Taco Day at school. So totally beyond disgusting, and of course, her mom hadn't packed her any lunch. For the last hour, she'd been thinking of nothing but the package of chocolate cookies waiting in the pantry.

"Mom and Dad," Ryan added.

Kelly kicked off her boots, and Ryan followed her across the front hall and into the kitchen. Her fuzzy blue socks slipped on the worn wooden floor. She dumped

her backpack and hunter-green parka on one of the mismatched chairs, then turned to stare at her little brother. "What are you talking about?"

At ten years old, Ryan delighted in taunting her with secrets. His days were spent scheming to possess more information, as if it made him smarter or more grown-up. He still hadn't clued in: She didn't really care. Usually.

Ryan watched her open the pantry and grab the foil package. She slid out four cookies. They were the oversize, hockey-puck kind. *Four seems like the right number to make up for lunch,* Kelly reasoned. She ate the first one and let him wait. She knew he wanted her to ask again. To beg for more information. Ryan fidgeted, trying so hard not to tell her anything until she asked.

She ate the second cookie, chewing slowly. "So?" she finally said.

"So . . . we're all alone," Ryan reported. He looked unsure.

"Meaning?"

"Meaning Mom and Dad aren't coming back. Just like I told you."

Kelly studied her brother's face. He wasn't smiling or smirking. Had something bad really happened? Her mind raced through the possibilities. Car accident. Plane crash. She grabbed his arm. "Ryan, come on. Tell me what's going on."

"Snowstorm," Ryan said, swatting her hand off his sweatshirt. "They're staying in Philly."

Kelly took a deep breath, annoyed that her brother had almost scared her. It was only for a second, but still. *That's my job,* she thought. *Everyone knows that I'm the best at scaring people.*

"When did they call?" Kelly asked, biting into another cookie.

"About ten minutes ago." Ryan grabbed a cookie from the package too. The elementary school bus got home before her middle school bus. Mom and Dad must have called just as Ryan let himself into the house. "There's a blizzard or something. They're going to call back."

And just at that moment, the phone rang.

"Guess that's them." Kelly hurried to the phone on her mother's desk in the far corner of the kitchen. Her mom referred to her desk as "Command Central." In the middle sat a huge calendar with all their activities, and scattered about were school directories, recipes printed from the Internet, magazines she hadn't yet read, and a whole mess of other papers. Kelly never understood what gave her mother the right to be on her case about cleaning her room when her desk was such a disaster.

"Hi," Kelly said, sitting on the wooden desk chair.

"Kelly, honey, I'm so glad you're home," her mother panted. She sounded strangely out of breath.

"Of course I'm home. Got to get ready for my party. Lots to do," Kelly reminded her.

"Oh, Kels." Her mother sighed. "Listen, about that. Daddy and I are stuck in Philadelphia."

"Ryan told me." She glanced above the desk at the enormous bulletin board covered with articles and downloads. Her mom, among a million other things, wrote a column for their weekly town paper called It Happened Here. It was about all the unimportant things masquerading as history that had happened in their little Vermont town since the French trappers first arrived. Kelly kept telling her mom no one cared. But the editors kept asking for columns. She guessed it gave the newspaper a reason to exist, because there was certainly no real news going on in her town. The bulletin board was like a mini history lesson, if anyone cared to read the columns, which she didn't. Kelly usually just read the captions to the photos while she was on the phone.

"It's snowing like crazy here. They canceled all flights out of the airport." Her mom sounded tired. She'd been up since dawn.

"What are you going to do?"

"We thought about renting a car, but the weather report says the storm is heading up the East Coast. A big nor'easter. Should be in Vermont by nightfall. The roads will be a mess." Kelly could hear her dad in the background, trying to tell her mom something. "The only sensible thing for us to do is to spend the night in a hotel here."

"Oh. Okay." Kelly had never stayed alone in the house overnight. She felt fine with it, though. She had babysat for little kids down the street, and that was no big deal. She could totally handle Ryan. Between the TV and his video games, he'd stay out of her way. Besides, Paige and June were sleeping over tonight. An early birthday celebration. She'd have company.

"Daddy and I will leave first thing in the morning to get back home," her mom promised. Kelly could hear the worry in her voice. "What, Dave? How can they not have rooms? Look, the meeting wasn't my brilliant idea. It's fine . . . whatever . . . anywhere . . ." Her mom argued with her dad in the background. They had a company together, Authentic Vermont Blankets. Supposedly there was something about the sheep in their state that made superior wool for blankets—or at least, that was what her parents advertised. They had flown to Philadelphia this morning to try to convince some big store to sell their wool blankets instead of Amish quilts.

Kelly peered at a photocopy of a news clipping on the bulletin board about a woman named Mary Owens. She had never noticed this one before. The picture showed a young woman wearing a mod 1960s minidress and tall white patent-leather boots. A one-of-a-kind homemade necklace was draped about her neck. She sat serenely on a sofa, a playful smile on her thin lips. A Christmas tree decorated with candy canes filled the space behind her.

Her mom sighed. "Your dad could only find us a room in some ramshackle motel." Kelly could hear other voices and the muffled reverberations of loudspeaker announcements. She guessed they were still at the airport. "Kel, listen. I need you and Ryan to stay put. No going outside. And lock the doors."

"Sure." She studied the perfect swoosh of Mary's chestnut hair across her forehead. She wondered if her shoulder-length dark-brown hair could do that too. Doubtful.

"Chrissie is coming over at six," her mom continued. "She's bringing a pizza for dinner."

Kelly tore her gaze away from pretty Mary Owens. "Chrissie Cox? Why is she bringing us dinner?" Chrissie was her best friend Paige's older sister.

"Chrissie will be staying with you and Ryan tonight."

"A babysitter?" Kelly cried. "You got us a babysitter? I'm way too old for a babysitter! I'm in middle school."

"I know how old you are," her mother said. "But I'm not leaving you and your brother alone overnight. It's not safe. Plus, a big storm is coming."

"But Mom, we won't be alone," Kelly reminded her. "Paige and June are coming for the sleepover."

"Kelly, that can't happen tonight. Not without me or your dad there."

"That's not fair! It's not my fault there's a storm. It's my birthday!" Kelly cried.

"No, it's not," Ryan piped in behind her.

She shot him an evil glare. He crossed his eyes at her. "Real mature," Kelly muttered.

"We'll move your birthday celebration to next

weekend," her mother said. "Besides, your birthday is really on Tuesday," she rationalized, as if Kelly didn't know when it was. "So next Friday will work just as well."

Kelly groaned. Typical of her mother. She always moved holidays to suit her own schedule. They often had Thanksgiving on a Sunday so her mother's whole family could drive in, and Easter on a Saturday so they didn't have to fight the weekend traffic home from Boston.

"But—" She had planned so many great things for tonight.

"No buts, Kelly. I'm counting on you. I'll call back later," her mom said. "Dad and I need to find this motel before the roads become impassable."

"Okay." She sighed. She wasn't happy, but she didn't have a choice. She knew that. No sleepover. She passed the phone to Ryan. As he babbled about some science project in school with pennies and sugar water, Kelly took a closer look at Mary Owens. The caption under the picture said the photo had been snapped at a Christmas party right before her untimely death.

Kelly stood on the chair and unpinned the article. She began reading from the beginning. All the while, she had the strangest feeling that the gaze of the young woman in the picture was fixed on her. Wanting her to know what had happened. Mary's story was so tragic. Killed in a freak avalanche. Suffocated under the weight of the snow.

Staring into her soulful eyes, Kelly wondered what it felt like, alone, buried under all that whiteness.

"Mom said we should watch the Weather Channel." Ryan had hung up the phone and was standing over her. "What's that?"

"One of Mom's articles. Scary stuff." She pinned it back onto the bulletin board before he could reach for it. "I'm going to my room." She glanced out the window over the sink. The sky remained its usual winter gray. Thick clouds but no storm.

All this craziness over nothing, she thought. *I've been looking forward to this sleepover all week, and now I have to sit here with a babysitter, totally bored.*

She had no idea of the horrors that lay ahead.

CHAPTER 2

Kelly made her way up the stairs, the floorboards of their renovated farmhouse creaking under her weight. Her bedroom was down the hall to the right. A vision in pink and green.

She'd begged her parents all year to let her redecorate, but her mom refused. She couldn't accept that Kelly had long since outgrown the plaid decor she had picked out when Kelly was still crawling. Kelly had the feeling she'd be living in preppy paradise until she left for college.

She tossed her book bag on the carnation-pink carpet, next to the rolled-up pair of jeans she'd tried on, then rejected, this morning. Pulling out the white chair that matched her desk set, she booted up her laptop, then quickly IMed Paige and June.

Kookykell2011: Hi. Bad news.

Juney206: ?

Kookykell2011: No sleepover tonight. Parents trapped in snow in Philly.

Paige4peace421: I heard. Can't believe your mom thinks Chrissie is gonna keep u safe! LOL

Kookykell2011: Spare me. So not my idea!

Juney206: U have a babysitter!!!???!! Chrissie!

Kookykell2011: Not my idea!!!!

Paige4peace421: It is kinda scary at night alone . . .

Juney206: Ooooooh! Better watch out!

Kookykell2011: So NOT scared!

Juney206: What about your sleepover?

Paige4peace421: Yeah. I have a present 4 u.

Juney206: Me 2.

Kookykell2011: Thx. U guys r the best. I have to move it to next weekend. Stinks. Had so many great scares planned for u tonight!

Paige4peace421: Maybe I'm safer at home! Ha ha!

A sudden, terrified shriek filled the house.

Ryan pounded up the stairs, taking them two at a time. "Kelly!" he cried. He burst into her room.

"What's wrong?" she asked, pushing back in her chair to see him.

"Look what I found." He gingerly held up what appeared to be a severed finger wrapped in a napkin.

"Ooh, gross." She shrank back. She could see all the tiny wrinkles in the skin and the nail still in place on the end. So alive. So real.

"Don't act all innocent," he said. "I know it was you."

"What are you talking about?" she asked. "Are you okay?"

Ryan sneered. "Like you care."

Kelly raised her eyebrows in confusion.

"I know you're the one who stuck this fake finger in the cookie package." Ryan's face reddened in anger.

"It's scary when kids get too greedy. Got to keep your fingers out of the cookie jar, as some people say." Kelly couldn't hide her triumphant grin. Ryan was such an easy target for a scare. There really was no sport in it. He fell for her frights every time. After all these years, she would've thought he'd wise up. But she was glad he stayed so gullible. She loved hearing his frightened cries.

"Ha-ha." He turned to leave. "I'm watching TV. Leave me alone tonight."

"Gladly," she replied, swiveling back to her screen.

SpenceX77: HEY.

Kookykell2011: HEY.

Spencer Stone logged onto their chat session. Kelly filled him in on the blizzard situation. He lived across the street from Kelly, and Paige lived behind her house. June Prendergast was only around the block. The four had been friends since tricycle days. There was a goofy photo of them all squeezed into a red wagon around age three in a frame on her desk.

Kelly's cell buzzed, and she wiggled her shiny blue phone out of her jeans pocket. There was a voice mail. *This phone has the worst service,* she thought. As Paige and June greeted Spencer, she listened to the long message from her mom. They had arrived at the motel, and her mom wasn't happy. *That makes two of us,* Kelly thought. *She's not getting any sympathy from me.* Then she grinned. Her mother's story gave her an idea. She instantly knew how to add lots of spooky touches to really freak out her friends. A classic Kelly scare. Her fingers flew over the keyboard.

Kookykell2011: YOU GUYS WON'T BELIEVE WHAT JUST HAPPENED TO MY PARENTS. THE TAXI LET THEM OFF IN FRONT

OF A RUN-DOWN BUILDING ON THE FAR EDGE OF PHILLY. THE
ENTIRE STREET WAS BLANKETED IN DRIFTS OF SNOW. EVEN IN
THE STORM, MY MOM COULD SEE THIS WAS THE KIND OF PLACE
YOU ONLY CHECKED INTO IF YOU WERE DESPERATE, WHICH
THEY WERE. THE BRICKS WERE CRACKED, THICK DUST LINED
THE WINDOWS, AND THE ROOF SLUMPED IN AT A DANGEROUS
ANGLE. THE TAXI PULLED AWAY, DISAPPEARING DOWN THE
STREET, LEAVING THEM ALONE. EVERYTHING WAS COMPLETELY
SILENT. THERE WERE NO OTHER CARS. NO SOUNDS. NOTHING.

Juney206: OMG! DID THEY GO IN?

Paige4peace421: I WOULDN'T.

Kookykell2011: THEY HAD NO CHOICE. THEY PUSHED
OPEN THE HEAVY WOODEN DOOR AND STEPPED INTO COMPLETE
BLACKNESS. NO LIGHTS. THEY CALLED OUT BUT GOT NO ANSWER.
MY FATHER REACHED AROUND DESPERATELY FOR A LIGHT
SWITCH. SOON HIS FINGERS FELT ONE, AND HE FLICKED IT ON
AND . . . BEHIND THE FRONT DESK SAT A SKELETON. WHO
KNEW HOW LONG THE BODY HAD BEEN THERE, ROTTING AWAY?
THE FLESH HAD DECOMPOSED AND ONLY THE BONES REMAINED
. . . SITTING THERE, WAITING TO GREET THE GUESTS. THEN THE
MOTEL PHONE RANG. IT RANG AND RANG. MY FATHER TOOK
A HESITANT STEP FORWARD AND LIFTED THE RECEIVER. HELLO?
HE SAID.

SpenceX77: WHO WAS CALLING? WHAT DID THEY SAY?????
Kookykell2011: HE SAID GOTCHA! KELLY RULES!

She laughed as her friends typed back, annoyed that she had done it again.

Kookykell2011: I AM THE QUEEN OF SCARES!

She'd been scaring her friends for years. In elementary school, she was mostly about fake snakes and eyeballs. And while those were still awesome, especially when skillfully placed in a lunch bag, she'd moved on in middle school to creepy stories about monsters and creatures and ghosts. The real spine-tingling stuff. Everyone agreed that she was the master.

Kelly glanced around her empty room, suddenly feeling a bit let down. A scary story wasn't the same when she couldn't see her friends' reactions. That was the whole adrenaline rush. The look of pure fear. She couldn't get that typing on a screen. *This no-sleepover thing stinks,* she thought. Everything was ready. Her green flannel sleeping bag was rolled out on her floor, with a plastic bag of scares tucked underneath. A fake fuzzy mouse to slip under June's pillow. A book of ghost stories. A tiny, handheld device that emitted bloodcurdling screams and vicious growls. *It would have been perfect,* Kelly thought. She didn't want to wait until next week.

That was when she had a brilliant idea.

Kookykell2011: Let's have a webcam sleepover tonight. All of us.

SpenceX77: What's that?

Kookykell2011: Just like a real one but virtual. We all put on our webcams so we can see each other and just hang like we would if we were together. Except with the computer. Spencer can hang too.

SpenceX77: Excellent! Never been to a girls' sleepover.

Kookykell2011: Eight o'clock! Wear pj's!

Paige4peace421: Awesome!

Juney206: C u then.

Kookykell2011: Before you guys go, I have to warn you about something.

Paige4peace421: What?

Kookykell2011: It's serious.

SpenceX77: Spit it out.

Kookykell2011: Get ready to be scared! Very scared!

CHAPTER 3

Kelly opened the front door that evening for Chrissie and immediately shivered at the drop in temperature. The air had plummeted to way below freezing, causing the snow of the past week to crust over into a shiny shell. Chrissie, pizza box in hand, slid a bit on the front walk. Her blond hair poked out of a knit cap, and a puffy navy parka swallowed up her thin body.

Glancing out into the early evening darkness, Kelly still didn't see her mother's big storm approaching. Just the same heavy gray clouds, the Stones' SUV pulling into their driveway across the street, and Mr. Golubic, wrapped in a thick wool coat, walking his black Labrador, weaving around the snowdrifts on the side of the road. The usual New England winter stuff.

A little before eight, Kelly stood up from the over-stuffed family room sofa, where Ryan and Chrissie were watching reality-show reruns.

"Time for the webcam sleepover?" Chrissie asked. She smiled knowingly.

"Paige told you?" Paige and Chrissie had this weird relationship. Sometimes they were the best of friends, and sometimes Chrissie went into superior-older-sister mode, acting as if Paige were an alien life form best to be avoided. The hard thing, for an outsider like Kelly, was figuring out which dynamic was playing out when.

"Yeah. Sounds like fun." Chrissie smiled, crinkling her blue eyes the same way Paige did.

Kelly had to admit that Chrissie was probably the best choice if she was forced to have a babysitter, which obviously she was. A senior in high school, Chrissie starred in all the school plays but wasn't a drama queen. She was actually pretty laid-back, and she seemed more into talking on her phone than the whole babysitter authority thing. She was fine with letting Ryan and Kelly do what they wanted, which worked for Kelly.

Chrissie's ringtone trilled an upbeat tune from a current Broadway musical. "Just come downstairs every once in a while, so I know you're still breathing," Chrissie said before she walked away to answer her phone.

Kelly closed her bedroom door and changed into striped flannel pajama pants and a long-sleeved sweatshirt with polka dots. She nudged Ezra off her desk chair. The ten-year-old black cat stared at her, then scampered along the windowsill to the top of her dresser. He was her dad's cat. She wasn't exactly sure what his problem was, but the cat refused to live on ground level. He'd climb to the highest point in any room so he could reign supreme, staring haughtily down at the humans below.

Kelly pulled her hair into a ponytail, then switched on her webcam and logged into the conferencing site. Paige's face peered out from the top box on Kelly's screen. As perky as ever, she bounced up and down on her bed. Paige always bounced. On the bus. In the cafeteria. During class. Paige's mom called it nervous energy. Kelly glanced enviously at Paige flopping on her new teal-and-gray bedspread. Totally sophisticated.

Kelly waved into her webcam.

"How's Chrissie?" Paige asked. "Did she play games with you? Is she going to tuck you in?"

Kelly screwed up her face. "Ha-ha. Very funny."

"I think it's so cute that Kelly has a babysitter," June cooed.

Kelly gazed at a second box on her screen that framed June's face. Forever the glamour girl, she wore pink satin button-down men's-cut pajamas. Kelly doubted June owned a pair of sweats, and if she did, they were probably the velour kind, jeweled with rhinestones. June held two fingernails up to the camera. One was polished in iridescent purple; the other in a matte baby blue.

"Color choice?" she inquired.

Paige and Kelly both chose the sparkly purple. Kelly watched June, sitting at her vanity, her laptop certainly nestled among bottles of perfume and tubes of lip gloss, meticulously polishing her nails. Her long auburn hair fell like a curtain over her face as she bent in concentration.

"Should we all polish our nails?" Paige asked.

"Or we can make beauty masks," Kelly suggested. "I read that if you mix avocado with honey and smear it on your face it makes your skin glow."

"You serving chips with that?" Spencer's voice broke through as he appeared in a third box on her screen. "I mean, seriously, we're not really going to sit here and watch you girls have some sort of spa session, are we?"

"You would look good in a green face mask," Paige quipped. "Might mellow out all those freckles."

"Whoa! Back off the freckles," Spencer warned. "You only dream of having this much character on your face."

Paige laughed. "Just joking."

"So what's the plan?" asked a voice from behind Spencer.

"Who's that?" Kelly spotted a silhouette hovering behind Spencer, just out of view of the camera.

"Show yourself," June commanded.

"You guess," said the voice.

"Well, from your voice I can tell you're a guy." June giggled. Kelly rolled her eyes. June had recently started using this fake flirting giggle. Didn't she know it was so transparent?

"Do you go to our school?" Paige asked, leaning into her camera to catch a closer glimpse.

"Yes," the voice replied. Spencer sat at his desk, his secretive grin broadcasting to all their screens.

"Are you in any of our classes?" June asked.

"Kelly's," he said. "Math."

Kelly quickly did a mental scan of her math classroom.

Who was Spencer friends with in that class? Everyone she thought of, she rejected. She couldn't think of anyone that Spencer would hang with. She threw out a few random names, but the voice said she was wrong, wrong, and wrong.

"I give up," she admitted. "You win. Who are you?"

"The mystery person is . . ." Spencer used his game-show-announcer voice. He moved away from the camera, and for a moment, all that was visible was the *Avatar* poster on his bedroom wall. Then a face filled the screen.

Kelly gasped.

His eyes were crossed and his upper lip curled back, exposing an expanse of gums and huge upper teeth. Gruesome!

She needed a few moments to recognize Gavin Mahon. He was new to their school. He sat in the back corner of their math class. She had never spoken to him. She wondered how Spencer even knew him—and why he was hanging out at his house.

Spencer squeezed back into the screen next to Gavin, who had now uncontorted his face, and introduced him to June and Paige. While they were comparing classes and saying hi, Kelly took a closer look at Gavin. He was so unlike tall, sturdy Spencer. Gavin seemed younger and skinnier than other boys their age. His arms were thin and his neck was wiry. He wore his black hair in a bowl cut, and she could make out a faint scar above his thick eyebrows.

"Gavin started Adventure Guides with me," Spencer was saying when Kelly tuned back into the conversation. *That explains it,* she thought. Spencer was into nature, hiking, and fishing. Adventure Guides was some sort of survivalist group. Of course, skinny Gavin looked like the last person to rough it in the outdoors. "He's sleeping over tonight. A *real* sleepover."

"This one is real too," Paige protested. "And you guys should be in pj's if you want to participate." She scowled at their jeans and T-shirts.

Kelly was going to agree, when she heard a knock at her door. "Come in," she called.

Chrissie pushed open the door and pranced in, a bowl of mint chocolate chip ice cream in her hand. "Hello, sleepover people," she chirped. "I brought a yummy bowl of ice cream. Your favorite flavor, right, Paigey-o? Sleepovers should have treats . . . oh, but, wait"—she poked her head in front of the webcam—"you're not

here to share it, are you Paigey-o? And I know there's no ice cream at our house. So sad for you."

Paige jumped up from her bed. "Get lost, Chrissie!" she yelled to the screen.

Chrissie continued to taunt her little sister. Kelly couldn't believe her mom was actually paying Chrissie. *I act more mature than she does,* she thought. Moving away from her desk, she let Chrissie slide into her chair. She stood alongside, watching Chrissie chat with her friends.

Suddenly Kelly sucked in her breath. "Oh, man. Chrissie, don't move. Seriously. Don't."

"W-what? What's happening?" Chrissie asked, her voice shaking.

Kelly tried to scream, but no sound came out. All she could do was point at the bare skin on Chrissie's neck. It was horrible. So horrible.

Chrissie stiffened. "Please. Tell me!"

"It's on you," Kelly whispered. She inched backward. "Oh, watch out! It's going to bite."

CHAPTER 4

"A spider." Kelly gulped. "There's a huge spider on you."

Chrissie jerked her head, trying without success to see the spider. Her cheeks flamed, and her scream rose throughout the house. Ezra arched his back in protest. Leaping from the dresser onto the desk, he shot out the door in a black flash of fur, raising the pitch of Chrissie's scream an octave.

"Get it off!" she wailed.

"I don't know. . . ." Kelly stared at the enormous black spider. "It's so . . . so hairy!"

"Help me! It's going to bite. I know it!"

Kelly took a deep breath. She reached over and, with the back of her hand, knocked the spider from Chrissie's neck. She froze as it landed on Chrissie's sneaker.

Chrissie shrieked again. "Are you crazy?"

"Gotcha!" Kelly cried. "Smile for the cameras!" All her friends laughed, as she waved the fake tarantula in Chrissie's face. Paige danced on her bed, delighted that her big sister had fallen for the lamest scare ever.

Chrissie scowled. "Ooh, that was bad. You freaked me out."

Kelly shrugged. "I am the master. With me, you should always be ready for a scare."

"Who's there? Hey, Kelly! Hi! Hi, June! Can you see me?" Spencer's six-year-old brother Charlie's gap-toothed grin filled the screen.

Charlie is way cute, Kelly thought. They'd all been friends since long before he was born, and Charlie kind of felt like a younger brother to her, too.

"Get lost," Spencer said, playfully pushing Charlie out of the way. "Aren't you supposed to be going to bed?"

"Take a hike, squirt," Gavin added. Kelly detected a slight edge in his voice. As if he didn't like Charlie.

"You're mean." Charlie's whine could be heard.

"Yeah," June agreed. "Be nice."

"Charlie, sweetie, leave your brother alone." Spencer's mom's voice sounded faint, as if she was down the hall.

The ringtone of Chrissie's phone filled the room. "Ugh, I hate that song," Paige said, leaning back against her oversize pillows and pulling out her own phone to check messages.

"I kind of like it." June stood and shimmied to the beat. "It's got a good groove."

"Not when you hear the same show tune every two minutes," Paige complained. "Chrissie's obsessed with Broadway musicals."

Chrissie glanced at the caller ID, then let the call go to voice mail. "Okay, I'm done here. I'll be downstairs watching TV with Ryan—" The Broadway hit trilled again. Chrissie screwed up her face. "Nobody has any patience. I gotta get this."

Kelly heard Chrissie talking into the phone as she padded down the stairs. Kelly plopped back onto her chair and kicked her feet up onto the desk. "What we need," she announced, "is a ghost story."

"Ooh, good idea," Paige said. "Everyone turn off the lights."

"Mood lighting," June agreed.

As she stood to reach for the light switch, Kelly glanced out the small window between her desk and her dresser.

Through the overgrown tangle of tree branches, frosted white from storms earlier in the week, she could make out the first flurries slowly falling. The storm was starting.

"Kel, don't you have a big book of ghost stories?" Spencer asked, his face lit by the greenish glow of his monitor, the room behind him completely dark.

Kelly nodded and was about to reach for it when Gavin said, "I know a story."

All eyes turned to him.

"It's a true story, though. Is that okay?" He sat on a chair next to Spencer, so the camera aimed on both their faces.

"True is better," June said, purple light surrounding her as if part of a surreal music video. June must have her bedside lamp on. The one with the purple bulb.

"What's it about?" Paige asked.

"You need some background," Gavin began. "I come from a small town in the way northern part of the state, right near the Canadian border. It isn't really a town. More like a bunch of cabins in the woods. My dad worked for a lumber mill."

He blinked several times. "Things were different up there. People weren't so friendly. Or so trusting. We pretty much kept to ourselves. Except for one night every year."

Kelly leaned closer, studying Gavin's face. It had an intensity she had never seen before.

"Every year, on January twenty-ninth, we'd gather at the old Richardson place. It wasn't that we much liked the company. It was just accepted that on a night like that, there was safety in numbers." He pushed his finger-tips together, methodically cracking each knuckle. "The howling started at nightfall."

"What howling?" Spencer asked.

"Animals. The attacks started small. Rabbits and squirrels. Then bigger animals. Foxes. Deer." Gavin swallowed hard. "The cries would then grow louder, more intense. The shrieks of geese. The wails of wolves."

"Why were they making all that noise?" Paige wrapped her arms around a pillow, hugging it close.

Gavin blinked rapidly. A nervous habit? "Death is painful. Vicious. Especially under the powerful grip of the Lagad."

"The what?" Was Gavin making this up? Normally Kelly would have thought so. But that cold, faraway look in his eyes was the stare of someone who had witnessed horrible things.

"The people who were natives to the woods called it—him—the Lagad. An ancient name."

"What was it?" Paige wanted to know.

Gavin paused. "Hard to tell. Some said it was a man who had turned into a hairy, ravenous creature. Some said it was a huge creature that had humanlike traits. Whatever it was, it was supernatural and deadly. It descended from the mountains on this one night every year as an act of revenge against the loggers who had destroyed its lair on that very day generations ago. The Lagad returned to settle the score."

"By killing animals?"

"It warmed up with animals," he explained. "As the hour grew later, it tracked people. The same way some people hunt deer . . . silently following tracks . . . scents. Alone in your house, you were no match for the Lagad. You would hear the crunch of its footsteps, maybe the crack of a twig, the scraping of its claws against your door, and then it was all over."

"Did you ever see it?" June asked.

His right eyelid twitched involuntarily as he measured his response. "Yes."

Kelly could hear herself breathing. Had the creature done something that had caused Gavin to leave his home? To move down here?

Gavin stared into the distance, remembering that terrible time. "My brother and I were home alone. We should've been at Richardson's place, keeping the vigil with everyone else. But we were waiting for my dad. His truck had broken down, and he was coming from the mechanic. To get us. It was too long a walk in the cold to Richardson's, so we waited. We waited too long."

Kelly pulled her sweatshirt sleeves over her hands. The darkness of the room cocooned her, transporting her to that desolate cabin in the northern woods.

"We were upstairs when we heard the noises at the back door. Grunts. Pounding. We huddled together. Terrified. It was here. It was coming for us. There was nowhere to hide. And then we heard the splintering of wood. . . ."

Kelly could hear the scraping of the creature's claws. The cracking of the door as the creature banged its way into the cabin. So close. Scraping, scraping.

She let out a low moan as the sound grew louder. The creature was coming.

Suddenly she knew. The scraping wasn't part of Gavin's story. She could hear the sound. In her room. Behind her.

Something was trying to get in. Something was try-ing to get her!

She whirled around.

Nothing.

She scanned the darkness. Her monitor threw off enough light to make out the outlines of her bed, night table, and dresser. Gavin continued to speak, but she tuned him out. Slowly she stood. Her legs trembled as the scraping came again.

From the window.

Her hands freezing with fear, she edged away from the desk and stepped silently toward the window.

CHAPTER 5

Kelly gazed though the window and jumped back. Bare branches slapped at the glass.

She shook her head at her own stupidity. How could she have gotten so sucked in by Gavin's story? It was just the wind causing the trees to scrape the windowpane. No one was there.

"Kelly? What happened? You okay?" Paige called out.

She was glad she was out of view. *I'm supposed to be the one doing the scaring,* she chided herself. *Not the one being scared. Such an amateur move.* From now on, she'd take control of the sleepover—at least, the scaring part.

She pulled the cord, closing her shade to the movements of the night. "Just checking on the storm," she called back. "Wind's picking up." She returned to her position in front of her webcam as if she'd merely taken a casual stroll across her room. She'd missed the end of Gavin's story. She wondered what happened, although now, by the grins on her friends' faces, she suspected he'd been making it all up. Figured.

"I have an idea." Paige leaned toward the monitor. "We should summon the dead."

"I like it." June nodded with a mischievous glint in her eyes. "Who should we bring back?"

"John Lennon?" Spencer suggested.

Gavin elbowed him. "Oh yeah, he's a real scary music dude."

"How about Cleopatra?" June said. "She had the coolest jewelry."

"No way," Gavin retorted. "A mummy would be creepy. Not a queen."

"I think we need someone we have a connection to. You know, to make it mean something," Paige said. "Someone from around here. Maybe someone who died a long time ago in a strange way or—"

"Guys!" Kelly interrupted. "I have the perfect person." She closed her eyes, bringing forth the pretty face in her mind. The clear, innocent gaze. She'd never been one to believe in fate and all that. She was a straightforward facts kind of girl. But this felt as if it was meant to be. As if there was a true connection. "We will call forth the spirit of Miss Mary Owens."

"Who?" all her friends wanted to know.

"I'll tell you about Mary." She paused as the old heater in the attic above her clanked, revving up to fight the cold creeping through the ancient wood siding. The wind gusted, and the branches rattled against the house. "She died on a night like this."

"How do you know about her?" Paige asked.

Kelly told them about the article she'd read that afternoon. "The year was 1966. Mary was young, like Chrissie's age. She'd come to our town to visit her aunt for the holidays. Her aunt lived out past the MacMaster farm, near the base of the big mountain. Back then there were no strip malls. Just houses and farms. And in Vermont, in the winter, there was snow. Lots and lots of it."

She paused to recollect the story. "Her aunt threw a large party. Lots of people. Caroling and food and holiday cheer. Mary had an eye for beauty. She decorated her aunt's tree with dozens of candy canes. She wove garlands with those round red-and-white peppermint candies and strung them throughout the rooms. Guests remarked on the scent of peppermint that filled the house. Mary even placed mints on a string and wore it as a necklace, surrounding herself with the holiday aroma.

"Now, crafty is nice where grown-ups are concerned, but Mary was beautiful, too. So, of course, the local boys at the party noticed her. And, of course, the local girls noticed the local boys noticing Mary, which didn't go over so well. Especially when some of those boys were the boyfriends of some of those jealous girls."

Kelly pictured Mary sitting by the fireplace, in her red-and-white dress, laughing lightly as a group of boys brought her punch and iced gingerbread cookies. Good for Mary. Not so good for the ignored girlfriends.

"During the party, the phone rang. The caller asked for *Miss Mary*. Mary took the call in the privacy of the kitchen, but she didn't go back to the party. No one noticed it at the time. She immediately went out the back door, wearing only her party dress. Snow had started to fall, and more was on its way. No one would ever know who called or what the caller had said. But something drove Mary to walk through the snow, without a coat, to the shed at the farthest part of the property in the darkness of a freezing winter night."

"What happened then?" Spencer asked.

"Before this, there had been days and days of storms. Wet, heavy snow was piled everywhere. A huge mound of snow and ice had accumulated on the shed roof. Mary entered the rickety shed alone. Why? Who knows. The door must've slammed behind her, setting off an avalanche of the snow on the roof. The rumbling was deafening. There was no time to run. Nowhere to go. Tons of snow crashed in a wave as the roof crumbled.

"Mary was found the next morning. The article said the smell of mint filled the destroyed cabin. She had tried to claw her way out of the suffocating whiteness, and her bare hands were frozen in place. Her mouth was forever stuck in a horrified scream. She had been buried alive."

The faint whirring of her computer was the only sound Kelly could hear. Her friends remained silent, their thoughts with the helpless girl.

Kelly continued. "Some of the girls from the party were suspected of luring her out there. But no one could prove anything. It could have been anyone. A secret past, perhaps? And no one could have known that all that heavy snow would have thundered down. The case is still unsolved." She took a deep breath and stared straight into the camera. "People say that Mary's spirit hasn't left the area. They say that she wanders about on the snowiest nights. They say that she strikes out at the young, trying to take their life the way her life was taken tragically early."

"I say we find Mary." June's eyes widened with excitement.

"Definitely," Paige agreed.

"But how?" Spencer asked.

Kelly waited for Gavin to say something, but he remained silent. She took this as agreement. "Here's what we do."

She frowned at Paige. Sprawled on her bed, her friend's fingers tap-danced across her phone. Paige was an obsessive texter. "Put down the phone. Put down everything. Full concentration is needed."

Paige rolled her eyes, finished her text, and rested her cell on her night table.

Only the dim, greenish glow from the monitors illuminated each room, casting sickly shadows on the friends' faces.

Kelly recalled all she knew about summoning spirits

of the dead. "Next we each need a reflective surface."

"What about our screens? I can sort of see myself in mine," Spencer said.

"That should work," Gavin said. His face appeared strangely pale. Bad lighting for them all.

"Okay, to call back Miss Mary, each of us must chant her name thirteen times as we spin in a circle. One chant per turn, our voices growing louder, drawing her to us. On the thirteenth time, stop spinning and stare at the reflective surface." Kelly surreptitiously placed the little scream machine out of sight on the edge of her desk. Her plan was to press the button and sound the bloodcurdling scream at just the right moment to freak out her friends.

"Clear your minds," Gavin instructed solemnly, as if he'd done this before. "Think only of poor Mary. Trapped in the snow. Alone. Focus on her tortured soul."

Kelly bit her lip in anticipation as they began. Standing in the darkness, she slowly turned in a circle. "Miss Mary."

"Miss Mary."

"Miss Mary."

Around and around they spun. Some standing, some sitting on revolving desk chairs.

"Miss Mary. Miss Mary." Their voices rose, calling the name of the dead girl. The eerie green glow was the only beacon in a spinning whirl of darkness.

"Miss Mary. Miss Mary."

Kelly was losing count. Losing balance. The face of Miss Mary swam before her eyes. Drowning in an avalanche of green light. Pulling her under. Down, down. Around.

"Miss Mary." Calling for her. "Miss Mary!"

Louder, louder, their voices crying out in unison. Reaching beyond the years. Reaching into the depths. The air crackled around them. An electric current sent jolts throughout her body.

The final dizzy turn.

The screech of her name ripped from their throats.

And then the gasps. Kelly blinked, disoriented, hearing everyone gasp. Desperately she tried to focus on her monitor. She was dizzy. Oh, so dizzy.

"Kelly!" June's face froze in wide-eyed horror. "S-she's behind you!"

CHAPTER 6

Swallowing hard, Kelly peered over her shoulder. Darkness greeted her. Her eyes roamed the room. Silhouettes of stuffed animals on her bed. The lump of her school bag on the floor.

No one.

She sank into her chair, pulling her monitor close. Her heart beat fast. "Who? Who did you see? There's no one here." She glanced again to be sure.

Shadows. The rush of the wind.

"She was there. Behind you." June trembled.

"I saw her too," Paige said. "For a second, she appeared on your screen. Then she was gone."

"That was so weird," Spencer murmured.

"Who? What did she look like?" Kelly wavered. Were

her friends tricking her? She wanted to believe so, but their faces told her otherwise. They had seen something.

"More of a shadow than an actual person," Paige murmured.

"But it was definitely a woman," June added. "I could see her silhouette. Hovering there. Just for a second. Oh, wow, Kel, she was totally in your room."

A chill ran down Kelly's spine. She hugged her arms around her chest, trying to make sense of it all. "Do you think it worked? Do you think we really brought her back?"

No one wanted to speak first. To say the thing they all felt, yet couldn't explain.

"I saw it . . . her . . . too." Gavin broke the silence. "The last time we said Mary's name. She was there. She was real."

"Awesome!" Spencer's spark returned. "We did it. We brought back the dead."

"I think it's creepy," Paige said. "Don't you, Kelly? I mean, she was in your room."

Kelly reached over and ran her fingers along the tiny black plastic box on her desk. She'd never pressed the button and sounded the scream. She'd never had the chance to pretend the supernatural could be contacted, because . . . it might have really happened. She shifted her weight in her chair. She was unsure of what she felt. She wished she had seen what they'd seen. "Let's do it again."

"What?" June sat straighter.

She shrugged. "To be sure. Let's see if it's really her. Do it all again. The chanting. All of it." She tucked a stray piece of hair behind her ear, suddenly excited by the idea.

"Sure." Spencer was up for anything.

"It was freaky, but okay." Paige was in.

"No way." Gavin nudged Spencer into the shadows, making sure Kelly could see him on her monitor. His beady eyes bored into the screen. His face remained grim. "You don't mess with the dead."

"Oh, please!" Paige snorted, no longer scared. "Let's do it."

"I'm serious. Once was enough." Gavin blinked quickly many times. "Trust me."

"Why? What makes you an expert?" Kelly wanted to know.

He cast his eyes downward for a moment, still blinking nervously. "Nothing." He paused, cracking one knuckle, then another. "You made contact. You've started things in motion—"

"What things?" she demanded.

Gavin shrugged. "Things we don't understand. Things from beyond. Things that should be left alone."

He's so weird, Kelly decided. She thought of texting Paige and seeing if she thought so too. It didn't feel natural to have him here with them. What right did he have to dictate what they could do?

"Well, I—" She stopped, suddenly hearing a faint melody. The notes repeated. An unsettling tune.

"You know," June began hesitantly, "I sort of agree with Gavin. I don't think we should do it again."

"Really?" Kelly asked. She was surprised. June usually liked adventure.

"I felt something," June whispered. She looked embarrassed.

"What?" Kelly and Paige asked in unison.

June gnawed a hangnail on her thumb. "Didn't you? A tingling kind of thing? Right before she appeared?" She gazed at them hopefully.

Kelly hesitated. Had she felt something? She wasn't sure. Maybe . . . maybe some static electricity. But did ghosts give off that kind of energy? And sure, she was dizzy, but that could've just been from the spinning.

"I felt it," Gavin replied.

Paige shrugged. So did Spencer.

Kelly shook her head. "No way. It's all in our heads. Come on. One more time." Suddenly, for some unexplained reason, she wanted to show her friends that it had just been a weird group hallucination. That it couldn't be true. She would do something the next time that would scare them—the fake growl, perhaps—and then they would know it wasn't real and—

The melody sounded again. Louder this time.

The same eight sinister notes. A haunting tune.

"What's that song?" Paige asked. "Kel, did you put music on?"

"No."

Everyone listened as the tune repeated twice more. So loud. As if right outside her door.

"Probably something Ryan is watching," Kelly guessed. "I'm going to check. Be right back. Don't do anything without me, okay?"

She walked across her room and rested her hand on the door handle. Straining her ears, she listened for the melody. The low buzz of garbled TV voices was the only noise she could make out from downstairs. The music had stopped. She pushed open her door and poked her head into the darkened hallway.

The smell immediately overwhelmed her.

Inhaling, she felt weightless, spiraling back in time. To a farmhouse in the snow. To a party filled with cheer . . . and despair. The scent surrounded her. Made her dizzy. She grasped the door handle to anchor herself.

She drew her breath in again, just be sure. The smell was undeniable. Peppermint.

The icy mint aroma filled her nostrils. And she knew: *Miss Mary is here.*

CHAPTER 7

She froze in the doorway, unsure of where to go or what to do. Her eyes darted about the hallway and over her shoulder, into her room. She had no idea what to look for. Her heart beat rapidly.

Peppermint. She smelled peppermint.

Would a ghost leave behind an odor? she wondered. Did it mean Mary's spirit was here? Now?

She wanted to run to her computer and tell her friends about the peppermint smell. She could hear the murmuring of their voices coming from her computer speakers. June's high-pitched giggle. The lower tone of Gavin. A sudden overwhelming wave of logic and disbelief prevented her from turning back.

She shook her head, trying to straighten out her

thoughts. *Get a grip. There is no ghost,* she reminded herself. *I told the story from the newspaper to scare everyone else. Not to scare myself.*

She inhaled again. The crisp scent of mint wafted around her.

Then it hit her. *Chrissie must be baking something with peppermint in it,* she thought. *Maybe chocolate mint cookies or hot chocolate with peppermint oil.*

Much relieved, Kelly padded down the stairs in her fuzzy socks. She stopped midway, her hand resting on the oak banister. Drawing in another breath, she noticed that the peppermint was no longer as overpowering. The farther down the stairs she moved, the more the scent weakened. At the bottom, it was almost nonexistent.

She glanced out the front window, watching as the wind swirled the flurries in crazy circles. Under the glow of the streetlamps, the snow appeared as a magical coating decorating the walkway. It reminded her of the silver glitter she used to pour onto school projects. Mounds of shiny flecks piled on gobs of white glue.

She turned toward the back of the house. To her left, she could hear the TV in the family room. Two men arguing on the screen. She continued into the kitchen, expecting to see Chrissie by the oven or stove.

"Whatcha baking?" Kelly called out.

She was met with silence. The lights were on, but the kitchen was empty.

She could detect the slight smell of the pepperoni from tonight's pizza. No peppermint. No aroma even vaguely like peppermint.

The large chrome stove and double oven on the far left wall of the farm-style kitchen was dark and cold. Nothing cooking. The granite counter on the center island held only today's mail and a pizza box with uneaten crusts. Her mother's desk on the far right wall appeared to be in the same state of disorganization as earlier. The door to the basement at the right of the desk remained firmly shut. Even though her parents had bought sofas, a Ping-Pong table, and a foosball table to make it into a "playroom," she and Ryan rarely went down there. Calling it a playroom did nothing to disguise the dank basement smell and the permanent chill. It was like playing Ping-Pong in Siberia.

The only sign of life in the kitchen was on the oversize wood table. At the head of the rectangular table, a high-backed chair was pushed away, slightly askew.

Her mother had bought the six mismatched chairs at yard sales. She'd delighted in sanding and staining each, and the contrast of each of their designs made them strangely go together in a homey kind of way.

A glass of clear soda sat on the table in front of the pushed-away chair. Kelly walked over to it. Tiny bubbles popped and floated along the surface of the fizzy lemon-lime liquid. The soda hadn't gone flat yet, Kelly realized. That meant Chrissie had just poured it. A sugar cookie lay beside the glass, a single bite taken out of it.

"Chrissie?" she called out. "You here?"

No answer.

She shrugged. Chrissie had probably gone to the bathroom or was watching TV with Ryan.

Then her eyes rested on the phone. Chrissie's cell with its distinctive holographic purple cover sat along-side the cookie. *Strange,* Kelly thought. She didn't think Chrissie ever went anywhere without her phone. Even to the bathroom.

She pulled open the refrigerator door and reviewed the contents inside. Same stuff as before. Nothing too good. She reached for the plastic bottle of soda, shut the door, and poured some into a fresh glass. She rested the bottle on the island counter.

The carbonation tickled her throat as she took the first gulp. Glass in hand, she wandered through the archway that led into the back of the family room. Ryan slumped alone on the plush overstuffed sofa, totally immersed in the action on the screen. Two greenish creatures, each with three eyes, circled a lone cow in a meadow. They prodded the animal with some sort of electric device that buzzed on contact. Then there was heated discussion about returning to the ship.

Kelly sighed. Another alien movie. Her brother had a thing for sci-fi. It was all he'd watch or read.

"Hey, spacehead," she called. "Where's Chrissie?"

Ryan grunted, barely acknowledging her presence. His eyes remained glued to the action on the screen. The cow was having convulsions.

Figures, she thought. A total TV android. Ryan was impossible to talk to with the TV on. It was as if he inhabited the weird worlds he watched.

"Fine. Be that way. See if I care." Then she heard it again.

Kelly listened as the eight-note melody repeated. It was louder than it had been upstairs, but it was the same

creepy song. The tune reminded her of the music played in horror films—right before the crazy guy leaps out at the innocent girl.

It's a ringtone, she suddenly realized. And it was coming from the kitchen. She hurried back through the archway toward the noise. Then she chuckled to herself. *I'm just like the girls in those horror films,* she thought. Running toward the creepy sound. Spencer would find this funny. She couldn't wait to tell him that she had fallen into the classic scary movie trap. He was really into those old Hitchcock films.

The melody stopped as she entered the kitchen. Chrissie was back—and she was talking on her phone.

She changed her ringtone, Kelly thought. She didn't particularly like this new one. Too creepy.

Chrissie didn't notice Kelly. She stood by the kitchen table, wearing navy sweats with her feet bare. Her back was to Kelly. Listening intently to whoever was calling, she stared out the large picture window overlooking the backyard. The outdoor spotlight illuminated the swirling flakes. Large evergreens sagged under the weight of the week's snow. The yard was an expanse of white. Nobody had been out back since the last snowfall.

Chrissie whispered into her phone. Kelly couldn't make out all the words, but she sensed that her babysitter was bothered about something. Chrissie remained turned with her shoulders slumped as she whispered somberly. Eyes still focused on the empty yard, she ran her hand along the square-panel window at the top of the back door next to the window. Huge icicles hung from the archway outside the door. "No. No way," she said into the phone.

Kelly hesitated, about to speak. Then she changed her mind. Chrissie was obviously involved in a private conversation. It didn't seem right to bother her now about smelling peppermint. Down here in the warmth of the kitchen, the whole spooky-odor thing seemed silly. She drained her glass of soda, placed the empty glass quietly on the counter, and headed to her room.

"Hey, everyone," she announced into her webcam as she slid into her chair. "I'm back."

Paige lifted her head and faced her screen. "Finally! That took forever. We're totally bored. I'm even polishing my toenails."

Kelly laughed. "Wow, you really must be bored." Paige was much more the blisters-and-bandages-in-cleats type than the pedicure-ready-for-sandals girl, especially in the middle of winter.

Paige smirked. She raised one foot to the camera. "Look how I've botched it." She wiggled her toes, the blue polish thick and bumpy.

Kelly grimaced. "Maybe you need a redo?"

"Nice of you to join us." Spencer's face appeared in the bottom box on her screen. "We'd almost given up on this whole sleepover thing."

"It was your idea," Gavin pointed out. He squeezed into the frame with Spencer.

"Sorry," she said. "My bad." She watched Gavin toss pieces of popcorn in the air. Spencer bounced up to catch each kernel in his mouth.

"See, no hands!" Spencer grinned, then gulped another airborne kernel. "Party games for the sleepover."

"Excellent. Maybe we should all make popcorn," she suggested. She then looked closer at her screen. Paige was battling with the goopy polish brush and the tiny surface of her small toenails. Spencer and Gavin were performing like the seals at Sea World. But June . . . she looked closer. . . . June's frame was empty.

"June?" she called. "You there?"

June didn't respond.

"Where's June?" she asked the others.

Paige lifted her eyes from her botched pedicure. Coloring inside the lines was not her strength. "I don't know. She was there when I got back from finding the polish. I had to nab it from Chrissie's room. Don't tell her."

"June was there when we returned from the kitchen to get popcorn," Spencer added.

Kelly shrugged. June probably went to get something too.

As Spencer told a joke, though, her eyes couldn't stop wandering to the frame where June should have been. Something about it felt wrong. She just didn't know what.

Spencer was on a roll. "What did the snowman and the vampire name their baby?"

"What?" Paige abandoned the polish, leaving one set of toes in their natural state.

"Frostbite!" Spencer grinned. Everyone else groaned. He'd been telling lame jokes since they were little kids.

"I've got one," Gavin said. "What do ghosts dance to?"

"Soul music." Spencer rolled his eyes. "That one's played out."

Gavin shoved Spencer. Spencer shoved him back. Kelly ignored them. Her eyes returned to June's screen. What was it? Then it hit her. She didn't know why she hadn't noticed it right away. June's frame had gone completely red.

"What do you guys see when you look at June's frame on your screen?" she asked her friends.

Everyone stopped talking and joking.

"Weird," Paige murmured. "It's all red."

"Is her room painted red?" Gavin asked.

"No. It's yellow," Spencer answered.

"So why are we all seeing red?" Kelly asked. "I mean, shouldn't we see her vanity chair, since her computer was on her vanity? Or something in her room?"

"Maybe something's up with her computer," Spencer ventured. "A weird electrical thing?"

"Did she say where she was going?" Kelly asked.

Paige looked perplexed. "No. It was kind of like one minute she was there and then she wasn't."

"Yeah," Spencer agreed. "One time I looked up and no June. Poof!"

"June?" Kelly called again. "Are you there?"

June's window on her screen remained red and silent.

"She'll be back." Kelly relaxed and watched Spencer do an impression of their earth science teacher. His accent was a little off but still funny. Paige joined in, making them guess which teachers she was mimicking. She had the phys ed teacher's quirky tics spot-on.

"You know," Gavin said after fifteen minutes had passed, "it's weird that June still hasn't come back. Shouldn't we try to find her?"

June's screen still glowed scarlet.

"She's fine," Kelly replied, annoyed that Gavin was telling them what to do. June was their friend, not his.

Nevertheless, she reached for her cell phone and quickly texted June.

She got no response.

"I texted her," Paige announced. "She's not texting back."

"Me too. I'll call," Kelly offered. June's phone rang three times before going to voice mail. "Hey, June, it's us. Where are you? Come back to your screen or call me. Bye."

Kelly shrugged to her friends. "I left a message."

"I think Gavin's right. It's weird," Paige said.

"It is kind of spooky after the whole Miss Mary thing," Gavin put in.

Kelly laughed. "So you really fell for the bringing-back-the-dead thing?"

"Didn't you?" he asked seriously.

"No way." She recalled the peppermint scent but pushed the unsettling thought aside. A coincidence, she figured.

The abrupt slam of a door and then a violent crash thundered through the house, breaking Kelly away from her thoughts.

This wasn't something she could just block out. Kelly jumped up and raced down the stairs, unsure of what she would find.

CHAPTER 8

"What was that?" she cried, skidding from the foyer into the main entrance of the family room.

Ryan stared at the aliens on the TV, completely engrossed in the movie.

"Did you hear me?" Kelly asked her brother. "Did you hear that noise?"

Ryan didn't answer. The sofa had molded to his unmoving body the way a worn glove cradles a baseball.

"You've got to me kidding me." She groaned. "I don't know what your problem is, but I'm not playing your silent game. I can't believe you didn't hear that!" She hurried across the room and through the back entrance to the kitchen. Chrissie sat in a ladder-back chair by the table, obsessively twirling a single strand of her blond hair.

"Did you hear that noise?" Kelly demanded.

Chrissie nodded. Twirling, twirling.

Why wasn't anybody talking? Kelly wondered.

She took a closer look at her babysitter. Still in her navy sweats, Chrissie was now wearing white snow boots. Flecks of wetness dotted their nylon exterior. Her face looked pale, ashen, as if she was worried.

"What's up?" Kelly pulled out the spindle-back chair next to her and sat.

"The icicles outside the back door fell," Chrissie said without feeling. The monotone sounded strange coming from her. Kelly was used to her peppy, chirpy voice.

Kelly glanced toward the door. In the glow of the outdoor spotlight, she saw that the row of huge icicles was no longer hanging. That would account for the crashing noise, she realized. But she wondered about the slam. Someone must have slammed the door to cause the icicles to fall so suddenly. They were the thick kind. It would've taken a lot of force to smash them to the ground.

"Were you outside?" she asked Chrissie.

"No." Chrissie stared at a far-off spot on the table as if suddenly interested in the vintage woodwork.

"Really?" she pressed. The snow caked on the treads of Chrissie's boots was obvious.

"No, I wasn't." Chrissie twirled her hair, wrapping a piece tightly around her index finger. She wouldn't meet Kelly's gaze.

Chrissie was lying. Kelly could see that. But why? "Someone must have slammed the door," Kelly began.

Chrissie didn't saying anything right away. She opened her mouth as if about to, but then seemed to think better of it.

Kelly's throat felt dry. She swallowed several times. The Chrissie she knew was always bubbly and happy. She didn't recognize this morose girl sitting next to her. "Are you okay?" she asked gently.

Chrissie nodded slowly.

"Really, if you're not, you can tell me." Kelly reached out her hand to touch Chrissie's arm, but Chrissie shrank back.

"Was that your boyfriend on the phone?" *Maybe it's a breakup thing,* Kelly thought. She didn't have any experience yet with boyfriends, but she'd seen enough TV shows with girls moaning over broken hearts.

Chrissie shook her head. That wasn't it. Again she

seemed about to say something but stopped herself, casting her eyes away from Kelly.

"Seriously. You're scaring me," Kelly said in a low voice. The air around them seemed heavy. As if a dark cloud had descended on the kitchen.

"She doesn't want you downstairs," Chrissie whispered suddenly.

"What?" Kelly leaned closer.

"She won't be happy," Chrissie murmured.

Kelly swallowed hard, trying desperately to wet her throat. "Who?"

Chrissie stayed silent for a few minutes, a shadow of fear clouding her gaze. "You should go back to your room," she finally said.

What was going on? Who was Chrissie talking about? "I don't understand."

"It's best."

"*What's* best?" Kelly's voice rose unnaturally.

Chrissie twisted that one chunk of hair so taut, it was in danger of breaking. "Just go. Please."

Kelly stayed seated for a moment, contemplating her babysitter. Something was definitely wrong. She debated calling her parents. But she knew they couldn't do anything trapped in the snow except worry. That wasn't good. She gazed around the kitchen. Nothing looked different. The TV blared from the family room. The wind shook the trees outside, and the snow fell faster. Everything seemed okay—except for Chrissie.

Kelly shrugged. Sitting with Chrissie made her uncomfortable. *I'll just leave her alone,* she thought. *Let her work it out, whatever it is. Maybe Paige knows what's wrong with her crazy sister.*

"Whatever," she said, getting up. "I'll be in my room."

Chrissie stared at her blankly.

"Okay then." Kelly couldn't get back to her room fast enough. She had to talk to her friends. Tell them what was going on.

The preppy plaid of her childhood welcomed her as she entered her bedroom. For the first time in a long time, the pink and green comforted her, gave her that secure, settled feeling. Maybe she wouldn't press her mom to redecorate.

She stood in front of her desk and gazed at her screen. Her mouth opened in shock.

In the bottom frame, Gavin and Spencer appeared to be having a whispered argument. Gavin's forehead was furrowed, and his dark eyebrows were drawn together in worry. Spencer's freckles seemed to darken against his suddenly pale skin.

June's frame was red and still empty.

And Paige's frame was now empty too—and filled with the same pulsing crimson color.

"Where's Paige?" she asked hesitantly.

Gavin and Spencer whirled their heads around to face her. She could see it in their eyes. Something had happened while she was downstairs. Something bad.

"Where's Paige?" she asked again.

"She's gone," Gavin said slowly.

"Gone where?" Her voice again sounded shrill.

"Kel, something freaky is going on. We were talking to Paige, and then, boom, her screen turned bloodred and she was gone. Totally gone. As if she was sucked up by some force," Spencer babbled nervously. "We tried calling her cell. You know she always has her cell. It just kept ringing and ringing. No voice mail or anything. She won't answer texts, either."

"Maybe she just went to the bathroom or another room," Kelly suggested.

"Both of them?" Gavin asked.

She stared at her screen. Both June and Paige's frames were a hot, pulsing red. Definitely strange. A seed of dread stirred in the pit of her stomach.

She flipped open her phone and hit Paige's name in Contacts. She listened to the ringing. Eight times, she counted, before she hung up. No voice mail. She pushed June's number. Her phone rang, then clicked to voice mail. She left another message, more urgent than the one before.

Where are they? she wondered. Her fingers drummed her desk. The heater clanked overhead, working to combat the chill of the churning wind.

I NEED U TO TXT ME!!!!!! NOW!! she wrote to Paige.

She watched her screen. Paige always answered texts at lightning speed. They joked about it all the time.

Not now. No text came back.

"Kel, there's something else." Spencer leaned toward his webcam. His eyes widened in her monitor.

"Don't tell her," Gavin cautioned.

"She should know." Spencer turned to Gavin.

"I don't think so. We don't know what we're dealing with," Gavin said as if she weren't listening.

"What shouldn't I know?" she demanded.

Gavin shot Spencer a warning look, but Spencer ignored him. "While you were gone . . . right after Paige went missing . . . we heard something coming from your room."

"What do you mean?"

"Whispering. There was the sound of a voice whispering in your room," he said.

"W-what was it saying?" she stammered.

"We couldn't be sure. It sounded like . . . like . . ."

"What?" she cried.

"It sounded like 'Miss Mary, Miss Mary.'"

CHAPTER 9

A sudden chill shook Kelly's body. She shivered, pulling her hands farther into her sweatshirt sleeves. As the wind moaned through the trees, the branches slapped her window in angry protest.

This sleepover wasn't turning out as she'd planned. She wished all her friends were here with her. All together in her room, laughing with the lights on. Sitting alone in the dark in the storm was creeping her out. And she didn't get creeped out. Ever.

"Are you sure?" she asked Gavin and Spencer. She straightened in her chair, trying to shake away her nerves.

They nodded.

She eyed them suspiciously. The clanking of the

heater had stopped, and a slight chill settled over her room. She pushed the bowl of uneaten melted green ice cream to the side of her desk.

"No joke. We heard it. Really." Spencer gazed unflinchingly.

After all these years, she knew Spencer could never meet her eye if he was lying. *But just because he believes he heard something doesn't mean he really did,* she assured herself. She was afraid to let her mind go down the other path.

"I know it doesn't make sense," Gavin said. "But something is going on."

"What kind of something?" she challenged.

"Something supernatural," he said calmly.

Kelly tried to laugh, but the croak that came out sounded more as if she were choking. Her throat felt unnaturally dry again.

"I think we did it," Gavin said. "I think, somehow, we brought back the spirit of that dead girl." His eyes gleamed with excitement, although his face remained grim.

Kelly stared at both boys. Spencer looked uncomfortable. He fidgeted in his chair. He gazed around his room. But Gavin looked, well, almost energized. His wiry body fidgeted expectantly. She wasn't sure what to make of this, especially since she barely knew him.

"Do you think we did, Kelly?" Spencer asked. "Do you feel anything weird?"

She rubbed her icy fingers together, then tried to warm them with her breath. The whole night had been weird. Paige and June were missing. Chrissie was completely off-kilter. And she had felt a strange sensation after they had chanted. Electric. Dizzy. She didn't know what.

But she wasn't going to admit it.

"No." She picked up her cell and dialed Paige. Nonstop ringing. June's number went right to voice mail. She didn't bother to leave another message, although she really wanted to scream at her friend. Where was she? Why were she and Paige doing this?

"So?" Spencer asked.

"So nothing," she replied. She tried to control her frustration.

"They're not answering my texts." Spencer held his phone up to the camera as if her seeing his phone would make her realize how odd it all was.

"Mine either." She sat quietly for a minute. The air

around her had grown frigid. She could faintly see her breath as she exhaled. The upstairs heater must have died, she realized. She hoped the downstairs one was still working. It was going to be a long, uncomfortable night if they didn't have heat.

"I'm going to call Paige's house phone," she told them. She almost never called Paige at home anymore. Paige always had her cell by her side. She dialed and listened as the Coxes' phone rang and rang. Where were Paige's parents? They wouldn't be out on a night like this. On the tenth ring, she hung up.

Rummaging about on her desk, she uncovered the slim school directory under a pile of notebooks. An absurd-looking moose wearing a sports jersey graced the cover. She'd never understood why they had to have the stupidest mascot ever. She flipped to the Cs to check the number. It was silly, really. She'd known Paige since she was born. She didn't have the wrong number. She knew that. But still.

She dialed again, pressing each number deliberately. Ringing and ringing. No answer. "No one's there," she reported.

"Isn't Paige's sister babysitting you?" Gavin asked.

"Maybe she knows where Paige went."

Spencer perked up. "Yeah, Kel. You should go ask her."

Kelly sighed. "I don't know if that's the best idea right now."

"Why?" Spencer asked.

She told them about how Chrissie had lied about being outside. She explained how disturbed and disconnected she seemed.

"She's possessed," Gavin said matter-of-factly.

"Oh, please," she scoffed.

"Think about it," he challenged. "Think about when her behavior changed."

It was true. Chrissie had started acting odd after the chanting. After the smell of peppermint.

Gavin's dark-brown eyes burned through the screen at her with an intensity that made her uncomfortable. "We did something," he said.

She stood and turned her back on the boys. She needed a moment to think. To try to make sense of it all.

She walked to her bed and grabbed the wool blanket folded at the end. An Authentic Vermont Blanket, of course. She wrapped the thick, bright-green blanket around her for warmth. Moving about her room, she came up with plenty of places her friends could have gone. She just couldn't come up with a lot of reasons why they hadn't returned her texts or answered their phones.

Pulling back her shade, she gazed at the falling snow. Frost inched up the windowpane. It was going to be a big storm, she realized. Her mother had been right. She hoped her parents were okay. She hadn't heard from them in a couple of hours.

She crossed her room and flicked on her light. The glow brightened the room and her mood. Her friends' disappearances suddenly seemed less scary. *There is an explanation*, she told herself. *I just have to figure it out.*

She glanced back at her monitor. Only Spencer's face was visible in the frame. Gavin didn't seem to be around. Spencer waved his hand, beckoning to her urgently.

She hurried back to her desk.

"I need to talk to you," he whispered. His eyes darted about anxiously. "Turn off your microphone. Use the keyboard."

She gave him a questioning look but followed his instructions.

Kookykell2011: WHAT'S WRONG?

SpenceX77: IT'S GAVIN.

Kookykell2011: ??? WHERE IS HE?

SpenceX77: WENT TO GET A DRINK. DON'T HAVE MUCH TIME. I'M REALLY FREAKED OUT.

Kookykell2011: ABOUT MISS MARY?

SpenceX77: WELL, YEAH, BUT ABOUT GAVIN, TOO.

Kookykell2011: WHY?

SpenceX77: IDK. IT'S A VIBE. HE'S ACTING REALLY STRANGE.

Kookykell2011: STRANGE HOW?

SpenceX77: NERVOUS. TWITCHY.

Kookykell2011: MAYBE THAT'S WHAT HE'S LIKE.

SpenceX77: THAT'S NOT IT. STARTED WITH THE MISS MARY THING. BEEN WEIRD SINCE. KEEPS MUMBLING STUFF UNDER HIS BREATH. TO HIMSELF, BUT I CAN HEAR. IT'S SCARING ME.

Kookykell2011: WHAT'S HE SAYING?

SpenceX77: STUFF THAT DOESN'T MAKE SENSE. COLD-NESS IS COMING AND YOU CAN'T BE HERE.

Kookykell2011: WHO CAN'T?

SpenceX77: IDK. HE DOESN'T SEEM IN CONTROL. IT'S AS IF HE CAN'T HELP SAYING THIS STUFF OR HE DOESN'T KNOW HE'S MUTTERING IT OR—

Kookykell2011: WAIT. IT'S LIKE—

Kelly stopped typing. She tried to swallow but couldn't. Her lungs felt as if they were being squeezed. She recalled the strange things that Chrissie had muttered just a few minutes ago. She hadn't told Gavin and Spencer what Chrissie had said. So why was Gavin saying the same sort of things?

She sucked in air, trying to inflate her lungs. To breathe normally again. In and out.

Kookykell2011: R U SURE?

SpenceX77: YES!!!

Kookykell2011: MAYBE HE'S PLAYING YOU. . . .

She kept coming back to her know-all-the-facts nature. She didn't buy into fortune-tellers and horoscopes and the other mystical things some of her friends believed. She liked science and reasoning. Everything for her always had a factual explanation. That was why she liked scaring her friends so much. All that supernatural stuff was fake, and she knew it.

Tonight was the first time she was having trouble making sense of things.

SpenceX77: MAYBE. I BARELY KNOW THE GUY. I DON'T WANT HIM HERE ANYMORE. SOMETHING ABOUT HIM IS WAY OFF. I DON'T TRUST HIM.

Kookykell2011: I AGREE. BEEN FEELING THAT WAY ALL NIGHT.

SpenceX77: WHAT DO I DO?

She wasn't sure. Maybe Spencer could fake sickness and ask Gavin to go home. She wished June would show herself. She was the best at these kinds of schemes. She'd create a believable story of why Gavin had to leave.

Kelly glanced at Spencer's webcam frame to judge how worried he was. She froze.

A dark shadow loomed behind her friend.

Spencer had no idea. His eyes stayed focused on his keyboard. He was typing. She stared in horror as the figure glided closer. She wanted to scream but could only watch in mute terror as it reached out its arms and slowly brought them down . . . down . . . toward Spencer's neck.

She had to warn him. She had barely seconds before . . . Her fingers flew across the keyboard.

She was too late. The attacker wrapped both hands around Spencer's bare neck. His fingers squeezed . . . squeezed . . . squeezed the air from Spencer's throat.

"Noooo! Stop!" she cried. Then she remembered their microphones were off. Spencer couldn't hear her. She grabbed her computer with both hands and shook it hard, as if she could somehow stop the horror with the force of her fear. She couldn't just sit here and watch her friend suffocate!

She wanted to cover her face, but she was afraid to let poor Spencer out of her sight. She stared in total helplessness as he weakened, growing limp.

Suddenly Spencer's eyes bulged. He twisted his body with a burst of renewed strength, jerking it left and right. The attacker's grip loosened, and he leaned toward Spencer.

Kelly narrowed her eyes and gripped her desk to steady herself. She stared at the face of Spencer's attacker. It was a face she recognized.

CHAPTER 10

Spencer jumped up and pushed his attacker back. Then he spun to face him.

Gavin.

Gavin's sinewy face broke into a huge grin. He laughed. "Oh, man. I totally scared you. Score!" He pumped his fist in victory.

"That was so not funny!" Spencer spat.

"It was just a joke."

Spencer's cheeks reddened slightly, but he forced a strained smile. "Y-yeah, you got me."

Gavin ran his hand through his spiky hair. "Who did you think it was, dude?"

Spencer shrugged. Kelly could sense him shrinking back as if he was putting up an invisible wall. It felt peculiar to sit across the street and watch the scene play out. Almost like watching a scary movie and not being able to help the victim.

"You are such a wimp," Gavin said. He gave Spencer a shove. Then another.

Kelly winced. She knew guys shoved all the time. Yet with Gavin, she wondered if there wasn't more to it. True, Spencer was way bigger than Gavin, but he was the kind of mellow kid who set ants free instead of squishing them. Gavin, though, had a barely contained aggression that pulsed right below the surface of his skin. She watched, still helpless, as Spencer backed himself up to the desk. She wasn't sure what he was doing. Was Gavin advancing on him?

For a moment, her screen was filled only by the heathered gray fabric of Spencer's T-shirt.

"Spencer!" she screamed. Was Gavin hurting him? Had he pushed him against the desk and hit him?

Then she heard a blip. SPENCEX77 IS OFFLINE appeared on her chat screen. His face slid into view, unharmed. She sighed, realizing that he'd blocked his screen so he could exit out of their conversation before Gavin saw it. She exited too and turned her microphone on. She was glad he hadn't heard her scream.

"Kelly? You there?" Spencer asked from the bottom frame. Gavin stood alongside him. The frames on her screen where June and Paige should have been continued to pulse red. *Danger*. The word suddenly popped into her head. Red is the color of danger.

"Yeah, I'm—" Her screen suddenly went blank.

Wrapping the wool blanket tighter around her, she pressed enter. The webcam sleepover didn't come back.

Her computer was still on. So were her lights. They hadn't lost power, she realized. She gazed at the screen. CONNECTION IS TEMPORARILY UNAVAILABLE. Her Internet service was down.

The wind slammed against the house, rattling the trees. The frozen branches clawed angrily at the siding. She fiddled with her modem, hoping she could bring up the connection. The storm might have shut it down for the night.

She watched the Internet icon at the bottom of the screen. It blinked, trying to connect.

INTERNET DOWN, she texted to Spencer. U OK?

MINE DOWN 2, he replied quickly. But he didn't answer her question.

She waited, watching the blinking icon search for a

signal, desperately wondering what was going on across the street. The scene kept replaying in her mind. She knew what she'd seen. It hadn't been a joke—no matter what Gavin said or how much he laughed. Gavin really seemed as if he was going to strangle Spencer. The glare in his eyes wasn't the look of someone joking. It was danger-ous. Unhinged. If Spencer hadn't fought back and turned around when he did . . . She shuddered to think about it.

After what felt like an eternity, although it was really only a few minutes, the Internet icon flashed green. She was back online. She signed in to the webcam confer-ence. Biting her lip, she wondered what she would find. Would Spencer be okay? Would June and Paige be back?

A single frame popped onto her screen.

The camera focused in on Spencer and Gavin sit-ting side by side. Spencer's posture seemed much more relaxed. Gavin leaned back casually in his chair. Every-thing appeared okay between them. They seemed like buddies again.

Her eyes roamed her screen. The frames where June and Paige had been—the frames that had turned bright red—were no longer there. She tried to dial into their computers. The connection failed repeatedly. No one was at the other end to link into the videoconference site.

"Can you guys see June and Paige's frames?" she asked. The panic began brewing again in her stomach. The red frames were disturbing, but at least they had been something. A lifeline of some sort. Without them, she felt very far away from her friends.

Spencer shook his head. "They disappeared. Can you see them?"

"Nope." She glanced at her cell phone. No texts. No messages. "I think we need to do something."

"There's nothing to do," Gavin replied.

"That's so wrong!" she cried. She'd had enough of him. Her fear and frustration bubbled up, congealing into anger toward him. "You barely even know us! And you have no idea where my friends are. I'm going to find them, and you can't stop me!"

Gavin threw up his arms in mock surrender.

"Calm down, Kel," Spencer said. "You're right. We need to do something. But this webcam thing isn't working."

"What do you mean?"

"Something is wrong. We need to figure this out together. Gavin and I will come over there. We'll all sit down—Chrissie, too—and make a plan."

"Good idea," she agreed. She wasn't thrilled about Gavin coming too, but decided not to let that get to her. She wanted company. "Hurry, okay?"

Spencer nodded. "Be over in a sec." He logged off.

She left her chair and flopped onto her bed. The chill had completely invaded her room, making her long to snuggle under her plaid comforter. She resisted. Spencer and Gavin would be here in a moment. She waited.

And waited.

She rolled over, watching the clock on her bedside table. Ten minutes had passed since Spencer had logged off. She wondered what was taking so long. She pulled her sleeping bag off the floor and draped it over herself. Staring at her ceiling, she let five more minutes pass. Then she sat upright.

Spencer had been running across the street to her house since they were in kindergarten. It took two minutes, at most.

She flipped open her phone. WHERE R U??? she texted.

She waited. No reply. No ringing doorbell. Nothing.

Maybe he's waiting at the door, she thought. *Maybe the doorbell is busted.* She leaped off her bed. How horrible of her to leave them outside in the brewing storm. She raced out of her room and down the hall. At the top of the stairs, she stopped.

The smell.

The bracing scent hung thickly in the air. She stood startled, as if slapped in the face. Every nerve tingled as she inhaled.

Peppermint. Again.

No one was in the hallway. The stairs were empty. She couldn't explain where the mysterious odor was coming from. Suddenly, more than ever, it felt urgent that Spencer be at the door. She needed him to smell the smell. To tell her she wasn't going crazy. To explain everything.

She hurried down the steps.

The temperature change was obvious as she reached the foyer. The heat was still on down here. The murmur of the TV reached her ears from the family room. She could still smell the peppermint, although perhaps more faintly than before.

Twisting the lock on the front door, she reached for the brass handle. She pulled hard. An enormous gust of frigid air swept through the house as she opened the door onto the storm. Her hair flew about her face, and she leaned into the wind.

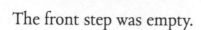

The front step was empty.

No Spencer or Gavin.

The outside lights on either side of the door cast a faint glow on the inky darkness of the night. Snow swirled about—the fat flakes carried in circles by the incredible wind.

She peered down the deserted walkway. It was covered by an untouched layer of fresh whiteness. No boot prints. They hadn't tried to come up to the door.

Still inside the house, she tried to see across the desolate street. The neighborhood was quiet, except for the howls of the wind. Everyone was inside, protected from the oncoming storm. She stared at the outline of Spencer's house. A shiver ran along the base of her neck.

The house was dark. Completely dark.

Twisting her head, she tried for a different angle. Her eyes teared from the icy gusts. But no matter how hard she squinted, the Stones' house continued to blend in with the blackness of the sky. No lights were on. No lights inside. No lights outside.

It was as if no one was home.

As if no one had ever been there.

The house was totally abandoned.

CHAPTER 11

Kelly slowly shut the front door. She stood motionless on the woven mat, trying to piece together the puzzle.

Spencer and Gavin had been in their house a few minutes ago. She was sure of it. And Spencer's little brother Charlie had been home too. And Spencer's mom. They wouldn't all leave suddenly in the night, would they?

As hard as she tried, she couldn't come up with a reasonable explanation. At this point, she was even willing to take sort-of reasonable. Maybe they all decided to go to sleep and shut every light—even the outside ones? Doubtful. Especially since Spencer had promised to run right over.

She hooked her mind around the promise. Of all her friends, Spencer was the one she could count on most to keep a promise. If he said he was coming, then he'd be here. He always came through. She would wait.

The hum of the television penetrated her muddled thoughts.

Ryan. She'd go hang out with Ryan until Spencer showed up, she decided.

She entered the family room from the foyer. The overhead light blazed brightly in here, and the heat seeped through the vents. Her mother had a passion for Americana crafts. A painting of an American flag done on a large, weathered, wooden plank hung over the sofa. The other walls held needlepoint reproductions of colonial samplers. Carved, narrow benches and cornhusk dolls decorated the area near the stone fireplace. On most other nights, Kelly felt as if she were living in a museum. She often teased her mom about it, calling it "Ye Olde Family Room." But tonight being surrounded by all her mother's trinkets felt soothing.

Ryan sat on the sofa, exactly in the same position as before.

"Hey," she said.

He continued to stare at the TV.

She was about to make a sarcastic remark about

whatever alien sci-fi movie he was captivated by when she stopped—and took a second look at the screen.

Three women in shorts and colorful tank tops stood in a row. They squatted in unison. Together they kicked their legs and counted the repetitions. Was Ryan really watching an exercise show?

She examined the women for another minute. They weren't even young or cool-looking. They looked like her grandmother's friends.

"Hey, you, why are you watching this?" she asked.

Ryan didn't answer. His eyes never left the screen. He appeared mesmerized by the middle-aged women, who were now jogging in place. Retro eighties music played in the background, but the women were hopelessly off the beat. There was absolutely nothing interesting in this show. And it wasn't bad enough to be funny. It was just bad.

Kelly narrowed her gaze at her brother. She was so not in the mood for his tricks. "Answer me," she demanded.

He stayed mute. Unmoving.

She studied him. Was this a joke?

"Stop it, Ryan." She waved her hands in front of his

unblinking brown eyes. He didn't flinch.

"Can you hear me?" she cried. Her heart began to beat rapidly. From anger. From confusion. "Move!" she screamed, her face centimeters from his. "Move!"

He remained frozen. She could hear him breathing. The air slowly traveling in and out of his nostrils. She grabbed his shoulders with both her hands and shook him hard. Again and again. "Answer me!" she screamed frantically.

His body felt limp in her hands. He gave no resistance. His glassy eyes focused vacantly on the TV. The three women crossed their arms and legs, counting out the fifteenth jumping jack. Their perky voices filled the silence of the room.

Her heart beat all over her body. Her thoughts jumbled around her brain. Nothing was making sense. Why was Ryan like this? It was almost as if he was . . . as if he was . . .

She hesitated, not wanting to complete the horrible thought. Fearful that if she thought it, it would be true. For the only thing she could come up with was that Ryan was . . . possessed.

She stared suspiciously at his zombielike figure.

He had never acted like this before. "Ryan." Her voice came out as a whisper. "Ryan, please." She could no longer disguise her fear. "You're freaking me out. Please."

He didn't respond to her pleas. Immobile, he stared into nothingness. Vacant.

She needed help. Now. She knew that.

She pulled her phone out of her pocket. Her fingers automatically dialed her mom's cell.

"Hi, sweetie." Her mom's voice, so near yet so far, made her legs weak.

"Hi, Mom." Her voice caught, and she swallowed hard.

"Is everything okay? What are you doing?" The line crackled.

"Well, you see—" Static filled the airwaves, then disappeared. It disguised the terror in her voice.

Kelly hesitated. She started to tell her mother that everything wasn't okay. That their babysitter was depressed. That her friends weren't texting her. That the house smelled weird. That her brother had become a zombie.

No. She couldn't tell her all that. She was the one who would sound crazy. Besides, what did she expect her mother to do so far away? She'd totally freak out and insist on driving home in this weather.

"Fine," she answered instead. "Everything's fine. Just watching TV."

"Good. Stay inside. The weather's bad." Her mom went on to tell her about the motel room and the lack of little shampoo bottles, soap, and shower caps in the bathroom. She hated motels without amenities. "Does Chrissie want to talk to me?"

Her mother's voice faded in and out. The line buzzed with static.

That was it! Chrissie would help, Kelly realized. She might be acting a little strange but she was older. She'd know what to do. She would confide in Chrissie. She didn't have to worry her mother.

"Can you hear me? Kelly, are you there?"

"We have a bad connection," she said. "I'll call back later. Everything's okay. Love you." She clicked the phone off, even though she suspected the call was dropped before she'd said good-bye.

With a backward glance at her brother—still sitting, still staring—she tucked her phone back into her pocket and headed across the room to the archway that connected the family room with the kitchen. Even from here, she could see the kitchen was dark. Was Chrissie even in there?

The babysitter's name formed on her lips, but she didn't call it out. She suddenly had the strangest sensation that she shouldn't scream. Slowly she treaded silently toward the entrance.

A breeze wafted across her body. She shivered. Where was the cold air coming from? What was in the kitchen?

She tiptoed into the darkened room. A biting coldness descended on her. Goose bumps tingled her skin. All the lights were off. But even in the dimness, she sensed that something wasn't right. The wind that had been beating against her bedroom window reached out its powerful arms and grabbed at her. The force of an unexplained squall pulled her farther into the kitchen.

She reached instinctively for the switch on the wall. Instantly the kitchen was bathed in the artificial overhead light.

Kelly clapped her hand over her mouth in complete amazement.

Her eyes followed the paper tornado churning about

the room, as if guided by a supernatural hand. White napkins rose to the ceiling, then circled back around, dipping down before another gust lifted them again. Sheets of paper—lined notebook paper, colorful school flyers, old receipts—twirled across the floor and the table. The lighter pieces joined the napkins in a crazy Tilt-A-Whirl of motion.

Kelly's gaze darted to her mother's desk. The surface was wiped clear by the windstorm vacuum. The piles of paper were now airborne.

The back door banged savagely against the wall. The door itself lay wide open to the approaching storm and the night. The wind rushed into the house as if shooting through a tunnel.

After a few seconds of shock, Kelly jumped into action. Racing across the kitchen, brushing the paper out of her path, she pushed at the door. The wind created a force she had to blindly throw her full weight against. As the door latch finally clicked into place, the paper storm died. Napkins fluttered lazily to the floor.

Kelly lay, panting, with her back against the door and surveyed the mess before her. Paper littered the kitchen. A cold wetness seeped through her fuzzy socks, chilling her toes. She gazed down. Small puddles of water dotted the floor near the door. Why had the door been wide open?

"Chrissie?" The urge to scream that she had suppressed only a few minutes ago let loose. "Chrissie! Chrissie!"

Her cries echoed through the empty house.

"Chrissie! Where are you?"

Only the faint undertones of Madonna's singing and the women counting off lunges on the TV could be heard.

The cool glass of the door's small window sent a shock through her body. Every nerve was alert.

What now? she wondered. *What do I do now?*

Her frantic gaze circled back to her mother's desk. With a jolt, she realized that the desk wasn't completely cleared of all its papers. She blinked in disbelief as she noticed one piece of paper sitting directly in the center, as if carefully placed or somehow attached.

She made her way through the carpet of trash and stood before the desk. Its distressed painted wood gleamed in the light. She rested both palms on the surface. Bending down, she stared at the lone paper.

The chills ricocheted throughout her body in an electric current much like the one she'd felt earlier in the night.

She carefully placed one finger on the paper. It yielded to her slight push. It wasn't taped into place. It stood squarely on the desk as if held there by unseen hands.

She wanted to flee but couldn't move. An energy—a force—pulled her toward the paper.

Down, down.

Kelly stared at the face on the page. The soulful eyes beckoned to her once again. The rest of the world faded into the distance. She and the girl were together. One. A bond unbreakable.

"Hello, Mary," she whispered.

CHAPTER 12

Mary Owens. The newspaper clipping that had once hung on her mother's bulletin board—the one she vividly remembered pinning up there just that afternoon—rested on the empty desk.

She couldn't explain how it had gotten there or how it had stayed there, but suddenly she felt sure of one thing: She and her friends had called back Mary's spirit. Upstairs, together, they had summoned the unhappy soul of a girl who had died a horrible, suffocating death.

Miss Mary, Miss Mary. She remembered how they'd chanted, their voices growing louder and louder.

And now all her friends were missing.

And her babysitter.

And her brother . . . was no more than a hollow shell.

Her hand rested on the receiver of the house phone. She would call the police. They would help her. They would *have* to.

Lifting the receiver to her ear, she listened to the steady buzz of the dial tone.

Did the supernatural count as an emergency? She feared they would laugh at her almost as much as she feared staying by herself in this house. She pictured the police cars skidding up the driveway. The blaring sirens and flashing lights rousing the neighbors. People gathering on the lawn, watching in curious fascination as the officers stormed the house. And she would tell them all about what had been going on tonight.

Bad idea, she knew.

Kelly gently returned the receiver to the base.

She wiggled her toes against the dampness of her socks and thought about the puddles by the door. *Maybe Chrissie went out,* she thought. She'd been wearing boots—and she certainly had been outside earlier. Chrissie could have left the door open by mistake. That was it.

An encouraging warmth spread throughout her body as the explanation unfurled in her brain. It was the same feeling she'd gotten when, at age five, her father reached for her mittened hand with an everything-will-be-okay smile every time she fell learning how to ski. She was overreacting, that was all.

She flung open the back door. The force of the wind struck her full on. Strands of hair blew about her face. She pushed them away from her eyes. Turning on all the lights in the yard, she saw that the snow hadn't begun falling too thickly yet.

She scanned the yard. The snow by the door looked trampled and kicked about. There was no question now that someone had been outside. A set of boot prints led away from the house, zigzagging across the white expanse. The tracks disappeared into the darkness. The spotlights attached to the back of the house shone only a short distance. There was no telling where the tracks led.

Still safely planted inside the doorway, Kelly scrutinized the boot prints. They weren't the deliberate prints of someone walking slowly through the snow. They were smeared and very close together. The snow was more compacted at the front of the boot print. The person had barely pressed any weight on the heel. Excess snow sprayed around the back of each print. She understood immediately. The person had been running. Fast.

Was it Chrissie? It had to be, she reasoned.

But why was she running? Was she running to something? Or was she being chased?

"Chrissie? Chrissie? Are you out there?" she yelled into the darkness.

The wind swallowed her cries.

"Chrissie?"

Her voice echoed back to her. Her throat grew dry and scratchy again. Panic pushed its way up.

The snowflakes fell silently from the sky. The yard remained frozen and eerily quiet.

Why would Chrissie leave?

"Ryan!" she screamed. "Ryan, can you hear me? This is an emergency!"

She waited. The television hummed in the house behind her. Her brother didn't come.

She strained her ears, hoping against hope that Spencer and Gavin would ring the doorbell. Everything would be okay if they'd just show up, she decided. As hard as she tried, she couldn't will the doorbell to ring.

She was overcome by the need to do something. She was fed up with waiting. Waiting for her friends to show up. Waiting to understand what was going on.

Her father's black rubber snow boots sat to the right of the door. He'd been outside shoveling yesterday. Suddenly it seemed like years since she'd seen her parents.

She peeled off her damp socks and shoved her feet into the oversize boots. The nubby, frayed lining scratched her toes. The boots were far too big, but she didn't want to waste time running to the front hall to look for her own boots. She grabbed her green parka with the faux-fur-trimmed hood off the back of the chair she'd thrown it on earlier. She pulled it on, not bothering to trouble with the zipper. She stepped outside, closing the door tightly behind her.

For a moment she stood, trying to formulate a plan.

But she realized she had none. The plan was to find Chrissie. Beyond that, she had no idea.

Unaccustomed to the weight of her father's boots, she wobbled as she moved into the snow. The frozen top layer crunched as her soles broke through it. The wet, heavy snow and the weight of the wind made each step forward feel as if she were pushing against a brick wall.

The cold cut through her thin flannel pajama pants, stinging her legs. She shoved her bare fingers deep into her parka pockets. Swirling snowflakes coated her hair.

Huddling against the cold, she pushed on.

Stepping in the boot prints left by Chrissie made walking easier. She placed each foot carefully, working her way farther and farther from the warmth and safety of the house.

The shadows of the trees tilted over the snow-covered yard, making it hard to follow the prints. She squinted through the frozen flakes lining her lashes. The light from the house grew dimmer and dimmer as she trudged forward. The moonless sky cast no light on her path.

Kelly concentrated on following the prints. Up, over, and down, she dragged each heavy boot. Her hot breath came out in puffs against the cold night air. Her cheeks tingled painfully. She knew they must be bright red.

"Chrissie?" she called again and again.

The wind howled mournfully. The trees shook their snow-caked branches at her. Never before had she felt more alone.

She shivered and dug her hands deeper into her pockets. She leaned into the gusting wind. Print after print. She followed the path, each step bring her closer to . . .

"Chrissie!"

CHAPTER 13

Kelly stood in the far corner of her yard and screamed her babysitter's name. "Where are you?"

She stared blindly at the snow.

There were no more prints.

Gone. The prints were gone.

The vast whiteness stretched unbroken by human feet. Turning in a slow circle, she squinted through the steady snowflakes. Though there was only the slightest glimmer of light this far from the house, she was sure: The boot prints had abruptly stopped.

Forbidding darkness pushed toward her from the evergreen-lined edges of her large yard. She wished she had thought to bring a flashlight. The pines whispered, warning her away.

She knew Paige's yard lay behind the thick expanse of trees her parents had planted years and years ago for privacy. But tonight it seemed miles away. She shaded her eyes with her hands, momentarily blocking the blinding snow. She looked at the last boot print. What had happened? Had Chrissie disappeared into thin air?

A wave of chills raced through Kelly's body, and she stood shaking. She remembered promising her mother after school that she wouldn't leave the house. Now here she was in the darkness, in the snow, outside, alone. If she had known back then how the night would turn out, she would've made her parents take a dogsled back home.

Turning, she began to trudge back the way she'd come. She kept her head down, eyes on the snow. She focused only on the warmth and light of her house. Everything else was too horrible. It was better not to think about it. Just move forward.

She had gone only a few feet when she heard the noise. A movement. A faint rustling in the trees. She jerked up her head, suddenly alert. The rushing wind made it hard to hear. She waited as the wind enfolded her, whistling about her. The gale skidded the fresh snow about the yard like a desert sandstorm. A covering of white dusted over her big black boots. She bowed her head, protecting herself from the icy squall.

Everything was silent again.

She began to move forward. One step, then two. And then the unmistakable crunch of snow, coming from her right.

She was not alone.

Kelly sucked in her breath, not daring to move a muscle. She stayed rooted to her spot in the snow.

Crunch. Crunch.

The movement was deliberate. Was it an animal? she wondered. She gritted her teeth, staring into the never-ending blackness. What kind of animal? *Please let it be something small,* she thought.

She squinted into the darkness, but she couldn't make out anything. The shadows morphed about her. Varying tones of gray and black obscured all objects in the yard. The branches bent and swayed under the weight of the wind. She focused through the falling snow on the tree line to her right. A thick row of pines bordered her family's property with their neighbor's. Something was working its way through the pines. Steadily crunching. Its steps heavy. It wasn't a small animal, that was for sure.

She eyed the distance to her house. The yellow glow of the light shining through the large kitchen window suddenly seemed miles away. She knew, though, that it was only about sixty yards. Safety wasn't far.

The movement in the trees grew louder. Heading her way. For a moment, she wondered if it was Chrissie.

"Chrissie? Is that you?" Her voice sounded thin in the wind. "Are you out there?"

She shivered and listened. The movement quickened. Thudding steps of some kind. Too heavy for slight Chrissie. Whatever it was, it was big—and heading for her. "No!" she cried. The force of her scream took her by surprise, waking her from an almost trancelike state.

Her feet started before her brain could catch up. She ran through the snow. She had to get away. Her father's big, heavy boots felt like cement slippers, weighing her down. Each step required extreme effort. Pulling the boot up, out, and over, then sinking back into the wet snow. Her legs trembled. Sweat trickled between her shoulder blades and coated her skin, leaving her clammy.

She pushed forward, running. The footsteps in the trees quickened their pace, and all at once she knew. She was being chased.

With a crash of branches, the something broke free of the trees and thundered across the open yard. Within seconds, it was behind her.

Kelly panted, struggling to breathe. All her energy was directed toward moving her feet. Faster. Faster. She had to get away—had to get back to her house. Her left boot stuck in the snow. She wobbled, and her knees began to buckle. She threw her arms forward to break her fall.

No, no, no, no! her brain screamed. If she fell, it would be all over.

She managed to right herself and regain her balance. The footsteps crunched faster through the snow behind her. Closer now. She could hear the creature's breath exploding in jagged puffs. So near. She wanted to look back but knew she couldn't risk it. She had to keep going.

Her chest heaved as she ran. Her side knotted in pain, but she could see the door now. The window with its glow of safety. Only feet away.

And then she was there.

Her hand reached for the door handle, and she twisted anxiously. Her frigid fingers, white with cold, slid about on the cold metal. At first nothing happened. Dread overcame her, as she tried the handle

again. Twisting and twisting. It wouldn't budge.

She frantically twisted the other way. It was stuck.

She was locked out.

She felt the creature's hot breath on her neck. She gulped, alarm overtaking her body. She squeezed the handle, refusing to let go of her way in.

"Please, oh, please," she whispered.

"Kelly, it's me."

She spun around. "Gavin! You almost gave me a heart attack."

"Sorry." His cheeks shone bright pink from the cold, but he wore a black parka and gloves. "Why were you running?"

Kelly hesitated, uncertain how to explain. "I was looking for Chrissie. She's gone. She disappeared in the snow out there."

Gavin nodded. He didn't seem surprised. He waited, not speaking.

She gazed over his shoulder, back toward the pine trees. "Where's Spencer?" Her hopes lifted at the thought of seeing her friend. She knew he'd keep his promise.

"I don't know," he said flatly.

"What do you mean?"

He shrugged. "I mean I don't know." His gaze jumped to her hand still gripping the door handle. "I'm freezing. Can we go inside?"

As much as she wanted to get inside, out of the wind and snow, she suddenly wasn't sure that she wanted Gavin inside with her. She squinted at him. "What's going on, Gavin? Where's Spencer?"

Just then a muffled noise broke through the whistling wind. She strained to hear. A song . . . no, it was a melody repeating.

The haunting melody from Chrissie's phone.

She listened closer to be sure. The muted, evil melody had to be coming from inside.

"Do you hear that?" she asked.

"Yeah." He took a step closer. "You should open the door."

"I think I locked myself out." She stayed where she was, blocking the path between him and the door.

She thought of Mary. Trapped in the snow. Freezing to death slowly, painfully. The snow draining the warmth out of her. Was that what was going to happen to her, too? Locked out in the snow . . . But how did Gavin fit in? Was he here to save her? Or was he here to—

She could no longer hear the melody. The phone had stopped ringing.

"Kelly, let's go inside," Gavin said. He stomped his boots impatiently in the snow. "Move over. Let me try."

She couldn't stay outside in this horrible cold. She knew that. "Where's Spencer?" she demanded again, refusing to move.

"He was behind me when we crossed the street. And then I looked back and he wasn't there," Gavin explained.

"But that was a long time ago," she said suspiciously. "You guys left his house a long time ago."

"I know."

"What were you doing sneaking around my yard in the dark?" She couldn't figure out what Gavin was doing here. Alone. Without Spencer.

"I wasn't sneaking around. I was searching for him."

"But you were chasing *me*."

"Because you started running." He stepped forward, and she let him pass. She wasn't sure what to do. Indecisive, she stood meekly behind him and watched over his shoulder.

He tried the handle. The cold metal slipped through his nylon gloves. He pulled off his gloves and shoved them into his parka pocket. Then he blew on his hands and rubbed them together. His hot breath loosened his fingers.

He tried the handle again. He threw what little weight he had into the door and twisted.

The door swung open.

They both nearly fell inside, stumbling into the brightness. Kelly closed the door behind them, shutting out the storm.

The house was quiet.

She blinked hard at the empty room. Her stomach dropped with disappointment. She'd secretly hoped that everything would have returned to normal—that she would have opened the door and been greeted by Chrissie and Ryan. That life would've gone back to the way it had been before she'd decided to play that silly game with her friends.

She shrugged off her coat and the boots, now dripping with snow. Her flannel pants clung damply to her legs. The front of her shirt was wet from where she had failed to zip her jacket. The chill of the storm clung to her. She longed to take a hot bath and wrap herself in her warm, fuzzy robe.

She scanned the kitchen, still littered with the contents of her mother's desk, for Chrissie's phone. She didn't see it anywhere.

The sound of someone behind her jerked her away from her thoughts. For a moment, she'd forgotten about Gavin.

He still wore his damp black parka, although his boots now lay beside hers. His white athletic socks were frayed at the heels. He stood, hands buried in his pockets, and watched her.

She stared at him for a few minutes, trying to figure out if she trusted him. His eyes held that same intensity that had unnerved her earlier in the night. He blinked several times in uncontrolled spasms. He seemed to give off an electric-like current that made the little hairs on her arms stand on edge.

Using her fingers, she brushed through her damp, tangled hair, slicking it back from her face. "So you don't know where Spencer is?" she asked again.

"No."

"June or Paige?"

"No." He gazed at her with glassy eyes. "It's just you and me now."

CHAPTER 14

"Coldness is coming," Gavin continued, his voice drained of all emotion.

"Huh? What are you talking about?" She gulped, trying to control the trembling in her voice as she remembered what Spencer had told her earlier about Gavin acting strangely.

"It's so cold out there. In the snow. Cold and dark." His voice was flat. His brown eyes held a haunted, faraway look.

"Y-yeah. Yeah, it is." Kelly stared in horror at him.

"You can't be here," he told her.

"What? Why not?" she demanded brusquely, but the squeaking of her voice betrayed her panic.

"So what should we do?" he asked suddenly. His tone

had changed abruptly, as if life had been injected back into it.

"About what?" She looked around. If she needed to, her best bet would be to run for the front door, she decided. She had a good twenty pounds on Gavin. *I could push him down,* she thought. *He may be crazy, but he doesn't look too strong.*

"I don't really know where to look for him anymore. I've been all over. I even went back to Spencer's house. It's like . . ." He hesitated, and his shoulders slumped. "It's like Spencer, his mom, his brother . . . It's like they completely disappeared."

"It's weird," she agreed. She took several steps backward, away from him. Flipping open her phone, she checked desperately for messages. Nothing. Not even a text. "Maybe they'll answer now," she said hopefully, more to herself than to him. She kept her eyes trained on Gavin as she tried each of her friends' phones again. She listened to them ring. Two rings. Five. Eight. No one was answering.

She and Gavin really were all alone.

That was when she noticed the silence.

The TV was quiet.

Had Ryan turned it off? Maybe he had snapped out of his trance.

"Ryan?" she called. She hurried toward the family room, leaving Gavin behind. Her bare feet slapped against the wooden floor. She burst inside.

And stared.

The room was empty. The television was dark. She could make out the faint impression of Ryan's legs on the overstuffed sofa cushions, but he wasn't there. No one was.

"Ryan!" she called again. She felt as if she'd been calling for people all night.

Silence once more.

Her heart began to beat so fast she was sure it might burst. The room started to spin. Slowly at first, but soon the colonial crafts were in full whirl. The floor tilted toward the ceiling. She had to sit.

She dropped into a blue gingham armchair near the sofa. The checkered pattern danced before her. She tried not to let the panic overwhelm her.

She had to find her brother.

She was in charge of him even though her parents had hired Chrissie. Not that she had done any good tonight.

She wondered what happened to a person's body once he or she was snatched by a spirit. Did the spirit claim just the person's soul or their whole being, too? And why had Mary—assuming it *was* Mary—come for everyone except her? Was she next?

And then she thought of Gavin. He was here too.

She remembered the bizarre things Gavin had been muttering. *Coldness is coming* and all that. What did it mean? Could the spirit of dead Mary have somehow gone into Gavin's body? And through him preyed, one by one, on her friends . . . ?

She shook her head violently. She had to stop thinking such crazy thoughts. Gavin was just a boy. A friend of Spencer's. Maybe he was little weird, but that was all. She had to get a grip.

A small moan escaped her throat. She had so many questions. She tried to order her thoughts. She gazed about the room, the dizziness going away.

She sensed him before she saw him. Gavin stood in the doorway, silently watching her. He waited and said nothing. She could feel the force of his gaze penetrating the back of her head. She willed herself not to acknowledge him, not to turn toward him. She didn't like him.

She wasn't going to obsess about why. He was probably harmless, but she couldn't handle his weirdness right now.

She stood shakily, holding the upholstered arm of the chair for support. She rested her phone on the cushioned seat. Then she walked to the television and stood directly before it. She raised her palm to the screen. It still felt warm. Ryan had been here not too long ago.

Upstairs. That was it. She sighed with relief. Ryan had probably gone upstairs to bed. She wanted to slap herself for being so silly.

"You okay?"

She turned toward him. Gavin had taken off his parka and was wearing the same T-shirt and jeans from earlier.

"I need to find my brother," she murmured, not meeting his questioning gaze. She headed through the foyer. Gavin stayed behind for a minute, then followed.

She climbed the stairs methodically. She could hear Gavin climbing two steps behind but ignored him. She wanted to tell him to stay away, but she didn't want to be alone, either.

Midway up, she stopped when she smelled the peppermint. The odor came from behind her.

Her fingers danced nervously on the banister. Gavin had stopped climbing too. He waited one step below. What did the odor mean, coming from Gavin's direction? she wondered.

"Kelly, what's wrong?"

Was the odor linked to the spirit of Miss Mary? she wondered. Then would that make Gavin—?

"Do you feel okay?" His voice betrayed genuine concern.

"Do you smell that?" she blurted out. "The peppermint?"

For a moment, he looked confused. "You mean my gum? Is it bothering you? Do you want a piece?" He slid a slim foil pack out of his back jeans pocket and held it up to her.

Kelly flushed, feeling like a fool. She noticed now that he was chewing gum. Mint gum, obviously. "No. I'm good." She continued up the last few stairs, refusing to look back at him.

At the landing, she turned left. Ryan's room was the first one. His door was closed. An old handwritten KEEP OUT sign from last summer was taped crookedly in the center.

She knocked. Twice.

Silence.

She pressed her face against the door. "Are you in there, Ryan?"

She waited. *Please,* she thought. *Please be in there.*

"I'm coming in," she warned.

She waited a moment, then pushed open the door.

The pain was immediate.

Sharp claws slashed through her sweatshirt, piercing the skin on her shoulders. She shrieked in agony. Her arms flailed frantically. She fought to release herself from the lethal grip.

And then she heard the high-pitched wail. A bone-chilling, inhuman sound like she'd never heard before.

CHAPTER 15

Was this how it was going to end for her? Had June and Paige been attacked too, before disappearing? She squeezed her eyes closed.

"Get away! Get off her!" Gavin cried. His quick hands grabbed the creature, releasing her from its painful grip.

The creature hissed violently, struggling to free itself, yowling in protest. Turning, Kelly caught a glimpse of thrashing black fur, whiskers, and bared teeth.

Ezra.

The cat must be totally spooked, Kelly thought. *Just like me.*

Gavin tossed the thrashing cat into the hallway, where it darted away, ears flattened, tail held high.

She knew she should thank him, but try as she might, she couldn't force the words out. Instead she gently rubbed her back where Ezra's claws had scratched. It throbbed slightly.

"There's some blood on your shirt. Not much. A few drops," Gavin remarked.

"It's more the sting. His claws don't cause too much damage," she said. "I've had it happen before."

"Do you want to get some Band-Aids or something? Or wash it off?"

"In a minute," she replied, suddenly remembering why she was in Ryan's room.

She lifted the light switch, and the answer was painfully obvious. Ryan wasn't here. He hadn't been here all day. The piles of clean, folded laundry his mother had set on his bed before rushing off to the airport remained undisturbed. His laptop was shut.

She swallowed hard. "If he's not here, where is he?" she cried.

"I don't know," Gavin said.

She hadn't meant to say that aloud. It hadn't been her plan to confide in Gavin.

"Ryan's your *younger* brother, right?"

She nodded. "I just don't understand. Where is he? And Chrissie? They wouldn't just leave me here, alone, unless something bad happened. Right? I mean, you don't think so, right?" She knew she was babbling, but for the moment it just felt good to have someone else there witnessing the craziness. She didn't care if it was Gavin.

"No. I don't think so," he said carefully. He eyed her with concern again, and she wondered why he wasn't looking more concerned himself. True, it wasn't his family, but his friend was gone too. "I told you what I thought, though."

She paused. "You think we did this—with the chanting and the spinning."

"I do."

"You think we brought her back. And then she . . . what?" Her voice sounded shrill even to her own ears, but she just needed him to say it—to say the outrageous things she'd been thinking.

"She was killed too young. Maybe it was an accident. Maybe it wasn't. Either way she was ticked off, you know? It wasn't fair." Gavin blinked quickly for a few seconds. "I think she's after a little justice."

"Justice?" she repeated sharply. "What's just about taking innocent people and . . . doing . . . well, I don't know what! Where *are* they?"

Gavin nervously blinked his eyes again. "I didn't say it made sense."

She looked sideways at him. "And what about you? Why are you still here . . . with me?"

"No idea." He reddened slightly, as if embarrassed. "It'll all be okay."

"Okay? Okay? You think this is okay?" She could hear herself screaming. It felt as if she were watching herself from the other side of the room. As if this scared girl were no longer connected to her. She squeezed her eyes tightly and let the waves of fear run through her body. She felt Gavin's hand lightly pat her shoulder, but she quickly pushed it away. She didn't want him touching her.

She walked across the bedroom, over to Ryan's window. She needed some space. She had to figure out what to do. She peered out. Since she'd come inside, the pace of the snow had picked up. She watched the whiteness blanket the yard, concealing all their footprints. Soon there would be no evidence that she had been there.

She would call her parents. Her dad, this time. He'd be calm and logical. He'd tell her what to do.

She glanced up. Gavin had stepped into the hall, right outside the door. He hovered in the shadows.

She reached around blindly for her cell phone. Where was it? She realized she'd left it behind in the family room.

She pushed past Gavin. She needed to get her phone and call her dad. It felt good to have a plan. Her dad would fix this. Somehow.

Gavin trailed her to the stairs. The slapping of their feet on the wood echoed throughout the quiet house. She paused halfway down, and Gavin tumbled clumsily into her. He grabbed the banister to steady himself.

"What is it?" he demanded.

"Shhhh. Listen."

They both stood silently.

Whispers. Whispered voices from down below.

Her hand gripped the banister so tightly her knuckles grew white. "Who is it?" she asked in a hushed tone.

He shrugged, leaning over to hear.

Faint whispers. In the house.

She took a tentative step. The stair beneath her creaked. She held her breath and stopped.

The voices had a rhythm. A hushed chanting. She listened hard but couldn't make out the words.

What were they chanting?

Then just as suddenly as they'd started, the whispered voices stopped.

She and Gavin waited, frozen. Silence overtook the house once again. The steady gusting of the wind was now the only background noise.

"I want to see," she declared, fear now driving her determination. "I want to see who's speaking." It suddenly seemed more important than anything to find the whispering voices. She scrambled down the stairs, no longer caring how much noise she made. Gavin followed at her heels. Rounding the front foyer, she headed back toward the kitchen and . . .

Everything plunged into total blackness.

Kelly gasped. Her heart thudded. She stood blindly, surrounded by crushing darkness.

"I think we lost the power," Gavin said quietly.

She blinked, trying to adjust her eyes to the darkness. She could hear his shallow, raspy breaths. He was so very close. Her mind flashed back to his hands reaching for Spencer's neck. Squeezing tight. His vacant gaze and strange mutterings.

Would he try to strangle her, too? Here in the dark?

She had to get away. The darkness gave him the

perfect cover to try so many horrible things. She trembled at the thought. She took tiny steps forward, reaching out her arms in search of the wall. She found it and groped along its smooth surface. Slowly she inched her way into the kitchen. Gavin trailed steadily behind her.

Suddenly his hand grabbed her shoulder, and she jumped. "Turn this way," he instructed.

"Don't touch me again," she snapped. She took a giant step away from him. She needed to keep distance between them.

"Whatever," he muttered.

I have to find a flashlight, she thought. She edged her way around the room and bumped into her mother's desk. Tracing its contours with her fingers, she located the bottom drawer and pulled out the emergency flashlight her father kept inside. With a flick of the switch, she blasted a beam of light into Gavin's surprised face.

"Whoa!" He raised his arms in mock surrender.

The melody sounded before she could answer.

She stiffened, listening to the familiar notes. The same sinister eight notes, playing again and again.

Gavin furrowed his thick eyebrows. "Weird song. The same one we heard outside."

She nodded, her eyes locating the phone in the middle of the kitchen counter. They watched the phone glow eerily in the darkness. It played the haunting ringtone over and over.

The phone definitely hadn't been there minutes earlier, when they had come in from outside. She was sure of that.

"Is it yours?" Gavin asked, his eyes trained on the phone too.

She shook her head. "Chrissie's." The phone continued to ring. A spine-tingling summons.

Together, they both stepped toward it, as if being drawn out of the depths of the ocean by a fisherman's line.

"Who's calling?" Kelly whispered. The phone pulsed with light, a tiny strobe in the blackness of the kitchen.

They bent over the counter and gazed at the illuminated caller ID screen. Neither dared touch the phone. "I don't know the number. Do you?" she asked warily.

"No."

The foreboding melody played again.

"Should I answer it?" she asked.

"Yes," he said, his eyes wide.

She wondered if she was making a huge mistake. She reached for the phone. "Hello?"

CHAPTER 16

"Hello?" she repeated into the phone.

For a moment, all she could hear was static. Then a female voice asked shakily, "Who is this?"

Kelly hesitated. She didn't know what to say. Gavin leaned annoyingly close, blatantly curious. She turned slightly, facing the refrigerator, resting the flashlight on the counter. "It's Kelly. Who's this?"

"It's Paige."

"Paige! Is it really you?" Kelly cried. An injection of relief spread through her veins.

"Yes. It is."

"I am so, so happy. I've been searching everywhere for you!" The words flew from her mouth. "Wow! You're okay!"

"I'm sorry."

"Sorry? Why are you sorry?" Kelly asked. She smiled at Gavin and mouthed, "It's Paige!"

He nodded.

"Paige. Paige?" Kelly said into the phone, when her friend didn't answer. "Are you okay? Where are you?"

"No, I'm not." Paige's voice sounded tight. Unnatural.

"What's going on?" The happy warmth of just seconds ago grew cold. "You don't sound like you."

"I need help." The words drew out of her slowly.

"Paige, what's wrong? You're scaring me." Kelly's voice quivered. "Please, tell me."

"She's here."

"Who?" Kelly cried, squeezing the phone in frustration.

"She has me trapped," Paige explained in a hollow tone.

"Who does? Where?"

A burst of static obscured the line, muffling Paige's reply.

"Paige, I didn't hear you! Where are you?" Kelly screamed, pronouncing each word so Paige could better understand.

"I'm in your basement."

Paige was here? In her own house?

"Help me." Paige's voice now a lifeless monotone. "Save me from her. Hurry."

"You're really in my—"

The line cut off.

"Paige? Paige, are you still there?" Kelly didn't bother to hide her desperation.

No answer. Paige was gone.

On the glowing touchpad, she quickly found redial and pressed. She listened as the numbers clicked in. Ringing. The phone kept ringing. Paige wasn't picking up.

Or couldn't pick up.

Someone was down there with her.

Kelly cradled the purple phone in her palm, testing its weight as if checking to be sure it was real. She began to rock slowly. Heel to toe. Back and forth. The rhythm soothed her, allowing her to block all the jumbled thoughts. Heel to toe. Back and forth.

"Where is she?" Gavin asked. He'd picked the flashlight up off the counter and was now shining the light at her face. "Are you okay?"

She stopped rocking and shielded her eyes from the spotlight with her free hand. Her gaze darted toward the door by the desk, hidden in the darkness. "She says she's down there. In the basement."

"So let's go." He turned toward the door.

"No." She reached out and actually touched his arm to stop him.

"Huh? Why?" Shadows danced across his confused face.

"She's not alone. Someone is with her. Someone has her trapped."

"But shouldn't we help her?" Gavin asked. For the first time, she heard panic in his voice.

"Yes, but . . ." One big part of her wanted to race across the kitchen and fling open that door and pull her friend to safety. But then there was that other part of her. The part that had listened to countless "never open the door to strangers" lectures from her parents, the part that had seen those late-night scary movies where opening a door meant walking right into evil, and the part that was *scared*.

Her thoughts were interrupted as a strange whirring that filled the kitchen. Then a beep. And another. In a rush, the lights flooded on and the appliances came back to life.

In the brightness, she immediately knew what to do. Paige was her best friend. She *had* to help her.

She moved quickly to the basement door.

"So we're going down?" Gavin asked, his voice loud. He stood by her side.

"Shh," she warned. "And yes." She had decided.

She peered at the crack at the bottom of the door. No light seeped out of it. The basement was dark, even with the power back on. Her hand rested on the doorknob.

Fear overcame her. She couldn't turn it. What was she walking into? Was she being stupid? Anything could be waiting for her behind that door.

"Weapon," she whispered. "We need a weapon."

Her eyes scanned the area by them. An umbrella stood propped by the back door. It was pointy but seemed silly. She knew there were mops and brooms in the cleaning closet off the back mudroom leading to the garage, but she couldn't imagine what good those would do. She had no idea what she was looking for.

Gavin raised his eyebrows. "You—you think we'll need a weapon?" he stammered.

"I don't know what we'll need," she shot back, her anxiety peaking. "I don't know who is down there."

"Or if it's human," he added quietly.

She froze. He had that intense, disturbing look again. She edged away.

She glanced down at Chrissie's phone, still cradled in her left hand. She pushed the keypad, and it blinked to life. Carefully she dialed the numbers 9-1-1.

Positioning her left thumb over the send button just in case, she twisted the knob. The basement door swung open, and she stepped down into the darkness.

CHAPTER 17

She tentatively took the first step. Her stomach twisted, and she paused. Was she really doing this?

Yes. Yes, she was. She had to help Paige. And Paige might know where her brother was, and Chrissie, and everyone else. *Come on, Kelly,* she coached herself.

Her hand reached for the light switch, but before she could touch it, the lights flashed on themselves and then—

"Surprise!"

Kelly screamed and reeled backward. She dropped the cell phone and frantically reached for the banister. Her knees wobbled from the shock. What was going on?

"Surprise!" the voices yelled again.

She stared dumbfounded at the smiling faces beaming

up at her from the bottom of the stairs. Paige, June, Spencer, Chrissie, Ryan, Spencer's mom, and his brother, Charlie.

"Wh-what?" She couldn't understand what they were all doing in her basement. Together. Looking so . . . happy.

"Happy birthday!" they all cried.

Her brain took a few seconds to compute the meaning of what was going on. Then she noticed the balloons and streamers decorating the usually blah basement.

"Go downstairs." Gavin gave her a gentle nudge from behind.

She glanced over her shoulder and gave him a questioning look. She still was too scared and confused to speak.

"It's a surprise party," he explained. "For your birthday."

"Really?" Her voice came out as a squeak. "Seriously?"

Gavin smiled widely. "Seriously." She noticed that it was the first time she'd seen him smile. His face looked different now. Warmer. Friendlier.

"Get down here!" June commanded good-naturedly. She hurried up the stairs and grabbed Kelly's hand. Kelly let June lead her. She stood surrounded by her friends.

"I had no idea . . ." Her voice trailed off, still amazed.

"Of course, silly," Paige teased. "That's why it's called a *surprise* party."

"We have cupcakes." Charlie, wearing his truck-printed pajamas, tugged at Kelly's pant leg. "And they're chocolate!"

She looked down at him and rumpled his staticky brown hair. "Really? I love cupcakes."

"Sit down, birthday girl," Mrs. Stone, Spencer's mom, said. She led the group to the sofa. Kelly sank into the cushions, letting her body relax for the first time in hours. She took in the display of cupcakes, chips and dip, and hot chocolate on the table in front of them.

"This is amazing." She looked at all her friends, no longer in pajamas but in warm winter clothes, gathered around. Then her eyes stopped at Chrissie, all happy and bubbly. "Wait. I don't get it. You were outside. And then you weren't. And you were acting all strange and wouldn't answer when I called you. . . ." Her gaze moved to Ryan, smirking as he shoved a cupcake into his mouth. "Hey, and you! Why wouldn't you answer me? I was so scared."

"Gotcha!" everyone shrieked at once.

"Huh?" Kelly said.

"We totally scared you," Spencer explained. "You're no

longer the Master of Scares, are you? You were *terrified*."

"We got you good!" Paige sang out, bouncing from foot to foot gleefully.

A joke. It was all a joke, Kelly now realized.

She nodded slowly. "Oh, wow. I was so freaked out." She thought back over the events of the night. "So it was all fake?"

"Yep," June said, sitting next to her. "And you fell for it all."

"I'm a good actor, aren't I?" Chrissie beamed proudly.

"Not as good as I am!" Ryan countered.

"Hey, I taught you everything you know. Who showed you how to do the zombie stare? I'm so good, I should open an acting school," Chrissie bragged.

"But I don't understand. . . ." Kelly tried to quickly tie all the pieces together but couldn't.

"When we saw how bummed you were at not having a party tonight, we came up with the idea of a surprise party. I told Chrissie, and she was cool with it," Paige explained. "She clued in Ryan."

"Then we decided that it was time to scare the Master of Scares," Spencer continued. "But it was Ryan who came up with the most genius idea."

Kelly stared at her little brother. He gloated and reached for his second cupcake. "How?" she asked.

"He showed me the article you were reading earlier about Mary Owens," Chrissie said. "Before the sleepover even started, we came up with a plan."

"We pretended that the summoning of Miss Mary worked," June added.

"Wait, so you didn't see anyone behind me?" Kelly asked.

"Of course not," June scoffed. "And then we started disappearing. Me first. Spencer found this program that made our screens turn that wacky red. Scared you, right?"

"Yeah," she admitted. "But who was Chrissie talking to on the phone?" She turned to the older girl. "You know, when you were acting all sad and weird."

"I should get an Academy Award, don't you think?" Chrissie beamed. "I was talking to Paige. Totally made all that stuff up to play with your mind."

"Actually, I was more awesome. Right, Kel?" Ryan asked. "I mean, you so fell for my zombie routine."

She punched him playfully on the arm. "That was so mean!"

Ryan laughed, and Kelly looked around the room.

That was when she noticed Gavin, standing slightly behind the others. "How does Gavin fit in? I mean, no offense, but I barely even know you."

"That was perfect, I must say." Spencer grinned, clearly pleased with himself. "I had invited Gav to stay over before I even knew about this whole webcam thing. His dad and brother had to go out of town. Anyway, we decided that since you didn't really know him, he could totally mess with you. We really wanted you to believe he was possessed."

"I believed that," she agreed.

Gavin chuckled, and Kelly cringed. "Sorry. You were way creepy. Especially when you came running out of the bushes. What was that about?"

"That wasn't planned," Spencer admitted. "You see, we each made our way over here, one by one, and sneaked into the basement through the side door, so you wouldn't hear us enter the house. Chrissie unlocked it for us. Charlie heard about it and really wanted to come too. And my mom wouldn't let us do all this without an adult, so that's why she is here." Spencer grimaced.

"I played along, but I was always looking out for you, Kelly honey," Mrs. Stone said. Her pale-blue eyes twinkled. Clearly she'd enjoyed herself.

Chrissie took over. "I made the boot prints to nowhere. Then I doubled back on the same prints—not easy, if you want to know—and hid in the mudroom off the kitchen to watch you. But when I saw you wandering aimlessly in the storm outside at night, well, I got scared that you would get hurt or frostbitten or something. We knew we had to get you back inside and to the party."

"So you sent Gavin after me?" she asked.

"Yeah," Gavin continued. "I snuck back out the side door and into the backyard. My appearing was creepy and still kept you scared. I really didn't mean to chase you like that, but when you just took off, I had no choice." He grinned. "You're fast. And boy, was it cold out there."

"And then?" Kelly asked, still working overtime to connect the dots.

"Well, I wasn't expecting the cat attack, that's for sure!"

Ryan and her friends laughed. Ezra's flying leaps were legendary.

"But I did manage to get you to the basement," Gavin explained.

"It helped that I called you," Paige interjected. "I used Mrs. Stone's phone. I figured there was no way you'd recognize her cell number on the caller ID."

Kelly shook her head. "Not at all. You sounded so . . . scared."

"Chrissie's not the only actor in the family, right?" Paige grinned; then her face softened. "And, hey, it's nice to know you'd come save me. You know, if anything ever happened for real."

"Of course," Kelly murmured, nodding at her friend.

"And that's the whole story," June concluded.

"Wow." She was completely in awe. She thought through their complicated plans, then smiled. "I've taught you all well. Good scare. No, excellent scare!"

"Ha-ha," Ryan said, smirking. "You'd think—"

Everyone stopped speaking as the familiar ringtone sounded. Instinctively Kelly froze, still freaked out by the haunting melody. Why was the haunting melody playing again? Her eyes darted about the basement.

Charlie jumped from the sofa and ran to the top of the stairs. He scooped up the little purple phone from where it had fallen on the landing. "Phone's ringing!" he called.

"Give it here." Chrissie hurried over to him.

"The creepy ringtone?" Kelly asked.

"Just put there to mess with you," Paige explained. "Good, huh?"

Kelly exhaled. She had the feeling it would take her a while to stop jumping at every little thing. "Ooh, look. Presents," she cried, suddenly noticing the little pile of packages alongside the sofa.

"Hi, Mrs. Garcia. How are you?" Kelly heard Chrissie greet her mother. "Everything's great here. Storm? Well, it's snowing a lot and all, but it isn't bothering us. We're having a great time." Chrissie smiled down at Kelly and her friends.

Kelly smiled back and began ripping open the gold wrapping paper on a little package. "This is the best birthday surprise ever," she announced. "Even if you all did scare me half to death."

It was after eleven when Spencer, Gavin, and Mrs. Stone, carrying sleeping Charlie, crossed the snowy street to return home. June and Paige trudged over to Paige's house. It was decided that June would spend the night there. The snow was too deep to even walk around the block.

Kelly yawned as she finally pulled open her dresser

drawer for a fresh pair of pajamas. A flash of black fur flew through the air, and she sucked in her breath. Ezra leaped off the top of the dresser once again and scurried out of her bedroom into the dark hallway.

"Good idea!" Kelly called after the cat. "Go bother Ryan."

She was exhausted. Her brother and Chrissie had already gone to sleep. She pulled back her plaid comforter and crawled into her warm bed. Even though the heat had miraculously turned back on, it was still cold upstairs. She snuggled into the sheets and smiled at how badly her friends had scared her. She still had trouble believing it was all a joke.

Rolling onto her side, she turned off her bedside lamp. The darkness was welcome for the first time today. She felt as if she'd come off the school bus a year ago. She groaned as she rolled back over and saw the glow. She stared at the greenish light of her laptop perched on her desk. She didn't feel like getting up. But she knew she should turn it off.

She pulled herself out of bed and wandered over to her desk. Resting her fingers on the keyboard, she squinted at the screen. Their webcam conference session from earlier was still up and running. Spencer and

Gavin's frame still appeared on her monitor.

Her friends, of course, weren't at their computers. The *Avatar* poster behind Spencer's desk filled the screen. Shadows covered the room. Spencer and Gavin were probably asleep.

She paused before logging off. Then she smiled slyly. She'd send an e-mail to the boys. A little something spooky to wake up to. Her fingers began to type.

MISS MARY. MISS MARY. MISS MARY.

She chanted the words under her breath as she typed. She was about to hit send when she glanced up. Her breath caught in her throat.

There, in the corner of Spencer's screen, a figure shimmered. A woman in the shadows. Reaching out. Reaching out to her.

The figure moved closer, gliding toward the screen.

Red dress. Translucent skin pulled tight over protruding bones. A skeletal hand reaching out. Pushing up against the screen, scratching and clawing as if trying to get through. To get out. To escape.

Kelly whimpered, then sucked in her breath. She slammed her finger against the power button on the side of the laptop. In a moment, her screen turned dark.

The ghostly figure was gone.

She remained motionless in her chair. She stared at the screen. Her heart pounded. Had she seen what she thought she'd seen? She shook her head. She couldn't have. It had been a long night. She was overtired. That was it. Definitely overtired.

She inhaled deeply. She had to calm down. Breathe. She had to breathe. She exhaled and then breathed in again. And began to shake.

Peppermint.

The overpowering scent of peppermint. The odor came from her computer. As if it was flowing out of the screen!

She couldn't stop shaking.

The smell. It was so strong.

She thought back on the night. She had never told her friends about smelling the peppermint. And now she realized with horror that they had never mentioned it either. The aroma surrounded her, invading her throat, her nose.

She thought about the words she'd just typed to Spencer.

MISS MARY.

WANT MORE CREEPINESS?

Then you're in luck, because P. J. Night has some more scares for you and your friends!

Kelly searches for her friends all over her house, but doesn't find them until the very end. P. J. Night wants to know . . . are you a better detective? Find all 30 words in this word search! Words can appear up, down, backward, forward, or diagonally.

BASEMENT	ICICLE	PHONE
BURIED	JUNE	PIZZA
CHARLIE	KELLY	POSSESSED
CHRISSIE	LAPTOP	RYAN
DARKNESS	MISS MARY	SCARE
EZRA	NEWSPAPER	SLEEPOVER
FOOTPRINT	PAIGE	SNOW
GAVIN	PARKA	SPENCER
GHOST	PEPPERMINT	VERMONT
HAUNTING	PHILLY	WEBCAM

READY TO SOLVE?
WE DARE YOU!

```
V H X E K E L L Y I T N I R P T O O F Y
A E G T N E M E S A B W E P A R K A S A
R C W B Z H X D S G Y D U Z R Y F H D T
Y L L I H P Q F F G O E E C P A I G E H
S I A I E D S B C V Z C U I O N U U X Y
A T R B P V R G M R Z T Z H S P L L U G
X E N U J P Y I A X M Z H O S C A R E O
B I N R Q T I B C V A F D J E N K O T P
H S S I I P C S B L I P K J S X C Q I E
R S R E E F I X E M A N H W S N I M N P
B I G D A L C O W N M M A S E N G I P P
C R Q F V F L M R W T N U F D E V S J E
G H O S T Z E E U M T O N E K W R S W R
T C S R Z Q V E R M O N T I L S Y M B M
C T N T F O A L U L R A I L K P M A A I
Q W X T P Q W P P D B N N R E A H R W N
P M S E Q L T O K L T K G A E P J Y S T
W J E O D A R K N E S S R H P E U V K W
C L E X D R Q J K S P E N C E R B W J
S K L Y M L A P T O P H O N E V I T E E
```

DID YOU FIND ALL 30 WORDS?
FIND THE ANSWER KEY IN THE FOLLOWING PAGES.

THE ANSWERS YOU SEEK ARE BELOW:

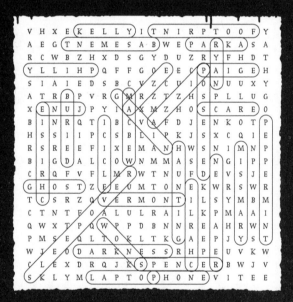

```
V H X E K E L L Y I T N I R P T O O F Y
A E G T N E M E S A B W E P A R K A S A
R C W B Z H X D S G Y D U Z R Y F H D T
Y L L I H P Q F F G O E C P A I G E H
S I A I E D S B C V Z C U I O N U U X Y
A T R B P V R G M R Z T Z H S P L L U G
X E N U J P Y I A M M Z H O S C A R E O
B I N R Q T I B C V A F D J E N K O T P
H S S I I P C S B L I P K J S X C Q I E
R S R E E F I X E M A N H W S N I M N P
B I G D A L C O W N M M A S E N G I P J
C R Q F V F L M R W T N U F D E V S J E
G H O S T Z E U M T O N E K W R S W R
T C S R Z O V E R M O N T I L S Y M B M
C T N F O A L U L R A I L K P M A A I
Q W X T P Q W P P D B N N R E A H R W N
P M S E Q L T O K L T K G A E P J Y S T
W J E O D A R K N E S S R H P E U V K W
C L E X D R Q J K S P E N C E R B W J V
S K L Y M L A P T O P H O N E V I T E E
```

YOU'RE INVITED TO . . .
CREATE YOUR OWN SCARY STORY!

Do you want to turn your sleepover into a creepover? Telling a spooky story is a great way to set the mood. P. J. Night has written a few sentences to get you started. Fill in the rest of the story on the lines provided and have fun scaring your friends.

You can also collaborate with your friends on this story by taking turns. Have everyone at your sleepover sit in a circle. Pick one person to start. She will add a sentence or two to the story, cover what she wrote with a piece of paper, leaving only the last word or phrase visible, and then pass the story to the next girl. Once everyone has taken a turn, read the scary story you created together aloud!

My last vacation was hardly a vacation—it was more like a nightmare. What had been advertised as a gorgeous hotel looked more like the set of a horror film. The windows shook in the wind, and the rooms smelled old

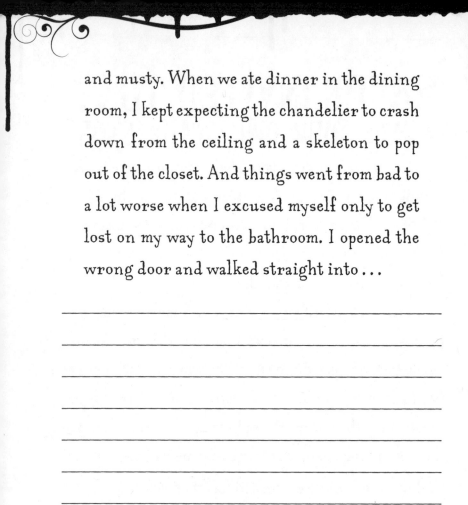

and musty. When we ate dinner in the dining room, I kept expecting the chandelier to crash down from the ceiling and a skeleton to pop out of the closet. And things went from bad to a lot worse when I excused myself only to get lost on my way to the bathroom. I opened the wrong door and walked straight into . . .

_____

_____

_____

_____

_____

_____

_____

_____

_____

_____

_____

_____

_____

_____

_____

_____

_____

_____

_____

_____

_____

_____

_____

_____

_____

_____

_____

_____

_____

_____

_____

_____

THE END

The Show Must Go On!

PROLOGUE

"You're fired, Ms. Wormhouse!" barked the principal of Thomas Jefferson Middle School. "And we are canceling your play, forever." He leaned forward on his desk and locked his piercing gaze on the eyes of the woman seated across from him.

Mildred P. Wormhouse stared back, her dark, sunken eyes blazing with anger. "Canceling?" she sneered. "I've worked on this play my entire life. Fire me if you wish, but the play will be performed!" Her curly shock of jet-black hair shook with every word.

"Maybe somewhere else," the principal said, standing now, his tone growing increasingly impatient. "But it will *not* be performed here, at this school—ever! Do you have such little regard for human life?"

"Bah!" Wormhouse snarled with a dismissive gesture. She stood, her long black coat flapping near her ankles as she turned away from the principal.

"A girl died last night, Ms. Wormhouse," the principal said through clenched teeth. "On this school's stage, playing the lead in the play you wrote and directed. And that was only the final terrible incident. The rehearsals have been marred with accidents and other troubles. In fact, strange things have been happening at this school since the day you arrived. I've heard rumors that your play is cursed. I'm not a superstitious man, but I'm starting to believe them. I've seen to it that every last copy of the play has been thrown out."

Wormhouse turned slowly back toward the principal. "Cursed?" she hissed, her lips curling in a slight smile. "You really shouldn't let your fears get the best of you—"

"This conversation is over," the principal interrupted. He marched across the room and threw the door open. A roar erupted from the angry mob of parents and teachers who had gathered outside the office.

"There she is!" one man shouted.

"It's her fault," a woman yelled. "Her play!"

Wormhouse squirmed out the door and through the

crowd; her head bent low, her black coat flapping with every step like a cape. She headed for a hallway that led to the front door of the school. Pausing, she turned back toward the irate crowd.

"You may fire me," Wormhouse cried. "But you cannot stop my play. The show must go on." Then she turned down the hall toward the front door of the building.

"Good riddance!" someone in the mob shouted.

"Don't ever show your face around here again!" screamed someone else.

Wormhouse disappeared from view around a corner in the hallway. But instead of turning left toward the front door, she turned right—toward the school's auditorium, where her play had opened last night and where the girl playing the lead had died.

Walking quickly down the center aisle of the empty auditorium, glancing back over her shoulder every few steps, Wormhouse made her way backstage. Spotting an old steamer trunk, she shoved a pile of costumes off the top, then yanked open the lid. Inside the trunk were props from all the years of school productions. She reached into an inner pocket of her long coat and pulled out the last remaining copy of her play. Burying it beneath the mound of props inside the trunk, she gently lowered the lid.

Seething, her breath now labored, she repeated her vow, muttering to herself, "The show must go on."

CHAPTER 1

PRESENT DAY . . .

Felix Gomez shoved aside a rack of hanging costumes and looked around backstage in the auditorium of Thomas Jefferson Middle School. He had been the drama teacher at the school for a few years now, and he really wanted to do something different this year. He would put on a new play, he decided, not just the same old, same old. Tasked with revitalizing the school's sagging theater program, he had spent weeks reading new plays, but so far nothing had grabbed him.

Then it started—an inexplicable urge, at first vague, then specifically focused on the backstage area of the school's auditorium. Gomez had no idea why he was drawn back there, but somehow he knew that the obsessed, panicky state of mind that had gripped him for days now could only be eased by searching there.

In a dark corner, buried under long-discarded props and scenery, Gomez spotted an old steamer trunk. He knew instantly that this was what had been calling out to him, driving his obsession.

Throwing open the trunk, his hand—feeling as if it were being controlled by some other force—reached in. He pushed aside old props and grasped a stack of pages, bound together by three rusted metal fasteners.

Blowing off a cloud of dust from the top, Gomez read the title of the play. *The Last Sleepover.* He slammed the lid of the truck and sat down in the dim light to read the play. It looked like it had been typed on a typewriter. "This is it!" he said to himself before he had read a single word. "I know it. This the play I have been looking for!"

But as Gomez read the play, the force that had driven him here battled with a new feeling, one of inexplicable anxiety and horror. The more he read, the more intense the feeling of dread grew. Somewhere deep inside, he knew there was something wrong with the play.

"No. This isn't right," he muttered to himself, staring at the script, fighting the urge that had been driving him. "I can't do it. I won't put on this play."

Gomez stood and hurried to the trunk to put the play back where he'd found it. Feeling a sudden sharp pain in his ankle, he tripped over a low stool that he was certain had not been there a moment before. He crashed to the ground and clutched his right leg in pain.

Bree Hart paced up and down the center aisle of the Thomas Jefferson Middle School auditorium and nervously twirled her curly dark hair around her finger. The meeting for students interested in auditioning for this year's play was about to begin. The auditorium was filled with energized students, busily chatting, eager to know what the play would be about. Bree had never felt this way before. She was equal parts excited and terrified.

"Trying to wear a hole through the carpet?" asked someone from behind Bree.

She spun around to face her best friend, Melissa Hwang.

"Oh, Lis, I'm so glad you came," Bree said, hugging her friend. "I'm so nervous!"

"I told you I would come," Melissa replied. "You think you're the only one who wants to be in the play?"

"I can't believe the time is here!" Bree exclaimed. "I've dreamed about acting for as long as I can remember, but I've never had the guts to actually audition for anything."

"Good for you, Bree," Melissa said. "You don't want to spend the rest of your life living in Megan's shadow, do you?"

Bree thought about her older sister, Megan, who had gotten the lead in every school play since the third grade. Melissa was right. It was time for Bree to take center stage.

"I wonder what's keeping Mr. Gomez," Bree said. "He was supposed to be here, like, ten minutes ago."

"Anxious to begin your new life in the theater?" Melissa quipped.

"Something like that, yeah."

Just then the auditorium door swung open.

"And here he is," Melissa said.

But instead of Mr. Gomez, a tall woman strode slowly down the center aisle, carrying a large briefcase. As she passed, Bree noticed the dark circles around her eyes and her jet-black hair.

"Who's that?" Bree whispered to Melissa. Melissa shrugged.

The woman climbed the steps to the stage and walked out to the center. Adjusting the single microphone that had been set up for the auditions, she spoke in a surprisingly pleasant and gentle voice.

"Ladies and gentlemen, if I may have your attention please," the woman began. "My name is Ms. Hollows. Unfortunately, Mr. Gomez had an accident yesterday afternoon. He broke his leg and will not be able to direct the play. I will be your substitute drama teacher for the next few weeks, and I will be directing this year's play."

A buzz went through the crowd. Mr. Gomez was one of the most popular teachers at the school—many of the students sitting in the auditorium that afternoon were there because of him. Bree could hear the sighs of disappointment throughout the room.

"I was really looking forward to working with Mr. Gomez," she moaned.

"Me too," Melissa concurred.

Having given the students a moment to digest this unexpected bit of news, Ms. Hollows continued. "The play I have selected for us to perform is called *The Last Sleepover*."

Ms. Hollows opened her briefcase and pulled out

a thick stack of papers. "I have copies of the play for those interested in auditioning," she said, placing the pile onto a stool next to where she stood. "Please form a line and come up and take a copy. You are to read the play this weekend and decide which role you would like to audition for. Auditions will be held after school on Monday. I will see you then."

One by one the students walked onto the stage, each taking a copy of the play. Bree felt a thrill run through her when she turned and looked out into the sea of empty seats in the auditorium. She pictured herself in the lead role, standing before a cheering crowd, taking her bows, curtain call after curtain call.

"Are you all right, Gabrielle?" someone asked, startling Bree back to reality.

"Oh, yes, sorry, Ms. Hollows," Bree said sheepishly as she picked up a copy of the play and hurried off the stage. Only after she left the stage did Bree realize that she had never told Ms. Hollows her name, especially not her real name. Everyone, except her mother sometimes, called Gabrielle Hart by her nickname, Bree. *How did she know?* Bree wondered.

"Weird," she said under her breath.

"What's weird?" Melissa asked, falling into step with Bree.

"Somehow Ms. Hollows knows my name already," Bree replied. "And not just my nickname. My *real* name. No one ever guesses that Bree is short for Gabrielle."

"Well, you are one of the top students in the school," Melissa pointed out. "Maybe she did some research about who she might want in the play."

"Yeah, maybe," Bree replied, not really believing what Melissa had just said. "Anyway, I'll see you later, Lis."

Melissa waved as she ran toward her bus. "Bye."

Later that evening Bree curled up in a big, overstuffed chair in her living room and opened the script. "*The Last Sleepover*," she read aloud. "By M. P. Wormhouse." Bree read on.

The play told the story of a house haunted by the ghost of a girl who had always wanted to attend a sleepover. As Bree got further and further into the script, she began to read aloud:

"(CARRIE'S BEDROOM IN HER NEW HOUSE. THE HOUSE IS AN OLD VICTORIAN THAT

IS BEING REMODELED AND HAS AN ABANDONED, HAUNTED FEEL TO IT. THE TWO OTHER GIRLS WHO HAVE GATHERED AT THE SLEEPOVER ARE HUDDLED AROUND CARRIE. CARRIE SITS IN THE MIDDLE, WITH HER BLACK CAT ON HER LAP.)

CARRIE: Thanks for coming tonight. Ready to hear something creepy?

RACHEL (EXCITED): Awesome!

LAURA (NERVOUS): What?

(CARRIE LEANS IN CLOSE TO THE GIRLS TO TELL THEM HER SECRET.)

CARRIE: Years ago, a girl named Millie lived in this house. She was a shy girl who kept to herself most of the time. Although she didn't have a lot of friends, the thing she wanted most in the world was to be invited to a sleepover. She dreamed about hanging out all night in her pajamas, in a sleeping bag, telling stories, eating, laughing . . .

RACHEL: Having pillow fights.

CARRIE: Having pillow fights. All the cool stuff we're doing tonight. Anyway, Millie waited and waited until finally a girl named Gabby had a sleepover. Gabby invited every girl in her class--every girl, that is, except Millie.

RACHEL: Mean!

LAURA: Poor Millie.

CARRIE: I know. Gabby was a bit of a bully. Millie begged her to be allowed to come to the sleepover, but every time she asked, Gabby said no.

RACHEL: Why?

CARRIE: I don't know, but that sleepover was only the first of many. At least twice a year, Gabby had a huge sleepover, and each time all the girls in the class were invited except Millie. Then Millie got sick. Very sick. In time she died, having never gotten her wish to attend a sleepover.

LAURA: That is so sad!

RACHEL: It is. But where does the creepy part come in?

CARRIE: I'm getting there. Millie's family moved shortly after her death and sold this house to another family. That family had a little girl. One night, that girl had a sleepover. And that's when the haunting began. Lights flickered on and off, and a strange face appeared outside her bedroom window.

RACHEL: Yeah, right. You're making this up.

CARRIE: I'm not. Promise. I heard the whole story from the old woman who lives next door. She remembers Millie. They went to school together a very long time ago.

LAURA: Creepy.

CARRIE: It gets creepier. Every girl who has had a sleepover in this house since Millie died has experienced the same things. It's said that Millie's ghost haunts this house and will keep haunting it until she is allowed into a sleepover!

RACHEL: Well, she's not getting into this one!

CARRIE: Nope. Not if I have anything to say about it.

(LIGHTS GO OUT ALL OF A SUDDEN. GIRLS SCREAM WITH FEAR.)"

As Bree continued to read the play, she began to get more and more creeped out.

"This play is so dark . . . and there's something else I can't quite put my finger on," she murmured to herself when she had finished reading. She set the script aside. "I wish Ms. Hollows was putting on a happy play, with singing or something. Maybe I should wait to

478

audition next year." But that didn't make Bree feel any better either.

Bree recalled her English teacher describing the feeling of being outside your comfort zone. That the best way to learn and grow was to do something that felt difficult or unfamiliar. Maybe this was the play for her, and maybe she was destined to play Carrie.

"Whatcha got there?"

"Oh, hey, Megan," Bree said absentmindedly, not bothering to look up at her sister. "It's a copy of the play we're putting on this year."

"Are you seriously thinking of auditioning?" Megan asked, unable to stifle a giggle. "The shy, fly-on-the-wall, always-stay-in-background Bree wants to step into the spotlight?"

"You're always such a drama queen, Megan," Bree replied. "It's just a play. It's just an audition. Are you nervous that you aren't the only one in this family with acting talent?"

"Okay, okay, don't get all riled up," Megan shot back. "I'm just teasing you. So, what's the play about?"

Bree described the strange story of *The Last Sleepover* to her sister.

"Sounds creepy," Megan said when Bree had finished recounting the plot.

"It really is," Bree said, hoping to get Megan's advice about acting. "Just reading it gives me a really weird feeling. Have you ever been in a play like this? You know, where it just gets under your skin?"

"That's nuts," Megan replied with a laugh. "It's just a play. It's just acting, you know, make-believe. I hate to break it to you, but there is no such thing as the boogeyman, or ghosts, or other silly stuff like that. You know what I think?"

"Enlighten me," Bree said.

"It's nerves," Megan said. "You might just not be cut out for the stage."

"Thanks for the sisterly advice!" Bree shouted as her sister left the room. Just when she thought Megan might be of help, she acted like, well, like Megan. "You know what I think? I think you just don't want to share the spotlight with me. Well, guess what? I *am* auditioning and I *will* get the lead!"

Bree picked up the script and stormed off to her room. She would show Megan!

But that night, as Bree drifted off to sleep, she had to

admit to herself that she did feel nervous. She couldn't shake the haunting presence of the play and its characters. They felt so real, as if they had entered her life, not as words on a written page but as real people, including a very real-seeming ghost.

She spent the night, tossing and turning, her dreams blending with her waking thoughts. It was the first of many restless nights.

CHAPTER 2

Bree was distracted during her classes all day on Monday. She could focus on one thing and one thing only—the audition. Each class period seemed like it lasted for three hours. She couldn't wait for the school day to be over so she could finally get her big chance.

When the last bell rang, Bree raced to the auditorium. She couldn't decide what she felt more: excited or nervous. She decided it was pretty much a tie. Reaching the auditorium, she took a deep breath, opened the door, and walked in.

"Bree!" Melissa called out as soon as Bree had stepped into the auditorium. She waved from the front, up near the edge of the stage. "Here!"

Bree hurried down the center aisle to join her friend.

"What did you think of the script?" Melissa asked. "Wasn't it spooky?"

"It totally creeped me out," said Bree. "I wanted to put it down, but it was like something forced me to keep reading."

"I know, I know!" Melissa exclaimed. "That Wormhouse must have been some kind of writer. I had to keep going until I got to the end . . . like, *had* to keep reading, not just because I wanted to. And the whole time I kept thinking, 'I really want to be in the play . . . but *this* play?' But then I got such a strong urge to do it, I have to at least try out.

"I'm going to read for the part of Rachel, Carrie's best friend," Melissa continued. "I need to set my sights on something I think I can handle."

"I'm going for Carrie, Lis," Bree said. "It's time for me to jump into the deep end."

"How cool would it be if we got to play best friends in the play?" Melissa squealed with excitement.

"Yeah, well, that's not going to happen," said someone right beside them. Bree didn't even have to turn her head to know who had spoken. It was Tiffany O'Brian, one of the most popular—and snobbiest—girls in the school.

"Really?" Melissa replied. "And why is that?"

"Because *I'm* getting the lead," Tiffany replied. "This audition is a waste of time. I'll be playing Carrie. This reading is merely a formality."

Bree never ceased to be amazed by the size of Tiffany's ego and her boundless sense of entitlement.

"Just because you've played the lead before doesn't mean you'll be the lead in this one," Bree pointed out.

"Well, look who's speaking up," Tiffany taunted. "Little Miss Wallflower, never dances at a party, never says two words. And you are suddenly going to get the lead. I think if anything you're more suited to play the ghost."

"Leave her alone, Tiffany," Melissa chimed in. "She's allowed to audition just like you are."

"Waste your time if you like, Wallflower," Tiffany said, tossing back her wavy blond hair. "But the part is mine." Then she turned and walked to the other side of the auditorium.

"She's the worst," Melissa said when Tiffany had gone.

"Must be nice being Miss Perfect," Bree added. "I wonder how it feels. Maybe I should ask my sister."

The door to the auditorium swung open, and Ms. Hollows walked down the aisle and up onto the stage.

"Ladies and gentlemen, did we all enjoy the script?" she asked, scanning the auditorium from one side to the other.

Murmurs, grunts, and nods of agreement passed through the assembled students.

"Very well then," she said. "Let's begin. Will those auditioning for the role of Carrie please line up to my left, here on the stage?"

This is it, Bree thought. *No turning back now.* She joined four other girls up on the stage. Tiffany, seeming to be in no hurry, was last in line. *She probably thinks she'll watch the rest of us, then go last and blow us all away,* Bree thought as she watched the first girl walk over to Ms. Hollows in the center of the stage. *And who knows? Maybe she's right.*

Bree glanced at the girl performing a scene, but she really didn't hear any of the lines. Her focus was locked on the script and the lines she was going to read.

"Next," Ms. Hollows called when the first girl had finished. Bree swallowed hard and walked briskly to center of the stage.

"And which scene have you chosen, Gabrielle?" Ms. Hollows asked. This time Bree was less startled when the drama teacher used her full name. She figured Melissa must have been onto something yesterday. *She must have looked me up in the school records,* she thought.

"I'm going to do Carrie's monologue during the 'floating objects' scene," Bree answered.

"Very well. Begin."

Bree had thought about who Carrie was. She wanted to become another person, not just be herself reading the lines. Megan was wrong. Acting was more than just pretending. She was going to *become* Carrie. Bree began:

```
I told you. This house is haunted by
the girl who died before she ever got
invited to a sleepover. Her name was
Millie, and now she shows up every
time someone has a sleepover in this
house. I feel kinda sorry for her,
but she is a ghost. And who wants a
ghost at their sleepover? I know, I
know, it sounds nuts that I'm stand-
ing here talking about a ghost like
she's just some girl who lives in the
neighborhood, but somehow I think
she's really connected to this house.
Well, it's my house now, not hers, and
she's just not invited. End of story.
I know you don't believe me about
Millie, but don't be surprised if--
```

Instinctively, Bree paused onstage, as the stage directions called for the girls at the sleepover to laugh and throw pillows at Carrie. Then a hairbrush and a small handheld mirror on the dresser float up into the air. The brush moves in long, even strokes. The mirror remains stationary. Suddenly a face appears in the mirror—and only in the mirror—the face of a young girl brushing her long jet-black hair. All the characters scream, except for Carrie.

After the brief pause, Bree continued with the lines:

```
I told you! I told you the ghost is
real. Millie, is that you? If so, you
are not welcome! This sleepover is
for the living only!
```

This was the moment Bree was waiting for in the audition. She was to pretend to be horrified as the brush stops moving and both the brush and mirror drop to the ground, the glass in the mirror shattering all over the stage. Then Bree let out her best horror movie scream.

"Thank you, Gabrielle," Ms. Hollows said when the scene was over. "Next!"

Bree left the stage and took a seat in the front row. She could feel the adrenaline that had fueled her audition still coursing through her.

She then watched as two other girls auditioned for the

role of Carrie. Although Tiffany did a good job, Bree was confident it was no better than the audition she had given. She suddenly felt sure of herself, thinking that she could really do this, that she was as good as anyone up there.

Auditions for the role of Rachel were next. Three girls tried out, including Melissa. When Melissa had finished, she rushed over and sat next to Bree.

"You were great!" Bree said.

"So were you!" Melissa echoed. "That was quite a scream. You were way better than Tiffany any old day."

One by one, Ms. Hollows called out the rest of the roles, and groups of students went up and read. When everyone had auditioned, Ms. Hollows spoke into the microphone.

"Thank you all," she said. "The cast list will be posted tomorrow." As Bree and Melissa got up to leave, Ms. Hollows brushed past them. She turned back, looked Bree right in the eye, and whispered, "The play has been waiting for you." Then she hurried from the auditorium.

"What was that?" Melissa asked, seeing that her friend was obviously shaken.

"I—I don't know," Bree murmured. "Does that mean I got the lead?"

CHAPTER 3

Bree lay awake in bed, staring at the ceiling. She turned her head and glanced at her alarm clock. It read two thirty.

Will I ever fall asleep? she wondered. She couldn't get Ms. Hollow's words out of her mind. *The play has been waiting for you.* What in the world did that mean?

She recalled the eerie feeling she'd gotten when she first read the play. As much as she wanted to put it down, another part of her felt drawn to the play. She felt as if she had to audition, and now she might actually be getting the lead. *Is that what Ms. Hollows meant?*

Bree looked over at the clock again. 2:35. Rolling over onto her side so she couldn't see the clock, she forced her eyes closed. Much to her surprise, she dozed off.

When the alarm went off at six thirty the next

morning, Bree woke with a start. She was confused for a moment about where she was exactly. She knew she had been dreaming—deep, intense dreams—but she couldn't remember anything about them. Realizing that she was still safe in her own bed, she threw off the covers and started to get ready for school.

"Today's the day," she murmured to herself as she slipped on her bathrobe. She didn't totally expect to get the lead, but just for fun, she imagined what it would be like to take her bow on opening night. She was stretching her arms way out and bending over when she accidentally knocked into the small handheld mirror sitting on her dresser. It shattered on the floor.

"Gabrielle, is everything okay?" her mom shouted from downstairs.

"Yes, everything's fine!" Bree replied.

Just seven years of bad luck, that's all, she thought as she quickly swept up the shattered pieces. She then headed downstairs for breakfast, her delusions of grandeur trailing behind her.

As she entered the school building a short while later, Bree glanced quickly at the time on her cell phone. She still had a few minutes before homeroom, so she dashed to the auditorium. Stepping up to the bulletin board outside the door, she took a deep breath and scanned the board. Nothing! No cast list yet. She'd have to wait.

Struggling to pay attention in her first class, Bree bolted from her seat when the bell rang. Navigating the hallways, cutting and skipping around past people like a quarterback on a football field, she hurried to the auditorium. There she found a crowd of students gathered in front of the bulletin board.

Before she could reach the board, Bree spotted Melissa, who shrieked, "You got it! You got it!"

Bree squirmed through the crowd and shoved her face up to the board. There, hanging by a pushpin, was the cast list. Next to the name "Carrie" it said "Gabrielle Hart."

Bree was stunned. Her wish had come true! She had gotten the lead!

"And I got Rachel!" Melissa added, pointing to her own name on the list, right below Bree's.

"I—I can't believe this," Bree said, for a moment not knowing whether to celebrate or to run and hide.

"If you think *you* can't believe it, wait until Tiffany finds out!" Melissa said.

"Wait until I find out what?"

Tiffany shoved her way to the front of the crowd. Her eyes opened wide and she pursed her lips tightly together as she read down the list. "Ugh. This is so wrong!" she whined.

"What's wrong about it, Tiffany?" Melissa asked. "You auditioned; Bree auditioned. She got the part."

"But I am so much better than her," Tiffany complained. "I have to be in this play."

"But you are in the play," Melissa pointed out. "You've been cast as Millie, the ghost who haunts Carrie's sleepover. It looks like *you're* more suited to play the ghost." She caught Bree's eye and winked, holding back a giggle at her own joke.

"It'll be fun to work together, Tiffany," Bree said. In a weird way she felt sorry for Tiffany. It meant so much to her to play the lead.

"I don't need your pity, Wallflower," Tiffany barked. Then she turned and stalked away from the crowd.

"See you at rehearsal, Tif!" Melissa called after her.

"Lis, don't," Bree said. "The more upset you make her, the more she's going to take it out on me."

"Oh please, Bree," Melissa said as the crowd began to break up and head off to their classes. "She's got to grow up. She can't always get everything she wants. You won that role fair and square."

"I wonder," Bree replied, her thoughts drifting back to the previous day. *The play has been waiting for you.*

"What do you mean?" Melissa asked.

"What? Oh, nothing. I've got to get to class. I'll see you at rehearsal."

"See you at rehearsal . . . *Carrie!*" Melissa called out.

"Good-bye, *Rachel!*" Bree shouted back. She was thrilled that her best friend would be there with her every step of the way. But there would still be Tiffany to deal with, not to mention the play itself.

At the first rehearsal the next afternoon, Bree made her way to the auditorium. Stepping inside, she found a bunch of students up on the stage, hard at work putting together the set for the show.

Many plays had been put on in this auditorium over the four decades since the middle school had opened. And so it was no problem for the students who had volunteered to work behind the scenes on the play to rummage through old scenery and props to make a new set.

The main set for the play was Carrie's bedroom. Bree stared at the stage, watching the set decorators hard at work. They had been at it for only a little while, but she could see that when it was completed, it really would look as if Carrie lived in a haunted house. The walls of Carrie's bedroom, which now stood stacked in a row waiting to be set up, were cracked and peeling. Cobwebs dangled from the corners.

A dusty, damaged chandelier sat on the stage, waiting to be hung. When it was fully wired, it would flicker on and off, as offstage, a student operated a light switch set up to control the chandelier.

A spotlight was being set up. It would be placed outside a fake window built into one of the walls. Turning this spotlight on and off quickly would create the illusion of lightning flashing outside during a thunderstorm scene.

On the back side of the window, a pair of tattered old shutters hung loosely. Poles attached to the bottom of these shutters would allow unseen students backstage to flap them during the storm scene, as if the wind were fiercely blowing them back and forth against the house. An old piece of tin with a handle on the bottom hung backstage. When a student shook the tin sheet, it sounded like thunder.

Bree smiled widely, picturing all these elements coming together on the finished set to create Carrie's bedroom—*her* bedroom.

"Boo!"

Bree jumped, startled by Melissa's sudden entrance.

"Don't sneak up on a person in a haunted house," Bree scolded her best friend. "Even if it's not finished yet. Don't you know anything?"

"I know that Tiffany is still sulking," Melissa replied.

Bree turned to face the back of the room and saw Tiffany sitting by herself, flipping through her copy of the play, shaking her head in disapproval.

Ms. Hollows entered the auditorium and hurried down the center aisle. She paused at the foot of the stage for a moment, taking in the vista of Carrie's bedroom. Then, giving a quick nod of approval, she climbed the stairs and walked out to center stage.

"Ladies and gentlemen," she began. The buzz of excited conversation that had been humming through the auditorium stopped instantly. "I thank you all again for volunteering to be a part of this play. Thank you to the set decorators and technical volunteers. Now, may I have all the actors up onstage, please?"

"Here we go, Bree!" Melissa said excitedly as the two made their way onto the stage with the rest of the actors, including Tiffany, playing the ghost; the boy playing Carrie's elderly neighbor; and the boy and girl playing Carrie's parents, as well as a few others.

"Yeah, here we go," Bree echoed, still unable to shake the twin feelings of excitement and nervousness.

"Ready to put on a fantastic play, everyone?" Ms. Hollows addressed the cast. The actors on stage nodded, some more vigorously than others. Bree was somewhere in the middle. Tiffany's eyes were glued to the floor.

"All right then," Ms. Hollows continued. "Let's start from the top. Scene one. Rachel, Laura, and Carrie. Places, please."

Bree, Melissa, and Dara Marinelli, the girl who'd been chosen to play Laura, sat in a circle in the middle of the stage. They began rehearsing the scene.

> RACHEL: Nice, Carrie. The place looks like it was decorated by a wrecking ball!

CARRIE: Cute. You know we only moved in a few weeks ago. My family and I haven't had a chance to fix it up yet. I just couldn't wait to have my first sleepover. It helps to make it feel like home.

LAURA: Yeah, if your home's been condemned!

CARRIE: Ha-ha-ha! Come on, you guys. We should--

(SUDDENLY LIGHTNING FLASHES AND THUNDER RUMBLES.)

LAURA: Eiii!

CARRIE: Laura?

LAURA: Sorry, I'm just a little afraid of thunder. I--

(THE THUNDER SOUNDS AGAIN . . . LOUDER THIS TIME. LAURA SCOOTS OVER CLOSER TO CARRIE. SUDDENLY THE CHANDELIER OVERHEAD FLICKERS ON AND OFF, AGAIN AND AGAIN.)

RACHEL: Okay, now I'm officially creeped out. I--

CARRIE: Look!

(CARRIE POINTS TO THE CHANDELIER. A FLASH OF LIGHTNING REVEALS THAT THE CHANDELIER IS SHAKING UNCONTROLLABLY. EVERYONE SCREAMS.)

"Okay, let's take a break, everyone," Ms. Hollows called out. "Very good start."

As the girls in the cast sat down on the edge of the stage to get their notes from Ms. Hollows, the lights in the auditorium began to flicker again. But this time it was not just the stage lights that flashed on and off. Every light in the room twinkled.

"Please leave the lights on!" Ms. Hollows shouted impatiently to the technical crew backstage.

"It's not us, Ms. Hollows!" Tyler Lahari, the boy running the lights, replied, sticking his head out from backstage. "We didn't touch the lights that time!"

Then the entire auditorium went completely dark.

CHAPTER 4

"Flashlights!" Ms. Hollows shouted out.

Several members of the backstage crew came running out with their flashlights blazing.

"I'm going to see if I can find out what's going on with the lights. Perhaps the whole school has lost power," Ms. Hollows said, and left the auditorium.

"Great, now what do we do?" asked Bree.

"I have an idea," Melissa said. "Why don't we sit in a circle and pretend this is a real sleepover?"

"We could even tell ghost stories to get us in the mood," Tiffany added. "Unless, of course, you can't handle it, Wallflower."

"I'm fine," Bree said. "I guess it can only help us get more deeply into our characters."

As the backstage crew settled into the front row of the auditorium, the girls onstage flipped on their flashlights and sat on their pillows.

"I'll go first," Melissa said. "Here's one I heard at summer camp.

"A girl went to a school dance. She was kinda shy and was sitting in a corner when a nice-looking boy came over and asked her if she wanted to dance. No one else had even come near her, so she jumped at the chance.

"The girl was surprised that she had never seen the boy at school before. He told her that he used to go to the school a few years earlier but had moved away and that he always tried to come back for the school dances, since he liked them so much and they always brought back so many good memories for him.

"The two danced every dance, and soon it was time to leave. The boy offered to walk the girl home, saying that her house was on the way to his house anyway. During the walk, the girl got cold, and the boy offered her his school jacket, which had his name stitched onto the front. He draped it over her shoulders, and she felt warmer right away.

"When they reached the girl's house, the boy kissed

her good night and went on his way. Once inside the door, the girl realized that the boy's school jacket was still on her shoulders.

"She turned to yell out to him, but he was nowhere to be seen. It had been only a minute since he'd left, but the street was now dark and empty.

"Then the girl remembered that while they were walking, the boy had mentioned where he lived. She hurried to his house, which was only about ten minutes away. When she arrived, the girl stepped up to the front door and rang the bell.

"A woman answered the door. The girl asked if the boy was home, figuring he had to be. Where else would he have gone? The woman's eyes filled with tears as she explained that the boy was her son and that he had died three years earlier.

"'But that's impossible!' the girl exclaimed. 'I just saw him at the school dance. In fact, he lent me his jacket. Here it is!'

"The woman took the coat and hugged it tightly as tears flowed from her eyes. 'Thank you for return-ing this,' she said. 'My son died due to an accident at a school dance three years ago. I've wanted his school jacket as a memento, but the people at the school said they never found it. Thank you for bringing it home!'"

The girls onstage breathed out a collective sigh. Each girl, without even realizing it, had slid off her pillow and was clutching it tightly.

"That was great," Bree said to Melissa.

"Pretty creepy," Dara added. "I heard one once that my cousin told when my family went up to my aunt and uncle's cabin by the lake. We were sitting around a campfire, and my cousin told us the story of a school tour group on a trip to Colonial Williamsburg.

"A small group of kids got separated from the main group and found themselves in front of an old house that looked like it hadn't been touched since actual colonial times.

"'This is not on the tour,' one of the friends said. 'I don't think we should go in.'

"'Come on,' said another. 'The tour is boring. Maybe we'll find something cool in there.'

"The group slowly pushed open the creaky old front door and stepped inside. The door slammed shut behind them loudly, startling everyone in the group. Then a man dressed in full colonial costume stepped into the entryway.

"'Good day to you,' the man said. 'Welcome to my home. My name is Jeremiah Hobson.'

"'I thought you said that this house wasn't on the tour,' one friend whispered to another.

'It's not supposed to be. I guess they added it or something.'

"As Jeremiah Hobson led the group on a tour of the house, he described the day-to-day activities of his daily life in colonial times. The friends were all impressed by his detailed descriptions.

"'This guy's the best actor yet,' one friend whispered.

"'Yeah, but you'd think they would clean the house up before they took people on a tour,' said another. 'This place is a filthy wreck.'

"Just as the tour ended, the kids heard the front door burst open.

"'Hey! Who's in here?' someone shouted.

"The kids ran toward the voice and found themselves face-to-face with a police officer. 'What are you kids doing in here?' he asked them as he stepped inside.

"'We were taking the tour,' one of the students explained.

"'The tour?' the officer replied. 'What tour? This

house has been closed up and condemned for years.'

"'But what about Mr. Hobson, the tour guide?'

"'Hobson? Jeremiah Hobson?' the officer asked.

"'Yeah, that's him.'

"'Jeremiah Hobson lived in this house two hundred years ago! You say you saw him?'

"'Yeah, he's right over—'

"The kids all turned to the spot where a moment before, Jeremiah Hobson had been standing. He had vanished. Turning back to the police officer, their eyes opened wide in shock as they watched the front door slam closed . . . with no one having touched it.

"'Good-bye, Jeremiah,' the officer said, which was when the kids realized that they had been given a tour of the house by its original occupant—or at least by his ghost."

"Cool!" Melissa cried. "I like it. But I wish the lights would come back on so we could keep rehearsing."

"I have one," Tiffany said with a sly grin.

"My story is about the very play we're performing," Tiffany began. "I did a little research and discovered that it was first performed thirty years ago. In fact, it was put on in this school, in this auditorium, on this stage where we are now sitting.

"A creepy drama teacher named Wormhouse wrote the play. She insisted that the school put it on, but she met a lot of resistance from parents and teachers who said it was too strange and too scary and that it didn't have a happy ending. They all wanted Wormhouse to do a safe, nice musical, something everyone knew and was comfortable with. But she would have no part of that. She insisted that her play be performed, and in the end she got her way.

"Right from the start, though, the rehearsals were plagued with strange incidents. Props would break, scenery would collapse for no reason right in the middle of a scene, and lights would go on and off by themselves—kind of like what happened to us tonight.

"Finally opening night came. But as soon as the girl playing Carrie stepped out onto the stage to begin the show, something fell from above. It struck her and killed her instantly."

All the girls onstage gasped.

Tiffany had them in the palm of her hand, and she knew it.

"Back then there were rumors that the play itself is cursed . . . and that whoever plays the lead is destined to die!"

As Tiffany said the word "die," the lights in the auditorium blazed back to life.

Bree looked around and realized that everyone on the stage was wide eyed—and they were all staring right at her!

CHAPTER 5

"Thank you, Tiffany, for that very entertaining piece of folklore," Ms. Hollows said as she came back into the auditorium. "As you can see, the problem with the lights has been resolved. Now if we can all get back to reality, I'd like to run through one more scene."

Bree did her best to focus as the rehearsal continued, but Tiffany's story had really shaken her. *Cursed!* she thought. *Could the play really be cursed? Was that what she had been feeling all along? Was such a thing even possible?*

Bree was by nature a pretty rational, straightforward person. She liked ghost stories but never truly believed in the supernatural. But a strange feeling of dread began to work its way into her subconscious. She was sure she wanted to be here doing this play. But there was something else . . . something she just couldn't put her finger on that was making her question that decision.

When rehearsal ended, she headed from the auditorium feeling unsatisfied. She thought that the first part of the rehearsal had gone very well. Then the lights had gone out and Tiffany had told her story. Bree was much less pleased with the quality of the scenes she had run through after that.

"You okay?" Melissa asked, catching up to Bree at the front door of the school. "You seemed kinda out of it during that last scene."

"I don't know, Lis, that story Tiffany told about the play really freaked me out," Bree explained.

"Oh, she's just trying to get under your skin," Melissa said. "She's still all bent out of shape about not getting the lead. She's probably trying to rattle you so Ms. Hollows reconsiders. Don't let her mess with your mind. You're doing a great job. You were born to be Carrie!"

"Thanks, Lis. I think," Bree said hesitantly. She knew that Melissa's comment was intended as a compliment, but it reminded her of what Ms. Hollows had said on the day of the auditions: *The play has been waiting for you.* Both statements carried a strange sense of destiny that made Bree very uncomfortable.

Bree and Melissa stepped out of the building and into a raging thunderstorm.

"Okay, well, that explains why the lights went out," Bree said, looking out at the wind-whipped trees and sheets of torrential rain. She felt relieved to find a logical explanation for the creepy incident that had so closely mimicked the events in the play.

"For sure," Melissa agreed. "I just hope I have power at home. I have tons of chatting to do online! See ya tomorrow, Bree." Melissa trotted over to where her older brother waited in his car to give her a ride home.

"Hi, *Gabrielle*," said someone from behind her. Bree spun around and saw Tiffany standing on the steps of the school.

"Tiffany!" Bree cried, startled to hear a classmate calling her by her full name.

"I have something to tell you," Tiffany said.

Bree thought she had said quite enough for one day already. Or was she actually going to apologize for always being so snotty?

"Okay," Bree said cautiously.

"You're going to *hate* playing the lead," Tiffany spat out, contempt dripping from every word. "In fact, you're going to be sorry that you ever even tried out for this play."

"What do you mean?" she asked.

"The amount of work is intense," Tiffany continued, stepping up right next to Bree. "Learning all those lines. All the pressure of the whole play revolving around you. Everyone is depending on you, you know. That's what comes with being the lead. And it's so easy to let down the whole cast . . . the whole school, actually. One little mistake, one tiny thing done wrong, and you could ruin the play for everyone."

Bree was startled, and for the moment, speechless.

"I'd quit now if I were you," Tiffany said as she brushed past Bree. Then she stopped and turned back toward her. "But fortunately, I'm not you."

Bree watched Tiffany disappear into the driving rain and darkness, stunned and confused. She got onto the late bus for students who were involved in after-school activities, her mind still reeling from the bizarre encounter with Tiffany.

Was that a threat?

After dinner, Bree hunkered down at her desk and dove into what felt like a week's worth of homework. As she plowed through her math and science assignments, she wondered how Megan had managed to be in all those school plays, for all these years, while remaining a straight A student.

"Have a good day, Superstar?" Megan asked, poking her head into Bree's room, startling her.

"Pretty good," Bree said. She was not about to share all that had happened with Tiffany that afternoon. Megan would probably say that Tiffany was right. *I'm not giving her any reason to put me down again. I'm sure she'd love to see me flop . . . or even better, quit.*

"Well, be sure to let me know if you need any acting tips," Megan offered.

"Yeah, right, Megan," Bree replied sarcastically. "You'll be the first one I'll go to."

Megan shrugged and closed the door.

After another hour of homework, Bree began to feel sleepy. She had gotten a good chunk of her assignments done and felt satisfied. Slipping into bed, she read for about five minutes before drifting off to sleep.

In her dream, Bree found herself sitting in the front row of the school's auditorium. The props and scenery for *The Last Sleepover* were set up on the stage. "How did I get here?" she wondered aloud.

A crowd of people filed into the auditorium and took their seats.

"What am I doing sitting in the audience?" Bree wondered. "I should be backstage, or up on the stage, or . . ."

At that moment she noticed that something was wrong. Glancing around at the people entering the auditorium, she realized that they looked strange. *What are they all wearing? And what's with that hair? They all look like they stepped out of another era.*

Was it an eighties theme night at the school? But why would they do that on the night of a performance? And why would they ask the audience to also play dress-up? None of it made any sense.

The lights went down and the actors made their way onto the stage in the dark. Dim stage lights set the mood, and the play began.

RACHEL: Nice, Carrie. The place looks like it was decorated by a wrecking ball!

CARRIE: Cute. You know we only moved in a few weeks ago. My family and I haven't had a chance to fix it up yet. I just couldn't wait to have my first sleepover. It helps to make it feel like home.

LAURA: Yeah, if your home's been condemned!

That's the scene we just rehearsed today, Bree thought. Then she focused on the girls up onstage. *Okay, now this is officially weird. Even the actors have hairstyles from another era.*

As the play continued, Bree grew more and more confused.

(SUDDENLY LIGHTNING FLASHES AND THUNDER RUMBLES.)

LAURA: Eiii!

CARRIE: Laura?

LAURA: Sorry, I'm just a little afraid of thunder. I--

(THE THUNDER SOUNDS AGAIN . . . LOUDER THIS TIME. LAURA SCOOTS OVER NEXT TO CARRIE. SUDDENLY THE CHANDELIER OVERHEAD FLICKERS ON AND OFF, AGAIN AND AGAIN.)

RACHEL: Okay, now I'm officially creeped out. I--

CARRIE: Look!

(CARRIE POINTS TO THE CHANDELIER. A FLASH OF LIGHTNING REVEALS THAT THE CHANDELIER IS SHAKING.)

Bree heard a sharp snapping sound that seemed to be coming from overhead. Looking up, panic flooded through her as she realized that a stage light had broken loose and was plunging down from above. The light was headed right for the girl playing Carrie!

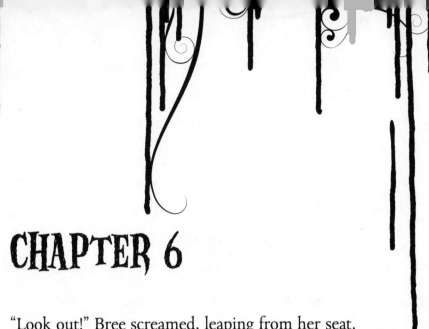

CHAPTER 6

"Look out!" Bree screamed, leaping from her seat.

The stage vanished, as did the girl and the falling light and the audience. Bree was sitting upright in her bed, her heart pounding and her hands shaking. After a few seconds, her mind cleared and she realized that she had just awakened from a terrible dream. She was in her room at home, and the sun was shining through her window.

It was like I was right there, when the play was first performed. And that poor girl getting hit by the light. Thank you, Tiffany, for planting that vision in my brain.

Trying to shake off the effects of the dream, Bree pulled herself together and headed downstairs for breakfast.

"You look horrible," Megan said when Bree joined her at the kitchen table.

"Thanks. I didn't sleep well. Bad dreams."

"About what?" Megan asked.

"The show," Bree replied through her sleepy haze. She immediately regretted having shared that with her sister.

"Stage fright, huh?" Megan said casually, shoving another spoonful of cereal into her mouth.

"No," Bree replied defensively. "I'm fine when I'm onstage. It's just the play itself. It's hard to explain, but it gives me the creeps."

"It's a scary play, Bree," Megan said, shrugging her shoulders. "Giving people the creeps is what it's supposed to do."

"Yeah, but it's supposed to give the *audience* the creeps," Bree pointed out. "Not the actors. I've had a nagging feeling that something isn't totally right with the play. Then Tiffany told us that story." Even mentioning the story sent a shiver through her.

"Story?" Megan asked, leaning in toward her sister.

Bree recounted the tale of the play as it had been performed thirty years earlier and the death of the girl playing the lead.

"And then last night I had a dream about it," she said, finishing her story. "And I saw it happen, Megan.

I was right there, sitting in the front row when the light fell down on that girl. It seemed so real."

"Sounds to me like that play is *really* getting to you," Megan said. Bree thought that her sister almost sounded glad. "You know, some people just aren't cut out for the theater. There's no shame in that. Maybe acting isn't for you."

"Thanks for being so sympathetic," Bree snapped, shoving her chair away from the table. "You're a big help."

She stormed back up to her room to get dressed. *That's the last time I go to her with my problems, she thought. I'm just going to get through this play and everything is going to be fine. It was just a dream. That's all. A dream.*

At school that day, Bree felt more focused than she had in a long time. The dream faded from her mind, and she didn't think about the play at all.

When the last bell rang, Bree hurried to the auditorium for rehearsal with a renewed sense of purpose. After her fight with Megan that morning, she had managed to push aside her uneasy feeling about the play and was once again excited about playing Carrie.

"You look positively perky," Melissa said as she and Bree headed to the stage.

"Perky, huh?" Bree echoed. She decided not to tell Melissa about her dream, preferring to forget it. "I guess I have been a bit serious about all this. I let that story Tiffany told us get to me, but I know she was just making up all that stuff about it being cursed to get me to quit the play. This is just a play."

"Uh-huh," Melissa said, looking at her friend a bit strangely. "Right, and this is just a stage, and this is just a chair, and this is—"

"Okay, okay," Bree said, sighing. "Never mind."

Ms. Hollows hurried into the auditorium.

"All right, ladies and gentlemen," she announced. "Let's run the Carrie and Rachel scene, please."

Bree was thrilled to notice that the set for Carrie's room was looking more like a real room than it had the day before. The set decorators had added more touches. Clothes, books, and general junk were strewn everywhere around the room. A few old, worn-out sleeping bags were arranged in a circle on the floor. *A complete mess*, Bree thought. *Perfect for the scene of a haunted sleepover.*

"Ooh, the sleeping bags are here," Melissa cooed when

she stepped onto the stage. "Now it looks like a sleepover!"

The scene they were about to rehearse featured only Carrie and Rachel. Bree was thrilled to be alone on the stage with her real-life best friend. They walked onstage, and Bree immediately let herself be transported into character. She was no longer Bree, she was Carrie. Melissa was no longer Melissa, she was Rachel. This was not the stage in the auditorium, it was Carrie's bedroom.

```
(RACHEL RUSHES TO CARRIE'S BEDROOM.
CARRIE IS PACING, OBVIOUSLY UPSET.)

RACHEL: All right, Carrie. Spill it!
What was so urgent that it couldn't
wait?

CARRIE: Remember when I told you
that I thought someone was following
me?

RACHEL: Uh, yeah. It was just
yesterday.

CARRIE: Right. Well, it happened
again. Only now, it's happening
everywhere.

RACHEL: What do you mean, EVERYWHERE?

CARRIE: Every time I walk down
the hallways, I can feel someone
following me. On every walk home
```

from school, I'm certain I can hear footsteps behind me but no one is there. Even when I go from one room in my house to another, I feel it.

RACHEL: Hold on. Hold on. You "feel" someone following you. I'm not sure I know what that means. Have you actually seen anyone?

CARRIE: I hear footsteps all the time, and when I turn around, no one is there. But I know it, Rachel. I just know it! And what's worse--

RACHEL: There's a worse part?

CARRIE: I'm positive that whoever is following me means to do me harm!

Walking toward the front of the stage, still fully in character, Bree heard a snapping sound from above. She really didn't want to break out of her character, but something told her to look up, even though it wasn't in the script.

Glancing toward the track of stage lights above her, Bree saw that one of the lights had broken off and was plunging right toward her.

CHAPTER 7

Bree flung herself out of the way. She landed hard on her shoulder, just as the light crashed to the stage floor.

"Bree, are you all right?" Melissa screamed, dashing to her friend's side.

Ms. Hollows and the entire cast rushed onto the stage.

"Gabrielle, are you all right?" Ms. Hollows asked calmly.

Adrenaline shot through Bree's body. She felt numb. The shock of what had just happened, and what had *almost* happened made her feel as if time was standing still. She could see the stage light snap, then fall through the air in superslow motion. The moment, stretched out over several seconds, replayed over and over in her mind. She saw the light hit the stage and explode into a million shards of glass. The slow-motion

scene stopped, and time accelerated back to normal.

"I'm okay," Bree said, pushing herself up into a sitting position. Her mind began to clear as the shock wore off. Her shoulder was a bit sore, but as she got to her feet she realized that she had not been seriously injured. She hadn't even been hit by any glass.

"How could that have happened?" Melissa asked Ms. Hollows in an almost accusatory tone. She peered up into the darkness of the catwalks and metal pipes that ran above the stage, but saw nothing and no one. By now the set decorators were running around, checking all the props. Everyone else was chattering about what had just happened and where they were when the light fell. Ms. Hollows stood in the middle of all this chaos, eerily calm.

"What was that noise? I heard a—" Tiffany said as she walked out onto the stage from the wings and spotted the smashed-up light and the crowd surrounding Bree. "What happened?"

Bree stared at Tiffany and wondered where she had just been. Why hadn't she rushed onstage with everyone else? What had she been doing? Then Bree caught herself.

What am I thinking? Even she *wouldn't try to hurt me . . . would she?*

"I'm fine," Bree replied. "It was just an accident. Let's try that scene again. This time without the falling light."

Bree's little joke broke the tension onstage. "Fantastic, Gabrielle," Ms. Hollows said. "The show must go on!"

A few minutes later the janitor had cleaned up the broken light and the rehearsal resumed. This time the scene between Carrie and Rachel went off without a hitch.

When rehearsal ended, Bree and Melissa walked from the auditorium, heading toward the front door of the school.

"So, Lis, I wasn't going to tell you about this, but after what happened today . . ." Bree's words trailed off.

"Go on," Melissa encouraged her friend.

"Last night I had a terrifying dream," Bree began. "I was sitting in the audience of a theater when I realized that it was actually our auditorium. Then a play began, and it turned out to be *The Last Sleepover*."

"So you were dreaming about us doing the show," Melissa said, sounding a bit relieved to learn that her friend's big news was only about a dream.

"But that's just it, Lis," Bree continued. "It wasn't *us* doing the show. In the dream everybody was wearing out-of-date clothes, like from the eighties or something.

Then the girl playing Carrie came out onto the stage to start the show, and *she* was wearing those same kind of clothes. I think I was watching the original performance—the one that Tiffany told us about."

"Just because of the clothes?" Melissa asked. "I mean, dreams can be pretty weird. Your brain takes stuff from a bunch of different places and mushes it all up together."

"Not just the clothes, Lis," Bree said, taking a deep breath. "I saw the accident Tiffany described. I was sitting in the audience, watching the light fall onto the girl who was playing Carrie. It was just like Tiffany had described it. And it was exactly like what almost happened to me."

"So what are you saying, Bree?" Melissa asked. "That there's some evil spirit connected to the play? Or that someone is out to get you? I think Tiffany made up that story, and it's getting to you. I mean, if a girl died right here on this stage, then everyone would know about it, right?"

Bree nodded.

"And the light falling today?" Melissa added. "Well, that was just a coincidence. Accidents happen. Even coincidental ones."

Bree kept nodding. It was easier this way. Melissa

made some good points, but that didn't explain away her uneasiness.

"Listen, I gotta go," Melissa continued. "My mom is picking me up. Are you sure you're okay? Do you want a ride home?"

"Nah, I'm going to stick around here for a bit," Bree said. She stood in the hallway and watched Melissa hurry from the school. Maybe Melissa was right. The whole thing—Tiffany's story, her dream, the accident at rehearsal—might be just a combination made-up story and wild coincidence, but somehow she didn't believe that. She was still very shaken up.

Bree knew that because this was a Thursday, Mr. Harris, the school librarian, stayed late to help students with their research projects. She turned toward the school library and marched down the hall, striding purposefully. She would get to the bottom of all this. And she would do it now, before another rehearsal took place.

Bree opened the library's large oak door and walked inside. Every time she came here she realized just how lucky she was. She had seen a few other school libraries while visiting friends, but the library at Thomas Jefferson Middle School was clearly a cut above.

She had almost forgotten how busy the place got on Thursdays after school. It had been a while since she'd had to come here for a research project.

Almost at the moment she entered the room, a short man with a thick shock of snow-white hair appeared from between two tall bookshelves and shuffled toward Bree.

"Bree Hart. How are you?" the man said.

"Hi, Mr. Harris," Bree said. "I'm fine, thanks."

Seeing Mr. Harris always made Bree smile. He had been at the school for more than twenty years. He loved his job, and though he'd long been eligible for retirement, he saw no reason to stop. This library, its books, computers, and vast archives, was the focus of his life. And he loved nothing more than helping students.

"I haven't seen you in a while," Mr. Harris said. "Now what can I help you with today?"

"I need to look into a bit of Thomas Jefferson Middle School history," she replied.

"Ah, one of my favorite topics, since I've been here for most of it!" Mr. Harris joked. "What are you looking for in particular?"

"Well, Mr. Harris, I'm in the school play," Bree began.

"Yes, I know," the librarian said. "Playing the lead,

if I'm not mistaken. I'm very much looking forward to seeing it."

"Yes," Bree continued, feeling a bit self-conscious. Until this moment she had been so focused on her work in the play that the thought of people she knew coming to see her perform hadn't crossed her mind in a while. "I'm actually here to research the history of the play itself. I believe it was performed at the school once before and only for one night."

"I see," Mr. Harris said, his curiosity clearly piqued. "That was a little before my time, and now that you mention it, I do recall hearing about some incident related to a play. Do you know why the play was performed only once?"

"Well, that's what I'm here to find out," Bree explained. "I heard a story about what happened back then, but I wanted to find out whether or not it was really true."

"To quote a cliché, 'You've come to the right place,'" Mr. Harris said.

Bree could almost see an actual twinkle in his eye. He loved his work, and a new project, digging around, doing what he liked to call "informational archeology," always made his face light up.

"I have every issue ever published of the *Jeffersonian*, dating from the beginning of the school's opening," Mr. Harris explained. "Follow me, Bree."

Bree trailed a few steps behind him as he wended his way through the stacks. She always marveled at how he seemed to know exactly where every single thing in this vast library could be found. And she had to walk at a fairly brisk pace to keep up with Mr. Harris, who was well into his sixties. Once he was on the trail of information needed to solve a problem or answer a question, he wasted no time.

"Here we are," he said, practically hopping onto a small stepladder at the base of a tall bookcase. "When did you say the play was performed?"

"I don't have an exact year, Mr. Harris, but I think it was about thirty years ago, so the early 1980s? The play is called *The Last Sleepover*."

Mr. Harris ran his finger along the wide spines of row after row of plastic magazine holders. Each container held a year's worth of the monthly school newspaper. "Let's begin with 1979," he said, handing a container down to Bree. She placed it onto the desk beside the shelf. "Here's 1980, 1981, and 1982."

He stepped down from the ladder. Much to Bree's

surprise, he took a seat beside her at the desk.

"I can do this myself if you have other students to help," she said, flattered by the special attention but a bit confused.

"Oh, anyone who needs help can find me," Mr. Harris replied, his eyes sparkling. "I'm a bit of a theater buff myself. And you know how much I love school history. Why don't you start with 1979, and I'll take 1980." Bree took the container labeled THE JEFFERSONIAN—1979 and pulled out the yellowed issues. She was immediately struck by the fashion and hairstyles of the students in the photos. Everyone looked as if they had stepped out of her dream.

Bree went issue by issue, carefully flipping through the delicate pages, scanning the paper for any mention of *The Last Sleepover*.

"It's not 1979," she said, when she had gone through the December issue.

"Nor is it 1980," Mr. Harris added. He handed 1981 to Bree and took 1982 for himself.

Bree repeated the searching process with the issues from 1981. When she reached March, her eyes opened wide. "Mr. Harris, here it is!" she cried, then looked

around to see if she had disturbed anyone in the library.

Mr. Harris pulled his chair up close to Bree's. She pointed to the page, then read the headline aloud: "'This Year's School Play Announced.'" She continued reading: "'The drama department has decided that this year's show will be a brand-new play called *The Last Sleepover*. The play was written by and will be directed by Thomas Jefferson drama teacher Mildred P. Wormhouse.'"

Bree paused. "Mildred!" she muttered to herself. "Millie is short for Mildred!" *Mildred P. Wormhouse, the playwright, must have named the ghost after herself. Was she a girl who never got invited to a sleepover?*

"Excuse me?" Mr. Harris said.

"Huh, oh, I'm sorry, never mind, that name just made me think of something," Bree replied. She continued reading: "'The first meeting of all students interested in being involved with the play will be held on March eighth in the auditorium.'"

Bree set March aside and pulled out the April issue. She unfolded the paper and there, running across the front page, was a headline twice as big as any she had seen so far: LEAD ACTRESS DIES OPENING NIGHT!

CHAPTER 8

"So it's true!" Bree cried. "The story Tiffany told me is true!"

"Tiffany O'Brian?" Mr. Harris asked.

"Yes," Bree replied, trying to regain her composure. "She's in the play with me. She told me that the girl playing the lead back then died in an accident on opening night."

"Hmm," Mr. Harris said, thinking aloud. "I remember some hushed whispers about a girl who had died at the school, but I never got the full story. None of the older teachers ever wanted to talk about it, and they're all retired now. This happened ten years before I arrived at Thomas Jefferson. What does the article say?"

Bree started reading: "'Tragedy struck on opening night of the school play when a stage light fell and killed

eighth grader Gabrielle Ashford, who was playing the lead role in the play *The Last Sleepover.*'"

Bree stopped reading. *Gabrielle! The girl who died was named Gabrielle.*

"Bree?"

"I'm sorry, Mr. Harris, I got lost in thought for a moment."

Bree continued reading: "'Playwright, director, and Thomas Jefferson drama teacher Mildred P. Wormhouse was quoted as saying, "The entire cast and crew are devastated. Working on this play, we became a family, and I could not have imagined anyone bringing the character I wrote to life any better than Gabrielle did. Our hearts go out to her friends and family."'"

Bree fell back into her seat.

"Are you all right?" Mr. Harris asked.

"I'm—I'm okay, Mr. Harris, thanks," Bree assured him. "This is all just so freaky. The play hasn't been performed since then. Until now. And I'm playing the lead, just like Gabrielle Ashford. And my name is Gabrielle."

"I don't think I've ever heard anyone at this school call you by your real first name," Mr. Harris said.

"No, and there's only one person who does. Thank

you so much, Mr. Harris. I really appreciate your help. I have to head home now."

"It's my pleasure, Bree. And come back anytime. It's always nice to see you."

"Thanks."

Bree hurried from the library, her mind racing.

Mildred is Millie the ghost. Gabrielle is me. I mean, Gabrielle played the lead and died. Tiffany's story was true. She also said the play was cursed and that I would die. Is that true too?

"I've got to talk to Ms. Hollows," Bree murmured to herself, heading to the auditorium.

She shoved open the big auditorium door and stepped inside. She saw no one.

"Ms. Hollows!" she called out. "I need to talk with you." Her voice echoed around the empty, cavernous room. "Ms. Hollows!" she yelled again, heading down the center aisle toward the stage. Again she got no answer.

Bree bounded up the stairs leading onto the stage and scooted backstage. It too was empty. She was completely alone in the auditorium. Or was she?

She got the strong feeling that someone was watching her. "Hello?" she called. "Is anybody here?"

Stop making yourself nuts, Bree, she thought as she

marched back up the aisle toward the door. *Go home. Get some rest. You are imagining—*

She spun around on her heels, certain that she would see someone behind her. The feeling of being watched was overwhelming. But she was alone.

Leaving the auditorium, she strode quickly along the long hallway. She headed for the front door of the school, her footsteps echoing down the empty corridor. As Bree listened to the sound of her own footsteps, she could swear that she heard a second set of footsteps mingling with her own. She stopped.

Silence.

Resuming her walking, she heard the second set of steps again. This time she stopped and spun around. She saw no one.

Reaching the front door of the school, Bree glanced back over her shoulder one more time as she grabbed the door handle. This time she caught a glimpse of a shadow disappearing around a corner. She threw open the door, burst from the school, and ran home as fast as she could.

As she ran, above the sound of her own hard breathing, Bree heard footsteps following her the whole way home.

CHAPTER 9

CARRIE: Someone is following me.

RACHEL: What do you mean?

CARRIE: I heard footsteps behind me as I was walking home.

RACHEL: Did you see anyone at all?

CARRIE: No, that's what I'm saying. I didn't see anyone. But I did have the strong feeling that someone was following me, AND I clearly heard footsteps behind me. When I took a step, whoever was following me took a step. When I stopped, the second set of footsteps stopped.

RACHEL: Sometimes having a good imagination can be a problem, you know.

CARRIE: It's not my imagination. Something strange is happening.

"Cut! Very good scene, everyone," Ms. Hollows shouted. "Let's take a ten-minute break."

Bree and Melissa were up onstage on Monday after school, rehearsing the play. Bree was struggling with her lines today—she hadn't slept again last night and was finding the lack of sleep starting to really affect her. She also found it a bit weird that they were rehearsing the scene in which Carrie thinks someone is following her home from school, so shortly after Bree had experienced the same thing. The play seemed determined to mirror her life—or was it the other way around?

And the events in the play seemed all the more real to Bree now that the set was completed. She caught the eye of Justin, the boy in charge of putting the set together. He was being extra cautious since the light incident and came out on the stage in between scenes to make sure everything was in order. Or in the case of the mess that was Carrie's bedroom, disorder.

"Everything looks great, Justin!" Bree said, trying

to take her mind off everything and focus on the fact that this was going to be a very good play.

"Thanks," Justin replied, tightening a clamp that held two sections of wall together. "It does look pretty cool."

"Now that the window is in, it looks like a real room."

"Check this out," Justin said, slipping back behind the wall in which the window hung. "Tony, do the lightning!"

Lights flashed on and off behind the window. The shutters whipped back and forth, slamming against the outside of the "house" as if the wind were blowing them during a storm.

"Very cool!" Bree exclaimed. "It's going to be great when an audience sees it."

"And we got the chandelier up and working," Justin said.

Bree glanced up and saw that the chandelier had been hung. It was dusty and covered with cobwebs. Its lights flickered on and off. She was standing directly beneath it.

A wave of fear suddenly swept through her as she relived the moment when the stage light fell right next to her. She took a step to the side so that she was no longer right under the fixture.

"Awesome," she said, regaining her composure.

Bree walked to the side of the stage, where she spotted the top of a staircase that the crew had built. The handrails and the top few stairs disappeared behind a curtain offstage, giving the impression that a person could walk downstairs to a lower level of the house.

"This looks so real!" Bree exclaimed, gripping the handrails and looking down, almost expecting to see a real staircase. Instead she saw a soft mattress a foot below, there to break her fall in the play's final scene. "You guys are good!"

Melissa, who had run off to the dressing room after their scene, joined Bree onstage.

"Doesn't it look incredible, Lis?" Bree asked.

"It's so real I'm almost scared!" Melissa joked.

Bree smiled, but Melissa's innocent comment reminded her of what had happened last week. She had tried to forget it. She didn't want to ever tell Melissa about it, but now she felt like she couldn't keep it to herself any longer. She pulled Melissa away from everyone and spoke in a voice barely above a whisper.

"This is going to sound so strange, but last Thursday, before I went home, I heard footsteps."

"Footsteps?"

"Yes. Well, first I thought that someone else was in the auditorium."

"Well, that sounds terrifying," Melissa said sarcastically.

"It was actually because no one else *was* in the auditorium. At least not that I could tell. And it felt like someone was watching me. Then, as I walked down the hall toward the front door, I was certain I heard another set of footsteps. Someone was following me. I could just tell."

"Uh, we're on a break, Bree. No need to continue rehearsing."

"No joke, Lis," Bree said, realizing as she said it how crazy this all sounded . . . and how much like the lines they had just rehearsed. "I'm not talking as Carrie now. I'm me. And I'm telling you that the same thing that happens to Carrie in the show happened to me the other day. Someone followed me home."

"Did you see anyone?" Melissa asked.

"Not exactly."

"What do you mean, 'not exactly'? You either saw someone or you didn't."

"I caught glimpses, a quick peek of something, like a shadow moving in the hallway."

"Bree, I think this creepy play is really starting to get to you," Melissa said. "All this so-called crazy stuff can be easily chalked up to coincidence."

"But here's the other thing," Bree continued. "I went to the library and found out that the girl playing Carrie thirty years ago did die on opening night. And, get this. Her name was Gabrielle!"

"Yeah, so . . ."

"Don't you see, Lis? It's all happening again. It's connected. There's something not right about this whole play. Tiffany was right!"

"Say it louder. I love when people say that," Tiffany said, stepping up behind Bree. "What was I right about?"

"The girl who died thirty years ago," Bree replied. "How'd you know?"

"Something I overheard my parents talking about ages ago. I told you the play was haunted," Tiffany said. "You should quit before something happens."

"Are you threatening her?" Melissa asked.

"I'm just saying," Tiffany replied casually, walking away.

"I can't believe she's still trying to get your part,"

Melissa said, seemingly more upset at Tiffany's words than Bree was.

"I'm starting to wonder exactly what I believe, Lis," Bree said softly, not quite sure if Melissa even heard her.

"Okay, everyone, the break is over," Ms. Hollows announced. "Places onstage, please."

Once again, Bree tried her best to shrug off her unease and put her mind back into the play.

The girls took their places for a key scene in the show. In the story, the sleepover was well underway. Carrie suggests they play a game.

CARRIE: The game is called "The Witch's Body." It's kinda creepy and kinda goofy.

(CARRIE PULLS OUT A LARGE PLASTIC BAG BULGING WITH ITEMS INSIDE IT.)

CARRIE: This is the story of the witch who was so old that her body began to fall apart. And it just so happens that I've got the body parts right here in this bag!

(CARRIE SHAKES THE BAG MENACINGLY AT HER FRIENDS. THE OBJECTS RATTLE AND MAKE SQUISHING SOUNDS.)

RACHEL: Body parts? Gross!

CARRIE: That's where the game part comes in. I'm going to pick a body part from this bag and put it in this smaller bag.

(CARRIE TAKES A SMALL PLASTIC BAG AND PUTS IT NEXT TO THE LARGER BAG.)

CARRIE: Everyone will take a turn reaching into the small bag and feeling a body part. Then you have to say what body part it is and what the object REALLY is. Okay, now, everyone close your eyes.

(CARRIE REACHES INTO THE LARGE BAG AND PULLS OUT ONE OF THE ITEMS. THEN SHE PUTS IT INTO THE SMALL BAG.)

RACHEL: I'll go first!

(RACHEL SHOVES HER HAND INTO THE BAG.)

RACHEL: EWW! I feel something round and wet and squishy. And it's bigger than my hand. Wait. Wait. I know. It's the witch's heart!

CARRIE: You got it. Okay, now what is it really?

RACHEL: A--a peeled tomato!

CARRIE: Two points for Rachel. Okay, Laura, you're up.

(SOUND EFFECT: TAP. TAP. TAP. THE GIRLS ARE ALL STARTLED BY A TAPPING NOISE AT THE WINDOW.)

RACHEL: What was that?

LAURA: Sounded like someone tapping on the window.

CARRIE: Yeah, but we're on the second floor. How could someone be up here?

LAURA: Maybe it was just the wind blowing a tree branch against the window.

CARRIE: Totally. Let's get back to the game.

(CARRIE PULLS ANOTHER "BODY PART" FROM THE BIG BAG AND PUTS IT INTO THE SMALL ONE. LAURA REACHES INTO THE BAG.)

LAURA: I feel two little round squishy things. I know. I've got the witch's eyeballs.

CARRIE: Great!

LAURA: And I know what they really are. They're peeled grapes!

CARRIE: Another two points. Excellent. I--

(SOUND EFFECT: TAP! TAP! TAP!)

CARRIE: Did you see it? Did you see it?

RACHEL: See what?

CARRIE: The face! There was a face in the window.

(LIGHTNING FLASHES, REVEALING THE FACE OF A LITTLE GIRL WITH DARK, SUNKEN EYES AT THE WINDOW. CARRIE IS THE ONLY ONE TO SEE IT.)

CARRIE: Look!

(ALL HEADS TURN TOWARD THE WINDOW, BUT WHEN THE LIGHTNING ILLUMINATES THE OUTSIDE, THERE IS NO FACE AT THE WINDOW.)

RACHEL: So now you're seeing things?

CARRIE: Seeing things? You all saw the hairbrush and the mirror, right? And I saw her face.

LAURA: The ghost.

CARRIE: Yes, the gh--

(THERE ARE TAPPING SOUNDS AGAIN AT THE WINDOW. THIS TIME THEY ARE EVEN LOUDER AND MORE URGENT. EVERYONE TURNS BACK TO THE WINDOW. THERE, STARING IN AT THEM FROM OUTSIDE, IS THE GHOST.)

EVERYONE: YIIEEE!

(THE GIRLS ALL SCREAM AND RUSH TO THE SIDE OF CARRIE'S BEDROOM OPPOSITE THE WINDOW, TRYING TO GET

AS FAR AWAY AS THEY CAN FROM IT.
CARRIE'S BLACK CAT ARCHES ITS BACK
AND HISSES.)

RACHEL: Who could it be? How did she
get up here?

CARRIE: Either someone is pulling a
prank . . .

RACHEL: Or?

CARRIE: Or it's the ghost of the
girl who used to live in this house,
trying to come to our sleepover!

"And fade the lights to black," Ms. Hollows said.
"Excellent, girls. Gather around for notes. Can we have
our ghost out onstage, please?"

Tiffany came walking out from backstage, still wearing her scary pale mask with black, soulless eyes. She
joined the others at center stage.

"Nice job, Tiffany," Melissa said as Tiffany sat down
beside her. "But next time you should try the scene with
the mask *on*."

"Very funny," Tiffany replied, pulling off the mask
and scowling. "Maybe you should be in a comedy instead
of a scary play."

"The ghost is an important character," Bree said.

"Don't placate me, *Gabrielle*," Tiffany shot back. "I know exactly what my role is in this production. I don't need your pity, and I don't need your pitiful attempts to try to make me feel better."

Bree turned away. She had tried being friendly to Tiffany at every rehearsal, even though it seemed at times as if Tiffany was trying to scare her into leaving the show. But enough was enough. She didn't like Tiffany. She didn't have to be her friend. She didn't have to make her feel better. She just had to work with her in the play.

Ms. Hollows gave the cast their notes. She was very pleased with how the play was taking shape, but there were always things that needed to be tightened up and fine-tuned so that the play would go off without a hitch when it was performed in front of an audience.

Following notes, Ms. Hollows dismissed the cast.

"I think Tiffany makes a great ghost, don't you?" Melissa asked Bree as the two left the school building.

"Why does she have to be so snotty all the time, Lis?"

"Hey, it just wouldn't be Tiffany without the attitude, now would it? Forget about her. With any luck, that mask will get stuck to her face and we won't have to listen to her whine anymore. See ya tomorrow, Bree. Gotta run."

"See ya."

Arriving at home, Bree found a note from her parents:

Out getting groceries with Megan. We'll be back in time for dinner. Snacks in the fridge.

Love, M & D

She threw open the refrigerator door and pulled out a plate filled with cut-up pieces of fruit and a few cookies, then headed for the stairs leading up to her bedroom.

Suddenly all the lights in the house began to flicker on and off.

What's going on? she wondered, pausing at the bottom of the staircase.

Again the lights flickered on and off. Then they went off and stayed off.

Placing the plate of snacks on a small table in the

hallway, Bree opened a drawer on the front of the table and pulled out a flashlight. Her family kept flashlights handy in case of power outages. But this was different.

She noticed that although every light in the house seemed to be out, they hadn't actually lost power. Digital clocks on the front of the coffeemaker in the kitchen and the DVR in the living room still glowed with the correct time. Only the lights seemed to be affected. Bree wondered if she somehow blew a fuse.

She flipped the hallway light switch on and off several times, but the lights stayed dark. Switching the flashlight on, she headed upstairs, thinking that maybe the lights up there would work. Reaching her room, she stepped in and tried the overhead light.

Nothing.

Then her bedside lamp.

Nothing.

Yet the numbers on her alarm clock still shone brightly.

Walking around her bedroom in the dark, carrying a flashlight, gave Bree a very creeped-out feeling. It was as if she were still walking around the stage in the dark, searching Carrie's bedroom with only a flashlight.

This is way too close to the play, she thought.

Bree swept the flashlight's beam across her wall. As the light passed the window, she spotted a face staring at her from outside. It had dark, sunken eyes.

CHAPTER 10

Moving exactly as she had just an hour earlier at rehearsal, Bree raced across the room, yanked the window open, and stuck her head out. But just as in the play, the face had vanished. Bree swept her flashlight down to the street. She leaned out the window and shone the beam left, right, down, even up, searching for that haunting face. But it was officially gone.

All right. This is going too far, Bree thought. *Maybe I'm really Carrie, and this whole Bree thing is a part in a play.*

"Bree! We're home!" her dad called from downstairs.

"Pull yourself together," she murmured to herself as she raced from her room and bounded down the stairs, following the beam of her flashlight. As she ran, a thought popped into her head. Maybe she wasn't crazy after all.

"Megan!" Bree shouted, storming right up to her sister, putting her face nose-to-nose with Megan's. "Were you just outside my window? Are you trying to scare me out of doing the play?"

"Outside your window?" Megan asked incredulously. "How would I get up there?"

"What are you talking about?" her mother said sternly. "Your sister has been with us for the past two hours. She came into the house with us just now. And speaking of the house, why are you here in the dark?"

"All the lights just went out at the same time," Bree explained. "I tried—"

Flick!

Bree was interrupted by the sound of her mother flipping on the light switch—the same switch that Bree had flipped up and down a bunch of time just a few minutes earlier. The lights came right on.

"The lights work just fine," her mother said. "Are you feeling all right?"

"I don't know about you, Mom, but it's clear to me that the pressure of doing this play is proving to be too much for poor Bree," Megan said, her voice positively dripping with condescension.

Their mother gave Megan a reproachful look, but she didn't say anything. Maybe she was starting to think Bree was cracking under the pressure too. And if she was being perfectly honest with herself, Bree was beginning to agree with her. She must have imagined the face in the window.

Normally she would have protested both the tone and content of Megan's comment. She would have whined to her mother about how Megan had been against her from the start, how her sister should be more supportive, and on and on.

But Megan was right. The pressure of the play, the weird connections between what happened in the story and what was happening in her life, were blurring the lines between where Carrie ended and where Bree began.

And thinking that, Bree finally came to a decision. Despite the fact that they were far into the rehearsal process, she would quit the play. Tomorrow.

Much to her surprise, she slept better that night than she had for a while. No bad dreams. No dreams of any kind that she could remember. The incident with the face in her window began to fade from her thoughts. Perhaps having made the decision to leave the play had calmed her mind, freed her from the craziness that had invaded her life ever since the moment she'd agreed to do the show. Whatever it was, she awoke the next morning rested and refreshed.

"Any more scary faces at your window?" Megan asked, munching a piece of toast.

"The only scary face I see is the one across from me now," Bree replied, feeling much more like sparring with her sister than she had the night before.

"Ha-ha, very funny," Megan replied. "But I still think you should quit that show before you completely lose all your marbles."

Bree just shrugged casually. Although she had made her decision, something in her mind told her not to say anything to Megan until the deed was actually done.

"Gotta run," was all she said, tossing her napkin onto her plate and pushing her chair away from the table. "You'll be a dear and put these in the sink for me, won't you?"

Before Megan could reply, Bree jumped up from the table and ran toward the door.

"Mom!" Megan whined at the top of her voice.

"She left already," Bree called back to the kitchen. "Bye!" Then she scooted out the door.

At the start of her classes, Bree felt confident about her decision. She imagined what she would say to

Ms. Hollows that afternoon. But as the day wore on, she grew more and more anxious about going into rehearsal and actually saying the words "I quit" aloud. By the time classes ended and Bree was walking to the auditorium, she was practically in a state of panic. She opened the door to the auditorium, stepped inside, and knew instantly that she wasn't going to quit the show.

There was something different about being in that theater. As if the place, or more accurately, the play, had a life of its own. And Bree felt as if it had some influence over her life. She decided not to fight it and to simply hope things would get better. That the weird stuff would stop and that she could find a clearer line between Bree and Carrie. But at this point, could that actually happen?

"Let's pick up the scene, girls, just before Carrie gets the phone call, shall we?" Ms. Hollows announced as the girls all took the stage.

> RACHEL: So do you really think that was someone at your window?
>
> CARRIE: I don't know what to think.
>
> LAURA: Let's just try to forget about everything and go back to that Witch's Body game.

CARRIE: Good idea. My turn.

(SOUND EFFECT: BRIIIING! BRIIIING! BRIIIING! EVERYONE JUMPS AS THE PHONE IN CARRIE'S BEDROOM RINGS LOUDLY.)

CARRIE: Who in the world could be calling me? It's so late.

(CARRIE PICKS UP THE PHONE. A VOICE STARTS SPEAKING.)

FEMALE VOICE ON PHONE: Leave now, and never come back . . . or you'll be sorry!

(CARRIE PRESSES THE SPEAKERPHONE BUTTON JUST AS THE MESSAGE REPEATS.)

FEMALE VOICE OVER SPEAKERPHONE: Leave now, and never come back . . . or you'll be sorry!

(SOUND EFFECT: CLICK!)

RACHEL: That was one crazy crank call.

CARRIE: Something tells me it wasn't a crank call. I'm going to use call return.

(CARRIE DIALS THE CALL RETURN NUMBER.)

OPERATOR'S VOICE FROM PHONE: The number you have dialed is not in service. No more information is available.

They ran the scene three times until Ms. Hollows was happy with it. Bree felt herself dragging a bit. After rehearsal, she and Melissa stood outside the school.

"Rehearsal was kinda slow today, don't you think, Lis?" Bree asked.

"Seemed okay to me," Melissa said, shrugging. "But I guess Ms. Hollows agreed with you, since she made us do the scene three times."

BRIIIING! BRIIIING! BRIIIING!

Bree's cell phone rang. She jumped a bit, realizing that it was ringing with the same old-fashioned ringtone that the sound effects engineer had chosen to use for Carrie's phone in the play.

Glancing down at her screen, she saw the caller ID: UNKNOWN NUMBER.

Bree pressed speakerphone.

A female with a hollow, distant voice said, "Leave now, and never come back . . . or you'll be sorry!"

CHAPTER 11

"It's gotta be a prank, Bree," Melissa said when Bree had hung up the call. "Someone who was at rehearsal and saw the scene we just did."

"And who do you think that might be?" Bree said, not even trying to disguise the anger in her voice. "The voice was kind of familiar. I just can't exactly put my finger on it, but guess who is number one on my list?"

"Tiffany," Melissa answered. "You know, Bree, I thought you were being a little paranoid, suspecting that Tiffany was actively trying to get you to leave the play. But now, this seems like a no-brainer. She's still inside, you know."

"Come on," Bree said, charging back toward the

front door of the school. "I'm going to put a stop to this right now."

Bree threw open the front door and marched toward the auditorium. Her sense of purpose was firm. She felt more committed to confronting Tiffany than she had felt about anything since her involvement in the play began. Maybe if she could get Tiffany to stop trying to make her quit, everything would be better. Everything might actually feel normal again.

Reaching the auditorium, with Melissa close on her heels, Bree burst through the doors and stomped down the aisle toward the stage. Tiffany stood at the edge of the stage, packing up her things and getting ready to go home.

"Tiffany!" Bree boomed.

"Well, if it isn't the star," Tiffany replied, smirking. "What's got you all in an uproar?"

"*You*, that's what!" Bree shouted. "It's got to stop, Tiffany! The other night it was the face at the window— did you use the mask from the play to do that? And now the phone calls! Enough!" Bree was amazed at herself. She had never felt so angry in her life. She felt as if she were watching another person explode in fury, blaming Tiffany for everything that had happened.

"What are you talking about?" Tiffany replied, dropping her smirky, above-it-all act, seeming to be genuinely startled by the blast of anger she had just received from the usually meek and mild Bree.

"Tell me you didn't just call my cell and say the same words that Carrie hears on her phone in the play," Bree demanded.

"Uh, okay, I didn't just call your cell and say the same—"

"I don't believe you, Tiffany!" Bree shouted. "Why don't you show me your phone? Show me what your last outgoing call was."

"I think that being in this play has made you snap," said Tiffany, unknowingly echoing the sentiments of Bree's sister. She opened the zipper to the front compartment of her backpack, pulled out her cell phone, and thrust it toward Bree.

"Here. Knock yourself out," she said as Bree snatched the phone from her hand.

Bree scrolled through the "call history" menu until she got to "recent calls made." The last call Tiffany had made was to MOM.

"Happy?" Tiffany asked, grabbing her phone back. "I

called my mom a couple of minutes ago to tell her I was leaving rehearsal and heading home. So I don't know what you're talking about."

Bree looked at Melissa, who shrugged.

That was when Bree's phone rang again.

BRIIIING! BRIIIING! BRIIIING!

Again the caller ID read UNKNOWN NUMBER.

Bree looked at Tiffany, who was standing right next to Melissa. Tiffany had already put her phone away. Bree answered the call.

"Leave now, and never come back . . . or you'll be sorry!" said the female with the same familiar voice.

"Who *is* this?" Bree screamed into the phone. She got no reply.

It was now clear that it could not have been Tiffany who had been making the calls. Tiffany was standing right next to her. Bree's mind flashed on Megan for a moment, as she ran through a list of who didn't want her to be in the show. But she knew that Megan had band practice at this time at the high school, where cell phones were strictly forbidden.

So who is it? Who is calling me with a warning? And should I listen to her?

CHAPTER 12

Bree decided to walk home. She could have taken the bus or called her mom for a ride, but she needed some time alone. She often did some of her best thinking on long walks, and this one might just help her sort out her thoughts.

Then again, it might not.

For what felt like the millionth time, Bree ran through the details of everything that had been happening and everything that she had been feeling since she first got involved with the play. She felt almost as if there were two different people living inside her head—regular Bree, who had simply decided that she wanted to break out of her shell and be in a play, and then another Bree.

Regular Bree was the one who had been determined to stay in the play no matter what, just to prove her sister wrong. But that was also the Bree who was beginning to feel that she should leave the play, despite any ridicule she might get from Megan or Tiffany or anyone else, when crazy things started to happen, like lights falling on her or seeing faces in windows. That Bree was practical and usually trusted her feelings. If that had been the only Bree, she would have left the play, no question.

Then there was the feeling of being drawn to the play as if it had some magical power over her. As if she were under some kind of spell. That Bree was the one who'd lost it on Tiffany as the other Bree, regular Bree, watched as if she were indeed another person.

That was it! That was the problem. It was all clear to her now. It was the two-Bree situation.

The two-Bree situation? she thought, frowning. *You really are losing your mind.*

As she approached her house, she realized that although she had clarified a few things, she still had no explanation for the phone calls or other mysterious things. So *I'm right back where I started,* she thought. *Still in the play. Still wanting to quit the play. Still not going to quit the play. Dealing with two "Brees" arguing in my head.*

That night at dinner Bree eyed Megan suspiciously. Logic told her that Megan could not have been the one making those calls, yet somehow she felt she couldn't trust her sister.

"So how're rehearsals going?" Megan asked.

Bree was startled. Was this really her sister being friendly, showing interest in her, making small talk? Maybe someone had taken over part of *her* brain too, and now there was a nice Megan living in there along with the usual self-centered one.

"Okay, I guess," Bree replied cautiously. The last person in the world she would confide in regarding all this craziness was Megan. "I'm remembering all my lines, and I like being onstage with the other kids. I think the show is going to be okay."

"Great!" Megan replied, getting up from the table. "I can't wait to see it."

"You're going to come see the show?" Bree asked incredulously.

"Of course. Wouldn't miss it!"

Bree couldn't help smiling. *There is definitely someone else living in that head of hers. I just hope that "nice Megan" sticks around for a while,* she thought.

After dinner, Bree went to her room and dove into her homework. She found it surprisingly easy to focus. She had always been a good student. Now she was using schoolwork to help get her mind off the play and relax.

As she finished her homework, she got a text from Melissa. ANY MORE WEIRD PHONE CALLS? MAYBE YOU SHOULD CHANGE YOUR NUMBER!

Bree wrote back. NOPE. TRYING TO FORGET ALL THAT. CAN'T WAIT UNTIL THE PLAY IS DONE. I'LL BE HAPPY WHEN MY LIFE RETURNS TO ITS NORMAL BORING SELF!

Melissa replied instantly. WELL, YOU ONLY HAVE TWO MORE DAYS TO DEAL WITH IT. G-NITE!

G-NITE!

Melissa was right. Opening night was just a couple of days away now. Bree really was entering the home stretch of this whole strange experience. Soon it would all be behind her—both the good parts and the creepy ones.

After reading for a while, she started to feel drowsy, the stress of the day—the past two weeks, in fact—catching up to her. She fell into a deep sleep, then tumbled into the most vivid nightmare she had ever had.

In the dream, the idea of "two Brees" came stunningly

alive. She felt herself floating in the air, looking down—
on herself!

She couldn't tell if she was actually flying or just seeing the world from a new point of view. But since this
was a dream, it didn't really matter. The laws of nature
and physics had no meaning here. All she knew was that
she was able to watch herself, as if she were in the high
balcony of a theater, watching her life like a play. And
the odd thing was, this new perspective felt perfectly
normal, as if it were an everyday experience that people
had all the time.

Bree watched herself wake up and slip out of bed.

Is my room really that messy?

She watched as she ate breakfast silently beside
Megan, who seemed to be completely self-absorbed.

Looks like the "real" Megan showed up for breakfast.

Bree was unable to shake the feeling that she was
simply watching a play. Actually it was more like a
movie, as the scene shifted from her house to school.
She had a perfect view of herself as she continued to
look down from above.

She watched herself walk to school. The closer she
got to the building, the more her sense of wonderment

at this new point of view on her life lessened. It was replaced by dread, as if something terrible was going to happen at school. She knew it, yet she was powerless to stop it. With each step she took, the anxiety grew more and more overbearing.

As she watched herself stepping into the school, a sense of evil and impending doom washed over her.

Stop! she thought, hoping that maybe she could command this "show" to end, as if she were pressing the stop button on a remote. But the "show" continued. She did not wake up, and images of her life did not stop playing out in front of her eyes.

She watched herself go through her day of classes. The slight thrill of "spying" on her own life, which she had enjoyed at first, vanished. All she could think about was how to turn the images off, how to stop herself from stepping into whatever she was certain was going to happen.

When classes ended, Bree watched herself walk through the halls on her way to the auditorium for rehearsal. Her dread ratcheted up to a new intensity as the Bree below grabbed the handle and opened the auditorium door.

Once inside, rehearsal of the final scene proceeded smoothly.

(THE GIRLS ARE OUT OF THEIR SLEEPING BAGS, PACING AROUND THE ROOM NERVOUSLY.)

CARRIE: This is not how I pictured my sleepover going.

RACHEL: Well, I don't believe in ghosts either, but what else could it be?

CARRIE: I know. What other explanation could there be? It all adds up--the girl who died, the face at the window, the floating objects--

LAURA: Don't forget the phone calls.

CARRIE: Ghosts making phone calls?

LAURA: I know how it sounds, but why is it stranger than ghosts doing any of the other things?

RACHEL: Why don't you just invite her to the sleepover and be done with it?

CARRIE: No, she is not welcome. She's a ghost. She's not one of us. She's not even alive. There's no way she's coming to my sleepover!

LAURA: Uh . . . I think you should tell HER that!

(LAURA POINTS OVER CARRIE'S
SHOULDER. EVERYONE TURNS AROUND
AND GASPS IN HORROR AS THEY SEE
THE GHOST WALKING INTO THE ROOM,
HEADING RIGHT TOWARD CARRIE.)

CARRIE: Get out! You are not welcome
here!

(THE GHOST IGNORES CARRIE AND
CONTINUES TO WALK TOWARD HER.
CARRIE BACKS AWAY, MOVING TOWARD
THE TOP OF THE STAIRS.)

RACHEL: Carrie, look out!

(CARRIE BACKS UP, RIGHT TO THE TOP
OF THE STAIRS. THE GHOST IS VERY
CLOSE TO HER NOW. CARRIE TAKES A
FINAL STEP BACKWARD AND TUMBLES
DOWN THE STAIRS, FALLING OFFSTAGE.
THE LIGHTS GO TO BLACK.)

Laura and Rachel: YIIIIII!!!!!!

THE END

Bree was fascinated by watching the play as if she
was part of the audience. She had seen plays before, certainly, but never one in which she was acting!

And she realized, oddly enough for the first time,
here in her dream, why the play was called *The Last
Sleepover*. All along she had thought the title referred to

the ghost's last sleepover, but she was wrong.

This was the story of *Carrie's* last sleepover, as if the ghost had wanted something bad to happen to Carrie from the beginning. As if the ghost was blaming Carrie for having kept her away from all those sleepovers. Now, in the end, in the play, the ghost, Millie—Mildred P. Wormhouse—had gotten her revenge.

Bree watched as the cast ran through the entire play again. She figured out that this had to be one of the final rehearsals. Everyone was so prepared, doing the play exactly as they would on opening night.

"Excellent!" Ms. Hollows said when the rehearsal was finished. "I have never felt more confident about a play I have been involved with."

"Opening night is tomorrow, ladies and gentlemen," Ms. Hollows continued. "Everyone please get a good night's sleep. I will see all of you for the performance."

Wow! Opening night. I wonder if I'll—

Before Bree's dreaming mind could even complete the thought, the scene before her switched. She was still looking down at the auditorium, only now it was filling up with people.

Her dream had shifted to opening night.

Bree spotted her parents and Megan, sitting right in the front row.

A hush fell over the audience as the houselights dimmed and the curtain went up. The stage lights came on, revealing the set for Carrie's bedroom.

A thrill ran through Bree. *Here I go! This is so exciting!*

She watched herself step out onto the stage. The audience applauded wildly. Perhaps the person clapping the loudest was her sister, Megan. A great feeling of satisfaction washed over her.

The audience grew quiet. Onstage Bree took a breath, then opened her mouth to start the show.

BOOOOOM!!!

A thunderous explosion rocked the auditorium.

Now Bree saw herself buried onstage in a cloud of smoke and debris.

CHAPTER 13

Bree bolted upright in bed, covered in cold sweat. She tossed her covers onto the floor, then followed them off the bed. Landing on the pile of covers, she wrapped herself up like a cocoon, rocking back and forth on the floor. A few moments later she realized that she was whimpering like a baby. She felt out of control, as if her life had been taken away from her and all she could do was watch from the sidelines—or the balcony.

The dream she had just had was no ordinary nightmare. It was a warning. Whoever or whatever was now controlling her life was trying to tell her that something bad was going to happen if she walked out onto that stage on the opening night of this play.

Bree rolled onto her side and pushed herself up to a

standing position. Her path was now clear. She had to get dressed, go to school, and tell Ms. Hollows that she could not do the play.

I know, I know, she began saying to herself, but in some ways it felt as if she were arguing with another person—more specifically, another Bree. *How can you do this? Opening night is tomorrow. You can't just walk out on everyone. The whole cast, all your friends, Ms. Hollows—the whole school is depending on you to come through. How can you leave them in the lurch like that?*

"No!" Bree shouted, then caught herself, hoping no one else in the house had heard her. She lowered her voice as she continued the conversation. "I can't let what everybody else thinks control my life anymore. That's one of the reasons I decided to do the play in the first place. Megan thought I wasn't cut out for the theater. Tiffany thought I didn't deserve to have the lead in the play. And now, if everyone thinks I'm a quitter, well, that's just too bad! I don't care what everyone thinks. I don't even care what *you* think!"

She stopped, realizing that she was now staring in the mirror, carrying on this argument with her reflection.

That sudden awareness acted like a splash of cold water in the face.

"Walk away from the mirror, Bree, eat a piece of toast, and go to school like a normal person."

But once again, on the walk to school, Bree's mind began to change. As if the school building—or more specifically, the auditorium—exerted some force, some control, over her thoughts. The closer she got to the school, the stronger the feeling that compelled her to do the play in the first place got. By the time she walked into school, she knew that she was going to that afternoon's final rehearsal, and that she would indeed walk out onto the stage tomorrow night, opening night, and perform the part of Carrie.

None of which lessened her anxiety. She could not get the image of the explosion out of her mind. Through each class, walking in the halls between classes, sitting at lunch, and talking to her friends, she felt distracted, her mind locked on that single, devastating image.

"Earth to Bree," someone said as she walked through the hallway on her way to rehearsal.

Bree spun around, practically jumping into the air.

"Melissa!" she cried. "You shouldn't sneak up on

people." She tried to joke her way out of the reality that her mind was far away, lost in her terrible dream.

"You've been in a fog all day, Bree," Melissa said. "Getting the 'I can't believe opening night is tomorrow' jitters?"

"Maybe," Bree replied flatly. She had already told Melissa too many weird things. She was not about to share her most recent nighmare with her too.

"Are you kidding?" Melissa said. "Even with all the bizarre stuff you've had to deal with, you have been the glue that holds this show together, Bree. You're a rock. You are going to rule tomorrow night!"

If I survive. Bree thought, grimacing.

"Thanks, Lis," Bree said, trying to sound happy—like her usual self. "I guess it is opening-night nerves. What else could it be? I mean, this *is* my first play, and I am playing the lead."

"You'll be great," Melissa repeated as they reached the auditorium. She pulled open the door, and Bree followed her inside.

"Ladies and gentlemen, please assemble onstage," Ms. Hollows said as Bree reached the front of the auditorium.

Bree joined the rest of the cast on the stage.

"This is our final rehearsal. Our dress rehearsal. We will be performing the entire play, start to finish, exactly as we will be doing it tomorrow night in front of an audience. Before we begin, I would like to let each and every one of you know that I could not be more proud of you," Ms. Hollows began. "You started as a group of individuals, each with your own ideas about what this play was and what your part in it would be. In the weeks we have worked together, we have become a unit, a team. Each of you has put aside any notion you walked in here with, for the good of the play, and your performances certainly reflect that. I could not have asked for a better cast.

"Watching you bring the author's words to life has been a rewarding experience for me. I believe in this play strongly, as strongly as if I had written it myself. And on that note, let's begin. Break a leg, everyone!"

As the cast headed backstage, the lights dimmed, and Bree stepped out from behind the curtain to begin the first scene. As she opened her mouth to deliver her first line, a wave of panic seized her. The image of the explosion played out in front of her eyes, as if someone

were projecting a movie of her dream right here, where it happened.

"I—I," Bree stammered. She was Bree, alone and frightened on the stage. She was not in character at all. She was certainly not Carrie. She was Bree caught in the grip of the deadly vision that now haunted her every waking minute.

Ms. Hollows stepped up to the edge of the stage. "Gabrielle," she said. "What is the problem?"

"I'm sorry, Ms. Hollows," Bree said, using every ounce of willpower to push aside the terror and the panic that shook her whole body. "Must just be nerves. Let's start again. I'll get it this time."

Bree walked offstage and took a deep breath. *You only have to do this a few more times in your entire life. You know the lines. You know what to do. Just do it!*

She walked back onto the stage. The lights dimmed, and this time she became Carrie. The play began, and she moved from scene to scene seamlessly. The further into the play she got, the more her sense of panic and impending doom eased.

She felt comfortable as Carrie.

It was even somewhat of a relief to lose herself in the

character, to become someone else for a couple of hours.

When the dress rehearsal had ended, Ms. Hollows called the cast together. "Excellent! I have never felt more confident about a play I have been involved with. Opening night is tomorrow, ladies and gentlemen," she said. "Everyone please get a good night's sleep. I will see all of you for the performance."

A rush of all-too-familiar anxiety overwhelmed Bree. *Those are exactly the same words Ms. Hollows said in my dream. And then . . . and then . . .*

All the calm and relief she had felt during the rehearsal vanished in a moment.

Struggling to hold herself together, Bree hurried backstage. She didn't want Melissa to see her like this. She didn't want anyone to see her like this. She just wanted it to all be over. The fear, the nightmares, the crazy masks and lights and phone calls, the play.

The play.

Ever since it had come into her life, Bree had felt as if the play was a really bad thing disguised as a really good thing.

Every time she had begun to feel good about the experience, something inside, something deeper, felt off, wrong, even threatened. The play would be finished soon and she would be free—free of the power it seemed to hold over her. And then she would never have to do it again.

"Coming, Bree?" Melissa asked, sticking her head backstage.

"Nah, my mom's coming to pick me up," Bree said, trying her hardest to act normal. "I'll hang here."

"'Kay," Melissa said. "See ya tomorrow for the big show!"

"Tomorrow," Bree repeated. Melissa left the auditorium, along with the rest of the cast.

Bree knew that her mom would be there in about twenty minutes. Enough time to do what she needed to do. She hurried from the auditorium and raced to the library, knowing it was unlocked. Slipping into the room, she was overwhelmed by the silence. It was so weird to be here without Mr. Harris, and without a roomful of studying students. But she didn't need Mr. Harris's help for this. She just needed a computer, and she couldn't wait until she got home to use her own.

Signing onto one of the library's computers, she searched for "Mildred P. Wormhouse." As she typed the name, she wondered why she hadn't done this earlier. It seemed to Bree that the key to all of this had to rest with the playwright herself.

After a few minutes of digging, she found a website dedicated to obscure playwrights. Searching through the names, she found what she was looking for—a short biography of Mildred P. Wormhouse.

Reading the bio, Bree learned that *The Last Sleepover* was the only play that Wormhouse ever wrote. Apparently, she had had a difficult, unhappy childhood. She had few friends and spent much time alone. The bio referred to the death of Gabrielle Ashford on the opening night of the play at Thomas Jefferson Middle School. And it also said that Mildred P. Wormhouse apparently disappeared shortly after the event and was never heard from again.

Her whereabouts, or even whether she was still alive, remained unknown.

Wormhouse was quoted in the piece as saying, "I was endlessly tormented by one particular bully. As a matter of fact, she was the inspiration for my play. She turned everyone at school against me, and there was nothing I could do about it. And so, since I had no control over events in my real life, I decided to get my revenge through my writing, through *The Last Sleepover*. Not to be too obvious, I shortened the name of the poor tormented ghost in my play from my own 'Mildred' to just 'Millie.' And I changed the name of my tormentor completely, calling her Carrie rather than her true name—Gabrielle."

Bree reached the end of the bio and sat, stunned. Not only was the girl who died thirty years named Gabrielle, but so was the bully who'd excluded young Mildred from sleepovers—the inspiration for the play itself.

"This whole play is about revenge," Bree said to herself. "Revenge against the Gabrielle who excluded Mildred. Was it also revenge against Gabrielle Ashford? Will it also be revenge against Gabrielle Hart—against me?"

She shut down the computer and hurried from the library. She still had a few minutes before her mom would be there, so she headed back to the auditorium to pick up her things, trying to digest what she had just learned.

The auditorium was silent. Bree was alone.

Or so she thought.

She suddenly heard the soft scraping of feet, the sound of someone running down the aisle.

"Who's there?" she called out, stepping from backstage out onto the stage. She saw no one. "Hello?"

A shadow moved at the back of the theater.

"Who is it?" Bree called again, staring intently into the darkness.

She saw a quick movement near the bottom of the stairs leading up to the balcony. Then a figure stepped into a small pool of light cast from above.

Bree caught a momentary glimpse of a face, half in light, half in shadow.

It was the face of a girl, a girl about her age, but Bree couldn't place her.

"What are you doing here?" Bree cried out.

The girl said nothing. She simply turned and hurried up the stairs leading to the balcony.

Bree chased after the girl, racing to the stairs. A mysterious stranger lurking in the shadows of the theater? Mysterious, yet familiar—just like the voice in the phone calls. In light of all that had happened, Bree felt certain that this was the person behind everything.

She was going to get her answers, and she was going to get them now, tonight, so that when the curtain went up tomorrow night, all this craziness would be behind her.

She dashed up the stairs, taking them two at a time. As she ran, she heard soft, steady footsteps charging ahead on the flight of stairs above her. Up she went, to the top level of the theater. As she rounded each turn on the staircase, Bree caught a brief glimpse of a foot, or a leg, or a flash of color vanishing around the bend ahead.

Once she reaches the balcony, there's nowhere else to go, Bree thought as her feet pounded the stairs. *I've got her. And she will tell me who she is and what has been going on!*

Reaching the top level of the staircase, she stepped out onto the balcony. Short rows of seats angled down toward the stage far below. A low railing ran across the front of the balcony. There Bree spotted the girl she had been chasing. The girl peered over the railing, looking down at the empty stage.

"There's nowhere to go, you know," Bree said firmly. "You can't run anymore. I know you're the one who's been messing with me, playing these tricks, trying to make me believe that I'm crazy or that I shouldn't be in this play or who knows what. Well, it ends here."

She rushed down the aisle, walked up to the girl, and grabbed her by the shoulders.

"Who *are* you?" she demanded, spinning the girl around. For the first time she got a good look at her face.

Bree released the girl's shoulders. Were her eyes playing tricks on her? How could this be? Bree stared right into the girl's eyes. The face belonged to . . . Bree! She was looking at her own face, staring at herself.

"I'm not dreaming, am I?" Bree asked.

The other girl, the other Bree, shook her head.

"Then what's happening to me?" Bree shouted, venting all her anger and frustration in one powerful outburst.

The other Bree spoke in a voice that Bree had come to know all too well.

"Leave now, and never come back . . . or you'll be sorry!"

Bree was so stunned by hearing those same words, spoken with that familiar voice—her own voice—that she stumbled backward toward the stairs. Trying to regain her balance, as her mind tried to make sense of what had just happened, she tripped at the top of the stairs.

She went tumbling down the stairs and hit her head on the landing.

That last thing she saw before everything went dark was her own face looking down at her from the top of the stairs. The other Bree was smiling.

CHAPTER 14

Bree opened her eyes slowly. At first she could not make sense of her surroundings. She felt her head resting on a pillow.

Her awareness then shifted from the softness of the pillow to the throbbing pain in her head. Her blurry vision began to clear, and she could make out a rectangular plastic light cover, the type used to cover fluorescent bulbs in office buildings and hospitals.

Bree next focused on the ring of faces looking down at her.

Mom? Dad? Megan? What's going on?

"Where am I?" she asked, finally mustering enough energy to speak.

"You're in the hospital, sweetheart," her mom

replied. "That was quite a fall you took, but the doctors say you're going to be just fine."

"Nice to see you awake, kiddo," her dad added.

"You'll do anything for attention, won't you, little sister?" Megan asked, smiling a genuinely warm smile.

"Fall? I really did fall?" Bree asked, still very confused. "That wasn't a dream?"

"No, honey, I wish it had been just a dream," her mom said.

"What day is it?" Bree asked, trying to sit up, but only managing to lift her head a few inches before falling back down onto the pillow. "What about the play? What happened to the play? Did the show go on?"

"Relax, honey," her mom said, gently stroking Bree's forehead. "You've been here for two days. The play was supposed to open yesterday, but of course, the opening was postponed after your fall."

"You can't put on a play without the lead, after all," Megan said.

"And, of course, everyone was so relieved that the play was postponed," her mom continued.

"What do you mean, relieved?" Bree asked.

"Because of what happened," Megan said. She

grabbed a remote and flipped on the TV, which hung above Bree's hospital bed. Megan dialed around until she found a news report.

"Crews are still cleaning up from the small explosion that took place yesterday evening in the auditorium of Thomas Jefferson Middle School," the news announcer reported. "The blast went off at seven thirty, which was the precise time a play at the school was about to begin. Fortunately, the play had been postponed, and so the auditorium was empty at the time of the blast. No one was injured. Cleanup crews have been working around the clock to get that section of the school open and safe for use again."

Megan shut off the TV.

"The blast happened exactly at the moment I would have gone onstage to begin the play!" Bree said, trying again to sit up and once again falling back onto her pillow.

"Don't get excited, honey," her mom said. "You were very lucky. I'm not happy you fell, but when I think about what might have happened if the play had gone on . . . "

"In my dream I saw myself out onstage," Bree began to rant. "And I watched from above as I was about to start the play. I saw that explosion happen before it happened!"

She paused. If it sounded strange to her, imagine how it must sound to her family.

"Get some rest, honey," her mother said. "You've been through a lot."

Bree closed her eyes and tried to make sense of everything. Could the other Bree she saw have placed that dream into her mind, the dream in which she saw what would have happened if she'd gone out to start the play? And when she didn't heed that warning, did her other self show up at the theater, while Bree was awake, to warn her in person?

With these questions swirling through her mind, and her body still weak and tired from the fall, Bree drifted off into a deep sleep. She gently fell into a dream, but this time the dream was calming and beautiful rather than terrifying.

In her dream, she was walking through a field of flowers on a beautiful, sunny day. As she strolled through the field, Bree was joined by her other self. It felt like the most natural thing in the world. It felt like an old friend had decided to accompany Bree on her stroll.

"The play is cursed, you know," the other Bree explained as they walked. "Whether by explosion, or a light falling, or some other way, whoever plays the lead is destined to die."

"Somehow I did know that, or I sensed it or something," Bree said. "But who are you?"

"It's a little complicated," the other Bree replied. "I'm you. Or rather, I am your spirit. I'm the ghost of the Bree who would have played the lead and died in the explosion if she hadn't tripped and fallen."

"So you died?" Bree asked. "I mean, *I* died?"

"Sort of," the other Bree said. "There are many timelines that run parallel to one another. They are based on the choices we each make a hundred times a day. Things like 'Do I walk or take the bus?' 'Do I go to my friend's house or hang out at home?' 'Do I go to see the seven o'clock showing of a movie or the eight o'clock showing?' Simple choices like that.

"Every so often two of the timelines intersect. In our case, I made them intersect. With your help. Each of the dreams you had in which you saw me opened a portal between timelines. That portal allowed me to pass back and forth between timelines.

"By the time you had that last dream, the portal was stable enough that I was able to come through and stay

in your timeline. That was how I was able to visit you in the theater. I know this is all kind of confusing."

"No, I think I understand," Bree said. "You are from the timeline in which I chose to go out onstage on opening night and do the play. And in that timeline, I died. You are my spirit from that timeline. You crossed over to my timeline, hoping to stop me from going onstage on opening night.

"I watched as the explosion happened and I was buried in rubble. I saw what was supposed to happen in my dream, but it was because of my other self—because of you—that the show did not go on and I didn't get caught in the explosion.

"It was you! You were trying to warn me all along. You were trying to keep me from walking out onto that stage, either by scaring me out of the play or by calling me and telling me to leave. All that, all these weird things that have been happening to me, was just *me* trying to warn *me*."

"Exactly," the other Bree said. "I tried to prevent you from being on that stage when the explosion happened. And because of the way the timelines worked, I could only really do things that were part of the play.

That's why it seemed like the scary things in the play were coming true in your real life. It was all I had to work with.

"I succeeded in getting you away from the stage on opening night, though your falling was never part of my plan. I also did it for selfish reasons. I did it to free myself and finally allow my spirit to rest."

"I don't understand," Bree said.

"It's part of the curse of the play," the spirit explained. "Not only does the girl playing the lead die, but she is cursed to be stuck inside the play, reliving it day after day, doing all the scary things that happen again and again, just like the girl who died thirty years ago, the first girl to ever play the role."

"That's why I was able to watch *her* performance in one of my dreams!" Bree suddenly realized. "She is stuck in the play, doing it over and over, dying again and again. One of those times I was able to watch her through my dreams. Just like I saw you die in my dreams."

"That's when I crossed timelines and was able to enter your physical reality in the theater that night," the other Bree said. "But I couldn't figure out how to warn you in any way you would actually believe me.

"And now that you are safe, I am finally free to rest in peace."

Before Bree could say anything else, her other self smiled and faded away, leaving Bree standing in the field of flowers with an overwhelming feeling of peace. Just before her dream faded, leaving her in the deepest, most restful sleep she had experienced in weeks, Bree thought about the good things that being in the play had done for her. She thought about how being involved with the play had given her the confidence to go onstage again and break out of her shell. Only next time, she would do it in a play that was not cursed!

After a few more days in the hospital, Bree finally went home. She rested at home for another week before she felt well enough to return to school. On her first day back, before classes, a meeting of the cast of *The Last Sleepover* was called to decide the fate of the play. With the auditorium still under reconstruction, the meeting was held in the gym.

Being back in school for the first time since her accident, Bree felt surprisingly calm. All the fears, doubts, and anxieties that had plagued her for weeks had vanished along with her spirit self when her dream had ended.

Stepping into the gym, Bree was greeted by a standing ovation.

"Welcome back, Bree!" Melissa shrieked, rushing over to Bree and throwing her arms around her. "This school is just not the same without you!"

"It's great to be back," Bree said.

"All right, everyone, please take a seat in the bleachers," boomed someone from the front of the gym.

Bree turned her head, along with everyone else. She knew from the voice that the speaker was not Ms. Hollows, but rather a tall man walking with a cane.

"Hello, everyone. For those of you who don't know me, I'm Mr. Gomez," he began. "I'm the drama teacher here at Thomas Jefferson. I was also supposed to have been your director for this year's play, but unfortunately, I broke my leg shortly before rehearsals were to begin."

"What happened to Ms. Hollows?" Melissa asked.

"She was only hired to direct that one play," Mr. Gomez explained. "And since the performance got postponed, and I was able to return to work, she has left the school."

"I won't miss her," Tiffany whispered, leaning close to Bree's ear. "She was weird."

Wow, even Tiffany's being nice to me, Bree thought, smiling.

"And so now we come to the question of the fate of the play," Mr. Gomez continued. Beside him, on a chair, sat a stack of copies of *The Last Sleepover*. "As you know, all future productions will be put on here in the gym until the repair of the auditorium is complete. Since you have worked so hard rehearsing *The Last Sleepover*, I thought maybe we could talk about restaging it here. What does everyone think?"

Before anyone could speak, Mr. Jenkins, the school janitor, walked into the gym.

"Sorry for the interruption, folks," he said, then went about lifting a large plastic bag full of garbage from the gym's trash can.

Without saying a word, Bree stood up and walked over to the stack of scripts.

"We may do a play in the gym, Mr. Gomez, but it won't be this play," she said, gathering up the pile of scripts in her arms.

"Wait a minute, please, Mr. Jenkins!" she called

out, walking across the gleaming wooden gym floor. Reaching the janitor, she pulled open the large plastic bag of garbage, then turned back toward Mr. Gomez.

"In fact, Mr. Gomez, no one will ever perform this play again."

Bree dumped every copy of *The Last Sleepover* into the garbage bag before returning to her seat. "Now," she began. "What play do we all think we would like to do?"

EPILOGUE
THIRTY YEARS LATER . . .

Bree slowed her car as she approached the school. She always enjoyed driving up to Thomas Jefferson Middle School. It brought back a flood of good memories about close friends and fun times.

Today Bree was here to pick up her daughter, Elle, following Elle's drama rehearsal. Bree was so pleased that Elle—short for Gabrielle—had shown an interest in theater, recalling how much her own involvement with school plays both in middle school and then in high school had added to her years as a student.

As Bree sat in the car with the window rolled down, she noticed an odd-looking woman standing near the entrance to the school. The woman was tall and had medium-length, jet-black hair. She wore a long, dark coat. *Who is that woman?* she thought. The woman turned around, revealing dark circles around her eyes.

"Ms. Hollows!" Bree gasped.

She paused for a moment and caught herself. This woman looked younger than Bree herself. "There's no way that could be Ms. Hollows," she said to herself. "That was thirty years ago, and Ms. Hollows would have to be in her sixties now."

Still, Bree was surprised, as she watched the woman disappear into the school building, by just how deeply the idea of seeing Ms. Hollows affected her after all these years.

A few minutes later Elle came bounding out of the school. She ran up to Bree's car, bursting with excitement.

"Hey, Peanut, how was drama rehearsal?" she asked as Elle slipped into the seat beside her.

"Fantastic, Mom," Elle replied. "You're not going to believe this. My drama teacher found an old play in a trunk in the basement of the school. She told us that no one has put on the play in years!"

"Really?" Bree asked, starting the car. "What's the name of the play?"

"It's called *The Last Sleepover*," Elle explained. "And I'm just dying to play the lead!"

WANT MORE CREEPINESS?

Then you're in luck, because P. J. Night has some more scares for you and your friends!

A TRUE TRANSFORMATION

Watch the creepy drama teacher transform before your eyes!

1. Write MILDRED P WORMHOUSE on the blank.

_____

2. Delete all vowels except O and U.

_____

3. Move the eighth and ninth letters to the end.

_____

4. U equals LL. Replace.

_____

5. Delete all Ds, Ps, and Rs.

_____

6. Insert an S between the first two consonants.

_____

7. Delete the third and fifth letters.

_____

8. Move the third letter to the last position.

_____

9. Move the seventh letter to the last position.

_____

YOU'RE INVITED TO . . .
CREATE YOUR OWN HAUNTED PLAY!

Do you want to turn your sleepover into a creepover? Writing and putting on a haunted play is a great way to set the mood. P. J. Night has written a few lines of dialogue to get you started. Fill in the rest of the scene and have fun scaring your friends.

You can also collaborate with your friends on this play by taking turns. Have everyone at your sleepover sit in a circle. Pick one person to start. She will fill in the first blank line of dialogue and then pass it to the next person. That person will fill in the next line of dialogue and pass it along. Once everyone has taken a turn, act out the scary play. Feel free to add as many parts as you have guests at your sleepover.

PERSON 1: I think I hear something coming from the attic. It sounds like someone is crying . . . or howling.

PERSON 2: It's probably just the wind, right?

PERSON 3: Perhaps, but haven't you heard the rumors? About ghosts appearing in attics late at night?

PERSON 1: Yes, but I don't believe in them. Who's brave enough to check out the attic with me?

_____

_____

_____

_____

_____

_____

_____

_____

_____

_____

_____

THE END

DO NOT FEAR—
WE HAVE ANOTHER CREEPY TALE FOR YOU!

TURN THE PAGE FOR A SNEAK PEEK AT

You're invited to a

CREEPOVER

There's Something Out There

CHAPTER 1

What happened in the woods that night changed every-thing, forever, and if the girl had known what was going to happen, she never would have left her house. Never left the safety of locked doors and windows, and the sound of laughter coming from the television, and the good smells of food cooking in the kitchen, and the warm glow of lights in every room.

But she didn't know, see? She didn't have a clue what was waiting for her, at the edge of the darkness, so when she heard the scratching, she thought it was the stray cat that had been coming around. The one with the tattered ear and the hungry eyes.

The sun was just about to set. She could see it still shining in the west, like an orange ball of fire on the verge of falling into space. So she thought, *I'll just put some food at the edge of the yard. For the cat.* She poured a cup of kitty chow into a plastic bag and grabbed her coat. Then she walked out the back door, into the dying light, like it was no big deal, because it wasn't . . . not yet.

That was a mistake, she realized later. She should have told someone—anyone—that she was going outside. Into the twilight. By herself.

At the edge of the yard, she looked for the cat by the tree where it usually waited for her. But tonight, the cat was nowhere. "Here, kitty, kitty," she called softly, kneeling down and snapping her fingers like she always did.

Still the cat did not appear.

The girl sighed. The air was damp, as if the fog were rushing in faster tonight than usual, hardly waiting for the sun to finish setting before blanketing the woods in a thick mist that was impossible to see through. She felt so sorry for the poor cat, sleeping in the woods all alone, even when it was cold or windy or wet.

Then she heard it again: the scratching. Just beyond the tree line. And—what was that? A whimper?

A cry for help?

The girl glanced behind her at the house, still all lit

up, so warm and cozy. She wanted to go back there.

So why was she walking toward the woods?

Because she couldn't bear it, the thought that the cat was sick or hurt, or in trouble. If she could help the little cat, she would. Of course, she didn't know then what was really in the woods.

"Here, kitty," she called again, pushing through the tree limbs. "I won't hurt you. Here, kitty."

Silence.

That the woods should be so chillingly quiet, the girl realized, was weird. Very weird. But instead of feeling afraid, she was curious. She should have been afraid.

On she continued into the woods, all the way to the clearing where she'd spent so many summer nights on campouts, telling stories in the flickering light of a campfire. She knew that clearing as well as she knew her own bedroom, but she'd never seen it the way she did tonight.

It was hard to see through the mist, but she could tell right away that the clearing was not empty.

And whatever was in it was a *lot* bigger than a stray cat.

The girl hid behind a thick-trunked tree, her heart thundering in her chest, and stared with wide eyes. She couldn't have looked away even if she'd wanted to.

Well, to be honest, she did want to look away. But her eyes were locked on the creature, and she wondered, suddenly, if she was dreaming.

But she knew that that was nothing more than a wish, an empty hope. Because nothing had ever felt this real—from the painful pounding of her heart to the bitter taste of fear in the back of her throat. She swallowed, hard, and held on to the tree trunk for support.

The monster was eating . . . something. Dark red liquid dripped from its mouth, soaking into the dirt beneath it. The girl's stomach lurched, but still she did not move.

And she did not look away.

Then, to her horror, the creature reared up on its hind legs at the same moment the mist cleared. In the dim twilight, she saw more of it than she ever wanted to:

An enormous lizardlike body, covered in scales and slime. Two tremendous, leathery wings, folded tight against its back. Two thick, stumpy arms; the end of each one curved into a razor-sharp talon, dripping . . . something. Something foul. Back legs that rippled with muscle. A knobby, bumpy head, with two red-rimmed, beady eyes, and a mouthful of fangs. And a tail that was studded with spikes as long as the girl's forearm.

Perhaps the worst, though, the memory she would never forget: Along its waxy underbelly ran an angry, raised scar that was barely visible in the fading light. It was obviously an old injury; she could tell from the way the skin puckered around it. Yet still it oozed as if it would never heal. The creature was like nothing she had ever seen before: part bird, part lizard.

All monster.

It tilted its head to the side, rotating slowly . . . slowly . . . until—no, it couldn't be—wait—it was—it was *staring right at her*, the pupil of that horrible eye dilating as it focused on what it wanted. Then, more powerfully than she ever could have imagined, the creature leaped through the clearing, directly to the tree she was hiding behind. One of its talons sliced through the darkness but somehow missed her, and got stuck in the thick tree trunk instead of in the girl's skull. Suddenly she was no longer rooted to the ground in terror; she was running for her life, crashing through the underbrush back to the safety of her house, the solid walls, the strong locks. The creature struggled to get free, screaming in frustration as it watched its prey escape. And it sounded like—

It sounded like—

CHAPTER 2

"*Aiiiii-ck-ck-ck-ck!*" Jenna Walker shrieked, so shrilly and bone-chillingly that all the other girls cried out in horror and clapped their hands over their ears. A satisfied smile flickered across Jenna's face. Her story was definitely the scariest one by far, and she hadn't even gotten to the really freaky part yet.

"Somehow, thanks to the trunk of that old pine tree, the girl made it back to her house," Jenna continued in a slow, quiet voice that made everyone else go completely silent. "She waited all night for the creature to follow her there, to smash through the windows. But it never did.

"And the next day, in the bright morning sun, she dared to step outside again. The woods were full of sound: chattering squirrels, chirping birds, scurrying chipmunks. If the woodland creatures felt safe enough to be out, she should feel safe too. So, one step at a time, she returned to the clearing." Jenna paused. She took a deep breath before she continued.

"There was no sign of the creature. No sign of whatever it had been eating, or the blood that had soaked into the ground. There weren't even any tracks. The girl started to feel embarrassed. Foolish. Had she imagined it? Was it all a dream? And then . . . she saw . . . this."

Jenna reached behind her back and whipped out an enormous talon, gleaming in the beams from the flashlights. Once more, everyone screamed, just as she'd hoped.

"Stuck in the tree . . . the claw of the Marked Monster!" she announced.

"*Ewww!* What is that?" Brittany shrieked.

"Jenna, wow. That was the scariest story, no doubt," Jenna's best friend, Maggie, said, shivering.

"True," Laurel chimed in. "Way to go, Jenna."

Jenna grinned at her friends. For the last three years, they'd been having sleepovers, and this was always her favorite part: telling scary stories. After the girls had eaten pizza and popcorn, after they'd watched movies and given each other pedicures, after everyone else in the house was asleep, they turned out the lights, lit up their flashlights, and tried to freak each other out. Sometimes Jenna spent the entire week before a slumber party trying to think up a scary story to top the last one she'd told, spending hours searching for creepy tales on the Internet. That's where she had learned all about the Marked Monster. Jenna had even read a description of its haunting shriek.

Brittany's face wrinkled up in disgust as she stared at the claw. "That is too gross. Where did you get it?"

"What do you mean?" Jenna replied. "I just told you. I pulled it out of the tree in the clearing behind my house."

"Wait—that was *you*?" Brittany asked. "*You* are the girl in that story?"

"Well, duh," Jenna said. "We've only camped out in that clearing, like, a hundred times."

Brittany shook her head. "No way. Not true. You probably just got the claw at the Halloween Store."

"You wish I did," Jenna shot back. "I mean, yeah, I didn't see the Marked Monster in the woods or anything—that part I made up. But I did find its claw in the tree. Trust me, the claw is the real deal. Here. See for yourself."

She leaned forward and dropped the claw in Brittany's lap. Brittany jumped up so fast that the claw clattered across the floor. "Get that nasty bird toenail away from me! It's probably covered in germs!"

Everyone cracked up then, and Brittany's face got all red. "You think it's so funny?" she asked, but when she started laughing, the other girls knew she wasn't really mad. "Here you go. Why don't you spend some quality time with this toenail?" She scooped the claw off the floor and tossed it toward Maggie, who shrieked as she caught it and immediately chucked it toward Laurel.

"Ack! Get it away! I don't want it!" Laurel cried, throwing it wildly toward Jenna. Too wildly.

There was no way for Jenna to catch the talon as it soared toward her; there wasn't even enough time for her to move out of the way. She heard the rip of her sleeve; she felt the burn as the talon sliced through her skin; and they all heard the *thunk* as the talon smacked against the wall behind her and plunged to the floor.

Jenna sucked in her breath sharply and grabbed her arm. She felt something hot and wet soaking through her torn sleeve.

"Oh no, no, no, are you okay?" Laurel asked in a rush. "Oh, Jenna, I'm so sorry, I didn't mean—"

"No, it's cool. It was just an accident," Jenna said,

biting the inside of her cheek as she tried not to cry. It was just a little cut. But it really, really hurt.

"I'll get a clean T-shirt for you to wear," Maggie said.

"Mags, where's your first-aid kit?" Brittany asked.

"Come with me; I'll show you," Maggie said.

"What can I do?" Laurel asked, hovering around Jenna. "Do you want some ice or something to drink or—"

Jenna forced a laugh. "Laurel, it's okay."

"I just feel so, so bad," Laurel continued. Her hands fluttered nervously in the air.

"Chill," Brittany ordered as she walked back into the rec room. "It's not Jenna's job to make you feel better."

Jenna flashed Laurel an extra smile. Brittany could always be counted on to tell it like it was, but sometimes, Jenna secretly thought, Brittany could *try* to be a little nicer. It wouldn't kill her—especially since they'd known Laurel for only a few months. She had moved to Lewisville in the middle of the school year, and even though she'd made friends pretty quickly, Jenna secretly suspected that Laurel still felt like the new kid.

"Here, Jenna," Maggie said, holding out a T-shirt.

"Thanks," Jenna said. She changed into Maggie's T-shirt, careful not to get any blood on the sleeve. Yep.

It looks like I'm gonna live," Jenna joked, and all the girls laughed. "Let's go get some—"

There was a sudden silence.

"Um, what?" asked Maggie. "Let's get some what?"

"Shhhhh." Jenna whispered as her face went pale. "Did you guys hear that? I swear I just heard, like, a growling sound or something." Jenna held up her hand. "Just—listen—"

All the girls were quiet, and then it came again, a soft *rrrrrrrrrrRRRRRRRRRRRRRR* that grew to a crescendo and made the hair on the back of Jenna's neck stand up. She could tell right away, from the scared expression in her friends' eyes that they had heard it too.

"Uh, Maggie?" Brittany whispered. "You didn't get a dog or anything, did you?"

Her eyes wide, Maggie shook her head.

rrrrrrrrrrrrrrrrrRRRRRRRRRRRRRRRRRRRRRRRRRRR.

Suddenly a shadow darted across the closed curtains. With a sinking feeling in the pit of her stomach, Jenna realized: *There was something outside the window.*

You're Invited to More

CREEPOVERS

A lifelong night owl, **P. J. NIGHT** often works furiously into the wee hours of the morning, writing down spooky tales and dreaming up new stories of the supernatural and otherworldly. Although P. J.'s whereabouts are unknown at this time, we suspect the author lives in a drafty, old mansion where the floorboards creak when no one is there and the flickering candlelight creates shadows that creep along the walls. We truly wish we could tell you more, but we've been sworn to keep P. J.'s identity a secret . . . and it's a secret we will take to our graves!